New Order

NEW ORDER

A NIGHT RUNNER NOVEL

MAX TURNER

HarperTrophyCanada™
An imprint of HarperCollinsPublishersLtd

New Order

Published by Harper*Trophy*Canada™, an imprint of
HarperCollins Publishers Ltd

First Edition

HarperCollins books may be purchased for educational, business, or
sales promotional use through our Special Markets Department.

HarperCollins Publishers Ltd., 2 Bloor Street East, 20th Floor,
Toronto, Ontario, Canada, M4W 1A8

www.harpercollins.ca

ISBN 978-1-44340-630-7

Printed and bound in Canada
WEB 9 8 7 6 5 4 3 2 1

For my family. You are my
greatest adventure.

IN *NIGHT RUNNER . . .*

ZACK THOMSON HAS BEEN living in the psychiatric ward of a hospital since his parents died. His degenerative blood disease, mood swings and strange allergies have all the local doctors baffled. Despite the occasional visit from his best friend, Charlie, and dinners with the intriguing Nurse Ophelia, his life is one of boredom, loneliness and isolation. Then Zack's Uncle Maximilian arrives out of the blue and reveals missing pieces from Zack's shadowy history: first, that Zack's late father, Dr. Robert Thomson, was a vampire hunter, not an archaeologist as he always claimed; second, that Dr. Thomson didn't die on an archaeological dig but was murdered by a vampire lord, Vrolok, who is now searching for Zack; and finally, that the same vampire infected Zack shortly after his father's death, making him a vampire, too.

As he waits for Maximilian to complete the process of adopting him, Zack is flushed from the ward by a police detective. Fearing that the detective is actually working for his father's killer, Zack escapes with the help of an elderly vampire, John Entwistle. But the older vampire is later trapped in a fire at a blood donor clinic, leaving Zack alone and uncertain.

Anxious to find a safe haven, Zack calls Charlie and they head to his friend's cottage at Stoney Lake. There, Zack meets a beautiful girl named Luna, and for a short time he gets a taste of ordinary teenage life. This comes to an abrupt end when a local cottager is murdered, and the police, believing Zack to be the culprit, taser him into submission.

En route to Peterborough with the police, Zack is rescued by Maximilian, who takes him to his place of business in Montreal, Iron Spike Enterprises. There Zack discovers that his uncle is very sick with lung cancer, and that his condition has prompted him to cut a deal with Vrolok, who turns out to be the notorious Vlad the Impaler. In exchange for his nephew, Maximilian has been promised eternal life and membership in the Coven of the Dragon, an elite vampire secret police. The extent of the betrayal intensifies when Vlad drags Charlie and Luna into the room and reveals his intention to impale them.

Enter Ophelia, Zack's nurse from the hospital. She also happens to be a vampire—and Vlad's wife. Fulfilling a promise she made to Zack's father, she tells Vlad to leave the kids and scram. A nasty fight ensues during which Zack bites Charlie to make himself stronger, inadvertently killing his best friend. Maximilian flees, but not before blowing out the windows and letting in sunlight. As things get toasty, Zack forces Ophelia from the room before he and Vlad die of exposure. Luna is left alone with their remains and Charlie's corpse.

Zack awakens in a hospital bed, following a massive blood infusion. Ophelia is there, along with Charlie. Having been infected with the vampire pathogen, Charlie had risen from death starving and fed from Luna, so now she, too, is a vampire.

AND IN *END OF DAYS* . . .

ZACK LEARNS ABOUT an ancient vampire prophecy. It foretells that an orphaned blood drinker and son of a great vampire hunter will die and rise again to lead his kind to salvation . . . or to destruction. This makes Zack the target of a mysterious creature called Hyde. Likened to the Beast of the Apocalypse, Hyde is killing both vampires and those who offer them support.

Following the suspicious death of a police inspector, Zack is once again arrested as a murder suspect. He is freed from jail by Charlie and Mr. Entwistle, who, to Zack's surprise, survived the deadly fire at the blood donor clinic and has been in England gathering information on the prophecy and an impending vampire war.

The three go to one of Ophelia's safe houses, where Zack learns that Mr. Entwistle, once called John Tiptoft, the Butcher of England, was an executioner who tortured and impaled his enemies during the Wars of the Roses. Unwilling to offer him shelter, Ophelia sends Mr. Entwistle away, then takes Zack to Tibet via the Dream Road, a spiritual highway that connects people who are dreaming. On the Roof of the World, Zack is introduced to Baoh, a twelve-hundred-year-old vampire prophet, who helps explain the prophecies and what Zack must to do survive.

The next night, after reconciling with Mr. Entwistle, Ophelia leaves to smooth things over with Detective Baddon, the man leading the police investigation into the crimes committed by Hyde. At the same time, Mr. Entwistle takes Charlie and Zack to meet Maximilian, who is looking to make amends after his disastrous dealings with Vlad. Following their strange visit, Charlie and Zack discover that Detective Baddon has a son convalescing in the hospital. His symptoms lead them to speculate that this boy, Vincent, is a vampire. As Zack and Charlie leave the hospital, Hyde appears and attacks them. Mr. Entwistle saves the day, but not before Zack is poisoned. He awakens to find that Luna and her sister, Suki, have joined them after driving up from their home in New Jersey. Following a failed search for Hyde, Zack and Charlie find themselves back in cottage country with the girls. Unbeknownst to them, Mr. Entwistle confronts Hyde alone and is killed.

The four teens return to Peterborough to regroup with Ophelia—only to discover that she's missing, their base of operations is on fire and Hyde has kidnapped Vincent, Detective Baddon's son. Charlie and Zack take up the chase, which leads them to the Warsaw Caves. In a confrontation there with Hyde, both are beaten badly, but Ophelia arrives and, using wolfsbane, turns Hyde back into his human alter ego, Detective Baddon, revealing that both he and his comatose son are werewolves.

Before the group can make an exit, the detective turns into the Beast again and tries to kill Ophelia, but Maximilian shows up and causes a partial cave-in. Hyde sacrifices himself so his son can be taken to safety. A larger cave-in follows, killing Hyde and Maximilian and burying Mr. Entwistle's corpse under millions of pounds of rock. Vincent also dies, but Zack is able to revive him, leading Zack to speculate that Vincent might be the true subject of the prophecies, given that Vincent is also the son of a vampire hunter and an orphaned blood drinker who has died and come back.

The story ends at Iron Spike Enterprises, where Zack becomes heir to Maximilian's fortunes. Two months later, the story continues . . .

CHAPTER 1

PARTY CRASHER

THE BOUNTY HUNTER arrived as I was setting the dinner table. I had a punch bowl in my arms, blood donor bags piled inside. As I made my way across the rooftop, my eyes strayed over the pool to the patio, eventually settling on the crystal goblet at my place setting. The man's reflection was fish-bowled across its surface, a tiny silhouette superimposed on the skyline of Montreal.

"A last supper," he said. "How fitting . . ."

His voice was peculiar, slow and deep, with just a hint of Southern drawl.

I set the punch bowl on a centrepiece of rose petals, then turned around. I don't know what part of his getup shocked me the most: the large, gem-encrusted rings that sat on each finger, his thick mutton-chop sideburns, his gold-rimmed aviator sunglasses, his white, rhinestone-studded jumpsuit that flared just below the knees or the matching cowboy hat embroidered with gold thread. He would have been a dead ringer for Elvis had it not been for his tanned skin and Arab features. And his guns.

7

Long-barrelled six-shooters hanging in snakeskin holsters. He started walking towards me, the wooden soles of his cowboy boots double-clicking on the patio stones.

It was Halloween. All week, my best friend, Charlie, and I had been planning a surprise dinner date with the lovely Abbott sisters, Luna and Suki. I'd left my sword-fighting lesson early so I could get things ready. There hadn't been time to remove my body armour, which was just dumb luck, but I wasn't armed for a gunfight. Against a normal man, I'd have fared well with a paper clip and an elastic band, but this guy moved with a fluid grace particular to a higher brand of killer. He was a vampire, like me.

"Aren't you a bit old to be trick-or-treating?" I asked, glancing over the tabletop.

Of the two guests we'd been expecting for dinner, only Suki, Charlie's girlfriend, was human. Her salad was at the far end of the table, along with the steak knife she'd need for her filet mignon. It was the only weapon in sight. Thinking to pull it closer, I put my hand on the tablecloth. It was meant to look like a casual gesture, but I was so rattled I probably looked less like 007 and more like the Tin Man from *The Wizard of Oz* after a good week of rain.

The bounty hunter stopped about six paces from me, placed a toothpick in his mouth, pushed up the brim of his hat, then removed his sunglasses and tucked them into his suit pocket. Normally, a vampire's eyes faded over time. His sparkled like amethysts.

"You sure you want to go that way?" he said.

The correct answer was no. What I wanted was a hot shower and some quality time with my Xbox, but there seemed to be little point in saying so.

His right hand moved closer to the handle of his pistol, his fingers undulating slowly so his gem-spangled rings sparkled red, white and blue in the candlelight. The toothpick rolled from one side of his mouth to the other. I tightened my grip on the tablecloth. He drew. I yanked the material towards me and raised my hand to catch the knife.

Nothing happened. The entire length of cloth pulled free. Everything on top stayed exactly where it was. The dishes, the punch bowl, the cutlery, Suki's salad. Even most of the rose petals. For a fraction of a second I stared in mute horror at the undisturbed place settings. Then he opened fire.

The bullets left a trail in the air. Gyrojet ammunition. Each round was like a rocket that sped up as it left the gun. A full clip cost more than a U2 concert, so you either had to be good or filthy rich to use them.

I twisted sideways and the first shot ricocheted off my shoulder armour. The second trimmed a lock of hair from over my ear. I spun the tablecloth like a cape to block his view, then dove to the far end of the table, rolled to my feet and reached back for Suki's knife. He stared at my hand with an expression of disbelief. I guessed he'd never seen a young vampire move so quickly.

I guessed wrong.

"You really think you can beat me with a fork?" he asked.

I glanced back at the table and blanched. Wrong cutlery. This was shaping up to be one of those nights.

Bullet number three hit my chest like a mallet. My armour stopped the round, but the force knocked me through one of the Plexiglas panels of the pool fence. I landed hard and rolled away as two more bullets shattered the patio stones beside me. Hoping to create some space, I leapt for the diving board and sprang onto the roof of the penthouse. My feet touched down on either side of the peak just as another bullet clipped the vambrace over my arm. I glanced behind me. The vampire smiled, holstered his gun and pulled out a short, curved dagger.

I took a deep breath and focused on the instructions Ophelia, my guardian and sword-fighting instructor, had given me.

Be like water. A thousand pounds crashing down the mountain. Fast. Fluid. And unstoppable.

The only part of me that felt like water was my stomach. The rest of my muscles were knotted rope. I could feel the fork deforming in my fingers.

Be like water . . .

The vampire leapt upwards, caught the edge of the eaves and slung himself over the lip of the shingles so we were staring at each other from opposite ends of the roof. He closed in at a run. I flicked the fork at him like it was a throwing star, then threw a desperate jab. He tapped the utensil aside, ducked my punch and swung his blade. A sound like a firecracker followed as it sparked against my armoured forearm.

The barrage that followed had me bobbing and weaving like a master of drunken kung fu. I should have been circling away from his knife hand, but on a pitched roof that would have given him the high ground, so I had to back straight up. In no time, I was dancing at the end of the peak. He thrust high. I ducked and slipped and would have tumbled over the side had he not grabbed me by the wrist. He pressed the tip of his blade against my throat and smiled. *"That's When Your Heartaches Begin."*

The pool was just beneath me. I twisted my hand free, kicked out hard and aimed for the deep end. My execution was slow and his blade sliced though my skin, sending ribbons of pain up and down my neck. This was followed by a shocking jolt when, instead of splashing gently down into the pool, my back landed flush on the diving board. One bounce later, two hundred pounds of flailing idiot was soaring over the patio.

I landed on the dinner table. The wooden legs collapsed. Blood donor bags burst, plates and crystal goblets shattered, tea lights spilled their wax and sputtered out, the smell of balsamic vinaigrette gummed up my nostrils. Suki's steak knife clattered to the patio beside me. By sheer luck, my hand came down over the handle. I turned it so the blade was hidden under my wrist, then tucked it up my sleeve.

The bounty hunter was doubled over, laughing on the penthouse roof. "And they say you're going to be T-R-O-U-B-L-E. *Trouble*." He straightened up to wipe his eyes. "All those crusty elders holed up in their tombs, too scared to face the night. Unbelievable."

I was lying on my side. Blood from my neck ran through my fingers and down the inside of my armour. A burst blood donor bag was lying on the patio stones near my hip. I picked up the bag and drained what was left. A short-lived euphoria carried the pain away. My heart was still stuck at the Daytona 500, but at least all my leaks were sealing.

The vampire leapt from the roof, hit the diving board, executed a perfect straight-legged front flip and landed like a rhinestoned ninja right in front of me. It was the coolest thing I'd ever seen. He drew his gun, cocked the hammer and put the tip of the barrel against my forehead. "Any last words?"

"Why are you doing this?" I asked.

"There's a bounty on your head. If you can match your price tag, I might forget I found you."

"How much?"

"Five billion dead. Ten billion alive."

I quickly did the math. "You're saying killing me is going to cost you five billon dollars?"

"A word to the wise, youngblood. Never wrong a person and leave them alive to take revenge on you. Five billion dineros is nothing to pay for peace of mind. And a good scrap is priceless. You're the first target who's ever tried to kill me with a fork."

He watched as I lowered the empty blood donor bag to the ground. As soon as his eyes lifted, I let the knife slide down into my palm. He took a quick step back.

"Ah-ah-ahhh!" he said. "*Too Much Monkey Business*. Drop it. NOW."

I raised both hands and spread my fingers. The knife slipped to the ground. "You don't miss much, do you?"

"Wouldn't be good at my job if I did."

"Did you know you were out of bullets?"

He peered down and noticed his chambers were empty. "So there's still room for improvement . . ."

I threw the salad bowl at him. It hit his chest. Dressing and lettuce flew everywhere. I grabbed the knife and rolled to my feet.

"Dagnabbit," he shouted. "You're *Steppin' Out of Line!*"

Balsamic vinaigrette dripped from the rim of his white leather hat. He flicked an olive from his lapel, then assumed an offensive crouch, the tip of his curved knife held aloft. We circled each other. My heart was beating so frantically I was amazed it hadn't bruised any ribs. The man faked a thrust. I moved to block it. He slapped my hand away and kicked me so hard in the stomach I went crashing back into the pool fence, knocking another Plexiglas panel loose.

He let me get up. I tried to tag him as he closed in. He leaned back, his suit snapping from the speed of his movements, then executed a perfect spin kick. The air was out of my lungs before I registered what was happening. Then he slammed his dagger into my sternum. By some bizarre miracle, the blade got wedged between two platinum armour plates. He tried to wrench it free and it snapped.

Inside the penthouse apartment the elevator pinged. As I circled away, chest throbbing, Charlie stepped out. He saw me and did a double-take. An instant later he was on the terrace, his dark hair matted, beads of sweat glistening on his forehead. He was still armed from his sword-fighting lesson and pointed the tip of his *katana*—a Japanese killing blade—at the bounty hunter.

"What is this, karaoke night? Who is this clown?"

"The last man you're ever gonna meet," the bounty hunter answered. "And you are . . . ?"

"Impressed with your costume. You know you're three thousand miles from Graceland?"

"The King lives, baby."

"Not for much longer." My friend stepped forward and raised the *katana* overhead. "Charlie Rutherford is going to send your sorry ass back to Vegas."

The man's forehead knit.

"You've never heard of me, have you?" Charlie asked.

"Should I have?"

My friend scowled and lowered his sword. "But I bet you've heard of Zack." It sounded like an accusation.

"Daniel Zachariah Thomson—the Child of Prophecy? Naturally. I'm lucky to have found him first. So who are you, his *sidekick*?"

Charlie snarled and threw his *katana*. The bounty hunter leaned out of the way, grinning as it swept past. Fortunately, Charlie wasn't trying to hit him. He was tossing the sword to me.

CHAPTER 2

THE UNBREAKABLE RULE

CHARLIE SMILED as my fingers closed over the sword handle. "Good luck," he said to the bounty hunter.

I went at the man like a berserker, the sword an extension of my body. It whistled through the air with deadly precision. I trimmed one sideburn, then the other. He managed to back up and pull his second gun, the one that was still loaded. Before he could take aim, I kicked his arm aside. Then I snapped the blade over his shoulder and stopped it at the edge of his neck.

"Drop it," I said.

The muscles of his jaw clenched. His gun was pointed sideways. If he swung it back my way, I'd have two options: kill him or take a round at point-blank range.

I was spared the decision. Charlie crashed into him and the two went down in a tangle of arms and legs.

"*Sidekick?* I'll show you *sidekick!*" my friend shouted. He started throwing haymakers. It bought me enough time to slip close and take what I needed.

The bounty hunter pushed Charlie away and rolled to his feet, only to find the barrel of his gun aimed squarely at his nose.

"Last words?" I asked.

He reached up slowly and pushed the top of his hat back so we were eye to eye. His purple irises sparkled mischievously. "You bet," he said. "*There's no tomorrow!*" His other hand was behind his back. It swung forward.

Charlie dove, hands outstretched, and pushed me sideways. "FLASH-BANG!" he shouted. A grenade hung in the air right where my face had been. I raised my arms as it detonated. My eyes were protected from the flash, but the bang shattered both eardrums. The world went silent and I tripped over the broken table. A smell of burnt metal filled the air as my ears started to ring.

I rolled over and tried to stand, but my balance was shot and I stumbled sideways, trashing another section of fence. Charlie was at my side. I expected him to help me up, but he pulled the gun from my hand instead, then staggered after the bounty hunter, who'd leapt from the edge of the roof. There was an apartment building across the street. Charlie took aim in that direction and the muzzle flashed.

I started fishing through the mess from the tabletop, hoping to find another blood donor bag, but my hands wouldn't go where I aimed them. Charlie knelt at my side a second later and found one with a few ounces left inside. I gulped it down, then waited for my hearing to come back online. Charlie sat down beside me and pulled my finger out of my ear—both were itching furiously. His lips moved.

"What did you say?" I shouted, clicking my jaw as my eardrums regenerated.

He muttered something I couldn't make out.

"Did you get him?"

"No." He jammed the gun in his belt, disgusted. "*Sidekick . . .*" His eyes bounced from the table to the broken pool fence. The only thing we hadn't ruined outside the apartment was an asphalt landing pad on the far side of the shallow end. "You know, when a guy shouts *flash-bang*, you've got to protect your ears."

"I'll know that for next time."

"Right . . . So, what did the Arabian Elvis want?"

"Apparently there's a ten billion dollar bounty on my head."

Charlie whistled, then pulled me to my feet. "That's *beaucoup de* moolah, Zack. Turn yourself in and you can pay for takeout. You made a total mess of our dinner."

He sounded angry about it, like it was my fault this had happened. My heart and stomach were still doing an acrobatics routine, but he seemed more concerned about his girlfriend's salad.

"In case you didn't notice, Charlie, that guy was here to kill me! Doesn't that worry you at all? I almost swallowed a bullet back there."

"But you didn't," he said. "We sent that loser packing." He picked up his sword. After examining the scoring on the blade, he slid it back into its sheath. "Why didn't you lop his head off? You could have handed him his hat, with his head in it."

What could I say? Years ago I had made myself a promise that I would never take another person's life. It was my unbreakable rule. Even in training, I didn't practise kill strokes.

"There has to be a difference between us and the bad guys, Charlie."

"I thought you didn't believe in bad guys."

This was true. Even the worst people had *some* good in them, though it might only be their taste in embroidered cowboy hats.

"You know what I mean."

Charlie turned so we were face to face. I was a few inches taller, and thick from years of weightlifting, but he was a year older, and had been shaving since he was fourteen, so he often acted less like a friend and more like a life coach. I sensed a lecture was on its way.

"This isn't a Batman comic, Zack. One day, someone's life will be hanging in the balance. Mine. Luna's. What if some dude is about to nix her and you hesitate? If anything happened, you'd never forgive yourself."

I clenched my teeth. "I'd feel nothing but pity for anyone who tried to hurt Luna."

"Yeah, but pity wouldn't stop them."

He was right, but I had to draw the line somewhere. Killing seemed a good place to start.

He began filling the punch bowl with ruptured blood donor bags. "Everyone has the right to self-defence. You've got to do what Ophelia says. Empty the mind and trust your instincts."

I understood the theory. But being empty-minded wasn't as easy as some people made it look, Charlie included. He could tell by my expression that I wasn't sold.

"If I hadn't shown up, you'd be in a body bag right now."

I nudged him in the ribs with my elbow. "But you *did* show up. 'Cause you're my *sidekick*."

I thought he was going to strangle me. Instead, he put his hand on my back, then shoved me towards the penthouse doors. "Let's get ourselves cleaned up before Ophelia finds out about this."

"Oh man, is she ever going to freak."

"You don't say. Well, that's exactly why you're not going to tell her."

"Charlie—"

"Look, she's got this place locked down tighter than the

Pentagon. I'm sick of it! If she finds out a bounty hunter came here, she'll put us under house arrest for good. It's bad enough that the whole building is full of security cameras and we're under surveillance twenty-four seven. It's worse than *1984*."

"Did you even read *1984*?"

"Just the SparkNotes, but that's not the point."

"Charlie, she's gonna find out eventually. If we don't tell her now, she'll go off like an A-bomb. Is that what you want?"

He tossed up his hands. Then his cellphone buzzed. He pulled it from his belt and scanned the display.

"What's the word?" I asked.

He flashed it my way. The message was from his girlfriend, Suki. It read: *r u free*.

He rattled off a quick response, his thumbs a blur. Then he pulled the bounty hunter's six-shooter from his belt and held it up like a trophy. "You wanna have a go with this?"

Firearms made me uneasy, so I shied away from the shooting range when the others practised there. If I had to suffer any more of Charlie's jokes about how good he was with his love-gun, or my being too shy to take my pistol out of the holster with a lady in the room, I was going to bite him.

"No thanks. I've got to find Ophelia. Any idea where she is?"

"Wep dep. She and Luna had some stuff to get for tomorrow."

The "wep dep" was the weapons depot, a name Charlie used to describe the sixth floor. It was where all of our guns, munitions and military equipment were stored.

Charlie turned back to stare at the mess, disappointment pulling his mouth down at the corners. "You sure you have to tell her?" I held his gaze. He sighed. "Too bad. Those rose petals were a nice touch."

Chapter 3

GERM OF CORRUPTION

I LEFT CHARLIE on cleanup detail and, after a rapid drop in the elevator, found myself in a long hall running along the edge of the building. Iron Spike Enterprises had once been an apartment complex, but my Uncle Maximilian had converted it into the sort of headquarters you'd expect to see in a spy movie. Since his death in a cave-in this past summer, it had been our home.

Floor six, the wep dep, was one giant storage room. I placed my hand on the palm-scanner outside the main door, then punched in a security code. When the light beside the lock turned from red to green, I turned the latch and muscled the door open. Luna was rummaging through a cupboard full of ammunition boxes, her copper hair falling in loose spirals past her shoulders. The sight of her helped settle my nerves. I was also relieved not to see Ophelia anywhere nearby. I wasn't looking forward to breaking the news about our recent visitor.

Luna glanced my way but said nothing. She was watching the camera on the wall. There was one in every room and hallway—part of my uncle's elaborate security system. Ophelia had deactivated the ones in our private quarters, but all of the others remained online.

"What's up?" I asked.

"Just getting some stuff for the shooting range so Charlie's father can show us how to use this gear. His flight comes in later this morning."

Charlie's father, Commander James Rutherford, was a master marksman. He was in between missions for the Canadian navy, so he'd agreed to fly down from Halifax to give us some lessons. He was also a member of the Underground, a covert group of men and women who shared the vampire secret and helped people like us stay hidden and supplied. My father had been part of the network too and had occasionally been tasked with hunting rogue vampires—those who suffered from Endpoint Psychosis. I knew very little about the Underground and how it worked, not only because it was a highly secretive organization, one my father never mentioned in his journals, but also because Hyde, a werewolf and vampire hunter, had wiped out all of the operatives around Ophelia and me, so I'd never had an opportunity to learn much about them.

Luna tucked a box of shells under one arm, then slipped a hand past my elbow so we were arm in arm. "Why'd you leave practice early?"

"About that . . ." I said.

Before I could explain, she pulled me behind a rack of assault rifles. It took us out of the camera's view. Her teeth were down. They pushed out her lips. Her hand rose to the base of my neck and she pulled me closer. Her pupils were so wide that only a slender ring of emerald was visible around them. I thought she was going to kiss me, but she didn't.

"We need to be alone," she said.

"We're alone now."

"You know what I mean."

I did.

"You need to talk to Ophelia," she said. "We aren't kids any more."

"I will."

She let me go, then put a hand on my chest and pushed me back. "You said that last week."

This was true. "The situation's gotten a bit complicated . . ."

Her eyebrows rose. "No kidding. Cameras everywhere. Constant training. We never get to go out and do anything. It's like a never-ending boot camp. I didn't agree to stay here so I could live like a hostage, or a nun. Suki feels the same. So does Charlie."

I couldn't picture Charlie as a nun, but I understood what she was getting at. Ophelia was overprotective to a fault. It hadn't seemed warranted until tonight.

"She just wants to keep us safe. And she's—"

"What she wants is to keep us apart."

This sounded melodramatic, but it was more or less true. Ophelia didn't like us to be alone. She'd never offered an explanation, and I'd never asked, but it didn't take a brain scientist to figure it out. Last summer, I'd bitten Luna. To my surprise, she bit me right back. And so we unwittingly shared our first *vampire's kiss*, an act we repeated often, not just because of the rush that followed, but because the mixing of our blood created a connection between us so strong that for a short time afterwards we could hear one another's thoughts. It was strange at first, but we quickly learned how to control it—like a kind of private telepathy. None of this was dangerous, at least not at the moment, but apparently as we got older things would change. The pathogen that caused vampirism would make us stronger, and we'd develop our vampire talents, those bizarre powers you find in Gothic novels and shows like *Buffy the Vampire Slayer*. Once that happened, sharing blood would become dangerous, perhaps even fatal.

Ophelia didn't like Charlie and Suki to be alone either. She was worried Charlie might pass on the contagion. And as much as I agreed with Luna that we weren't children any more, to other vampires we were considered abominations, so young that any vampire who saw us was duty bound to kill us. Helping us was a criminal act. It was why Ophelia had stopped letting any of us venture out at night. We might be discovered by others of our kind and killed. And if Suki got infected, she'd share that risk.

Luna crossed her arms. "Look, just ask her if we can go out on a date, like two normal people."

"Funny you should say that," I said. "Charlie and I had planned a nice dinner, but—"

I didn't get to finish. The door opened and Ophelia walked in. A look of surprise, then disapproval came over her face. I stepped away from Luna, but she stayed close, her head next to my shoulder. Faint traces of her floral shampoo laced the air.

"I didn't expect to see you two here," Ophelia said. There was more than mild reproach in her voice. She tucked a lock of blond hair behind her ear.

Luna held up the box of cartridges. "I was just getting these."

"I can take them," Ophelia said.

Luna handed them over. "Zack wanted to ask you something," she added. "I'll let you two talk privately." She slipped out the door. The patter of her feet faded in the direction of the elevator.

"What was that all about?" Ophelia asked.

I felt my tongue grow two inches thicker. "Well . . . Luna and the others are feeling trapped. She wanted me to ask for a night off." I almost added, *So we can have some time alone together*, but my mouth decided at the last second that it didn't want my foot in there.

"I see," Ophelia said. "I thought you four were having dinner on the roof."

"Yeah, well . . ."

"Well what?"

"Well, someone crashed the party."

Ophelia fixed me with an intense stare. "Who? What happened?" She started inspecting me.

"I'm fine. A few bruises. Nothing to worry about."

"What's that smell?"

I sniffed at the air around my shoulder. "Residue from a stun grenade."

She noticed the hole in my armour from the vampire's knife. "Tell me everything."

So I did, although I left out a few of the more embarrassing details, like my flight off the diving board.

"Do you know who's offering the bounty?" I asked.

"No."

"Could we raise that much—ten billion dollars?"

"Probably not. Why?"

"I just thought . . . maybe we could buy ourselves out of trouble. If it's a matter of money—"

"It isn't," she said. "No sum in the world will get you out of this. You toppled Vlad, whose reign made the name Dracula more feared than any in our history. Until Hyde appeared, but you stopped him, too. To anyone seeking power, you are more threatening than the sun."

"Because of the prophecies."

"Yes. You are a perfect match: an orphan risen from the dead, a blood drinker, your father's fame as a vampire hunter

23

unparalleled. You are destined to rule. It will make you a target to any vampire hoping to fill the power vacuum created by Vlad's death. It is the reason for this bounty."

"What about Charlie and Luna? Is there a bounty on them?"

"I don't know. Does it really matter?"

"Of course it matters!"

"That's not what I meant." She paused. It was so quiet I could hear both of our hearts beating over the hum of the lights. "Have you read *Victory*?" she asked. "It's a Joseph Conrad novel."

"No," I said. "Why?"

"It contains an interesting passage. 'I only know that he who forms a tie is lost. The germ of corruption has entered his soul.'" She looked at me as if I should understand what this meant. I didn't.

"You are connected to all of us. We are your ties, Charlie and Luna especially. It doesn't matter if there's no bounty on your friends. If any of them venture out and are taken, you can be leveraged. If you didn't do as you were asked, they would be made to suffer. It would tear you apart." She raised the box of shells and tapped the corner of it against my chest. The rattling of the bullets inside made me uneasy. "You need more training. There's barely been enough time since the summer for us to cover the basics. You know next to nothing about the enemies you'll have to face. Their talents. How to protect yourself. You want to risk a movie or a night at a dance club? Forget it. Those things will still be waiting when this is over."

"And when will that be?"

"When we end it. After you've trained more. When we have a better sense of who we're up against. And after our enemies spend a bit more time wiping one another out. It might take a year. Maybe two. Maybe ten. I can't say for certain."

I resisted the urge to throw up my hands, a gesture I some-times borrowed from Charlie, but it wasn't the time for theatrics or complaints. Not with Ophelia. I owed her too much.

"There has to be some middle ground here. I haven't had a decent run in months. And my friends feel like prisoners. It isn't fair to put them through this. Not because of me."

"No, it isn't fair, but that's the way it is. This danger is real. After tonight, you can't pretend it isn't." She held my gaze until she was certain the message had settled in. "Your friends will understand."

A moment later she left, and I was alone with the weapons and equipment—everything from construction tools to night-vision goggles and laser tripwires. Most of it we'd probably never use. My eyes came to rest on a long silver tube. It was six feet long, two feet wide and rounded at the edges. Charlie called it the photon torpedo because it looked as though it belonged on the starship *Enterprise*, but none of us had any idea what it was for. I'd once asked Ophelia about it, but she'd been vague, almost dismissive. "Nothing we can use at the moment," she'd said, or something like that.

As I took the elevator up to the penthouse, I considered what to say to Luna and the others. After my father's death, I had grown up in a mental ward, with routines and rules, security guards and medical staff. Nurse Ophelia was central to that. The others weren't used to her, or to such unusual restrictions. And now there was a bounty on my head. I wondered who had offered it and how much longer we'd have to wait before some-one else came around to collect.

Turned out, it wasn't long.

CHAPTER 4

CHARACTER FLAW

WHEN THE ELEVATOR reached the top of the building, the doors slid open. I heard a distinctive giggle echoing down the hall from Charlie's room. It was Suki. The girls weren't even supposed to be up there—part of Ophelia's no-nonsense house rules. Our dinner on the roof was to be the first exception since we'd moved in.

"Is that you, Flash?" Charlie shouted.

I stayed in the hall. "Yeah. It's me. What are you guys up to?"

Charlie laughed. "Well, there are only so many things you can do on a bed."

I heard the whump of a pillow. I reached in to close the door, but someone yanked me into the room. Luna. She didn't look happy.

"Why didn't you tell me?" she asked.

I glanced at her, then at Charlie, who was lying on his bed in his housecoat, his hair dripping wet. Suki was standing over him, poised to hit him with the pillow again. Everyone was looking at me.

"Tell you what?"

Luna crossed her arms and gave me a stern look that might have been borrowed from Ophelia. "A man came here to kill you, and you didn't even think to mention it to me?"

"I was about to. You never gave me the chance."

"Don't blame this on me!"

Charlie rose from the bed. "If you two are going to fight, do it somewhere else."

Suki hit him again with the pillow. It flew out of its case and crashed into his dresser, upsetting a photo of the two of them at Charlie's cottage on Stoney Lake. He caught it before it hit the ground, then examined it for a second before setting it back. It had been taken before his infection.

Suki had been a different person then. Confident, bubbly and athletic. But after witnessing the gruesome murder of a friend, then suffering the disappearance of Luna and Charlie, she fell apart, dropped out of school and stopped seeing her friends. According to Luna, she saw a therapist regularly, but no amount of counselling could fix the real problem—her confused and angry parents. Dr. and Mrs. Abbott fought constantly, which made the house more a pressure cooker than a home. I understood. One of their daughters was suffering from a post-traumatic stress disorder and the other was a vampire, a condition medical science couldn't understand, or even put a name to. It was too much for the Abbotts, and their frustration amplified Suki's distress. And so she went from being the most likely candidate for prom queen to being so nervous she didn't like having people look at her. She chopped off most of her hair, dyed it black and started dressing like every day was Robert Pattinson's funeral.

But things were improving. Charlie adored her—that helped. So did moving away from home. And she was our only set of eyes in the daytime, which meant once the sun was up she was the only one who could look after Vincent, a lycanthrope we'd more or less adopted. I took it as positive sign that she'd gone back to dressing in colour. And the dye had disappeared from her hair. It was still short, a bit boyish even, but she was blessed with a face that would never be hard to look at, especially when she smiled, which she did often now, despite all the constraints in place under Ophelia's watchful eye.

Charlie tossed a balled-up sock at me from across the room. "Snap out of it, Sleeping Beauty. What did Ophelia say?"

I knew better than to start that conversation. Luna was waiting for an apology. "Sorry," I said. "I meant to tell you about the bounty hunter. I was just waiting—"

"Well, that's the trouble," she said. "You're always waiting. You know, it wouldn't kill you to be more assertive."

I frowned.

"She's right," Charlie said. "You dither all the time. You've got to tackle things head-on."

"Dither?"

"Yeah. You could have turned that bounty hunter into a corpse, but you didn't, so he got away. If he puts a bullet through you tomorrow, you'll have no one to blame but yourself." Charlie looked around at everyone. There seemed to be some consensus about this. It was suddenly obvious that they'd been discussing this character flaw of mine right before I'd come in.

A tired breath escaped my chest. I felt like a deflated balloon. "Let me see if I understand you correctly. The bounty hunter got away—and that's my fault because I could have cut his head off. And so if he comes back, it's on me. It won't be *his* fault, or the fault of the guy who *hired him*. It will be *my* fault?"

"Well, there's no need to get sarcastic!" Charlie said. "I'm just saying you could have stopped it."

"What about you?" I asked Luna. "Do you think I should have killed him?"

"Maybe," she said. "I don't know." Her eyes flickered over to Suki, who was watching us all with a nervous expression on her face. "I'm not going to judge because I wasn't there. But that guy came here to kill you. He forfeited certain rights when he made the decision to do that."

"Exactly," said Charlie.

"I get that," I said. "But I don't want to kill anyone. Not ever."

"None of us *want* to," Luna said. "It isn't about *want*. It's about necessity, and the right to self-preservation."

"And who decides when it's necessary? Who has the right to do that?"

"We do," Charlie said. "When someone threatens us—we have that right."

"I can't accept that," I said. "It feels . . . I don't know, just wrong."

"You're being naive," said Charlie.

"And you're . . ." I didn't know how to finish.

"Hey, it's just my opinion," he said. "You'll get over it. Now give us the bad news. What did Ophelia say?"

"Don't try to change the subject," I said.

"I'm not *trying* to change the subject. I *am* changing the subject. It's part of my assertive nature. Did she flip out, or what?"

"No, she didn't flip out, actually. She's just worried about what could happen if we leave."

Charlie scowled. "What—like we might have some fun? You know, she ought to be worried about Endpoint Psychosis. Isn't that what your father called it? When a vampire goes mental and bites everything in sight?" He opened his closet and started rummaging through his clothes.

"Maybe she'll change her mind when your dad is here, and we have a bit more protection."

"We don't need my dad's protection. We can look after ourselves. We proved that tonight. Ophelia worries too much."

She had ten billion reasons to be worried, and so did I, but I wasn't in the mood to argue any more. I just wanted to be alone with Luna. "Can't we talk about this later?"

"It's always *later* with you," he snapped. "Now *is* later."

I looked at Luna.

"I'm with him," she said. Her arms were still crossed. She pointed an elbow in Charlie's direction. "You always want to put things off, especially when it might upset Ophelia."

"Can't you be on *my* side for once?"

Her face softened. "I *am* on your side. I totally freaked when Charlie told me what happened on the roof. But he's right too. None of us are happy living like this."

"It's better than having someone kill us."

"Someone?" Charlie asked. "Like the nitwit in the Elvis costume? Do you really think anyone's going to show up that we can't deal with?" He shook his head in disgust. "I need to get outta here. One night—that's all I'm asking for. What have I got to do, strap a bomb to my head and run screaming down the halls? I'm going nuts!"

That much was obvious. I stared at his bedroom windows. Even with a thick layer of black paint over the bulletproof glass, and a set of shutters, blinds and curtains in the way, I could feel the night dying outside. The sunrise was minutes away. I finally felt like a thousand pounds of water crashing down the mountain. I just needed my bed to break the fall.

"This isn't a problem we're going to solve tonight. I've got to get some sleep. We can whine all we want. I agree with Ophelia on this."

"So do I," said Suki. She avoided Charlie's gaze. Her face started to redden. "It might be Halloween, but staying alive trumps a dinner date."

"That depends on who you're dating," Charlie said. He gave her a look. She smiled and glanced away. It seemed his good humour was making a comeback.

It was time to make an exit. Luna and I walked out the door and into the hall. We were finally alone. Then her phone buzzed.

"Please don't get that," I said, but she was already scanning the text.

"Oh, shoot . . . Ophelia says Vincent's up and he's hungry. I gotta go."

My face drooped.

"What's that look for?"

"Nothing . . ."

"It's not like Ophelia would let us stay together anyway. Haven't you noticed how she always shows up when we're alone for more than a minute?"

I thought she was exaggerating, then I heard the clump of the elevator doors opening down the hall.

"See what I mean?" She turned and sprinted for Charlie's room to save him and Suki from whatever mischief they might have been considering.

I slipped into my room to avoid Ophelia. The air of disapproval around her would just bring me down. She'd want to take Suki and Luna downstairs—especially now that Vincent was up. He was Hyde's son, and, like his father, had been infected with lycanthropy. Although he could subsist for a short time on normal food, to stay healthy he needed a regular dose of blood. Ours was preferable, so we had to donate regularly, then replenish ourselves from blood donor bags my

Uncle Maximilian had stolen. Vincent always turned when he fed this way, and so he had to be restrained within an elaborate matrix of steel manacles. Even chained, he was terrifying. Just the scent of him as a beast made my teeth drop. Vampires and werewolves were natural enemies. It was one of the reasons there were so few of them. It was also why the girls fed him, Suki most often. He didn't feel as threatened by her.

I entered my room and removed my armour. It was similar to a suit my late friend John Entwistle had worn. Until his death at the hands of Hyde, Vincent's father, he'd been the oldest vampire in the West. His body was buried in the same cave-in that killed Maximilian. If things were as bad as Ophelia implied, we might need their expertise. Since both were vampires, we could raise them up once we managed to find them. All that stood in the way was time, lots of blood, a few million tons of rock and Ophelia's reluctance to venture out from our high-rise sanctuary.

I debated having a shower, but I was feeling the groggy pull of sleep. I lay down, pushed my head into my pillow and started thinking about the tunnel of light. This was another part of our training. Ophelia had us focus on the same mental image whenever we needed to restore our inner harmony. We were supposed to choose something deeply personal. For me, it was the warm glow I saw each time I died. A healing light that made me feel whole.

A few moments later I was dreaming of Charlie's cottage on Stoney Lake. I was on the dock, sword in hand, my armour tight against my skin. The night was cool and crisp and deadly quiet. Mist rolled in off the water, the chill of it raising goosebumps on my arms. I sensed that something sinister was approaching. Soon the air was so thick with fog I could barely see more than a few feet away. A shadow flickered in the corner of my eyes. I spun but saw nothing. A pain in my gums followed as my teeth dropped. The presence was drawing nearer. I could feel it.

I turned in slow circles, scanning the fog, but it remained out of sight. Then my armour started to fall apart. A shoulder plate slipped out first, then the metal over my chest. I tried to stop it and dropped my sword. As the blade disappeared through a crack in the dock, I dove for the handle. It detached. One quiet splash later, I was holding an empty piece of leather-wrapped wood. I sensed the evil presence behind me and spun to face it. Woven Kevlar unwound. What was left of the moulded platinum inside tumbled out like so many tin plates. My underwear was missing. It left me naked in the moonlight.

Someone laughed behind me, then a man's voice crackled like dry leaves. "A naked dream. I know what that means!"

I quickly used my hands to cover myself, and turned. A vampire was floating in the air. His legs were crossed. Each hand was buried in the opposite sleeve of his orange habit. His eyes looked closed, but I knew otherwise. This was Baoh, the prophet. He had no eyes. Skin grew over his empty orbits. His large eyebrows, which I'd once likened to insect wings, floated gently on the breeze.

"A word to the wise, young man. If you find yourself naked with an audience and you wish to remain anonymous, cover your face. Very few of us are recognized by our privates."

He had a point, but I kept my hands where they were.

He snapped his fingers. Jeans and a simple T-shirt appeared where my armour had been. "I didn't come here for a skinny dip, *gweilo*. You are in danger. Enemies gather in the shadows. The bounty is just the beginning. Come. There is little time."

CHAPTER 5

THE NEW ORDER

BAOH DROPPED SILENTLY to the dock, cocked an ear to the wind and listened. I heard nothing unusual—waves lapping the shore, crickets, the patter of moth wings, the hum of mosquitos, bats hunting overhead, the creaking of the pines and the swish of needles.

He moved closer, his slippered feet soundless on the wood. We were walking the Dream Road, a spiritual highway that connected people who slept. At Ophelia's request, we'd met in similar circumstances during the summer so we could deal with the werewolf Hyde. Baoh and I had played Wii Boxing together and discussed the prophecy. He was about as weird as a guy could get without adding extra heads.

"You need to take us somewhere safe," he said.

"Isn't this place safe?" I asked.

"Safe? This is a dock. It doesn't even have walls. Bah! Even a blind man could find you here."

I looked at his eyeless face. "Good point."

"We aren't the only ones who travel the spirit planes, you

know. A new power is rising. The New Order. Not a terribly original name, but they are incredibly dangerous." He took me by the arm, his bald head level with my shoulder. "Quickly, get us somewhere you've been that no one else knows about. Didn't you have a secret hiding spot as a kid?"

As soon as he asked the question, the dock and the landscape around us blurred and shifted. I remembered that from my last visit to the Dream Road: whoever was dreaming had the power to alter the surroundings.

Baoh turned and bumped his head against a hook in the wall. "Oooh!" He took a step back and his foot came down on a stack of comics, which slipped out from underneath him. "Whoa! What is this place, a death trap?"

"It's the closet in my old bedroom."

"Is there somewhere we can sit?"

I looked around at the comics, shoes, *Star Wars* figures, unmatched socks and green plastic army men scattered everywhere. "Um . . . not really."

He didn't seem pleased with my answer so I pushed everything to the far end of the closet to make space on the floor. His joints cracked as I helped him sit. Vampires, even old ones, didn't usually have that sort of trouble.

"I have not fed in months. Big mistake. I'm beginning to feel my age."

He was over twelve hundred years old. I couldn't imagine how that felt.

"I have come to warn you," he began. A long pause followed as he listened. I opened my mouth to ask for an explanation, but he held up a finger to stop me. "They are searching for you, Zachariah, these agents of the New Order. I'm sure you know why. Child vampires are forbidden. Most reach Endpoint Psychosis very quickly, you know? Young carriers have done much damage to our species in the past, inciting the mob against us with their reckless behaviour."

I understood. The possibility of going insane was one of the reasons Ophelia had raised me in a mental ward. I'd gotten the help I needed to cope with my anger and loss. It had also kept me safe from the prying eyes of elders, who would have made short work of me.

"And you know about the prophecies—about the hunter's son who would be orphaned and born again, a blood drinker who will lead us to salvation or destruction. If you are the One of whom the prophecies speak, then you are a threat to anyone who seeks power."

"I'm harmless. And I don't even think the prophecies are about me."

The long feathery tendrils of one eyebrow rose in a doubtful arc. "Really?"

The truth was, I wasn't sure. I think a part of me wanted the answer to be yes. Everyone wants to be special. To be a hero. And in a way, it would have made up for all that I'd lost—not just my mother and father but a chance at a normal life. On the other hand, how could a guy who couldn't find two matching socks be qualified to lead anyone?

"You want me to confirm that you are the One. Well, in life, are there any certainties?"

"I guess not."

His head rocked back as if my answer was a personal insult. "Don't be silly! Of course there are certainties! A mother's love for her child, for one. Ophelia is terrified for you, and for good reason. An elder who calls himself the Changeling has declared himself the next Grand Master. The bounty on you is his doing."

I'd never heard of the Changeling. "What can you tell me about him?"

"Very little. No one knows who he really is, but rumour has it that he is a wizard."

A wizard? That was a stretch, even for me, and I was a veteran of the World of Warcraft.

"I don't mean a wizard. That is not the right word." He paused to think. "Alchemist. Yes, that is the correct translation. Sorry. English is my forty-third language. I am not as proficient as I should be."

"What does that mean?"

"It means I don't speak it as well as I should."

"No, I mean that the Changeling is an alchemist."

"I am not saying he is. But others think so. It is the only way to explain his many talents. Like Vlad, his powers stretch the imagination. Some say he can assume any form. That he can copy anything he touches. Any person. Any animal. Any thing. And they say he is poisonous, like a serpent. That when he kills, there is no coming back. His resources appear to be limitless. For your head, he has promised enough money, deeds and titles for a person to start his own country. It is fortunate that I found you before he did."

The way he spoke made me wonder if he was interested in collecting the bounty himself. The thought had barely passed through my mind when he laughed. "You are not so innocent as you used to be. But do not fear Baoh. He has not stayed alive this long by taking sides."

"Aren't you taking sides now?"

His eyebrows fluttered upwards as if considering this for the first time. "Well, I hope you're good at keeping secrets. And I hope you atone for your sins, or the Changeling's Horsemen will kill you."

"Horsemen? What sins? What are you talking about?"

"The Four Horsemen," he said. "War, Pestilence, Famine

and Death. Haven't you read Revelation? You can't have an Apocalypse without the Four Horsemen."

"Who are they?"

"Elders. The most lethal of the Changeling's followers. It is said that together, they are unstoppable. The only way you can save yourself is to make redress for all the wrongs you have committed. Atone, seek forgiveness, and perhaps then you will survive. Perhaps . . ."

CHAPTER 6

FAILED RESPONSIBILITIES

I KNEW I WASN'T a perfect angel, but Baoh made it sound as though I was due to be the next celebrity guest on *America's Most Wanted*.

"What do you mean, I need to atone? For what?"

"You broke the law when you infected your best friend. He was, what, fifteen at the time? The same night, he infected Luna. She was too young, also. But even if she'd been older, it would have been unlawful. In a family of vampires, only two generations can coexist. You cannot make another vampire while your progenitor lives or your line of infection grows too long."

I was a bit lost. "What does that mean, exactly?"

"As a vampire, you can make only *one* other vampire, and you cannot do it as long as the one who infected you is still alive. Charlie should not have turned Luna while you lived. You should not have turned Charlie while Vlad lived. Vlad should not have turned you while Ophelia lived."

"Wait a second," I said. "You mean Ophelia infected Vlad?"

"She never told you this? Perhaps she is ashamed. He was a monster in the end. Before that, however, he was a very effective Grand Master. And not a bad ballroom dancer."

He started talking about the pathogen and how it had to be controlled, but I missed the particulars. My mind was stuck on Vlad and Ophelia. I'd known they were husband and wife, but I'd no idea that she'd created him.

"You're drifting, *gweilo*," Baoh said, poking my shoulder. "Pay attention. There are now four vampires in your family. Ophelia, you, Charlie and Luna. According to ancient law, this is unacceptable. The infection line cannot exceed two. You must fix this situation, quickly."

"How?"

"You must put Charlie and Luna into a state of undeath. That way, you have only two vampires active in your family, you and Ophelia."

I was having trouble wrapping my head around the word *undeath*. In most vampire fiction I'd read, we were thought to be soulless creatures, cursed to remain trapped forever between this life and the next. Neither living nor dead, but undead forever. In my experience, this was a bunch of baloney.

"What do you mean by undeath?"

There was a flicker of movement beneath Baoh's skin-covered orbits. He seemed surprised by the question. "Undeath is much as you would imagine it. A dreamless sleep. All of the body's functions stop. You don't breathe. Your heart doesn't beat. Muscles don't move. Nerves don't fire. None of your senses perceive. To others, you appear dead, but you are not, because your soul will not move on to the next life nor will your body decay."

The word *decay* dislodged something from my memory. Years ago I'd read that people in the Middle Ages sometimes dug up bodies to make certain that they'd started to spoil. A rotting corpse could be safely reburied. It wasn't going to rise from the grave. But any corpse that was found to be well preserved was assumed to be a vampire and would either be burned or staked to the inside of the coffin to keep it from wandering around.

"Your friends will not suffer in undeath. Ophelia can help them with the process. It is quite simple."

I stood up. The clothes hanging in my closet forced me to hunch. "I can't do that. I'd sooner cut off my own hands."

"A waste of time," Baoh said. "They would just grow back." He fumbled for my arm. "Listen to me. I am speaking to you as Ophelia's friend. As your father's friend." He gently took hold of my wrist and pulled me back to a sitting position. "Yes. I knew your father well. He trusted me. More than once I offered him counsel, and it saved his life. Until the end, when he wouldn't listen."

I reached up to my throat and my fingers settled upon the full-moon charm of my necklace. It was the last thing my father gave me before he died. There was another piece to it, a golden crescent that snapped to one side, but Luna wore that, as my mother had before her. Originally, the necklace had belonged to Vlad and Ophelia, but she had given it to my father, and he'd passed it on to me before he left to explore a temple near one of his archaeological digs. At least, that's what I'd been told at the time. He was really hunting Vlad. When his colleagues returned to camp and told me my father had been killed, I refused to believe it and rushed off to find him. I could still remember the pile of huge square stones under which he had been crushed. I was so shocked all I could do was run. The streets were sand. The buildings in ruin. Frantic, and blind with tears, I ran until I stumbled past something dying in the shadows. Thinking it was a dog, I crept too close. Vlad crawled out and bit me above the ankle. My blood revived him. And so

I unwittingly saved my father's killer and became a vampire myself. I still had the scars. The last I would ever have, now that I was immortal.

"I have survived for over twelve hundred years, Zachariah," Baoh said. "I know the nature of men. Despite what the prophecy says, the Changeling and his Horsemen will never follow a boy. All you can hope for is amnesty. But you must correct this problem you've created. Your friends, Luna and Charlie, they must be put to rest."

I shook my head. "I can't ask them to do that."

Baoh sighed. "If you don't, they will most assuredly be killed. Once they are undead, you can fulfill the more difficult of your tasks. The vampire pathogen has spread out of control. Overseas, at least. Hyde did much to contain its spread here, but not so in the Old World. Failure to address this outbreak is your greatest crime, and it must be remedied."

Ophelia had hinted that the pathogen was spreading in some parts of Europe, but I'd never been there. "That has nothing to do with me."

"Nonsense," snapped Baoh. "You toppled Vlad but assumed none of his responsibilities. Under his direction, the spread of the contagion was tightly controlled. After you destroyed him, you should have done the same. So here we are, with too many vampires, and something must be done . . . by you." He tapped his finger against my chest. "Or you will have difficulty convincing anyone that you deserve leniency."

"Why didn't you tell me about this before, when we first met? You knew what had happened with Vlad!"

"True. But you had enough on your plate with Hyde. And frankly, I thought he was going to kill you."

He nearly had. "Why didn't Ophelia ever mention this?"

"She's put you on a pedestal. She did the same with Vlad. It is regrettable, but it doesn't change your obligations. You must address this problem immediately, or the Horsemen are going to kill you."

A nervous breath escaped my lips. If I had this right, the most lethal vampires in the world had been sent to kill me by the Grand Master, who was poisonous and could appear as anyone, at any time. No wonder Ophelia didn't want us leaving the high-rise.

"What am I supposed to do?"

"Run," Baoh answered. He stood. His eyeless orbits were staring at the door of the closet. "RUN!"

"What? I thought you said I had to atone?"

His fingers closed over my arm. They felt like talons. "The New Order—they have found us. Go! GO!"

I looked back over my shoulder. The air in front of closet door was shimmering, like an image on fabric that someone was shaking. An instant later, it ripped open. Long white fingers reached in through the hole and tore it back. A vampire unlike any I'd ever seen stepped from the inky darkness. His arms were extremely skinny. So were his legs, which looked as though they might buckle under the weight of his bulging stomach. A roll of neck fat spilled over his frilly collar. In all other respects, he looked like a plague victim. His face and hands were swollen and covered in open sores, and his skin was as white as bone. There was a deep crimson rune on his forehead. It looked like a brand. As he moved closer, I could see past him to the rip in the dreamscape. Many sets of eyes peered from the darkness there. They were other vampires, shifting, restless and hungry.

"It's too late," Baoh said. "Pestilence has found us."

CHAPTER 7

TRAPPED IN A NIGHTMARE

B AOH TOOK A deep breath and planted a hand on my sternum. Then he spoke something indecipherable, with such intensity that it was as if he were trying to force the words through a stone. I shot backwards. The walls of my closet rippled and lengthened as I flew past.

Baoh's eyeless orbits were still locked on me when several sets of clawed hands took hold of him from behind and pulled him into the darkness. A ghastly chorus of snapping and tearing followed. It left me alone with the vampire at the far end of the closet. Pestilence.

The vampire raised a hand and I stopped in mid-air. It happened slowly, as though gravity were suddenly optional. I put a foot down to test the floor; the hardwood felt solid. The closet had stretched to become a long tunnel. It gave me an idea. If I could change the landscape, and get us back to the shooting range at Iron Spike Enterprises, perhaps I could turn this around. I imagined the room perfectly, right down to the tile floors and the soundproofed walls, but nothing happened. Somehow, I'd lost control of my dream.

Pestilence laughed. It was a grotesque, raspy sound. Each of his teeth had been filed to a sharp point. They punctured his gums so that blood was crusted on the inside of his lips and covered his tongue. He raised his arms until his hands were touching the closet walls on either side. Long, thin, spider-like fingers slipped through the drywall as if it were water, sending out a ripple of warped rings. He pulled his hands back and the tunnel shortened several feet, drawing me closer.

I started to sink. My feet were slipping into the hardwood as though it were quicksand. The floor was soon past my knees, then my thighs. I reached out, but nothing around me was solid. At the same time, Pestilence kept walking towards me, anchoring his hands in the liquid walls and pulling my section of the closet closer. He stopped when he was a few feet away, right on the edge of the puddle. I was past my waist by this time. His face started twitching again. It was covered in sores and scabs and purpled veins. None stood out so much as the rune on his forehead. I had been mistaken in thinking it was a brand. The mark had been carved into his skin. It was still raw. He smiled, then bit into a pustule on the back of his index finger, giggling as if the sight of me drowning was too hilarious to bear.

I pumped furiously with my legs, stuck my hands into the liquid floorboards and tried to push myself away. I succeeded only in getting my arms stuck. Then, while I watched, helpless, he placed the sole of his foot on my head and pushed me under. I closed my mouth to lock the air in my chest. Pestilence's wavy silhouette hovered above the floor like a ghost image filtered through murky water. He started snorting and chuckling again—a squeamish, sucking gargle.

I tried to swim back to the surface, but the more I kicked and pulled the farther down I sank. The air in my lungs started losing its potency. My head buzzed—it felt as if a spider were crawling just under the base of my skull. Pestilence was digging around in my mind, searching for something. I bent my thoughts towards him and tried to push him out, but he squirmed away. The sensation was horrible, like something slithering through the soft tissues of my brain. It made my head quiver, and I nearly lost my breath. He dug further. I tried to pry him out, but it was like pinching an earthworm in my fingers. I couldn't quite get hold. I was running out of time. Without help, I was going to drown. I needed Ophelia.

Pestilence's laugh intensified. Something about her must have amused him. Or perhaps it was my helplessness. As his serpentine presence kept wriggling through my head, images of Ophelia and me flashed across my mind's eye. The two of us at the Nicholls Ward when I'd thought she was just a nurse. Later, when she confronted Vlad. Then at our home on Hunter Street before Hyde turned our world upside down. Pestilence was sifting through my memories for ones of her.

He wanted to know how she sounded. How she looked. How she thought. He wanted to know how to find her on the Dream Road.

I was already panicked. My fear of drowning was stronger than my fear of the sun, but the thought of anyone hurting Ophelia was greater still. I couldn't let that happen.

I imagined my skull shrinking around him like a net. There was solid resistance. I squeezed harder and pushed. Then my lungs erupted. I tried to inhale, but there was no air around me, just a fluid so thick it choked off my mouth and throat. My diaphragm bucked and my chest caught fire. Then something yanked at my arms. People were shouting.

". . . suffocating."

"What the . . . ?!"

"Help me!"

I recognized the last voice. It was Luna's. All I could see was her blurry shadow. Something was covering my head. I clawed at my face, but Luna pulled my hands away. Something passed through my mouth and I sucked in a painful breath. A moment later, my bedsheet passed over my head. I sat up and retched. All that came up was blood. I could hear Charlie swearing.

"You were choking on your sheet," Luna said. She was kneeling beside me. "It was all the way down your throat."

There was blood all over me. My bed was ruined. I'd ripped the mattress to pieces trying to free myself.

"It's a good thing you didn't need mouth-to-mouth," Charlie said. "That is the grossest—"

Suki whacked his arm before he could say any more. She was standing behind him. It didn't look as though she wanted to get any closer.

Luna nervously rubbed the golden-crescent charm of her necklace, the one that matched the full moon that I was wearing. She let it go, then reached out and touched my face. Blood stained her hands and pyjamas. There were flecks of it on her cheeks.

"Normally, a guy has to drink a lot of beer to get that kind of distance."

"Charlie, you're not helping," Luna said. She kept her next words private. *What just happened, Zack?*

I wasn't sure if I wanted her to know.

Her eyes narrowed just slightly. It was enough that Charlie noticed.

"No, no, no, no, no," he said. "Not that silent talking again."

Luna sighed and I flopped backwards, cracking my head on the headboard. Hunger had taken root in my belly, and my lungs felt as if I'd inhaled a handful of glass.

"I need a drink," I said. I looked at Luna. Luna looked at Charlie. Charlie looked at Suki. She folded her arms over her chest.

"Okay, okay," Charlie said. "We've got lots. Just don't start the show without me."

He returned a minute later with a blood donor bag that I devoured instantly. The discomfort of healing gave way to the rush. When the aftershocks passed, I got up to change. My friends peppered me with questions. I did my best to answer, starting with Baoh and his news, and ending with my encounter with Pestilence and his attempts to read my mind.

Charlie threw up his hands. "Great. Just great. So you're saying some fat bag of sores can kill us while we're asleep?"

"Seems that way."

"We need to get you downstairs," Luna said.

"Why? What time is it?"

Charlie had to wipe the front of my alarm clock to see the numbers. It was just after 8:00 p.m. I'd been asleep all day. It felt more like a few minutes.

"I need more sleep," I said.

"Are you telling me you want to go back to bed?"

I looked at my ruined mattress. "Not in here."

"Is it safe?" Suki asked. "What if that guy comes after you again?"

"I don't know. Ophelia might have some suggestions."

"You can ask her about it now," Charlie said. "She and my dad are expecting us in the conference room. If they hadn't sent Luna here on wake-up detail, you'd be a corpse. If we take too much longer to get down there, she'll probably put us under house arrest till the world ends."

"I think that's the least of our worries. If Baoh's right, the most dangerous vampires in the world are coming here to kill us."

"Good," he said. "I'm sick of all this waiting around."

CHAPTER 8

MEETINGS

SUKI TOOK HOLD of Charlie's hand. "Didn't you say we should hurry?"

"Yeah," he said, but he didn't move.

She started pulling him gently towards the door. "You're going to have to see him sooner or later."

She must have been referring to his father, whom Charlie hadn't seen, face to face, since Christmas. Apparently, it was a disaster. Charlie's father was still furious that he was infected, and although that was my doing, Commander Rutherford had a way of blaming his son for whatever happened, regardless of who was responsible.

"I know what you're thinking," Charlie said to me, "and don't even start. Making me a vampire is the smartest thing you've done since learning to floss. Don't feel guilty. Not for a second."

It was a bit late for that. Suki gave his arm another tug.

"Are you going to be long?" he asked.

I looked around the room. Unless Mr. Clean showed up with a power washer, I was going to be busy for a while.

"I'll take care of him," Luna said, waving Charlie and her sister out the door.

"Wait, you guys," I said.

He and Suki paused in the hall.

"Can you keep this to yourselves, at least until I figure out what to say to Ophelia?"

"No problem here," Charlie said.

Suki pulled him out the door.

"Do you think he'll be all right?" I asked.

Luna laughed. "You're worried about Charlie, after what just happened to you? You're a piece of work, Zack." She walked to my closet, grabbed a towel and offered it to me. "Are *you* going to be all right?"

"How much trouble can I get into taking a shower?"

"Not as much as the two of us could together." She smiled, then headed out after Charlie and Suki.

"Luna?"

"Yeah?"

"Thanks."

She looked back over her shoulder. One of her canines was pressed against her bottom lip. "You can make it up to me later."

MY LATE UNCLE Maximilian had some extremely impressive hardware in his collection, including a car that could break the sound barrier and enough guns to storm the White House, but the most useful device to me was the penthouse shower. In less than five minutes, it could turn you into a new man.

After a quick cleanup, I jumped on the elevator, then decided to take a detour to Vincent's room. He was a very unusual kid, not only because he was the son of Hyde, a vampire hunter the likes of which the world had never seen, but because he was also an orphaned blood drinker, and, like me, he'd died and come back. It made me think the prophecies could have been about him. I wanted to know how he was doing before making any decisions that might put more on his plate than he could handle.

The short hall to his room led past the Vault. This was where he fed. Inside was a mess of chains heavy enough to raise the *Titanic*. It was the only way to keep him from ripping the place apart when he turned. His bedroom was farther along. From behind his door, I could hear the scratching of a pencil. The smell in the air was an odd blend of women's shampoo and Vincent's plastic Lego. I went straight to his door, knocked a few times, then pushed it open slowly.

"It's Zack," I said.

"I know," Vincent answered. "You knock the same as Ophelia, but your footsteps are heavier."

He was hunched over his desk, colouring. Although he was only eight, he was almost as tall as Luna. If you passed him on the street, you'd put him somewhere in the fourteen or fifteen range, at least until he spoke. His mind was like that of a third-grader, but he aged physically at a rate that was alarming. This was typical of lycanthropes—another reason they were scarce. Since he'd moved in with us, every week was like a year. Some days when he got out of bed you'd swear he looked older than when the girls had tucked him in. And his strength was alarming, at least when he turned. Unlike the werewolves you read about in stories, his transformations seemed to have nothing to do with full moons. Blood did it. When he smelled it or saw it. Sometimes when he just thought about it. It also happened when he got stressed or emotional, which was the most frequent trigger. Until two months ago, he'd been in a coma. When he awoke, we had to break the news that his entire family had been killed. He handled it remarkably well, but no kid, no matter how resilient, can overcome such a loss without the occasional temper tantrum sneaking into the script. Without the Vault, he would have reduced the building to rubble.

I peered over his shoulder, relieved to see him calm and focused. "What are you drawing?"

A red-and-blue figure with black lines on his face was dangling from a rope. Another man, with fangs, wearing a dark coat, stood beside him. He appeared to be holding two swords that dripped blood. There was also a metal robot.

"I haven't finished that one yet," he said, reaching for a green pencil crayon.

"Who is it?"

"Doctor Doom," he answered. He went to work on the cape.

"Where are his arms?" I asked.

He pulled back from the picture and cocked his head to the side. "Charlie's holding them." He tapped the fanged character that I'd thought was holding two blades. "He says that if anyone ever hurts me, he'll rip their arms off."

"Charlie's very colourful that way."

"That's Spider-Man," he continued, pointing to the blue-and-red figure with the dark lines on his face. "But I kind of wrecked his mask. My hands are clumsy again."

Sometimes he grew so quickly there was an adjustment period during which his coordination suffered.

"I think it looks great," I said. There was an empty chair beside his desk, so I pulled it out and sat down. "I have to go to a meeting. I just wanted to know how you're doing."

He stuck his tongue between his teeth while he filled in Doctor Doom's cape. "I'm fine. Charlie came by already."

"If you get nervous or need anything—"

"He gave me Suki's cell so I could call him." Vincent searched under several pieces of paper, then spied the phone on the floor and grabbed it.

"You know how to use the touchpad?"

"Yeah. Charlie showed me."

I smiled. Vincent seemed fine, so I rose and told him I'd drop by later with Luna and the others.

"And Charlie, too. Right?"

"Of course."

I scanned the wall by his desk on the way out. There were drawings of all of us mixed in with superheroes, characters from *Star Wars* and someone fat, round and blue, who might have been from a Japanese anime. Charlie was in all of the pictures, and he was always the largest. Hardly surprising. It was sort of that way in real life. He threw himself into things with reckless abandon, and the results, good or bad, were usually worth a picture or two.

I gently closed the door, then made my way down several floors to the conference room, where a full debate was in play.

"That's crazy," Charlie was saying as I entered. "I don't want to spend another six hours cooped up in this place, let alone six months."

Ophelia was seated at one end of the table; Charlie's father, the other. He was a huge man, over six and a half feet tall, and bald as a cue ball. In jeans and a leather coat, he looked more like a UFC fighter than a naval commander. He and my father had been best friends—close enough that I'd been calling him Uncle Jake since I was a kid, back before I knew about vampires or the Underground or my father's secret profession.

Uncle Jake's frown deepened when he saw me. I glanced at Luna, who was sitting beside Suki on the far side of the table.

Charlie was alone on the side closest to me. "About time you showed up," he muttered.

"I was just checking in with your biographer. He's illustrating your crushing defeat of Doctor Doom."

"What can I say? The boy has an eye for talent." He kicked a chair out for me.

"What have I missed?"

Luna, Uncle Jake and Ophelia all started talking at the same time. I got the gist right away. We were going to hole up here while Charlie's father went overseas to look into the bounty.

"That won't work," I said. "Staying here is no longer an option. We have to go out and get our noses dirty."

Charlie let out a quiet "Yeah" of approval. Ophelia glanced quickly at Charlie's father. They started to speak at the same time.

"You'll be dead within an hour . . ."

". . . won't last a night . . ."

Both stopped, then Uncle Jake waved for Ophelia to continue. "We've just been informed that a legion of vampires is coming here, hoping to make good on that bounty. The fellow you fought on the roof will be the first of many. Mercenaries. Ex-Coven spies. Assassins. Killers from all corners of the globe."

"Who told you this?"

"A vampire named Istvan," she explained.

"And you trust this person?"

"Istvan? Yes. He's saved me more times than you have years to your life."

"He's one of the good ones," Uncle Jake added. "An old friend of your father's."

My father seemed to have a lot of old friends I didn't know about. "Did you hear from Baoh?" I asked.

Ophelia seemed surprised by the question. "Baoh rarely makes contact with others. He is vulnerable because of his age."

"I thought the older you got, the tougher you got," Charlie said.

"That's true," Ophelia replied, "but the trade-off is that you must sleep longer. Baoh often rests for years at a time. While he does, he's at risk. He might be the oldest living vampire in the world. He is certainly the most secretive."

"He visited me last night on the Dream Road," I said. Then I passed on what I'd learned about the Changeling and his Horsemen, and about our family line being too long. The news shocked Charlie into a tense silence. He and Luna looked mortified.

"Ours is hardly the first family to extend past two generations," Ophelia said. "To suggest that anyone should be put into undeath is ludicrous. I will not support it."

"That wasn't all," I said. I then explained about the pathogen, and how I was being blamed for its spread.

I thought Ophelia was going to explode. She rose from her seat and started pacing.

"This is preposterous! No sane person would expect someone your age to assume the near-impossible task of policing our kind. Vlad and his Coven were taxed beyond endurance more times than I care to remember, and that was with the Underground supporting them. To imagine a teenager could manage it right after Vlad disappeared, with Hyde running wild, killing everything in sight, the Underground in shambles . . . These claims are completely absurd."

"Absurd or not, it explains the bounty," Charlie's father said. "With a prize like that on offer, few will care that Zack's been made a scapegoat. Did Baoh tell you anything more about him?"

"The Changeling? Just that he could appear as anyone. And that he's poisonous. Apparently, if he kills you, it's permanent."

A hush fell over the room. My eyes were on Ophelia. She had her forehead pinched between a finger and thumb and was chewing gently at the inside of her cheek.

"It's okay," I said. "I've been thinking this over. We need to go to the Warsaw Caves. My uncle and John Entwistle are buried there. With their help, we have a chance. It's time to dig them up and bring them back."

CHAPTER 9

A HOUSE DIVIDED

THE DISCUSSION that followed about my uncle and Mr. Entwistle was painfully short. No one wanted to raise Maximilian from his resting place, because nobody trusted him. About Mr. Entwistle there were other concerns. During his long life as a vampire, he'd evolved into a man as principled as any I'd ever met, but it hadn't always been that way. In ages past, he'd been so cruel that others called him the Butcher of England.

"You raise up a man like that," Uncle Jake said, "and you don't know what you're getting."

"It's true, Zachary," Ophelia added. "Death changes everyone, and not always for the better. Resurrect John, and you might find he's reverted back to older ways of thinking."

"That never happened to Zack!" Charlie said.

"No, but he hasn't changed enough in his short life for that to be possible. Entwistle lived over six and a half centuries. He's got a lot of baggage. And even when his intentions were good, he was far too reckless. His head-on approach isn't the best for this situation."

"I disagree," I said. "He told me this would happen. That a new order would be established, and they'd send an army. I think his head-on approach is just what we need."

Are you sure that's why you want him back? Luna asked.

I was relieved that she chose to keep this question between us. We'd had this conversation before. She was convinced I wanted Mr. Entwistle back because, deep down, what I really wanted was a father.

"We're sitting ducks here," I said. "And I need to get out and address the issue of the spreading contagion."

Uncle Jake frowned. "Venturing anywhere is too great a risk right now."

"And I won't allow it," Ophelia added. She fixed Suki and Luna with a stern gaze. "I made a promise to your parents that I would keep you out of harm's way. It's the only reason they agreed to let you stay with us."

I pushed my chair back and stood. "If we wait here, we're toast." I wanted to add more—that it was my fault that Charlie and Luna were infected and in trouble, and that maybe this outbreak really was my fault too—but nearly everyone started talking at once. Only Suki said nothing. She looked as though she wanted to bolt.

"One at a time," Uncle Jake said. "One at a time . . ." He gestured to me with an open hand. "You mustn't take all of this on your shoulders, Zack. And it isn't as hopeless as you think. There's another player in the game. He calls himself the Baptist. Word in the Underground is, he's a bona fide power. And he's preaching about the rise of a child vampire who will topple the New Order to make one of his own. Sounds like the kind of ally we need."

"Have you heard of this guy?" Charlie asked Ophelia.

"The Baptist? Yes. He's relatively young and has been trying to restore the Underground since Hyde's death. I will look into a possible alliance, while Commander James travels overseas to learn more about this bounty and what's happening with Vlad's old Coven. Any information about the Changeling and his Horsemen would obviously be useful. Until we know who they are, and what they can do, the rest of you need to stay out of sight."

I started to object, but Uncle Jake cut me off. "Zack, your father would never forgive me if I put your life in danger. And, Charlie, neither would your mother."

"Forget it," Charlie said. "You can't expect me to sit around this place waiting for a legion of assassins to show up, one after the other. Attack. *Always attack.*"

He'd said this before. It had been a mantra of sorts for Alexander the Great. It suited Charlie's disposition.

"It's not your responsibility," I said. "It's mine. Baoh told me that I have to be involved."

My friend spun his chair, then stood so we were face to face. "So it's okay for you to go out, but not the rest of us?"

"This isn't about dinner and a movie. This is life and death."

Luna glared at me. Her rage hit the inside of my head like a nail. *You're such a hypocrite. Would you let us put ourselves in danger while you hid here?*

She was right and I knew it, but with Charlie barking at me, I couldn't back down. Not after he'd called me a ditherer and said I needed to be more assertive. "Charlie, I'll duct tape you to the ceiling if I have to. I'm not going to see you killed because of me."

I felt Ophelia's hand on my arm. "The decision has already been made. All of us will stay. We can train. Lord knows we need it. Charlie's father will go."

That wasn't going to solve our problems. "Don't you understand? It has to be me!"

"This isn't your fault," Charlie's father said. "Vampires in every corner of the world were waiting for Vlad to show a sign of weakness so that they could replace him. This fight was centuries in the making. The best thing right now is to stay out of the spotlight. I'm going to take care of things."

"I'm not going to sit on my hands while you take all the risk."

"I'm not sitting this out either," said Charlie.

"Yes, you are," his father and Ophelia said at the same time.

Luna started walking away from the table. "Well, this is productive."

"Where are you going?" Suki asked.

Luna didn't get to answer. A white strobe started to flash above the door, then something in the room beeped. Ophelia pulled out her cell. Her eyes ran quickly over the display.

"What's that?" I asked.

"Trouble," she answered. "I'm patched into the building's security system. Someone has just broken in."

CHAPTER 10

INVASION

OPHELIA SHUT OFF the alarm. It started beeping again right away.

"What does that mean?" Charlie asked.

"It means there are break-ins at several different locations."

Charlie pulled out his cellphone. "When you said a legion was on its way here, I assumed we had a couple of nights."

"So did I," said Ophelia. "And I would have thought the bounty would discourage co-operation." She shut the alarm off. It started beeping again. Her eyes were frantic as she read the cell display. "We need to move. You kids get upstairs to the control room. It's the safest place at the moment."

"Does anyone know how to monitor the security cameras?" Uncle Jake asked.

"I do," I answered.

"Someone needs to get Vincent," Ophelia said.

Charlie was already dialling. "I'm on it."

I jumped over the table and grabbed Luna's hand. She was pulling Suki towards the door. "We'll take the stairs. It'll be faster."

"We'll all take the stairs," Ophelia said. "I'm shutting down the elevators." She and Uncle Jake shared a quick look, then moved for the door.

"Where are you going?" Charlie asked.

"To the equipment room," his father answered. "We're going to need—"

The shrill beep of the alarm drowned out the rest of what he said. He waved for us to get going. We headed up. He and Ophelia headed down. Before he was out of sight, he pulled an automatic from his belt. "Keep your cellphones handy. We need to know how many, and where."

Charlie tossed me his cell and had Suki jump up onto his back. "Vinny's not answering. You keep trying."

He started bounding up the stairs a half-dozen at a time, with Luna and me right behind him. When we reached the twenty-seventh floor, he and Suki headed for Vincent's room. I still hadn't gotten an answer. I kept trying until Luna and I reached the control room, three floors above. This was the nerve centre of the building, where all of the security cameras were hubbed. Luna placed her hand over the palm-scanner while I keyed in the code to unlock the door.

Inside, dozens of monitors were set into the wall. Facing these was a desk covered in dials, switches, keypads and buttons. There was also a small fridge that Ophelia had stocked with blood and other essentials. We weren't inside for a second when all of the monitors fizzled to a flat line, then went black.

"What just happened?" Luna asked.

"Someone shut down the power."

"What do we do?"

"We stay cool." I took a deep calming breath and reminded myself that Ophelia had been doing this sort of thing for centuries. "The emergency generators should kick in any second."

Charlie's cell buzzed. I picked it up and his voice crackled in my ear. "What's going on?"

The lights flickered back on. So did the monitors.

"Someone cut the power," I told him. "We're running on backup generators."

"Perfect."

"Is Vincent okay?" Luna asked.

I repeated the question to Charlie.

"Yeah," he answered. "He's on his way up."

I set the phone down. "Okay. Everyone will be here soon. We'll be fine . . . really."

"You think?"

"How bad could it be?"

I got my answer when I started flicking switches to see what was happening on the floors below.

"Oh my God!" Luna's eyes jumped from monitor to monitor. "They're everywhere!"

I stared in disbelief. Hundreds of vampires swarmed the halls and lower rooms. Baoh hadn't exaggerated when he'd said the pathogen was out of control. "This is crazy. Every vampire on earth must be here."

I quickly checked the monitor for the sixth floor hallway. Dark shapes shot past the camera and it went fuzzy. I started flicking switches for the lower and middle floors. One by one, the monitors blinked out. Soon we were looking at nothing but static.

"They're smashing all the hall cameras," Luna said. "We're blind."

Blind and woefully outnumbered. Unless Buffy showed up with the cast of *Twilight*, this was going to end badly. "We've gotta grab the others and get out of here."

"What happened to *we'll be fine*?"

"That was before. Now I'd say it's time to panic."

Luna flicked the switch so we could see inside the weapons depot. Ophelia was hastily removing the long silver case from its housing.

"Why do they want the photon torpedo?" Luna asked.

"I have no idea. Has anyone figured out what it's for?"

"You mean it's not a bomb?"

"I don't think so. It just looks like one. Didn't you watch *Star Trek* as a kid?"

She looked at me as though the answer should have been obvious.

On the monitor, Uncle Jake moved for the door, an assault rifle in his hands.

"We've got to warn them," Luna said. She reached for Charlie's cell.

"Wait," I said. "We'll use the intercoms." In front of me were a row of switches that my uncle had installed before everyone and their dog owned a cellphone. That way we could talk, while both Uncle Jake and Ophelia kept their hands free. I found the one for the weapons depot and flicked it down. "Get ready," I warned the two of them. "There's a swarm on their way. They'll be kicking your door in any second."

Uncle Jake started shouting. I pushed the switch the other way and it cut in, mid-sentence. ". . . many? Over."

"We can't tell. They've smashed the hall cameras, but there are hundreds here." I pushed the button back to listen.

"Why is the fire alarm ringing? Have they set part of the building on fire? Over."

Luna glanced down at a row of red lights on the console. One of them was flashing. In all the confusion, I hadn't noticed. "Yes," she answered. "In the garage."

Uncle Jake swore so loudly I'm amazed it didn't set off one of the thermite bombs in the crate beside him. Ophelia carefully set the long silver tube on the floor. I wondered what was in it that it would be so important. "Stay in the control room," she told us. "No matter what."

She removed a rapier from a rack beside her and drew out the blade. The image on the monitor started to get cloudy. Something was pouring out of a vent in the adjacent wall.

"Is that smoke?" Luna asked.

"Yeah."

Her face knotted up. "Why is it dropping? Isn't smoke supposed to rise?"

It was. But I sensed this wasn't ordinary smoke. "Uncle Jake, behind you! Something's coming through the vent."

Charlie's father turned. The barrel of his gun flashed. Then the camera winked out and all we saw was static.

CHAPTER 11

DESCENT

I STARED AT the fuzzy monitor, muscles jittery, eyes restless, heart pounding at a fight-or-flight tempo. When the palm-scanner beeped outside the door, I snapped my head around so quickly I'm amazed my teeth didn't fly out. Suki and Vincent hurried in. My relief at seeing them quickly fizzled.

"Where's Charlie?"

"Didn't he call?" Suki asked.

"I have his phone," I said.

"Yeah, but he has mine."

A heartbeat later his cell buzzed. Luna answered. Charlie's voice was faint but frantic. "Where's Zack's armour?"

It was in the penthouse. Charlie must have gone up to get it. "Are you *nuts*?" I shouted, accepting the phone. "Get down here before you get swarmed."

"Where is it?"

"Beside my bed."

I turned to a cabinet in the wall and flipped a release switch. A panel slid up. I punched in the security code. A second later, the metal doors unlocked. Behind them was a small arsenal. Vincent let out a slow "*Coool.*"

I pulled out a broadsword, then reached for a gun that Optimus Prime might have used. It had a spear sticking out the bottom and a grenade launcher on one side, and it fired about six hundred rounds a second. I handed it to Luna. "If anyone comes in . . ." I wasn't certain how to finish, so I pointed to a dial on the console. "That electrifies the door and the hall outside. It should keep you safe until I get back."

"Where are you going?" Luna asked.

She already knew the answer. Charlie was alone. And there was no way Ophelia and Uncle Jake were going to make it up here without help.

We heard footsteps outside the door, then someone started pounding against the metal. Suki yelped. Luna nearly shot a hole through it.

"It's me," said Charlie. "Open up."

Suki undid the lock and my friend tumbled in, a suit of armour draped over each shoulder. "Did someone die?" he said. "You guys look like the world's about to end."

"It might if we don't get moving," I said. We started suiting up. My hands were shaking. "There have to be hundreds here, Charlie. I was about to go get you."

He stopped and stared at me. "So this is what Entwistle was talking about . . . the army?"

"Looks like it."

"We making a run for the roof?"

"No," I said. "There's trouble downstairs. Your father and Ophelia need some backup."

"This is insane," Luna said. "You'll never make it."

Charlie opened the fridge. "Not without some fuel." He tossed me two blood donor bags.

Suki stepped in front of Vincent and clapped a hand over his eyes. "Is that really necessary? You know better than to pull that stuff out around him."

Charlie grabbed two more bags, then opened the door to the hall. "Sounds like we're going to need all the juice we can get."

"Are you supposed to take that much?" she asked. "What if you go crazy, like in the movies?"

"A little crazy wouldn't hurt at the moment. If anyone gets through that door, you feed some to Vinny."

She looked uncertain. Vincent never fed without being chained in the Vault.

Charlie winked at him. Vincent smiled.

"If anyone threatens you or the ladies, Vin, it's feeding time, you understand? Don't be afraid to turn, because if you don't, they'll kill all of you."

Vincent's smile vanished.

Is he for real? Luna asked me. *Vincent can't control himself when he turns.*

That's why you need to stay.

"I'm coming with you," she said aloud.

Charlie started grabbing weapons from the cabinet. He handed two pistols to Suki. "You can't *all* leave," she said.

Luna scowled.

Charlie pulled me out the door. "If there's as many as you say there are, without armour, it would be suicide." As he closed it behind us, I heard Vincent speaking to her.

"Don't worry. He'll be with Charlie. No one messes with Charlie."

OUTSIDE THE STAIRWELL, Charlie poked a hole in the first bag of blood, drained it, then polished off the second. I did the same with mine. Our eyes glazed over and our teeth dropped as the rush took hold. Once it passed, Charlie double-checked his belt. It was loaded with everything he could carry. Flash grenades, fragmentation grenades, incendiary grenades, tear-gas canisters, a pistol, a knife, even a gas mask. He pulled back the bolt on his M16, his pupils so wide he looked more shark than human. "Are you ready?" he asked.

"No," I said, unsheathing my blade. "But the coast is clear—outside the door, at least."

"You sure?"

"Yeah." I could feel Luna's frustration behind me in the control room, but for the first time, I could also sense others closing in from below.

What is happening? Luna asked. *I'm losing you.* Her voice was faint. Her presence was fading. I wondered if it might have been because of all the vampires nearby. The air was charged with anger. It was overwhelming.

Charlie paused at the door to the stairwell. "I know you, Zack," he said. It sounded like a criticism. "You don't want to hurt or kill anyone. That damn near got everyone wasted when we faced Hyde. These freaks are here for one reason: to kill you. And they will, if you don't turn up the whup-ass. I'm talkin' full bore."

He kicked the door open. "You need to show these Horsemen what it means to mess with the Chosen One."

I was bigger than Charlie. Stronger and faster, too. And I could beat him with anything but a deck of cards. I just wished I had a fraction of his confidence.

He jumped down the stairs. I was right on his heels. At the next landing, I stopped to test the air. A vampire was approaching. I sensed him before he leapt over the railing. Others followed. The first rushed forward, a dark blur of leather and long hair, his face twisted with rage. I swung my sword, but he reached up with one hand and caught my wrist mid-stroke. The other hand clamped around my throat and squeezed. My vision started to go spotty.

Charlie's gun rattled. The vampire used me as a human shield. Several rounds slammed into my back, each like a blow from a pickaxe. Other bullets made it past. One pierced his neck. He stiffened. Charlie kept shooting. When my vision cleared, I saw blood splattered on the walls and pooling on the floor. A row of bullet-ridden corpses lay unmoving in the centre of it. I backed away and started hyperventilating.

"Snap out of it," Charlie said, pushing me against the wall. "What's the matter with you?"

How could he even ask? He'd just killed half a dozen vampires. My insides railed against the wrongness of it. Even if I'd known how to put it into words, I couldn't keep enough air in my lungs to speak.

"Are you having a panic attack?"

My breath came in spurts. I was about to pass out. "Maybe . . ."

"You need to visit the light, pronto."

I closed my eyes. Instead of the warm glow of the tunnel, though, all I could see were dead faces twisted in hatred. My head started spinning. "It's not working."

Charlie snarled and pulled me ahead. He was turning to jump down the next flight of steps when a lean arm reached up through a shadow on the floor. The fingers were covered in pustules. The air froze in my chest. Pestilence was here. But this was no dream.

The hand closed around Charlie's ankle and upended him. He dropped his gun and it clattered down the stairs. Then a tall vampire with jet-black skin appeared at the top of the landing. I stumbled into her. It bought Charlie enough time to stand up.

More vampires appeared, some from the adjacent hall, others from below. I was moving beyond panic, into a kind of shock. I couldn't see anything but the black mass of enemies all around us. They were frenzied, like starving animals. There was no way we were going to survive this.

Then the dark-skinned vampire caught fire. In an instant, orange-yellow flames covered every inch of her skin. I thought Charlie must have tossed an incendiary grenade, but the woman had done it to herself. She didn't scream. There was no expression of pain on her face, not even a whiff of burnt flesh, just the faint odour of dry air. The heat forced me to turn away. She reached out to grab me, but Charlie hauled me backwards and lobbed something past my ear. It hit the wall with a clang. An explosion followed that nearly deafened me.

The blast sent us sprawling down the stairs. Vampires screamed. I rose to my feet and a bullet took me flush in the chest. More shots followed. My armour stopped the rounds, but the impact knocked me back down. Someone kicked the sword from my hand. Charlie tripped over me. He was trying to keep a vampire from ripping out his throat. Another vampire crawled over and started pulling at his belt. He loosened a grenade. It tumbled to the floor, pin missing, and rolled in my direction. I had no time to rise. Several vampires swarmed over me and tore at my arms and face. More than their weight, it was the feeling of them that crushed me—their senseless, mindless anger.

I was freed by a concussive shock wave that hit me like a battering ram. The security doors beside us blew apart and a blast of hot, angry air sent me rag-dolling down the hall. Ribs broke. Vertebrae broke. Even my teeth. Had it not been for my Kevlar suit, there would have been nothing left of me but a crimson stain and a bit of hair. I tried to raise my head, but I couldn't move.

A blurry shape appeared above. "Come on, lard-butt, get up." Charlie took my hand. Thankfully, he had enough sense not to yank me to my feet. It would have pulled me apart. "Holy hamburger, Zack. You're a mess."

I groaned.

"Come on, we gotta move."

I tried to stand and passed out. When I came to, Charlie was dragging me across the floor. His face was covered in burns and scratches. The rest of his skin was chalk white. I heard the beep of a palm-scanner and a door closed behind us. He put his back to the wall, slipped to the ground and closed his eyes.

"We have to go back," I whispered. "We have to get Ophelia."

He opened one eye. "Zack, we made it down three flights of stairs. Three! There's almost twenty more to go. We're dead if we go back. There's too many . . ." He ran out of breath. "How did they come at us so quickly? Were they phasing through the walls?"

Maybe. And jumping from the shadows.

"That door won't hold them long. Can you stand?" he asked.

I tried to rise.

When I came to, he was dragging me again. "No," I said. "Not here. Anywhere but here."

We were in a long rectangular office. One wall was a wide mirror flanked by windows. A couch sat opposite. Adjacent to that was an oak desk. Around the room, antique busts, weapons, armour, masks, vases and statuettes were on display, as well as an old oil painting of a Spanish battle that had once belonged to my grandparents. The sight of it filled me with a cold dread. This was Maximilian's office, where he had betrayed me to Vlad the Impaler. Later, I'd burned alive saving Luna. There were nothing but bad memories here.

"I don't want to die in this room, Charlie. I want to die outside."

He leaned against the wall to rest. "Don't talk that way. Nobody's going to die."

I started crawling towards the desk. Charlie stumbled past me. A pair of sconce lamps were mounted on the wall to either side of the painting.

"Which one is it?" he asked.

"The right one."

He pulled the right lamp down. A secret panel in the wall opened. It was where Vlad had been hidden the night my uncle sold me out. I started hyperventilating again.

"Come on. On your feet. We've got to get back to the girls." He scanned the desktop and started opening drawers. "Where is it?"

I had to answer in between gasps. "Top right."

He took out my uncle's automatic pistol. "Is there a way upstairs from here?"

I was struggling to get onto a knee. "I don't . . . know."

He helped me to my feet. "Deep breaths. You can do this." He inspected my armour. "Do you have anything to fight with?"

I shook my head. "If you take off my boots I could throw them."

"And unleash that foot odour? You'd kill us both." He tried to laugh, but it turned into a coughing fit. Then, with him grunting and me groaning, we hobbled into the dark.

CHAPTER 12

SON OF THE BEAST

WHEN WE STEPPED through the secret door, it closed behind us, leaving us in total darkness. No shadows. In the end, that saved us. And Ophelia. Always Ophelia.

"What the devil?" she said.

Charlie jolted in surprise and let go of me. I slipped against the wall and the impact knocked me out again.

When I came to, Ophelia was hunched over me, rapier in hand. The blade was bloodied right down to the hilt. She was furious. "I told you to wait in the control room!"

Despite her anger, the sound of her voice was like a balm. Relief flooded every limb.

"Where did you come from?" Charlie asked, coughing.

"Never mind that. Where did *you* come from?"

"Upstairs," he answered.

"Charles Rutherford, don't be coy with me. How did you get down to this floor?"

"We took the stairs."

"The stairs! Have you two lost your wits?"

Before I could say yes, something moved behind her. Uncle Jake emerged from an opening in the wall. There was a gun perched on his shoulder large enough to have been torn from the deck of a battleship. The barrel was slightly wider than a bazooka and stank like a firecracker. His eyes were hidden behind a pair of night-vision goggles. The right sleeve of his leather coat was shredded and the front of his T-shirt had a burn hole in it.

"Charlie, of all the idiot moves! Why can't you ever do what you're told?"

"Nice to see you, too, Dad."

His father growled, then lowered the gun from his shoulder, reached into the space he'd just vacated and pulled a metal case into the room. It was the photon torpedo.

"What's that?" Charlie asked.

"Later," his father answered, handing it to him. Charlie shouldered it with a grimace.

"Does this mean the others are alone?" Uncle Jake asked. Then he swore. "We need to keep moving."

"We can't go back that way," I said. "We'll never make it."

"We don't have to," Ophelia said. She moved to another section of wall, then pushed something. The panel beside her slid up. At the same time, another closed, sealing the wall where Uncle Jake had emerged.

"How many secret doors does this place have?" Charlie asked.

Ophelia raised a finger to her lips, then ducked into the new space. A set of spiral stairs rose into the darkness.

No one spoke. Through the walls, we could hear vampires scrambling in search of us. After a mercifully short climb, we reached the top landing. A keypad was mounted in the wall. Ophelia punched in the right code and a panel slid open. She walked into the hall and stopped dead.

"Dear Lord . . ."

"What is it?" Charlie whispered, leaning forward to see past me. The hallway was a bloody mess. Bits of clothing and hair and things I had no wish to identify were plastered across the floor and walls. The air was so thick with the smell of blood, each breath went down like a small meal. Charlie stepped around me for a better view and his foot slipped on something that might have been a glove with a hand in it.

"Wait here," Ophelia said. She slipped ahead to the control room, her sword dangling loosely in one hand. Her feet made squelching noises on the floor. "Luna? Suki? Vincent? Is anyone in there? Can you hear me? Open up."

The door buzzed and the lock disengaged, then I heard Luna's voice. "Thank God!"

She stepped aside to let the others past, then picked her way over towards me. The Optimus Prime gun was hanging from her shoulder. Judging from the smell of burnt gunpowder, she hadn't been shy about using it. She stopped with a good inch of space between us, which was good, since I probably would have shattered from the impact. My armour was holding me together.

"What the . . . ?" She reached up to touch my head but stopped short. I winced anyway. "Your ear's missing."

I hadn't realized that, but it helped explain my headache. "The hall . . . What happened?"

"Vincent happened."

"He did this?"

"Yup." She looked around at the mess. "We got stormed. One of them came right up through the floor. I'm not kidding. Like a ghost. It was freaky. Ugliest vampire I've ever seen."

"White face? Fat neck? Boils everywhere? Mark on his forehead?"

"That pretty much describes him."

"Pestilence. The guy from my dream. Did Vinny get him?"

"No. He was too fast. He just appeared, opened the door, then sank back into the shadows. The hall was full of vampires. They rushed us. That's when it really hit the fan."

I glanced around. Hitting the fan was an understatement. It looked like a whole brigade of vampires had taken turns jumping through a wood chipper.

"You look terrible," Luna said.

"I *feel* terrible. If it weren't for Charlie, I'd be in pieces right now. I was useless."

Uncle Jake poked his head into the hall. "Here." He held up a blood donor bag, then tossed it to me. Luna caught it after it bounced off my shoulder.

"Drink up," he said. "We're getting out of here." He stepped out and handed me another broadsword. "No sense in leaving this behind."

I took it, thinking it might serve me better as a cane. Everything but my hair was hurting. I felt terribly sorry for myself until Ophelia stepped from the control room. Vincent was draped over her back. I didn't see any injuries on his body, but he was unconscious, and his skin was a sickly grey. "Is he okay?" I asked.

"He might be out of commish for a while," Luna said. "He was out of control after he cleaned house. I had to hit him with a pretty big dose."

I glanced down at her belt. Hanging from it was an aerosol can. It contained a pungent extract that Ophelia distilled from monkshood, or wolfsbane, tiny yellow flowers that were extremely poisonous. It was the only substance we knew of that could turn Vincent quickly from a beast back into a boy. He got sick if the dosage wasn't right, so we used it only in emergencies.

"Can we flip on a light?" Suki asked.

Charlie was leading her into the hall, her arm in one hand,

the other cradling the case on his shoulder. They moved awkwardly. She was carrying enough guns and ammo boxes to outfit a small militia. "Trust me," he said, "you don't want to see any of this. Bad enough we have to smell it."

"No lights for now," Uncle Jake said. "We have to keep it dark."

"Why's that?" I asked.

"They have shadow-jumpers with them."

I thought he might explain, but instead, he waved for us to get going.

"What is that thing?" Luna asked him, staring at his shoulder cannon.

"Canister gun. Zack's father designed it. Best defence against smokers."

"Because cancer's not fast enough?" Charlie said.

His father sighed and shook his head. "A smoker is what Zack's father called a vampire who can assume a gaseous form. The canister gun forces them to solidify. Then you can take them out with conventional small arms." He shouted ahead to Ophelia. "Can you see anyone?"

She peeked out the door to the main stairwell. "No. But that doesn't mean we're alone. We'll have to chance it."

"It's okay," I said. "There's no one out there."

She responded with a flat stare. So did Luna.

"It's something in the air," I explained. "Like an aura of malice. It just feels wrong when they're around."

Ophelia paused, thinking. "You can feel it?"

"Yeah."

"Strange that I cannot."

"Maybe it's got something to do with the bounty," Charlie said. "It's Zack they're after."

Ophelia's eyes were troubled. "I suspect it has more to do with his heightened sense of empathy, but mark my words,

Charles, a sinister force is at work here, and it goes well beyond money. The man who showed up last night ran off when you two turned the tables on him. It wasn't worth it for him to stay. No reward would have changed his decision. But this mob, did any of them show the slightest interest in self-preservation?"

"No," I said.

"And that makes no sense. A vampire's instinct to survive is stronger than any other. The thoughtlessness of these intruders, it defies reason. Your foray onto the stairs—it's a miracle you two survived."

I didn't owe my life to any miracles. I owed it to Charlie. Before I could say so, Vincent started to groan. His eyes fluttered open. He looked around, then managed a weak smile. "See?" he said. "I told you Charlie would take care of things."

CHAPTER 13

PLAN B

CHARLIE AND I fed before leaving the hall. When the rush had passed, I nodded to Ophelia. There was nowhere to go but up, so she led us to the rooftop exit, deactivated the lock, motioned for us to stand back, then pushed the door open with her foot. A draft carried the smell of pool water onto the landing. The sight of the night sky and the cool air on my skin brought a feeling of instant relief. It wasn't to last.

"Why isn't anyone up here?" Luna asked.

"We're not sticking around long enough for it to matter," Uncle Jake said. He removed his night-vision goggles and started to get angry. I could smell it, even before he opened his mouth. "Where's the helicopter?"

Luna and I looked at one another. Charlie shrugged. "What helicopter?" Suki asked.

"Maximilian's Battlehawk. It's supposed to be on that landing pad." He pointed to the pavement beside the pool. There was a circle drawn in the centre of it. "Why didn't you tell me it wasn't here?" he said to Ophelia.

She glared at him. "There's never been a helicopter here. Perhaps if you'd asked . . ." The steel edge to her voice raised the hackles on my neck.

Uncle Jake seemed oblivious. "How in the seven hells are we supposed to get away now?"

"Don't you have a Plan B?" Charlie asked. "Hang-gliders, maybe?"

I thought his father was going to throw him from the roof.

Ophelia waved me over to the edge, then looked towards the apartments across the street. "Do you think you and the others could jump across?"

"No," I answered. "Without jetpacks, we'd just end up ruining the sidewalk."

"Does this mean we'll have to go back in and fight our way out?" Charlie asked.

Uncle Jake looked as if he was about to say something, but he was cut off by a gigantic explosion. Glass shattered. Chunks of concrete and steel shot from the innards of Iron Spike Enterprises. A burst of flame lit up the windows of the neighbouring buildings. It was as if we were suddenly standing inside a giant propane barbecue. Then the earth groaned, the floor lurched and the building started to crack.

I was too young to remember the day the Twin Towers went down, but like every kid on the continent I'd seen the footage and felt my mind go numb trying to understand all the whys and wherefores. Just like those massive buildings in New York City, Iron Spike Enterprises didn't collapse right away. If it had, we'd have been finished.

"Anyone have a rope?" Uncle Jake asked.

Charlie looked around as though he might find one hidden in the mess of last night's dinner. "We need a grappling hook. Where's Luke Skywalker when you need him?"

"A grappling gun would be better," his father said. "Maximilian must have one someplace."

"Does it look like this?" Luna asked, holding up the Optimus Prime gun. There was an attachment at the bottom with a spearhead sticking out.

Charlie's father accepted the weapon from her, gave it a rapid inspection, then smiled his approval. "Luna, I'm going to have you canonized." He took aim at a steel door on the roof of the apartments across the street. The harpoon shot out with a dull pop. This was followed by a short *whooloop* kind of noise as the thin cable uncoiled, and it ended with a metallic clink. "Let's hope that holds."

While Ophelia secured the near end of the line around the pool fence, Uncle Jake showed Luna and Suki how to slide down using an assault rifle, with one hand on the barrel and another on the handle.

"Boy, you two really trashed this place," Ophelia said, eyeing the table and broken sections of Plexiglas.

Charlie shrugged. "Hardly matters now."

A second later, the building groaned. Ophelia herded us to the edge. "Suki and Luna first. Move it!"

I held my breath as Luna slid down. She wiped out when she hit the roof, but the cable held. Suki was next in line.

"I'll carry you," Charlie said.

"No," she replied. "I can do this."

Ophelia smiled and Suki disappeared with a whoop. Luna was there to catch her.

Charlie stepped up next with Vincent on his back. "Geez, Vin," Charlie said, "what you been eating, bricks?"

Vincent looked like a corpse. He managed a weak laugh, then the two slipped from the edge and shot across the street.

Uncle Jake handed me the large silver case and motioned for me to hurl it to the other building.

"Won't that wreck it?"

"I don't think a nuclear bomb would damage that case. For all his faults, your Uncle Maximilian was not a man to take chances."

"What's in it?" I asked.

Ophelia cut me off with a wave of her hand. "Later. Get moving."

For its size, the case was extremely light. It sent up a shower of pea gravel when it hit the far roof.

Ophelia quickly handed me one of the metal posts from the pool fence. She'd torn it loose and bent it in a *V*—a perfect handle for our makeshift zip line. I stepped to the edge of the roof and paused. Something in the air wasn't right. The discharge of the explosives had given everything a burnt odour, but my nose caught something else. It was foul. I turned to ask Ophelia if she noticed it too, but as I started to speak, a lean white figure covered with pustules rose up from behind her and attacked.

CHAPTER 14

CASUALTY

O N OUR TRIP down the stairs, neither Charlie nor I had been able to figure out how we'd been swarmed so quickly. He'd made an offhand comment about vampires phasing through the walls. This wasn't too far off. Pestilence actually climbed out of Ophelia's shadow, as though the dark space was a hole in the floor. His speed was shocking.

Ophelia managed a surprised yelp before he put a hand on her face and pushed her into the ruins of the dinner table. I was still holding the metal fence post. As he charged me, I swung it at him like a baseball bat. It struck his neck. For all his fat and boils and pustules, his body was like a piece of iron. He didn't stop, but the blow moved him sideways just enough that instead of plowing me off the roof he hit my shoulder and spun me like a turnstile. He flew past the edge. For a fleeting instant, I thought I was going to be okay. Then he grabbed my collar and pulled me off.

I let go of the post and reached for the cable. I missed. Then I hit the ledge of the top-floor windows and managed to hook my hands over. A wrestling match followed. Pestilence yanked at my collar, laughing, blood gargling in his mouth. I held on for dear life.

My struggles would have been short-lived if Uncle Jake hadn't leaned over the roof and started shooting. Bullet number one hit Pestilence's wrist. Number two hit his shoulder. He let go and fell. The drop lasted a good four seconds. I risked a glance down, expecting to see a gruesome splat on the sidewalk, but he plunged into the shadow of a garbage can as if falling into water.

Uncle Jake reached down to help me up. Before I could grab his hand, Ophelia appeared at the roof edge and yanked him sideways. The sounds of metal on metal followed, and more gunfire. Luna and Charlie started shouting to me from the apartment building across the street. Their voices were drowned out by the shattering of glass. Iron Spike Enterprises was shifting. A row of windows cracked. Then another. Charlie pointed frantically. "Get up there!"

I hoisted myself over the lip. Ophelia was surrounded. As I drew my sword, a deafening boom hit my eardrum like a slap. Uncle Jake was right beside me, the canister gun on his shoulder. A thin ribbon of smoke drifted from the barrel. My eyes followed the metal cylinder as it arced over the penthouse. A dark cloud of swirling smoke had gathered there. Something solid was taking shape in the centre of it. The canister exploded like a giant Roman candle and a shower of bright red sparks tore through the air, filling my nose with the reek of burnt metal.

"Out of the way," Uncle Jake shouted.

I could barely hear him. My ears were ringing. He pushed me to the side, then fired several pistol shots into the cloud. It started to spin around, like a miniature cyclone.

"There," Uncle Jake said, pointing. He fired several more rounds, but the bullets passed harmlessly through. He set the pistol down and started loading the canister gun with another tin-sized cartridge. "You can hit him only when he materializes. I'll light him up; you finish him off."

I didn't know what he was talking about.

On the other side of the roof, Ophelia was fighting for her life. Pestilence rose up from her shadow again. Blood dripped from his injured shoulder and hand. He tried to grab her sword arm but she jumped clear. I started towards her, but Uncle Jake pulled me back. "She can take care of herself. We need to deal with this smoker. He's far more dangerous."

He dropped to his knee and took aim down the barrel of the canister gun. I followed his line of sight to the funnel of smoke overhead. Right in the middle was the ghost-like outline of a man's torso. The twister started spinning faster and shot forward.

Uncle Jake fired. The canister entered the twister and exploded. Tiny fragments of burning metal hissed through the smoke. For an instant, the man inside was cast in silhouette. Something was on his head. A helmet or a turban, I couldn't tell. In one of his arms was a curved sword. It made me think of the *Arabian Nights*, stories my father had read to me of dervishes, djinns and demons.

Uncle Jake raised his pistol and emptied the clip. The vampire went fuzzy and dropped his sword. The bullets passed right through him. Then his silhouette hardened and his scimitar returned to his hand as though pulled by an invisible thread. The man and cyclone headed straight for Uncle Jake. I leapt between the two, sword raised. Smoke and dust swirled past, filling my eyes with hot grit. At the last second, I resolved the man's shadow and met him, blade to blade. My sword sparked and I got knocked to the ground. The man flew by, the cyclone roaring like an angry wind.

Uncle Jake put a hand under my shoulder and helped me to my feet. "Good timing," he said. "Just like your father. Now get ready, he's going to make another pass."

"Who is it?" I asked, blinking furiously.

"I don't know. But I've never seen a smoker like this. Usually when you burn them they solidify long enough to take them down."

After roiling overhead for a moment, the cloud began to spin again. As it dropped, a shadowy outline of the man's head and torso appeared at the leading edge of the funnel. He reached out and his curved scimitar spun straight into his hand. I raised my own sword just in time to avoid being cut in half. The impact shattered my blade and sent me crashing into the pool fence.

"This is my last one," Uncle Jake said. He was loading the canister gun. "When it explodes, finish him. You have only a split second—when he's solid."

I stared down at the useless handle in my hands. There was barely enough metal attached to cut a sandwich. The building shuddered. I could hear more glass raining onto the street below. Cracks appeared in the mortar of the penthouse walls.

Suki was shouting from across the street. I glanced over and saw the cable was moving frantically. Charlie was climbing in our direction, hand over hand. Ophelia shouted for him to go back but he didn't listen. I was amazed that she'd even noticed with all of the activity around her. Two vampires lay still at her feet, but three others were closing in, warily. I could see no sign of Pestilence. One of the vampires tried to circle around behind her and strayed too close to the edge of the building. Bullets cut through the air. Luna was shooting from the far roof. The vampire stiffened as several rounds found their mark. Ophelia wasted no time cutting him down.

"Focus," Uncle Jake shouted. "Here, take this."

There was a knife in his hand. I needed something with more heft, so I kicked a Plexiglas panel from the fence and tore one of the steel posts from the concrete pad around the pool. The vampire of smoke dropped. This time there was no cyclone, he just surrounded us like a patch of dense, sulphurous smog. I couldn't breathe. It was like being on the stairwell again. I clamped my mouth shut as the shadow of his torso drifted past. I swung, but the post went right through him and he disappeared.

"Zack, he's behind you," Charlie shouted. He'd cleared the edge of the roof, gun in hand.

One of the vampires near Ophelia broke away to engage him. I didn't see what happened because the smoke around me thickened. Something crashed down on my wrist, and the fence post I was holding clattered across the patio and splashed into the pool. Then the vampire's blade hit the armour over my stomach and folded me in half. I sucked in a mouthful of foul air and started coughing. His next stroke would have taken my head off, but I was saved by the familiar boom of the canister gun. The air around me caught fire. Smoke burned. I raised an arm to shield my eyes. Sparks flew everywhere, burning my face and neck.

The cloud thinned and the man took shape again. His body was charred. Steam hissed from the bloodied cracks in his skin. He faced Uncle Jake, who was standing on the edge of the building, pistol in hand. He fired until he was out of bullets. All of them were perfectly aimed, but each passed though the man's smoke-like body and slammed into the bulletproof windows of the penthouse.

The vampire moved forward. He was limping. Uncle Jake pulled a second pistol from his belt. While he fired off another magazine to no effect, I closed in on the man from behind.

He spun, his blade raised. I blocked it with the armoured plate of my forearm, then brought my fist crashing down across his wrist. He looked so much like a shadow that it surprised me to hit something solid. He dropped the sword. I caught it before it hit the ground, then swung. The blade passed right through him, leaving a small ripple of turbulence across his chest.

I was now close enough to see the man's features. He had heavy cheekbones and large oval eyes. There was a suggestion of a moustache and close-cropped goatee. He scowled and drifted backwards. At the same time, a torrent of sulphurous ash billowed in front of me. I started coughing again and lost sight of him.

Then two dark hands took firm hold of me from behind. I was hoisted from the ground and hurled into Charlie's father. I thought we were both going to spill over the edge of the roof, but Uncle Jake was a large man, and strong. He stood with his feet braced wide and held his ground. I heard a deep grunt and felt his hands under my arms, keeping me on my feet.

"Now!" he shouted.

His eyes were wide and staring right behind me. In his dilated pupils I saw a blurry man-shaped shadow closing in. I turned. The man had retrieved the handle of my broken sword and was stabbing it down towards my unprotected neck. It seemed to be happening in slow motion. The outline of his person was as solid as I had seen it, and his whole body was exposed. I was still holding his scimitar and used it to knock his weapon aside. As he flew by I raised one arm in front of my face to shield my eyes. He took hold of the scimitar and tore it away. Uncle Jake was still behind me. The cloud hammered into him, and he was lifted off his feet and carried past the edge of the building.

I heard Charlie shout in alarm. The crack of his gun followed. Bullets whizzed through the torrent of smoke, but none found their mark. The cloud dissipated. For an instant, it left Charlie's father suspended in mid-air. Then he cried out and fell.

CHAPTER 15

PARTING WAYS

I DOVE FOR the lip of the building and reached out my hand, but Charlie's father was too far away. The next thing I remembered was getting hauled to my feet.

"Get moving," Ophelia shouted. She pushed me back towards the cable that was still strung from the pool fence to the far roof. "There's nothing we can do now. The building is going to collapse."

Charlie was beside me. His face was blank. He must have been in shock. We both were. Ophelia grabbed him by the arm and pulled him around.

"I have to see," he said.

Ophelia tightened her grip. I'd seen her like this before: when her husband, Vlad, threatened to kill my friends and me. She was like a piece of granite. Unyielding. Charlie stopped struggling and she led him to the edge of the building. I then noticed all the bodies on the rooftop. There were a dozen dead vampires around the pool. Ophelia's handiwork.

". . . you listening to me?" she shouted.

I hadn't been listening. I'd been searching for Pestilence. His corpse was not among the dead. "Where is he?"

Ophelia gave me a confused look, then handed her rapier to Charlie and sent him zipping across the cable.

"I'll go after you," I said.

She was about to argue, but two white, pustule-covered hands rose from her shadow and closed over the tops of her boots. A surprised "What?" burst from her mouth, then she began to sink into the roof. I grabbed both of her arms. We pulled, but she sank farther into her shadow, first to her knees, then to her thighs. It was just like the floor of my closet when Pestilence had nearly killed me in my dream. But this was real life. I was losing her.

I pulled harder, but it made no difference. She kept slipping down. Then the building shifted. Her eyes widened, and she twisted her arms free.

"What are you doing?" I shouted.

She answered by pushing me backwards. I was right on the edge of the roof so my foot came down on empty air. I reached out and grabbed the cable. It was still attached to the pool fence, but with all the damage the panels had sustained it couldn't hold me. The line pulled free.

The far end was still firmly secured, so I swung like a wrecking ball across the street and smashed into a balcony railing three floors below the top. The metal buckled, but I held on. Luna leaned over the side of the roof. She said something to me, but it didn't register. My mind was stuck on Ophelia and the sight of her being dragged away into the darkness. I started to get dizzy. It was all I could do to hang on.

Luna started hauling me up. I did my best to climb as she pulled. "What just happened to Ophelia?" she asked.

I couldn't answer.

Charlie appeared at the edge of the building. I thought he would help, but he didn't. "What happened to my father?" he shouted. "What happened?"

I flopped over the side. He grabbed my armour so the chest plates were sandwiched between his hands, then jerked me to my feet and started shaking me. "You had a chance to kill that smoker, didn't you? I was watching. You could have taken his head off, just like that idiot bounty hunter last night, but you didn't do it. Why?"

I opened my mouth, but nothing came out. Was he right? In my mind's eye, I could see the smoker streaking towards me as he made his final charge. He'd been solid. My broken sword was in his hand. I had his longer, heavier scimitar. My first thought had been to protect myself, but if I'd gone for the kill instead of knocking his weapon aside, it might have ended things. And Charlie's father would still be alive. I felt my face go numb.

Charlie pushed me away in disgust. I'd never seen him so angry.

"Where's Ophelia?" Vincent asked. He was standing beside Suki, staring back at the building.

As if in answer, Iron Spike Enterprises let out a terrible groan. The ground shook. A noise followed that was like an earthquake, then the entire structure dropped straight through the street as though it were being sucked into a giant hole. As I watched, shocked and helpless, a thick cloud of dust rose high into the air.

Charlie waved his hand in front of his face, then turned and glared at me, his eyes red-rimmed and furious. "Tell me he got away. Tell me he's not splattered on the sidewalk or buried in that rubble with the rest of those freaks."

Those freaks had taken Ophelia. She would have been buried, too.

"I shot that smoking vampire with at least a dozen armour-piercing rounds," Charlie said. "He didn't even flinch. That pasty one fell thirty storeys and came back like nothing happened. How are we supposed to beat vampires like that? How? HOW?"

"We aren't supposed to beat them," I said. It was a battle keeping my voice steady. "We were supposed to die."

He looked back at the dust cloud that had once been our home. We'd just lost everything. Our blood. Our weapons and equipment. Our sanctuary. All of our things . . .

"We haven't lost everything," Luna said.

"No," I agreed. "We still have the silver case."

"I meant we still have each other."

"Oh, right. Of course."

I looked over at Vincent. His face was still a sickly grey. He was petrified.

Suki took him by the hand. "Come on. That fat-faced vampire with the sores can come right out of the shadows. We're not safe here."

Vincent resisted. "I don't want to leave without Ophelia."

I didn't either. Luna reached out a hand to steady me. The rooftop was spinning. My legs felt weak. I thought my knees were going to buckle.

"Where can we go?" Vincent asked.

Charlie didn't answer.

Luna fixed me with a silent stare. *Where?* she asked.

There was no answer for that. Without Ophelia, I had no idea what to do.

CHAPTER 16

A SHORT REST

WE HAD TO get out of sight, so once we'd kicked our way in through the rooftop entrance of the apartment building, we scrambled down to the underground parking lot.

"What now?" Suki asked.

Charlie scanned the rows of parked cars and walked over to a rusted minivan. "This is too old to have an alarm." The door handle wouldn't engage, so he smashed his fist through the driver's side window and unlocked it. Once inside, he tore the cover off the steering column and turned the ignition. "Get in."

No one argued. Suki rode shotgun and the rest of us climbed in the back.

He pulled out of the lot slowly. We had to wait while an automatic door opened. It seemed to take forever. I kept thinking another wave of vampires was going to wash over us. Instead, we drove out through a dust bowl. A few spectators milled about in confusion, texting madly and taking video with their cellphones. We put them behind us as quickly as we could. Fleets of emergency vehicles were soon racing everywhere. The thought that they might find the corpses of Ophelia and Uncle Jake in the wreck of Iron Spike Enterprises made my stomach spin.

Vincent kept asking where we were going. No one had any answers. I made the mistake of asking Charlie if he had any ideas. He came to life just long enough to lose his temper.

"Do you think I care? Just . . . look . . . whatever. Don't talk to me right now."

So we didn't talk. We just drove down René Lévesque Boulevard, the air so tense it took all of my concentration just to breathe. Then Charlie swore.

"What?" Suki asked.

"The tank's almost empty. Anybody got cash?"

The collective answer was no.

"Well, that rules out leaving town, unless you want to get out and push?"

This started a debate about what to do. The girls were convinced we should try to find a hotel room so we could decompress and plan our next move. The lights of the Sheraton were visible down the street. "Do you have any other ideas?" Luna asked.

I didn't. "If we don't have any money, how are we going to pay for it?"

"Zack, your uncle left you so loaded you could buy this place," she said. "I'm sure we can work something out."

Charlie slid to a halt in front. "I need to ditch this van."

Luna and Suki climbed out. Vincent didn't move. He looked at Charlie. "I want to stay with you."

I sensed Charlie wanted to be alone. Suki noticed too. "You should come with us, Vin. You've got that poor orphan look working for you right now. We might need it if we're going to convince anyone to let us stay here."

I undid my seat belt. Luna stood outside my door so I couldn't open it. I rolled down the window.

"Let us handle this," she said. "Two guys with bloodstained body armour are just going to make everyone nervous." She fixed me with a stare. *Do what you can for Charlie. He's a mess right now.*

I swallowed hard.

Charlie drove around the block, then slipped the van into park. "What happened?" he asked me.

I knew what he wanted to hear. That I could have saved his father by killing that vampire. He might have been right. If I'd practised kill strokes during our training sessions and programmed myself to act differently, when my instincts took over I might not have been so defensive.

"I had no idea that would happen."

"My father is dead and that's all you have to say?"

"I don't know what else—"

"How about, *I'm sorry, Charlie. I could have killed that guy, but I let him live and he greased your dad.* How about that? How about, *I should have listened to you after the Arabian Elvis showed up, Charlie, so I didn't blow it when people were depending on me.* My father was counting on you and you let him down. Thirty storeys down. After all I did saving your bacon on the stairs, the least you could have done was put up a decent fight."

Disgusted, he climbed out of the van and slammed the door with such force the windshield cracked.

A part of me wanted to chase after him and argue, but I realized that he was right. People had been depending on me, and I'd failed them.

When he was about a block away, I slipped out and followed him to the hotel. My feet were so heavy it seemed a miracle I could walk. Charlie had just lost his father, and it might have been my fault. And Ophelia was gone. I had no idea how we were supposed to survive without her. My eyes started to water. I didn't fight it, I just watched my friend's back as he pulled farther away.

When he reached the Sheraton, he sat down on the curb at one side of the entrance. I sat on the other side. Seconds became minutes. They seemed to drag on for years. I wondered what would have happened if I'd killed the smoker. Would Charlie's father have had time to get across to the other building? Would he have been able to keep Ophelia from being drawn into the darkness? Was there even a chance she was alive?

Eventually, Luna poked her head outside the hotel and waved me over.

"Tell me you have good news," I said.

She tipped her head back and forth as though she wasn't certain. "The concierge says none of us are old enough to rent a room, even if we had the cash or some plastic to pay for it."

"Great . . . so what now?"

"Keep your chin up, Zack. If you were anyone else, I'd be worried."

I didn't get what she meant by that, so she explained. I was a person of means. The hotel was in the service industry. All it was going to take to grease the wheels was money. I was going to have to wire the hotel a damage deposit large enough to cover the cost of remodelling half the downtown and leave a healthy gratuity for the concierge. Luna handed me a slip of paper with a number on it. "This is all he's asking. For you, this is chump change."

"Gratuity? What . . . like a bribe?"

"*Tomayto, tomahto.*"

I looked at the number on the sticky note. I was so desperate to put this night behind me, I would have paid the sum if he'd added three zeros to the end of it. Fifteen minutes later, we were punching our room card into the door lock of a suite.

Charlie didn't speak, and he didn't look at me. He just picked up the remote, turned on the TV and started mindlessly flipping channels. Luna settled Vincent into bed.

"He's going to need blood when he wakes up," I said.

"Yeah. I used way too much wolfsbane to settle him down."

Suki was opening and closing the cupboards in the kitchenette. "He didn't give you much of a choice."

"No," Luna agreed. "But Zack's right. He'll need blood from one of us."

Charlie flicked off the television and threw the remote at the armchair across the room. Then he stood and made his way to the door.

"Where are you going?" Suki asked.

"I'm not anteing up any blood unless I can replace it." He glanced at the fridge beside Suki. "There won't be any in there."

"So you're going to go out?" she asked. "After what just happened? You can't be serious!"

Charlie looked around as though he wanted to rip the place apart. "I don't want to be here right now. There has to be a blood bank somewhere in town. I'll find it and get what we need." He took out his phone and started scrolling.

"What about Ophelia's contacts?" Luna asked me. "That Istvan guy? She said he was a friend of your dad's. And there was someone else. The Baptist. It sounded like he might help us. Is there some way to get in touch with them?"

I'd forgotten all about them. "Your guess is as good as mine."

Suki walked over to Charlie and picked something from his hair. "Don't go right now."

He turned and kept his eyes on his cell display.

"Zack and I can take care of it," Luna said. "If Vincent wakes up, he'll want you here."

Suki was standing behind him. "You're his hero, Charlie. You heard Luna. She and Zack can go." She slipped an arm around his waist. He flinched, then his expression shifted from irritation to a tired sadness. She rested her chin on his shoulder. "We'll have some privacy . . ."

That cinched it. He tossed his phone to Luna. She handed it to me so I could see the display. He'd been searching for blood donor centres.

Charlie closed his eyes. "I just want this night to be over."

I think we all felt that way. I inventoried the equipment we still had in our possession. It amounted to five-eighths of sweet diddly. A pistol with one full clip, a knife, Ophelia's rapier, four grenades and a can of tear gas. We also had two assault rifles and the Optimus Prime gun, but so few bullets that we'd be using them as door props before long.

Don't forget the case, Luna reminded me.

We don't even know what it does.

No, she thought. *But Ophelia risked her life to get it, so we know it's valuable.*

I picked up the rapier, tossed Luna the pistol and headed for the door. She stepped in front of me. Her eyes flicked over to Charlie. He was leaning against Suki, looking like a crash-test dummy with half the stuffing removed.

You need to say something to him.

She was right, but he'd just lost his father. Nothing I said could fix that. And he'd been adamant about not being in danger. He was finding out how wrong he was. Nothing I said could fix that, either, so I decided to focus on the practical.

"You have fifty-three rounds left, so I've set the assault rifles to semi-automatic. Keep them close. I don't know how long we'll be gone, but if you sleep, do it in shifts. If you have time, see if you can find out what's in that case." I tossed his phone to Suki. "If we get into trouble, we'll call."

CHAPTER 17

PARADIGM SHIFT

IT SEEMED UNLIKELY that we'd been followed from Iron Spike Enterprises, but there was no way to know for certain. Being cornered in an elevator with a vampire like Pestilence definitely would have ruined our first night in a hotel, so we made for the stairs.

"We need a plan," Luna said.

I leaned against the railing. "To get the blood, or for after we get the blood?"

"Both."

"How hard can it be to break into a blood donor clinic? As for afterwards, you know what I want to do. I just have no idea how to do it."

"Mr. Entwistle?"

"Yeah."

"You're going to have to move a whole lot of rock."

"I know. But I can't see a way forward unless we get some help. Not with Ophelia gone."

My voice broke as I spoke those last words.

Luna moved closer. She had this peculiar talent for standing right in front of me so that it seemed I couldn't breathe without our bodies touching. "There has to be some other option."

"There is," I said.

She waited for me to answer. It took a while.

"If I surrender to the Changeling, I might be able to buy you some time to hide. Maybe go back home to Jersey."

She fixed me with a cold stare. Her eyes had lost some of their colour—less emerald, more bleached ivy. It made them look frozen.

"You can't mean that. You'd just give up?"

"I didn't say give up."

"What's the difference?"

"I don't know. I just . . . I can't help but think that if I were out of the picture, you guys would be safer. And Charlie is furious with me right now."

She slipped her arms around my waist. "He'll come around. He just needs time."

"We don't have time," I said.

"Not if you turn yourself in."

"It was just an idea."

"And what do you think Ophelia would say about it?"

I felt myself cringe. She would have gone ballistic.

"She'd expect you to soldier on. It's what she trained us for. She believed in you, and so do I."

"I appreciate what you're saying. But how confident could she have been? She wouldn't let anyone go outside."

"She's not a risk-taker. You know that. It doesn't mean she wasn't confident about your abilities."

"What abilities?" I asked. "Neither of you were on the stairs with Charlie and me when I went to pieces. I couldn't breathe. I was a washout. If Charlie hadn't kept his head, we would have been torn apart."

"But you both made it out."

"It was luck."

"Or something else," she said.

"What does that mean?"

She glanced away, then looked back at me with an expression that could have been frustration, resolve or both. "How can you doubt the prophecies after all we've been through? Vlad. Hyde. This."

"It isn't that I don't believe them," I said. "I'm just not convinced they're about me."

"The rest of us feel otherwise. You can't just fold your tent and give in."

"If I could buy your freedom that way, it would be worth it."

"Worth it for whom?" she asked. "If you disappeared, what do you really think would happen to us? Without you, we'd have no chance. They'd just hunt us down and kill us. You can't jump ship. Not now. Not ever."

She leaned against me, her cheek resting on my chest. I closed my eyes and inhaled a deep breath, marvelling that after all we'd been through her hair could still smell so good. It reminded me of the first time she'd touched me. That was before she knew I was a vampire, when I was an escaped mental patient running from the police. Just a kid with some bizarre problems. It seemed an eternity ago.

"I don't think Charlie will forgive me for what happened to his father," I said.

"Of course he will. You're his best friend. Just let him be for a spell." She nestled closer. "It might take more than that, actually."

"Another gratuity?"

She laughed. "No. You're not getting off the hook that easily. It could be time to re-examine some of your ideals. I understand why you don't want to kill. Mercy and forgiveness. I get it. But these people aren't looking for forgiveness. They have no remorse. And they're going to obliterate us if we don't stop them."

I felt the comfortable pressure of her body against me as I quietly inhaled. She closed her eyes and waited for her words to take root. There was little I could say to refute them. On the staircase, I'd nearly been ripped limb from limb. Charlie had saved me. And now Ophelia was gone. Uncle Jake was dead. Our home was ashes. How much of this could I have prevented if I'd been more like Luna and Charlie in my thinking?

"So it's time for a paradigm shift."

She hummed an affirmative. "I think so."

"Okay."

Her eyes found mine again. She was probing for signs of uncertainty. I didn't give her any. She slipped her arms around my neck. "We haven't been alone enough."

"No."

"We're alone now." Her breath was hot on my neck. "You seem to need a reason to stick around . . ."

I reached down and cupped the back of her head. Her long copper hair was soft against my fingers. I pulled her head back and winced as my teeth stabbed through my gums. Then I kissed her, and for a time I forgot the danger we were in and lost myself in the person I loved most in the world.

CHAPTER 18

THE SPY

M Y PLAN WAS simple. Rent a car, drive to the blood bank, steal what we needed, then get back to the others. On paper, it seemed about as easy as ordering a pizza. In real life—well, it never ceases to amaze me how complicated things can get.

I was hoping to get the car through the hotel. I shouldn't have been so presumptuous, but I had this vague notion from the movies that they pretty much took care of you once they figured out you were made of money and were willing to spend like an idiot to impress your girlfriend. This wasn't the case. The rental agency affiliated with the hotel was closed, and that was that. Luna's eyelash batting and my vampire charm got us nowhere.

In the end, I had to buy a set of wheels from a night watchman—a Ford Festiva that was so old they probably stopped making parts for it when Justin Bieber was still in diapers. I'm sure I paid three times what it was worth. This took over an hour. It might have been easier to build one out of papier mâché.

I didn't have a driver's licence, so Luna drove. Two blocks from the hotel I saw a vampire. He was an elder, and he reminded me instantly of Vlad. He had the same kind of confidence that probably came from outliving his enemies by about four hundred years. His eyes were deep set, his nose fine. A moustache, like two half moons joined together at the tips, curled out over his mouth. His brown hair was long and gathered in spirals around his shoulders. He had a witch's lock—a streak of white hair on the left side. Luna saw him too and looked away, nervously.

"Pull over," I said.

"We should just keep going."

The Changeling's spies were undoubtedly all over the city looking for us. This guy was a block from our hotel. If he found out where we were staying and reported our where-abouts to the New Order, we'd definitely lose our damage deposit. And maybe this one knew what had happened to Ophelia.

"I'm not comfortable with this. He's too close to the hotel."

She kept driving.

"Luna, pull over. Please."

I probed her surface thoughts, but she'd closed herself off. I felt my stress meter go haywire. Aside from her and Ophelia, the only people in the world I cared about were back at the hotel.

I undid my seat belt and opened the door. Even with the car moving at eighty klicks, I would have stepped out onto the street. Luna pulled over to the curb, threw the car into park and glared at me.

"Okay, what's your plan?"

"I'm working on it."

"Great—"

"Give me a second to think." Cars whizzed past. Rain started to fall, spotting the windshield with tiny dots. "Let's try this. You turn around and pull over in front of him, then step out so he notices you. While he's distracted, I'll sneak up behind."

"And then what?"

"I'll improvise."

Luna rolled her eyes. "That's something Charlie would say."

It didn't sound like a compliment. "His judgment isn't the best, in case you hadn't noticed."

"I'm alive right now because of Charlie," I said. "If not for him, you'd be making this trip alone."

She looked away. The golden crescent charm of her necklace was in her fingers. "What about the blood?"

"The donor clinic isn't going anywhere. I'd say this takes priority."

"And what if this one has powers, like those two vampires from the roof? What if he does something and we can't stop him?"

I put my hand over her fingers, then gently pried the charm loose and let it fall against her shirt. "These elder types have a code. They don't reveal themselves in public. If things get out of hand, smart money says he'll bolt."

She stared out at the passing cars. The rain began to fall harder. The dots on the windshield turned into splotches, then rivulets. "This doesn't feel right," she whispered.

I sensed things wouldn't feel right for a long time. It was no reason not to act.

One U-turn later, she was heading the car back towards the hotel and I was running through the shadows in pursuit of the vampire. He was hard to miss. He walked down the centre of the sidewalk like he owned the city. Not much of a spy, if you asked me.

Luna pulled over to the curb about a half block in front of him and got out of the car. Her long copper locks sort of swirled

107

around, then fell over her shoulder, revealing the perfect contours of her face and neck. She flashed her pale emerald eyes his way. It was so distracting, I nearly ran into a lamppost.

The vampire saw her and sped up. She turned her back to him. He raised a hand like a sorcerer casting a spell, then moved it back. Luna jerked around as if a fishing line had snagged her shoulder. An expression of surprised panic came over her face.

I put my feet into high gear. It didn't take a genius to figure out what had just happened. The elder must have been a telekinetic—a person who could move objects with his mind. I thought of all the things he could do with a talent like that. Send her cartwheeling into traffic. Raise her up in the air and smash her onto the ground. What was most distressing was that he could do it all from a distance, without implicating himself, and so the whole idea of him bolting to avoid attention was poppycock.

I should have thought twice about using my girlfriend to bait a trap. Now it was sprung, and if I didn't move quickly, she was finished.

CHAPTER 19

A SHORT INTERROGATION

RAIN WAS FALLING hard. Cars raced past. A few people scampered by, anxious to get out of the deluge. The vampire didn't hear me as I approached. My canines were down and I was so stressed my heart was probably making more noise than my boots. I thought of Charlie's father and Ophelia, and how I'd failed them, then put all of that anger into an overhand right and dropped it on the base of his neck. Vertebrae snapped. His head tipped back and his body stiffened, then he toppled to the ground.

People had seen me, but I was more worried that the vampire might recover before I had a chance to get him back to the hotel so we could immobilize him. I draped him over my shoulder and ran for the car. Luna was fumbling with the keys.

"Hurry!" I said.

She unlocked the doors and I stuffed the vampire's body in through the hatch, then slipped into the passenger seat. She was shaking and pulled out into busy traffic. Someone honked. She had to hit the brakes hard to keep us from being broadsided.

"What's going on?" I asked. "Are you hurt?"

She pressed herself back against the seat and took a deep breath. "No. But that thing he did. It caught me off guard. I thought I was finished. Then you came flying out of nowhere. And your face. It was so angry. I've never seen you like that." She let out a tired breath. "Well, I asked for it."

"For what?"

"For you to examine your ideals. Suppose I ought to be more careful what I wish for." She glanced at me and her lips twitched into a nervous smile.

"We'll be okay," I said.

She didn't look convinced. Her eyes darted to the vampire lying unconscious in the back. "What do we do now?"

"Circle around the back of the hotel. We'll sneak him in. He might know something."

"He'd better," Luna said. "Because my sister's gonna flip."

A few minutes later, I was carrying the man's body up the back stairs of the Sheraton. We got to the room undetected. Luna swiped her key and we snuck in to find Charlie crouched behind the armchair with an assault rifle trained on us. Suki and Vincent were fast asleep, their breathing slow and heavy.

Charlie lowered the gun and stood. "What's going on?"

"We found a spy," I said.

"And you brought him *here*?"

I set him on the floor at the foot of the beds. "I figured we could tie him up and ask him some questions."

"Tie him up with what?" he asked. "We don't have any rope."

I'd gotten so used to living at Iron Spike Enterprises, with whatever I wanted at my fingertips, I'd forgotten that we didn't have anything in the room but a complimentary bar of soap.

Vincent stirred, his face twisting with discomfort. His body was still wrestling with the wolfsbane in his system.

Suki was curled up on top of the comforter. When he shifted, she awoke, saw her sister and sat up. "Did you get any blood?"

"There wasn't time," I said. "We'll have to hope Vincent's okay without it. Unless we can go out later."

She swung her feet to the floor and yawned. "He killed enough of those vampires to feed for a week. Maybe he'll be fine once he sleeps things off." Then she noticed the body at my feet, and her eyes, puffy with sleep, bugged open. "Who's that?"

"We don't know," Luna said. "But we're gonna find out."

Charlie unclipped the canvas strap from his assault rifle, then did the same with the other two. "Put him in the desk chair."

We used the gun straps to tie the vampire's wrists to the arm-rests, then Charlie pulled a bedsheet out of the closet, tore it into strips and used them to bind the man's ankles. He wasn't gentle.

"Will they be strong enough?" Suki asked.

"No," Charlie answered. "But it will slow him down." He took out his knife and started sharpening it against the gun bar-rel. I could smell his anger. It might not have been prudent to let him take the lead here.

The vampire stiffened, then started to convulse.

Suki peered over Charlie's shoulder. "What's he doing?"

"Healing," Charlie said. He kept sharpening the knife, the rasp of metal on metal loud in my ears.

Luna had her pistol out and stepped up beside me. "How much longer?"

As if in answer, the vampire's neck cracked. His eyes opened, then widened slightly as he took in his surroundings. Charlie moved behind him and pressed the knife against his throat. The vampire had to tilt his head backwards to avoid getting cut. His eyes wandered over us, then settled on me. A smile flickered up one side of his face.

"Finally. The famous Zachariah Thomson. The spitting image of your father. Who does that leave us with? The alluring Luna Abbott. Every bit as beautiful as her description. That would make you Suzanne, but you prefer Suki, don't you? And the charming young man behind me must be Charles Rutherford."

"How do you know our names?" Charlie asked.

"I know all about you. Just how many child vampires do you think there are in this part of the world?"

"What were you doing outside the hotel?"

His smile widened, exposing his long canines. "Taking a walk."

Charlie pressed the knife more firmly against his skin.

The vampire's teeth ground together. "My patience isn't inexhaustible, young man. I am accustomed to a higher brand of courtesy from my hosts."

There was a power in his voice that stunned everyone.

I waved for Charlie to put the knife down, but he didn't move. He was too nervous. We all were.

"Who are you?" I asked.

The man looked at me, then exploded into action. Just as we had hoped, the gun straps held. Surprisingly, the linens did, too. But the chair came apart as if it were made of matchsticks. Before Charlie could move, the vampire grabbed the knife from him. At the same time, he reached back and pulled the gun from Luna's hand. He wasn't even looking at her.

I sprang at his undefended back, but the muscles in my legs spasmed and that threw me off balance. An instant later, the barrel of the pistol was pressed against my throat.

"I am Istvan," he said. "A friend. And you are all very fortunate. Children your age should know better than to venture out at night unescorted."

CHAPTER 20

SHORT-TERM PLANS

ISTVAN HANDED THE pistol back to Luna, then spun the knife in his other hand, caught it by the blade and passed it to Charlie. "This is utter foolishness. Does Ophelia know you've run off?"

Charlie scowled. "We didn't run off. We were chased off."

The short conversation that followed was partly an apology and partly a description of the night's drama.

"I assumed you were a spy," I said, embarrassed.

He was picking up pieces of the chair he had ruined. After a cursory attempt to reassemble it, he realized it was beyond repair. "Your overcautiousness is understandable, however inconvenient."

Talk then turned to the disaster on the rooftop. The news of Ophelia and Uncle Jake left Istvan visibly distraught. The expression of sadness on his face reminded me of Ophelia. Her eyes had the same quality when she spoke about my father.

"A dolorous stroke. Commander Rutherford was a trusted friend. And Ophelia . . . I owe her more than I could ever repay.

We must hope the New Order recognizes their value as hostages and has kept them alive, though it pains me to say . . . we must prepare for the worst. That they are gone and can no longer help us."

I didn't want to think about that.

"You had best pack your things and come with me. The New Order has eyes everywhere. We must get you out of the city. I was planning to leave by ship. Commander Rutherford was to accompany me. You are under no obligation to follow his course, but coming to Moldavia would be safer than remaining here. Of course, it is for you to decide." He excused himself so that we could talk it over privately.

Luna closed the door behind him, then waited for his footsteps to fade as he walked down the hall.

"Well?" she asked.

Charlie sheathed his knife with a surly expression on his face, as if extremely disappointed he'd had no opportunity to use it.

"What if this guy's really the Changeling?" Suki asked. "We have no idea what the real Istvan looks like."

"I think if this guy were the Changeling, he would have finished us when he escaped from the chair," I said.

Luna agreed. Charlie said nothing.

"So, what are we going to do?" Suki asked.

"Well, we can't stay in Montreal. Did you two want to go back home to New Jersey?"

Suki and Luna both said "No" at the same time.

Ophelia still had safe houses in Peterborough, but that option had little appeal, since it was the first place the New Order was likely to begin searching for us. I was still set on a trip to the Warsaw Caves to look for Mr. Entwistle's corpse, but no one took up my cause. When it came time to vote, everyone else wanted to throw in with Istvan.

"We'll have time to explore more options once we're safely out of trouble," Luna said.

I didn't think we'd ever be out of trouble, but I kept that to myself.

"So it's decided?" Charlie said.

No one answered. He opened the door and padded off down the hall. When he returned with Istvan, we gathered up our things.

"What about this one?" Istvan asked, staring down at Vincent, who was still tossing in his sleep.

"He stays with us," Charlie said.

"Werewolves are dangerous creatures, Charles. Their bite is fatal to most vampires. The Changeling and his servants will kill him if they find him. He has no rights under our laws."

"I thought they wanted to kill all of us," Luna said.

"Given your age, it is likely, but one can never be certain. One often receives better treatment from one's enemies than from those who should be friends."

I wondered for a moment if this was a rebuke for tying him up, but he might have been talking about something else. There was an air of uncertainty about him. His eyes flitted nervously over Vincent, as if he were afraid.

"I'd rather not wake him unless we have to," Charlie said. "He's had a tough night."

Istvan nodded. "It would be a deception to say that things will get any easier for you, Charles. You have entered the eye of the hurricane. In every direction, there lies a storm of chaos."

CHAPTER 21

L'ESPRIT SAUVAGE

W E MADE OUR WAY to the underground parking lot where the car was waiting. Vincent remained groggy, so Charlie piggybacked him down. I shouldered the silver case. Apparently, Charlie and Suki had tried to open it after Luna and I left but couldn't find a latch or hinge. Short of ripping it apart, there seemed to be no way to get inside.

When we reached the car, Charlie couldn't hide his disapproval. "You could have built a better set of wheels out of Play-Doh. Tell me it didn't cost you more than a handful of loonies."

"We didn't have a lot of options," Luna said.

"Why did you need a car at all? The donor clinic's minutes away. It's a five-minute run, tops."

"I wanted to go to Warsaw afterwards," I said.

Istvan glanced over at me, his eyes slightly narrowed. "You were planning to go Warsaw? The caves near Peterborough?"

"No one else is keen," I said. "But I still want to go."

Istvan's head moved slightly in the affirmative, as if he understood my reasons. "A bold move, but it would not have ended well, I'm afraid. The New Order already has agents there." His eyes drifted to the eastern horizon. "We should be going now. The sun will be rising within the hour."

I could tell by his voice and manner that he meant well, but without knowing it, he'd dashed my hopes that we could get my uncle and Mr. Entwistle back into the mix. Until that moment, I didn't realize how much I'd wanted their guidance, and to be surrounded by a few more familiar faces. Everyone who had helped us in the past was either dead or missing. It left me with a sick feeling of dread.

I helped Luna strap Vincent into the back. She crawled in beside him. With Charlie and Suki in the front, there wasn't room for anyone else.

"Zachary will come with me," Istvan said.

Luna wasn't comfortable with this. *Remember what Baoh said. The Changeling can be whoever he wishes to be.*

If Istvan was the Changeling, we were already done for. It seemed the best option was to stick with the plan. "Are we going to run to the ship?" I asked.

"Nothing so intensive," Istvan said. He pulled a cellphone from the pocket of his coat. "I'm calling us a cab."

THE SHIPYARD WAS deserted when we arrived. Istvan pointed to an enormous cargo vessel. The name *L'Esprit Sauvage* was written on the hull in large white letters. Its hold was full of truck-sized, rectangular metal boxes stacked on top of one another like giant pieces of multicoloured Lego.

"How do we get aboard?" I asked. "Can you levitate us up there?"

Istvan raised an eyebrow. "Levitate you? I don't understand. You mean float you through the air?" He wiggled his fingers like a magician.

"Aren't you a telekinetic?"

"Like a Jedi Knight?"

Suki snickered. I felt my face redden. "I saw you spin Luna around in the street. It was just before I hit you."

"Oh, that," he said dryly.

I felt a slight pressure in my head. One leg spasmed. It was exactly what had happened back in the hotel when I'd tried to pounce on him. At the same time, my back muscles fired on one side, twisting me sideways.

He reached out to steady me so I wouldn't fall over. "Is that what you saw?"

"Yes."

Luna stepped over from the car. "How did you do that?"

"Your muscles twitch when they receive an electrical signal from your brain. I can encourage you to send that signal if your thoughts aren't properly shielded. I don't do it often. Like influencing someone's behaviour, or how they think and feel, it is an invasion into personal domains. Unless there is an emergency, a person's thoughts should remain private."

Luna was incredulous. "You make it sound like you can control a person's mind!"

"It isn't a matter of control so much as influence. I can't radically alter a person's perspective, nor can I compel them to do something that violates their sense of right and wrong, but if a person is already inclined in a certain direction, I can push them a bit further along. It is a subtle thing."

This was hardly good news. I could sense a sudden feeling of angst radiating from everyone, especially Charlie. "Can other vampires do this?" he asked.

"Most elders, yes. But it probably seems more fantastic than it is. Undoubtedly you have met people who could sway others with logical argument. This is much the same. The only difference is, the persuasion is non-verbal, and often unrecognized."

Istvan's eyes passed over each of us. "I can see this alarms you. There are ways to protect yourself. Once we are aboard ship, I will make this a priority. It is rumoured that the Changeling has a mind-flayer in his employ—a woman who can compel you to act in whatever way pleases her. I doubt it could be so, but the possibility is unsettling."

He looked over his shoulder at the wharf. Large steel containers similar to the ones sitting on the deck of the ship were stacked in neat rows beside a closed warehouse. Parked on the near side was a small convoy of clamp trucks and forklifts, and a giant-sized loading crane. Fog was rolling in off the water. Under the lights, it made everything shine with a hazy glow.

"I'll go first," Istvan said. "Wait for my signal, then follow one at a time."

He disappeared behind a pyramid of wooden crates. A short time later, we saw his silhouette moving up one of the mooring lines at the back of the ship. He climbed over the railing and disappeared. A minute or so later, a rope ladder uncoiled down the side of the hull. He waved us forward. One after the other, we snuck up the ladder and over the side. I thought we'd have trouble with Vincent, but his connection to Charlie was so strong that, even sick and tired, he would have swum the harbour if we'd asked.

"That was too easy," Charlie said.

Istvan's eyes were focused on the top of the hold. The fog gave everything a grainy appearance. "I fear you are correct," he said.

A man's silhouette appeared on the highest cargo box. He was large, and he wore a turban on his head. He limped to the edge of the stack, then dropped. The height was over sixty feet, but he landed with barely a sound. With no smoke obscuring his face, I finally got a clear look at the man who had killed Charlie's father. His burns were gone, and his skin was tanned and weathered, especially around his cheekbones and deep-set eyes. He had a dark moustache and beard, both of which were oiled and spun to fine points. His garments were black silk and fit loosely over his broad frame. Around his waist was a belt of hammered gold. The gem-encrusted scabbard of his scimitar hung from it.

The vampire's eyes drifted over us. His attention lingered on Charlie. "It has been a long time, Istvan, but I see the lapdog still keeps his master close by."

He's looking at the case, Luna thought.

"What do you want, Timur?" Istvan asked.

The vampire folded his arms across his chest. "The children and the case."

"Impossible."

"The Changeling makes all things possible, Istvan. He has assured me that you will have a place in the New Order if you take his mark. Decide quickly. We will not be alone much longer."

"What is he talking about, taking his mark?" Luna asked.

Istvan's voice was a quiet whisper in our minds. *And he causeth all, both small and great, rich and poor, free and bond, to receive a mark in their right hand or in their forehead.*

Timur's brow was hidden by his silk turban, but when I looked closely, I could see a mark on the top of his right hand, similar to the one Pestilence had on his forehead.

Charlie glared at him. His eyes were black. He slipped the assault rifle from his shoulder. "Who is this freak?"

He is War, said Istvan. *One of history's most feared generals, now a Horseman of the Apocalypse.*

"Decide, Istvan," Timur said. "Take the Changeling's mark or die. You cannot win."

Istvan stared through the fog. Dark shapes shifted along the edges of cargo boxes, scuttled along their tops and flashed in the spaces between rows. Istvan put a hand on my arm to steady me. Then his eyes drifted to the gun in Charlie's hand.

"They will kill you if they catch you, so make every shot count."

CHAPTER 22

THE FOUR HORSEMEN OF THE APOCALYPSE

TIMUR'S SKIN DARKENED and his legs became a column of swirling smoke. He rose into the air.

"Your choice pleases me, Istvan. You have delivered the orphan and the case into our hands. Your death will complete our triumph."

An aura of malevolence emanated from the fog behind him. Shadows moved like ghosts along the walls and containers. I started pulling at my collar.

Take deep breaths, Luna said, raising her pistol. *Focus on the light.*

I filled my lungs, closed my eyes and imagined the tunnel of light, first as a distant circle, then as a warm glow all around me. My heart started to settle. I pressed my teeth together and opened my eyes. Suki was on my other side, the Optimus Prime gun pulled tight to her chest. Vincent rubbed at his eyes, then stepped up beside us.

"It's go time, Vin," Charlie said. "We could use your alter ego right about now."

I drew Ophelia's rapier from the sheath. Luna pulled back the sliding mechanism of her pistol to load a round into the chamber.

"Really, Istvan," Timur said. "You're going to overthrow the New Order with a handful of children?"

"Run!" Istvan shouted.

The sound that followed was guttural, like a growl. He lunged into the air. His legs and arms shortened and shifted underneath his body. His nose and mouth lengthened. In the next instant, I was staring at a huge wolf, his tawny coat streaked with white over his left ear and shoulder. He hit the ground on all fours and launched himself at Timur, who drew his scimitar and rose out of range. The column of smoke beneath him took the shape of a rearing horse.

A wall of vampires streamed forward. Survivors from Iron Spike Enterprises. Charlie, Luna and Suki opened fire. Flashes lit up the hold.

We have come for you, Zachariah, said a voice. A beautiful lady draped in wisps of white silk stepped out of the mist. The others didn't seem to see her. She was tall, with large eyes and full lips. Her limbs and torso were so slender she seemed almost alien. The Changeling's runes were carved into the skin across the top of her chest, running shoulder to shoulder, then down to the tip of her right hand.

Do not be troubled, she said. *I am here to help you.*

I heard more gunfire and snarling. It seemed muted, as though it were happening a great distance away. The air was thick with clouds of spent gunpowder. The odour, normally pungent, was fading, as was the smell of vampire blood that spilled with each burst of Charlie's gun.

Someone roared. Vincent had turned. He was the Beast now. Stronger, faster, hungry. He fell upon a group of vampires surrounding Istvan, his claws and fangs like razors. Luna was beside him. Pestilence sprang from the shadows behind her. She turned and fired and he melted back into the darkness. An instant later, he emerged next to me.

Leave him, said the beautiful woman.

Pestilence vanished. To my left, Charlie was being smothered in a cloud of smoke. I caught a glimpse of turban and metal, then the sparking of swords. War's scimitar moved in a foggy blur. Some of the strokes Charlie blocked. Some he slipped. Some glanced from his armour. For each blow delivered, he swung back or shot or stabbed. There was a lot of rage in him. And Istvan, too. He was a terror to the vampires, who melted from the shadows to attack him. And there were many. I stood watching, my feet paralyzed. I tried to take a step, but it was as if my boots were bolted to the floor.

Rest now, the woman told me.

A deep lethargy settled into my bones. Time seemed to have slowed. One of the girls cried out. She had copper hair and pretty green eyes. I struggled to recall her name, but my mind was tangled. The lean woman with the dark eyes was right in my head, demanding my attention.

Rest . . . she insisted. *Let your mind be at ease . . .*

Luna . . . the girl's name was Luna. She was staring at me. I could tell she was shouting by the way her mouth moved, but I heard nothing over the quiet strains of the woman's voice.

Rest . . .

Luna stopped speaking when a vampire with a fat, pasty face emerged behind her and clamped his hand around her throat. His other arm circled her waist. She pointed the gun behind her and pulled the trigger. It would have put a round through his spine, but the clip was empty. I should have been helping her, but that would have displeased the woman with the raven hair. Her dark, bottomless eyes were fixed on mine. As the chaos swirled around us, she stood as calm as a pale reed. Elegant and hypnotic.

Rest . . .

My sword felt heavy. So did my eyelids. I fell against one of the cargo boxes, then slid to the floor.

It is not your desire to harm others . . . Put your sword aside and close your eyes.

I placed the sword beside me. My eyelids began to droop. They rose again when someone beside me shrieked. It was another girl, not the pretty vampire with the green eyes, a blonde with dimples. She was being dragged, screaming, behind a row of metal boxes. I could tell by her movements that she was human. On her own, she would not survive.

There is nothing you can do to help her, the woman said. *And why should you? She is nothing.*

She is a friend.

You will make new friends. And they will honour and fear you.

I didn't want to be feared, and I didn't want to rest. The night was dark and cool. I was a vampire. This was not the time for sleep. I tried to push myself to my feet, but my limbs were too weak.

A tall, dark figure emerged from the fog. He looked like a spectre, his face hidden beneath a black cowl. A sickle appeared from somewhere inside his billowing shadow. He was going to cut me down. A terrible fear took hold of my mind, drowning out the woman's voice. But the figure passed by, drifting towards a strange-looking wolf with a streak of white over its shoulder. The wolf changed into a man and grabbed a duelling blade from one of the dead vampires at his feet.

Death has come, said the woman. *Our triumph is at hand.*

War, Pestilence and Death. Three of the four Horsemen were here. I remembered what Baoh had said on the Dream Road: *together, they are unstoppable.*

One was missing. Famine.

No, said the voice. *We are here, all of us. And your thoughts are true. Against the New Order there can be no victory.*

Her voice was musical. I could feel her sense of elation. But something about it was wrong, like a chord with one dissonant note echoing deep beneath its fellows, throwing off the feel of things. She was not to be trusted. I should not have been listening to her. I had to help my friends.

There is nothing to be done. It will soon be over.

I pushed at the woman's voice to get it out of my head, but she dug deeper. The soothing richness of it changed. An intense pain followed. I screamed and pressed my hands against my head, but I couldn't make it stop. I shouted for her to get out and pushed harder. It made the cargo hold spin. I tipped sideways to the floor. Shadows flitted past. More vampires were coming. My friends were surrounded. They couldn't hold out much longer.

It is pointless to resist.

I gathered my strength and pushed one last time against the voice. It was not like Pestilence, a squirmy, crawling presence I could net and drag out. This was more like a deeply rooted barb. Each time I tried to pull it loose, it felt as if I was tearing my own mind apart. As I pushed, the pain grew. Then my mind said *enough is enough*, and I collapsed into darkness.

CHAPTER 23

FAILED RETREAT

I DON'T REMEMBER much about my mother. She died when I was two. My father became the only permanent fixture in my life, so when he died, things fell apart. I woke up in a mental ward surrounded by strangers, with no sense of what was wrong with me or how to cope. I often went days without speaking. It happened at those times when I felt most alone, when I missed my father terribly and couldn't accept that I would never see him again. I wouldn't eat or sleep or move; I simply retreated into my mind so I could speak to him in private.

Even dead, my father was a constant presence in my thoughts and dreams. So when I passed out, I shouldn't have been surprised to see him standing over me, fedora in hand, his khaki shirt and pants covered in dust. He reached down to help me to my feet. "In a pickle again, aren't you, son."

I glanced around. Suki was out of sight. Vincent was bleeding, dead vampires at his feet. Istvan was cornered, the phantom of Death bearing down on him. Luna was nose to nose with Pestilence, fighting for her life. Charlie looked positively rabid, battling in a noxious cloud. The woman, Famine, was staring at me, her black eyes wide with malice. All of them were frozen, as if someone had stopped time at the instant I'd fallen unconscious.

"She's in my head. I can't push her out. I blacked out from the pain."

"Pain is a good thing, son. It reminds you that you're still alive."

I had a bit of trouble swallowing this.

"Pain is temporary," he said. "But loss . . . loss is permanent. Quit now, and everything that matters to you will be gone forever. What is pain compared to that—to be haunted by cowardice till the end of your days?"

I thought the word *cowardice* was a bit extreme.

My father pointed his fedora towards my sword, still sitting on the ground. "If you stay here, in the comfort of your own thoughts, while others around you suffer, what else could you call it?"

I had no answer for that.

"You'd better wake up now, Zack. Your friends need you."

"How can I help them? I can't even stay conscious."

"You're only helpless if you believe you are."

"So what do I do?"

"Stop making excuses, son, and do what is right. The rest is just details. Now get moving. People are counting on you."

He reached out and ruffled my hair the way he always did. Then he smiled.

My eyes popped open and the pain came back. Famine was standing over me, only a sliver of white visible around her dark pupils.

"Stop making excuses, son, and do what is right . . ."

I closed my eyes and tried to imagine the tunnel of light, thinking it might break the hold Famine had over me, but she was there, in my mind's eye, staring the same baleful stare. I couldn't look away, but I knew that my sword was somewhere beside me. I started groping along the cold, steel floor.

Do not touch that weapon! Do not even think it!

Every nerve in my body caught fire. I screamed. My back arched until I thought it would break. I'd only experienced this kind of pain once before, the night I'd burned alive saving Luna from Vlad. An image of him dying in the sun flashed through my mind, my hand around his throat, the heavyweight champion of all vampires at my mercy. The image rattled her. My pain abated for just an instant. In that moment, my fingers fell upon the sword hilt.

Do not touch that!

The burn intensified. I kept screaming.

Drop it, or you will suffer pain without end.

Then I would suffer. I stood and raised my sword. My whole body was shaking. I took a step towards her.

STOP!

I took another step, then another. A shadow rose up in front of me. The fire in my limbs died. I caught a glint of white from the corner of my eye and moved just in time to stop Pestilence from slashing at my face with his long-fingered hands. His intervention seemed to break Famine's hold. He tried to grab me, but I kicked him away, then followed with an overhand stroke that would have taken his right arm off at the elbow had he not slipped through a shadow on the floor.

Famine was gone. Her voice was quickly replaced by the sound of Suki screaming. I stumbled past Istvan, who was locked, blade to blade, with Death. Sparks flew as they circled one another, their weapons crashing together like shafts of silver lightning. Vincent was still fighting. Bloodied and limping, he growled in rage at the ring of vampires surrounding him.

The smell of blood was all around. I could feel the *killing urge* rising in me—a kind of blood lust that affected vampires who were starving. Or crazy. I'd been caught in its grip twice before. Once when I hunted for the first time and killed a deer, and again when I tasted human blood for the first time. The intensity of it, then as now, was like a maelstrom. All I felt was a desire to kill.

I didn't resist it. I had failed to act aggressively on the roof of Iron Spike Enterprises and others had paid for it. I wasn't going to make that mistake again. I stepped forward. My blade sang in deadly arcs as I swept the vampires away from Vincent with the power of a tidal flood. Like a thousand pounds of water crashing down the mountain. Fast. Fluid. And unstoppable.

Some escaped. I let them go and made for the vampire who'd taken Suki. He was tearing at her collar. He saw me, and his hunger turned to fear. I cut him down before he could scream.

The next thing I remember was setting Suki at the base of a container. Vampires were all around me. I kicked and stabbed and snarled and they melted away. I didn't pursue anyone. The battle would be decided by the Horsemen. They were the ones I had to stop.

Luna called out. Pestilence was trying to pull her into the darkness. She punched him again and again, but he wouldn't let go. I charged at him. His eyes widened in alarm, then he vanished into the dark space between two cargo boxes.

I heard my name. Charlie was shouting at me. I spied him in an aisle between two towering rows of boxes. Vincent was draped over his shoulders, unmoving. He was a boy again, fragile and thin. Blood seeped from a wound in his back.

"Zack, help Suki!" Charlie said, running. Luna and I followed after him. Suki was moving slowly just ahead of us, her pace hampered by a gash in her thigh. Luna put a shoulder under her arm. I looked back. The shadow of Death filled the aisle. He was closing quickly, sickle in hand. I slowed to wait for him. The space was narrow. I could hold him off and buy them time.

Luna turned back. *Don't lag behind! Run!*

Running wasn't an option. Death was too fast. I had to block the exit or Suki would never make it out.

"Where is Istvan?" I shouted.

He took the case and fled.

I ground my teeth and tightened my grip on the sword. For a fleeting instant, I wondered if this whole thing had been a set-up, if he'd led us here on purpose so he could get the case and whatever was inside.

"RUN!" Luna screamed.

Pestilence emerged from the shadows again. Instead of grabbing Luna, he took hold of Suki's arm and snatched her away. Luna tried to yank her back but was pulled off balance from behind. It was Istvan. He had reappeared and was shouting for us to run.

Pestilence bit down on Suki's neck. She screamed. Charlie stopped when he heard the noise. He set Vincent's body on the deck and started running back. I lost sight of him as more vampires dropped from above and walled him off.

"Zack," he shouted. "Zack, help her!"

I couldn't. Death's shadow passed over me. I felt the chill even before he struck. He was taller than I was. Heavier. Stronger. His sickle fell against my sword with the weight of a boulder. The impact forced me to the ground. I rolled to my feet and parried his next few strokes. Then our blades crossed so we were chest to chest. My feet were splayed wide. My balance was perfect. I felt strong. And ready.

He pushed me to the ground like I was a child.

Suki was still screaming. I risked a backwards glance. Luna and Istvan were defending the unconscious Vincent. Through the fog, more vampires came crawling down the cargo boxes, black silhouettes within the darkness. Suki's blood was like a lure. They swarmed around her.

Charlie was hacking like a madman. "Zack! ZACK! I can't get through."

I rolled to a knee, my blade high. Death moved in. A rapid exchange followed that sent me sprawling again. By this time, a group of vampires had circled behind me. None of them made any move to attack. They glared at me instead, like a wall of giant carrion birds, eyes ablaze. Through their legs I could see Charlie. He'd fought his way closer to Pestilence. War descended from the other direction, his legs a horse-shaped cloud.

Suki stopped screaming and her head flopped backwards. The front of her torn shirt was scarlet. Charlie reached out to snatch her away, but Pestilence pushed her towards War, whose scimitar snapped forward in a lethal arc. Suki's body tipped sideways. A part of her fell the other way, a flash of blond. Then the swarm of vampires surrounded her corpse and started tearing it apart.

CHAPTER 24

DEATH

LUNA SCREAMED. I'd lost sight of her. Charlie shouted and attacked Timur, his sword a reckless streak of silver. The Horseman turned into smoke and spun away. Istvan was at Charlie's back and pulled him towards the others. Both disappeared from view as more agents of the New Order, rabid and hissing, appeared from every nook and cranny of the ship to chase them off.

I was still lying prone, frozen by what I'd just seen. I was so shocked by Suki's death, I don't think I moved for several seconds. I just stared back and forth between the place where she'd been murdered, and Death, who watched, unmoving, his eyes hidden beneath the shadow of his cowl.

Pestilence stepped from the shadows on my right. He was licking Suki's blood from his fingers, snickering. Tendrils of smoke gathered on my left, then solidified into War. He folded his hands over his chest. Famine returned last and stood behind Death, her dark eyes and raven hair faint shadows in the fog.

The Four Horsemen—unstoppable.

I rose to my feet. Death stepped forward. My knees and hands were trembling. Fear was taking hold. I squeezed my sword grip to steady myself, then forced my left foot forward and assumed the standard guard position, my blade pointing at his torso.

Empty your mind, someone said.

The voice belonged to a young man. I didn't recognize it, but he had to be somewhere nearby. I quickly glanced around, but only the faces of my enemies were visible.

Empty your mind.

I'd never really understood this. How did a person think of nothing? The very notion seemed impossible. And after what had just happened to Suki—

The past cannot be changed. You must stay in the moment. There is only you and your opponent. His appearance, his words and contempt, they mean nothing. Hope, fear, pain, fatigue—set them aside. Clear your thoughts and feelings, so all that remains is your skill against his. In the end, this is all that matters.

I felt limp. The killing urge was gone. So was my confidence. All that remained was a cold terror. I took a deep breath and tried to clear my thoughts, but all I could see in my mind's eye was Suki's headless body being ripped apart.

Empty your mind.

Death attacked. Our blades met once, twice, three times. He battered my sword away then chopped down on my wrist. The plates of platinum within my Kevlar suit took the brunt of the blow. It still hurt, but his sickle didn't cleave flesh or shatter bone.

He swung again. I met the stroke with an armoured forearm and countered. I faked high but changed the path of the blade so that it would fall across his thigh. He jumped back and I missed.

He is reading your thoughts, the stranger told me. *Put your fear aside. Empty your mind . . .*

I had no idea how to follow this person's advice. All I felt was more panic. If Death could read my thoughts, how was I supposed to beat him?

Empty your mind.

In my moment of confusion, Death struck quickly. My mind wasn't empty. It was full of distress and all the reasons I wanted to live. I blocked the next stroke, then countered clumsily, overextending myself. Death smashed his sickle into my stomach. I crumpled. He raised his arm for the killing stroke. Then something struck him flush on the back and threw him off balance.

Run!

The voice in my head was loud. The speaker was right in front of me. He was young in appearance—perhaps ten or so years older than me. His hair was light brown and tied back in a ponytail. He grabbed me by the arm and jumped on top of the nearest container.

"Go, go!" he shouted.

I started sprinting across the top of the containers. The vampire stayed at my heels, step for step. Not an easy feat. I was the Night Runner.

Who are you? I asked.

He turned to a vampire closing in from the shadows and knocked him aside. *I am he who goes before and prepares the way.*

Other vampires appeared, shrieking and howling behind us. I didn't look back as we ran across the boxes towards the bow of the ship.

Are you ready? he asked me.

For what?

A leap of faith.

We'd reached the last box in the stack. It was too foggy to see past the edge. The vampire sped past me and jumped.

I looked back over my shoulder. Death was behind me, his cowl snapping. War was hovering in the air over his shoulder, his legs a funnel of smoke. I kept my eyes on them for a fraction of a second too long. A thin, bone-white arm covered in pustules reached from the shadows and grabbed my foot. I pitched forward and dropped the rapier. As I slid over the edge of the box, I twisted my body so that my legs and feet were dangling over the side. I heard a splash. The other vampire had landed in the river, which was far enough away that only an inhuman leap would get me there.

I started to pull myself back up, but the hand of Death clamped over my wrist. He hauled me forward and leaned closer so our eyes were inches apart. Then he slashed me cleanly across the throat with his sickle. I had just enough time to pull my hand free before the pain arrived. Then I fell backwards through the air in a painful state of confusion. The face I'd seen was familiar. Whiskers of white and grey and black. Skin weathered like old leather. A forehead marked with the same rune as the Changeling's other servants. But it was his milky-blue eyes that were the most troubling. The windows to his soul. I remembered the first time I'd seen them, years ago, when he'd crashed through the front doors of the Nicholls Ward on a stolen motorcycle to warn me that Vlad was coming to get me.

Death was my old friend, John Entwistle.

CHAPTER 25

AWAKENINGS

A MAN DOESN'T live long with his throat cut open. Neither does a vampire. I had just enough time to wonder why my old friend had killed me, then I hit the deck and was dead before the first bounce.

After the pain and darkness came a feeling of warmth. I saw a light in the distance and drifted towards it. Soon its glow surrounded me, cleansing me of worry. Others were there. I felt a sense of togetherness. And I discovered again that all things are good—that, in the end, we will all come to the light and be made clean and whole again.

I awoke later in darkness. I felt diminished—small and disconnected. The warmth of the light was gone, as was the sense that things were as they should be. The smells of damp earth and stone, and of blood, were all around. I heard a bubbling noise and the air rattling in and out of my chest. My vision returned and I saw that I was in a small, dark space. A coffin. I reached up and pushed open the lid.

My armour was gone. In its place was a brown robe, like a

monk's habit, belted at the waist with rope. My feet were bare. The room around me was strangely lit. Red, orange and yellow light bounced off the stone walls. In the far corner, several thick candles poured grey, waxy smoke up to the ceiling. Fires were burning under jars of chemicals that bubbled steam into the air. Bowls and beakers sat next to mortars and pestles stained from use. Everywhere there were bottles and herbs and bits of things I could not identify. Corpses in various states of decay lined the walls. All were men and, judging by the teeth, vampires. Expressions of pain and terror covered their grey and flaking faces. Something about that sat uneasily with me. Vampires weren't supposed to rot in death.

"Old friends, once loyal to me, victims of that usurper, the Changeling." The speaker's voice was deep and powerful, and seemed to echo through the room and my head at the same time. I'd only met one person who could do that, but he was dead.

A shadow moved and I started. A man in a dark cloak was hunched over a counter running along the far side of the room. His body was short and thick. Long black hair spilled past his collar. He turned so that one large green eye stared past his shoulder. It was Vlad the Impaler. I caught my breath and froze.

Do you fear me, pup?

I did. This man had killed my parents. He'd tried to kill my friends and me.

Far better that this Prince be feared than loved. Fear is a whetstone for the mind. Let it keep your wits sharp. You will need your head about you in the hours to come.

What was he talking about? And how was it possible that he was even alive? When I'd last seen him at Iron Spike Enterprises, he was little more than ash and bone. But his remains had disappeared.

How I came to be here is far less important than why. I am here because I am needed.

I needed him like I needed a knife in the back. I couldn't stand his voice in my head, so I closed my mind and envisioned the calming light of the tunnel.

"That's better," he said aloud. "A man should be the master of his own thoughts." He stroked his moustache, two thick ribbons that stretched halfway across each cheek, then turned back to his workstation. His breathing slowed, as if he were engaged in something that required all of his concentration.

Something pulled at my arm. A needle had been inserted under the skin near my elbow. It was connected to a long tube that was channelling blood into my body. I carefully removed it and drank until the tube ran dry. The rush swept over me and I lay back. Above, the vaulted ceiling stretched out to the tops of the walls like the legs of a giant spider. We were deep in the earth. I could feel the weight of it pressing down on me.

"Where am I?" I asked. "And how did you get here?"

Vlad didn't answer.

A feeling of faintness came over me. The room spun and my vision blurred. I sat up too quickly. An intense nausea followed. My stomach started to heave and blood filled my mouth. I swallowed it down and stepped out of the coffin. My balance was off and I fell to the floor.

"What have you done to me?"

Vlad loomed above. I hadn't heard his footsteps or felt their vibration on the stones. I had forgotten that he could change his location without seeming to move. It was alarming.

"Not all who die go to the light," he said. "Death improves some souls. Others not at all. I could not chance you, little cub, so I have improved you myself." He shifted back to the counter and spoke over his shoulder. "I have given you my blood, pup, and the blood of a *night stalker*. It will accelerate the development of your talents."

My stomach lurched. Vampires weren't supposed to mix their blood. It was possible for Luna and me only because we were both young and our talents hadn't yet manifested. This was awful. It took both hands and all my abdominal strength to avoid erupting.

"You are decades from maturation. A shortcut must be taken. It comes at a price."

Vlad reached into a cage on the floor beside him and pulled out a rat. It squealed and squirmed as he forced a small eyedropper down its throat. A moment later, it stopped moving. He set it down, grabbed a syringe from the table, stuck it into a small vial and drew out a few drops of liquid, which he injected into the rat's belly. After a few seconds, it began to squirm again, then shuddered and was still. Vlad snarled. The room seemed to dim, as though a dark cloud had passed over the lights. He grabbed the dead rat by its hind end and hurled it into a basket that was filled with others just like it, mouths twisted and eyes bugged out. They had not passed gently into death.

"What happened on the ship? Where are my friends?" I tried to stand, but my body wasn't ready.

Vlad ignored the question. He adjusted a vertical tube that was dripping liquid into a beaker, then removed a flask from its place above a hissing burner. "Istvan mentioned a boy in your safekeeping. A shape-changer. Who is he?"

"Is he alive?"

"For now. But he is unclean. Who is he, and why does he travel in your company?"

"He's a friend. Someone Ophelia and I agreed to look after."

Vlad turned. His eyes dug into me. It felt as if his thick fingers were sliding under my skull. I gasped. Images of Vincent's father flashed through my mind, then others of Vincent, when he died and when I brought him back by feeding him from a cut in my hand.

"You will regret that decision," Vlad said. He turned and grabbed another rat. After administering more drops and another injection, it died just as the other had, although it struggled a bit longer. Vlad seemed to consider this progress. There was less anger in the room when he discarded it.

"Istvan is tending to your friends," he said. "If you are a God-fearing soul, you should give thanks that my cousin was able to lead them to safety."

"Your cousin?"

"Yes. Istvan is kin, though few remember him as Dracula's cousin. To the world, he was Stephen the Great of Moldavia, Champion of Christ, Scourge of the Heathen Turk. He is with your friends, readying them as I am readying you."

I wasn't ready for anything but a long nap. And all Vlad was doing was torturing some helpless rodents. I would have given both arms to be somewhere else. Luna would be sick with worry.

"What happened to everyone? Where's Luna?"

Vlad made some adjustments to the equipment in front of him, then removed the flask under the vertical tube and began to heat it. "Your friends are safe. All but the girl."

He must have meant Suki. The image of her being torn apart was still vivid enough to make my head quiver. No one deserved a death like that. "Is there any chance she survived, that she might come back as one of us?"

Vlad's gaze passed over the grey-skinned corpses at the edges of the room. "By Istvan's report, there was little left of her at the end. Another casualty of this war. One of many."

There was no hope for her then. She was gone.

Life is unfair. How many times does a guy hear that in his life? I understood. I was an orphan. But I still expected there to be justice in the world. There was nothing right about this. I felt sick.

Poor Charlie. How much worse it must have been for him—to lose his girlfriend and father within a day. And Luna. She must have been a wreck. I had to focus on breathing deeply for a few seconds before I could speak again.

"Where are they?" I asked.

"Your friends? Istvan took them to his castle in Moldavia, although they have since been moved."

"To where?"

When Vlad didn't answer, I glanced at the vaulted ceiling as if it might hold a clue as to where we were. Vlad had mentioned Moldavia, which I knew was in Europe. That meant we were overseas. Hoping Luna was nearby, I reached out with my mind the same way I would if I wanted to hear her thoughts, but there was nothing around me but stone and earth and corpses.

"I cannot disclose the exact location of your friends, but they are safe. Charlie is surprisingly resilient. I understand he lost his father and was connected to the girl who was murdered. Their deaths have birthed a great anger in him. With the proper guidance, it can be channelled, wielded like a weapon."

Vlad's tone was surprisingly mild, as if he were talking about an old acquaintance and not a stranger he'd once tried to murder.

"As for you," he continued, "Istvan was coming back when you were cut down. Call it luck, providence or divine intervention, but he got to you before our enemies did. Had he not been so swift, you would be under the Changeling's control now, a mark on your hand and a head stuffed with lies."

He spat out the last words with surprising vehemence. Then he calmed. "You are where you belong. Did I not say when we first met that you should not connect yourself to anyone but me? Our destinies are intertwined. I have always known it."

There was nothing I wanted less. He had no right to be alive. I thought of what he'd done to my father and instinctively reached up to grab the necklace he'd given me. It wasn't there.

Vlad reached under his shirt and removed the silver moon. The golden crescent was snapped to the side. He must have taken that part from Luna.

I was outraged. "That's mine!" I said.

In a flash, he shifted to my side, grabbed the collar of my robe and hauled me to my feet. "You are mistaken, pup. This is mine. And around my neck is where it will remain, until I give it back to Ophelia. You were never meant to have it. Neither was your father."

I tried to push him away, but he was back at his bench before I could move.

"I don't expect your forgiveness or your understanding," he said. "But if you cannot let bygones be bygones, it is Ophelia who will suffer."

"So she's alive?"

"Yes."

I could scarcely believe it. If Ophelia was alive, she could make things right. But I should have known better than to be hopeful.

"The New Order has her, and her execution is imminent. Only with our combined resources can we hope to save her. I am proposing that we call a truce. If you cannot accept it for your own sake, then consider hers."

Before he could say more, there was a knock on the wall. Vlad reached up to a lever over his workstation and pulled it down. I heard a metallic groan, and a section of stone rotated inward. Istvan appeared in the space behind. He looked exhausted. His hair was sweaty and stuck to his forehead in clumps.

"Cousin," Vlad said.

Istvan saw me and nodded. He seemed neither surprised nor pleased. Just tired. He pushed the section of wall closed.

"Well met," Vlad said. "Are your wards safely tucked away?"

"Do you mean my friends?" I asked. "Where are they?"

Istvan started to answer, but Vlad cut him off. "Circumstances permitting, you will see your companions shortly. But before that happens, there is a task you must perform."

CHAPTER 26

GOOD COP/BAD COP

V LAD LEANED BACK against the counter and spoke to
Istvan. "I was explaining to our young guest that we must
work together. He seems reluctant to accept this simple fact. I
am hoping reason will prevail."

Istvan pulled a stool over and collapsed onto it. "All in good
time." He looked at me, his face heavy with fatigue. It took him
a moment to speak again. "I imagine you have questions. Now
is the time to ask."

"Where am I?"

"You are beneath Castle Dracula in Romania."

"How long have I been dead?"

"Three weeks less a day."

"How did I get here?"

"I chartered a plane to cross the Atlantic. The overland route
from Paris was quite convoluted. Do you need details?"

"No. I meant, how did I get off the ship?"

"I slipped your body overboard, then let it sink. Thankfully
your armour was heavy, and the fog, thick. Had you not been

dead, I never would have managed it. After the ship left port, I went back. And here were are."

I had imagined something more heroic, but I had no right to complain, except that I was here with Vlad. I wanted to ask why he'd been resurrected and where his body had been all this time, but I couldn't with him glaring at me, arms crossed in disapproval.

"This man saved your life, pup," Vlad snapped. "A small measure of gratitude would be appropriate."

Istvan smiled, his eyelids at half-mast. "There is no need. Arguably, it was I who led him into trouble. Had we stayed at the hotel, the night would have ended much differently."

Vlad scowled. "It would only have delayed the inevitable. But we're wasting time. Ophelia's trial is six hours away. We need to know who we are up against."

Both men were looking at me. Istvan leaned forward. "You have some information we need, Zachary, regarding Death."

"It is rumoured he reveals his face only to his victims," Vlad said. "Did you see him? Did you recognize him?" He shifted closer.

I looked away. John Entwistle was an old friend. But centuries ago, he'd gone by the name of John Tiptoft. He'd been a mercenary and an executioner, a man who tortured and impaled his enemies. Uncle Jake and Ophelia had suggested back at Iron Spike Enterprises that it was possible for vampires his age to revert back to older ways of thinking when they were raised from the dead. Obviously this was what had happened. What I didn't know was whether any part of him remained John Entwistle and if he could be changed back. I didn't want to implicate him until I knew one way or the other.

"Who is Death, pup?"

I clamped my mouth shut. An instant later, an intense pressure built in my skull. Vlad was searching my memory. I pushed against him, my teeth clenched from the strain. Then I heard Istvan whisper to him, his voice muffled and distant, as though coming from another room.

Vladislav, this is not the way.

The pressure stopped, but Vlad continued to stare, his eyes smouldering. "Now is not the time for secrets. You have no idea what is at stake."

He was wrong. Having witnessed Suki's death and the death of Charlie's father, I knew exactly what was at stake.

"Rule number one in any conflict is to know your enemies," Istvan said. "Identifying the Horsemen will be critical if we are to best the New Order. War we know already."

"You called him Timur," I said, relieved that Istvan had changed the subject.

"Yes. Timur Lenk—Timur the Lame."

"Perhaps you know him by another name," said Vlad. "The Mighty Tamerlane, founder of the Timurid Dynasty. It is said that during his campaigns, nearly five per cent of the world's population was sent to the grave, although I think those numbers, like his prowess, are exaggerated."

"He is more formidable than when you last faced him," Istvan said. "Doubtless, when the Changeling raised him up some vile sorcery was used to augment his power. We would be wise not to underestimate him."

Vlad grumbled. "I have plans for him, and for Bathory."

"Who is that?" I asked.

"The Countess Elizabeth Bathory," Istvan said. "Once a living vampire, she has the power that inspires the mindless hunger of the horde. Hence the name Famine. She makes them positively ravenous."

I understood. A vampire who was starving would do just about anything for blood. It was a perfect explanation for the savagery Charlie and I had witnessed at Iron Spike Enterprises. So, Famine was behind it.

"It is said that only the most practised elders can resist her voice," Istvan continued. "That you were able to do so is unprecedented."

It must have been a trick of the light, but it seemed a smile flickered across Vlad's face. "I would expect nothing less from my progeny."

I wasn't sure if he was complimenting me or himself. "What about Pestilence?" I asked.

"I believe he is Donatien Alphonse François, the Marquis de Sade. The physical resemblance is uncanny, but his mind is too twisted a labyrinth for me to navigate, and he has given up his voice, so his identity has been impossible to confirm."

"What does that mean, given up his voice?"

"As Ophelia's ward, you must know something of the Dream Road. To find a dreamer, you must follow their voice. The voice of the Marquis has been taken from him—his master's doing, no doubt. Since he cannot speak, he cannot be found. It leaves him free to stalk the Dream Road, torturing rival vampires in their sleep without fear of reprisal."

Vlad bristled. "I should have had the body of that pus-filled worm destroyed centuries ago."

"He should be pitied," Istvan said. "I doubt he even remembers who he is. What remains of him is more animal than human."

"He was barely human in life!" Vlad said. "If his talents are so impressive, perhaps he'd like to visit me on the Dream Road. That would put an end to his meddling."

"And so that leaves us with Death," Istvan said, his eyes on me expectantly.

A nervous tension crept back into my bones. I stalled. "What about the Changeling?"

"Of the Grand Master we can be sure of nothing," Istvan answered. "Each time I think I have discovered something valuable and dig further, I find a contradictory set of facts. He is from the Far East, the Middle East, Europe, the north of Africa, the New World. He is a Zoroastrian, a Buddhist, a Muslim, a Sikh, a Christian. He is a wampyr, an alchemist, a revenant, a golem, a ghoul. He is the First Emperor of Qin returned, Genghis Khan, Murad the Conqueror, Cortez the Killer, Attila the Hun, the incarnation of Quetzalcoatl. He could be any of these things and none of them. He has saturated our networks with so much misinformation, I have no strategy for sorting through it. As if we were not burdened with enough trouble." He glanced at the desiccated corpses lining the room. As his eyes passed over each, he named them: Matthias Corvinus, John Hunyadi, Radu the Handsome, Stephen Báthory, Mihály Szilágyi. I recognized some of the names from a biography of Vlad that Ophelia had given me to read. Some of these men had supported him; some had betrayed him.

"We will be reunited with our friends soon," Vlad promised. "There is a way, Istvan. There is always a way." His eyes moved to me. "Mark my words, pup. We will twist the very fabric of reality if we must." He turned his attention to a beaker, removed it from its burner, then set it under a vertical tube and began to add another mixture to it. "But the question that concerns us at the moment is Death. Who is he?"

I couldn't trust him with that information. "You still haven't told me where my friends are, or why I can't see them."

"Your friends are close by," Istvan said. "Their exact location must be kept a secret."

"Why?"

Vlad was suddenly towering over me. "You are not so strong that your mind can't be opened. If we tell you where your friends are, you might just as well announce it to our enemies.

You will be reunited with them later, once Ophelia is safe. Now tell us what you know."

Reunited with them later? I didn't believe a word of it. I looked into Vlad's eyes for some sign that he was telling the truth, but all I could see was darkness. In Istvan's, I saw only pity. Hardly encouraging.

"Your friends are safe," Istvan said. "Our concern must be for Ophelia."

"They should be involved," I said.

"Impossible," snapped Vlad. "They are not equal to the task. And I have no intention of compromising my efforts by acting nursemaid to a gaggle of children."

"We were outmatched on the ship," Istvan said. "If we bring your friends with us, they will be easy targets. It does not serve our cause to place them in peril."

I suddenly understood why the good-cop/bad-cop routine was so effective. It really threw you off to have someone in the room you liked and wanted to trust, and another whose aggression inspired fear and hatred. I resisted the urge to engage with Istvan. Vlad was my enemy. I couldn't become complacent about that.

"I don't trust you," I said to him. "If you know where the Changeling is keeping Ophelia, tell me. I'd rather try this on my own than have you stab me in the back."

"Try this on your own? Did you hear that, cousin? The little cub wants to save Ophelia by himself. Well, good luck. You are free to leave and pit your skills against the New Order. Perhaps, in your next encounter, you'll manage to stay alive for more than a few minutes."

He turned back to his potions, then took his eyedropper and forced what must have been poison down the throat of the next rat in line. Once it stopped moving, he injected his newest concoction into its stomach. The rat shuddered and convulsed, then sat up and nearly scurried off the counter. Vlad's hand shot out so quickly I barely saw it. I could feel his sense of triumph. Then, after a few short seconds, the rat hissed, shook wildly and grew still. Triumph turned to rage. Vlad drew his fist back and would have smashed the entire apparatus in front of him had Istvan not grabbed his arm.

"We are out of time," Vlad growled. "Ophelia's trial is at sundown. If the Changeling is there, how will we survive this?" He raised his hand as though referring to the corpses. Istvan seemed to know what he was talking about.

Vlad turned around and glared at me. "Why do you linger?" He reached up and grabbed the lever above the counter. A second later, the door in the wall rattled open for me. "If you aren't going to help us, be gone."

I couldn't believe he was going to let me go. I wondered if it was a trick. I took a cautious step forward. My head screamed for me to lie down. The foreign blood was still causing havoc in my system.

Istvan waved for me to stay still. "We have one chance at this," he said to Vlad. "Let me prepare him. It will make a difference to have him involved. Consider Ophelia. She will take great comfort in knowing he is under our protection. And our enemies . . . what a terrible doubt we could sow in their ranks with the weight of the prophecy behind us and you two fighting side by side, elder and younger together. Leave Zachariah here with me. Get yourself some rest. I will proceed as you have planned."

Vlad glanced back, then returned to his work. "And what of Death?"

Istvan's eyes bounced quickly to me and then back to Vlad. Something passed between them.

"I will meet you here after the sun sets," Vlad said. Then he shifted through the exit and was gone.

CHAPTER 27

ONE TALENT TO
RULE THEM ALL

I STVAN CLOSED THE door of stone. With Vlad gone, the air in the room felt suddenly lighter.

"You must understand the pressure he is under. If he fails, our cause is finished, and he knows it."

"He . . ." I didn't know where to begin.

"I trust you've heard the old adage 'The enemy of my enemy is my friend.' The Changeling has no greater rival than Vlad. Try to think of him as an ally. Perhaps, in time, you will appreciate his strengths and forgive him his trespasses."

"After what he's done?" I took a deep breath to try to calm myself. The result was more nausea. "I can't imagine why anyone would want him alive again."

"You don't have to imagine." His eyes flickered over the corpses. "Look around you. Our list of allies grows shorter by the day. Do you think we can stop the New Order without him?"

I would have been willing to try. "How is he even alive?"

Istvan sighed, then sat slowly, as if the weight of his troubles might crush the stool beneath him. "His remains were in the silver case. The one your uncle was hiding."

The silver case . . . Should I have known? Probably. What other reason could there have been for all the secrecy surrounding it? "So Ophelia knew?" I asked.

"Yes," he answered.

"Was she going to bring him back?"

Istvan paused, thinking. "Had that been a priority for her, I'm sure it would have happened before this."

He stood, then started dismantling some of Vlad's equipment. "I know this must be hard for you. Vlad is a complicated man . . . And his history with your father is a complex tapestry. Years later, I am still having trouble unravelling the threads." He waved me over, then handed me some glass tubing. "Help me with this, would you?" He nodded towards one of the cabinets mounted on the wall.

"Vlad believes strongly in the maintenance of order, as do I. When he led the Coven of the Dragon, vampires who broke the law, particularly those who threatened to expose our existence, were dealt with harshly. Then your father came along and things changed."

He squirted some dish soap into a basin and began filling it with hot water.

"Dr. Robert Thomson . . . We often found ourselves hunting the same quarry."

I remembered reading this in my father's journal two summers ago.

"Needless to say, his approach was very different from ours. We offered death or undeath. He offered redemption, a chance to start over—something Vlad believed these vampires had forfeited by wilfully disobeying our laws. So we tried to stop him."

Istvan handed me a dish towel. He washed. I dried.

"It wasn't personal. Not at first. It just wasn't proper that a human, even one as well intentioned as your father, was interfering in our affairs."

This didn't make sense to me. "I thought my dad was part of the Underground. Wasn't he supposed to be doing that stuff?"

Istvan paused to scrub the scoring off the bottom of a beaker. "The Underground was a different beast back then, in the days before the Internet and cellphones and instant global communication. It was more of a loose affiliation. A network that evolved into being because some vampires needed help, and others got noticed. But the Underground had no charter back then, no clear mandate. Certainly none of the internal structures you'd expect to see in a modern institution. President. Board of directors. That sort of thing. Do you understand what I mean?"

"Not really," I said.

He laughed quietly, then handed me the beaker. "I suppose it isn't relevant. What matters is that we found ourselves, Vlad and I, at odds with your father. We came close to catching him several times, but Dr. Robert had an aptitude for slipping through our fingers. It was almost amusing at first. We were two of the most powerful vampires in the world, with a global army of informants at our disposal. But as we continued to fail, Vlad became more and more obsessed. In the end, paranoia set in."

For a time, he was quiet. All I could hear was the clinking of glassware and the squeak of my drying towel.

"I should have seen how it would end, and I am ashamed for not preventing it. Vlad became convinced that someone within our organization was abetting your father's escapes. He soon saw a traitor in every face around him. In time, he even suspected me and Ophelia. Once he stopped listening to her, his descent into madness began."

He shook water from his hands, then waved for the towel and dried them.

"You know the outcome." His voice slowed. "I am sorry for it. And in his moments of lucidity, Vlad is sorry, too. But you must not press him about your parents, Zachariah. He is a proud man and quick to anger, all the more so when challenged, or when his failings are exposed. When Ophelia is back, she will help restore some measure of calm. But for now, do as he says, because we cannot save her without him."

He opened a cupboard and starting stacking crucibles on a shelf. "Vlad is under considerable duress. We are weeks, perhaps months away from an antidote, assuming one can be found."

"An antidote for what?"

Istvan stared at the grey-skinned corpses along the wall. "The Changeling is venomous. His poison is so powerful we cannot bring our friends back, no matter how much blood we use. Think on that. Death forever, from a mere scratch. This weapon is in the hands of a vampire who could be anyone, at any time, and who now commands a legion. We are badly outmatched."

I was suddenly mindful again of why Ophelia had wanted my friends and me to stay indoors. "Where is Luna and everybody?" I asked. "Is Vincent all right? He was bleeding badly."

Istvan began disassembling the burners, then pointed to a drawer under the counter so I could put them away.

"Vincent and the others are hiding. They are as safe as we can make them."

"What about Suki? Is there nothing . . . ?" My tongue got stuck and I couldn't finish the sentence.

Istvan's face took on a sombre cast. "I am afraid she is gone."

I knew this already, but a part of me insisted that this must have been a mistake, that if I thought hard enough, some solution would present itself. Istvan's face told a different story. Tears formed in my eyes. I closed them and turned to the wall. It was a while before I could speak.

"Charlie . . . is he okay?"

"No."

"And Luna?"

"Devastated. The situation with her parents is tense. They want details, and we can't provide them. It's tragic. But what can be done in such situations? There is no time to mourn. We are at war."

"Can I see them?"

He sighed, then collapsed back onto his stool. "Vlad will not allow it, and I will not cross him. He claims it is for their safety, which is true . . . in part. There are those among our enemies who could pry their location from your mind. But I suspect the real reason is that with your friends as hostages, he can compel you to aid us. This includes providing us with information. You have seen the face of Death. If you are not willing to tell us who he is, I have little doubt that Vlad will threaten to kill them."

That sounded more like the vampire I knew.

"If you don't wish to tell *him* who Death is, perhaps you could tell *me?*"

I sealed my mind as tightly as I could. I wasn't ready to declare John Tiptoft our enemy knowing his death might also mean the death of Mr. Entwistle.

"We will speak of it later," Istvan said. "We must get you ready to travel."

Unless I was going to the nearest bed and breakfast, I didn't want to go anywhere. "I need more rest. I can't even stand."

"We have no choice. You heard what Vlad said. Ophelia's trial begins at sundown. The New Order plans to execute her. It must be done legally, if they wish to authenticate their position as caretakers of our species. Ready or not, we must press forward."

"What is the matter with me?"

"Vlad has given you some of his blood. Because of his age, it will accelerate the development of your talents. Regrettably, it will behave, at least in the short term, like a poison. Dizziness, nausea, what you're feeling now."

"I thought a vampire's blood was fatal to another vampire."

"The dose Vlad gave you would certainly have killed me or anyone else, but you are his progeny. Have you never wondered why it is that Vlad can do so many exceptional things?"

He stood and crossed the room, then examined the rat cage. "Their food is in that cupboard." He pointed to my right. There was a box inside that said *Mâncare Pentru Pisici*. It had a picture of a cat on it.

"You seem to have inherited his talent," he said.

"I thought you just said he has many talents."

"Let me explain. He has but one: he is immune to vampire blood. As are you."

"It doesn't feel like it."

"Your discomfort is to be expected. This first time will be the worst. But you will not die from it. In fact, from this one immunity springs near limitless power, because for a time afterwards, as a kind of side effect, you will gain the talents of those from whom you have fed. So it is with Vlad. Turning to mist. Shapechanging. Slipping like a shadow through cracks. Moving from one area of darkness to another. Compelling others to obey. Reading thoughts. Phenomenal strength and speed and endurance. Many talents, all spawned from the one."

He shook some dry cat food into a row of containers, then handed the box back to me so I could put it away.

"For over five hundred years he has collected the corpses of vampires who broke Coven law. His dungeons overflow with the undead. He need only raise them up, feed from them, and his power is renewed. Every possible talent is at his fingertips. And now they are at yours."

I could scarcely believe what I was hearing. Any vampire talent at Vlad's fingertips. And mine! The one thought was horrifying; the other, unbelievable. For the first time since the disaster on *L'Esprit Sauvage*, I felt real hope stirring within me. Rescuing Ophelia was now more than just wishful thinking.

"It is not adequate compensation for what has been taken from you," Istvan said, "but it will facilitate your survival. Now, you must tell me about Death. For the sake of your friends, you must put your reluctance aside, for if you do not tell me, I cannot predict what Vlad will do to compel you."

I understood. It seemed a small concession for their security. "Death is John Entwistle," I said. "But I don't think he remembers who he really is."

Istvan hummed a disconcerted note while he considered what I'd said. "So, he has reverted back to an earlier persona."

I hadn't heard the term *persona* used before, but I could guess its meaning. "He's gone back to being John Tiptoft," I said. "The Butcher of England."

Istvan glanced at the corpses and, for a second, I could see fear written plainly on his face. "It is no wonder you did not wish to speak of it. This is dire news. We must find a way to deal with him. It will not be easy. Do you know his talents?"

"Yeah," I said. "He can see things, visions of the past, and the future."

"It is troubling enough that a man who sees the future chooses to throw his lot in with our enemies, but there is more. He has *true sight*. It makes him a particular bane to Vlad."

"Why is that?"

"You must have noticed the way Vlad shifts from place to place," Istvan explained. "He doesn't seem to move, then is suddenly elsewhere. It is a trick of the mind. He projects an image, just as the rest of us do, but somehow, it stays frozen in your mind's eye. Then he moves and your senses do not perceive the change. He can also present himself differently. No doubt you have noticed that he often appears larger. He can be near but appear far or be far but appear near. In combat, it makes him terribly dangerous. How do you strike a man, or stop his blade, when you have no true sense of where he is? But John sees things as they truly are, so to him, Vlad is where he appears to be. When they fight, it will be skill against skill alone, and with a blade, Tiptoft is the best I have ever seen."

I could feel a heaviness in the air again. A kind of gloom. "We must have some chance against all of them?"

Istvan stood a little straighter and took a deep breath. "With an antidote, and all of us working together, yes, we have a better chance than most. Will we prevail? God only knows. But He seems to value a good struggle, for He is testing us all very sorely at the moment."

"All the more reason to get my friends to help us."

"They are not yet ready. I have done my best to further their combat training and have introduced them to some basic principles in psychic defence, but more practice and time is needed."

"What about that other vampire, the one from the ship?"

"I don't know who you mean."

Of course he wouldn't. Istvan had been gone before the

stranger showed up to help me. "He was young-looking. I would have been a goner if he hadn't shown up."

Istvan smiled. "You *were* a goner. But your friends didn't mention anyone else. Are you certain your memory is clear?"

"I think so."

"And he didn't say who he was?"

"Not exactly. All he said was . . . something about preparing the way."

Istvan looked surprised, then pleased. "I am he who goes before and prepares the way."

"That was it. Then he led me to the edge of the ship and asked me to take a leap of faith. If I hadn't looked back, I would have made it."

"A leap of faith." Istvan pressed his lips together and let out a satisfied hum. "This is promising . . . very promising."

"Why?"

"It seems we have an unexpected ally. You were saved by the Baptist. *The one who goes before and prepares the way.* He chose those words carefully. They were first spoken by John the Baptist, who prepared the way for Christ." He looked at me and smiled. "This improves our chances."

Uncle Jake had mentioned the Baptist back at Iron Spike Enterprises. "Do you know who he is?"

"No. But if he is watching over you, all the better." He motioned for me to get into the coffin. "Now we need to get to work. The night will soon be upon us, and we have not yet prepared you for your role in this crazy scheme. Lie down, and I will explain."

I was reluctant at first, but there was something in Istvan's patient demeanour that assured me I would be safe, so I climbed into the coffin. The room began to spin.

"Are you comfortable?"

"I'll be fine," I said.

"You have been given Vlad's blood and the blood of an exceptional night stalker."

"What is that?"

"A vampire with a rather remarkable talent. Now, close your eyes."

I hesitated.

"It will make this easier. Do not be afraid."

I closed my eyes.

"You are a vampire, Zachariah. A creature of blood and shadow. In a moment, I am going to ask you to separate these things. To rise as a dark essence from your body of flesh and then, like a living shadow, become one with the night."

CHAPTER 28

THE OFFER

BECOME ONE WITH THE NIGHT. That sounded like something straight out of a Hollywood movie. Hopefully not a horror flick that left the narrator in tiny, microwavable pieces.

"How do I do this?" I asked.

"Concentrate," Istvan answered. He placed his hand over my forehead so his thumb and fingers were gently pinching my temples. "Imagine yourself as you would appear in a mirror."

I pictured myself as a buff monk with a belt of rope and a passable head of hair.

"Now remove the colour. Remove the light. Leave only the silhouette. Your shadow."

My imaginary brown habit turned black. My face, my eyes, my hair, my legs and hands, all of it.

"Slow your heart."

"How?"

"Relax and take deeper breaths."

Easy enough.

"Now push," Istvan said. "Push your shadow against the wall."

I furrowed my forehead and pushed outward, the same way I did when I felt an unwanted intruder in my head.

"You are pushing against me, against my presence," Istvan said. "Ignore me. Focus on yourself. On your shadow image. Push it outward from your centre."

I tried again. This time I pictured my shadow rising from my physical self. It didn't work.

"Do not imagine it as if you were a spectator. *You* are the shadow that is rising. Push, and leave your body behind."

I pictured the coffin around me, and Istvan standing above. Then I pushed outward, imagining myself as a shadow breaking free from where I lay. At the same time, I felt his fingers slide away, as though he were pulling an idea from my head.

I opened my eyes, or rather, my shadow eyes, free from my body, saw the room around me. I looked back at the coffin. My body might have been asleep. Or dead. Something about that thought brought on a sense of panic and everything went dark. My eyes opened. Istvan was standing over me. I was back in my body. The acrid smell of the corpses was suddenly more potent, as were the sounds in the room—the rats scurrying over one another in their cage, Istvan's quiet breathing, my heartbeat.

"Almost," he said. "Try again. This time, concentrate on keeping your shadow essence outside of your body, even when you perceive the room around you."

And so I kept trying. Only once did I come close. My shadow separated itself completely from my body, then I began to float. I was weightless. Formless. Without a sense of touch I had no connection to anything. I panicked and fell back inside myself.

"You are almost there, Zachariah. Close enough that we can afford to take a few hours and gather our strength. We will refocus after you have slept. These things are always easier at night, when the sun is gone."

Istvan slumped into a chair. I wondered if the break was more for him than for me. He looked as if Atlas had just dropped the weight of the world on his chest.

"You look exhausted, Istvan," I said. "You need rest."

He didn't answer. He was already asleep. I shut my eyes and joined him.

Some time later, I awoke to a grating sound, like the movement of metal gears. Istvan stood at the counter, his hand on the lever that opened the door in the wall. In the next instant, Vlad was standing two feet inside the room.

"How have you fared?" he asked.

"Better than expected," Istvan answered. "One or two more attempts ought to see it done."

Vlad rested a mailed hand on either hip. He was wearing thick armour made from black metal plates overlaid with grey, like tarnished silver. It looked like something Sauron would have dressed his Black Riders in. The breastplate was decorated with a profile of a dragon's head. His long hair had been combed back over his shoulders and his moustache had been groomed. A bearskin cloak was pinned to his shoulders with a matching set of brooches. I recognized them as the symbol of his old Coven: a dragon, carrying a broken cross in its mouth.

"Time has caught us, my friend," he said. "Your strength has waned and you must feed. Leave the cub with me. I will join you when we are done."

Istvan looked relieved. He nodded to me, then left. I felt a chill run through me. Regardless of how much I might have needed Vlad's help, his presence unnerved me.

Vlad eyed me closely. For all of his hardware, he seemed

lighter. I wondered if he had fed, and what strange talents he might have acquired.

"My cousin is not prone to exaggeration," he said. "If he says you are close to being ready, I trust that is the truth."

Vlad shifted towards me. My necklace was strung between his thick-fingered hands. He'd removed the golden crescent so that only the silver full moon charm was present. "It was wrong of me to take this heirloom from you and Luna. Ophelia would insist upon its return. I am sure we can agree there is no better judge of right and wrong than she."

He slipped the necklace over my head. He was about half a foot shorter than me, but for an instant looked down on me as if he were twice as large. One blink later he was himself again.

I took the charm between my fingers and examined each side, as surprised by the gesture as I was by that fact that it seemed heavier than I remembered.

"We will continue your lesson," he said. "But before that, I have an offer to make." He held out his hand. There was a black dagger in it. The pommel was a dragon's head. In its teeth was a ruby the size of a hen's egg. The dragon's neck formed the handle. Bat-like wings of the same dark metal stuck out to form the guard. Above this was the dragon's tail—the blade. It was a perfect match for the sword he was carrying.

"This dagger is of exceptional quality, sibling to my Dragon Blade. Search the world over and you will find no weapons like these." He held the dagger so I could see it better. The sheath was black leather, inlaid with a silver symbol identical to the brooches he was wearing: a dragon with a broken cross in its teeth, the sign of the Coven of the Dragon.

"I have poisoned the blade with the venom of a water snake native to Polynesia. The faint-banded sea snake, *Hydrophis belcheri*.

It is the deadliest toxin nature has produced. Only the Changeling's venom is stronger."

He shifted closer, so he was right in front of me. "In ancient times, it was proper to seal contracts with a gift. Rings. Gold. Weapons. Land. In offering this dagger I am pledging my trust. Take it and you are pledging yours. It is no small thing. We will put aside our differences in the interests of saving Ophelia, even at the cost of our own lives." He held the dagger up. "Will you accept?"

I hadn't expected gifts. Giving me back my own necklace was one thing, but this extravagance put me on edge. For all its splendour, I knew this blade would cut two ways. But I also knew I was supposed to be forgiving, and to believe that people could change for the better. Still, this was Vlad. I didn't want to be tied to him.

"I have nothing to offer in return," I said, stalling.

"You are offering me your support. You might even save my life. I am buying that help in advance. Do you accept?"

If I did, would it imply that I had forgiven him? I hadn't.

He held out the dagger, hilt first. The dragon's eyes were black pearls. They seemed to stare at me no matter where the weapon moved. I felt as if I had been backed into a corner, with Ophelia's life in the balance. I thought of all she had done for me, and accepted.

"Keep it close."

I clipped the sheath to my belt of rope.

"That is a choice you will *not* regret." His eyes dropped to the Dragon Dagger. "I have spoken with your friend Charles about this gift. He told me of your reluctance to kill, even in self-defence, but it seems your behaviour in Montreal aboard *L'Esprit Sauvage* is strong evidence of an ideological change."

I didn't want to talk to him about killing or my moral code. What I'd done aboard the ship had been an aberration, and it had backfired. Suki had died, just as Uncle Jake had died. I wasn't a big believer in fate, or any kind of cosmic justice, but if I had been, it would have been easy to argue that her death was a punishment connected to my broken promise. I'd told myself after infecting Charlie that I'd never take a life again, and my actions had made a liar of me.

After a few awkward seconds Vlad continued, glancing from me to the grey, dead-eyed corpses along the wall.

"I was born in an age when religion suffused all aspects of life. When every occurrence, grand or trivial, rare or commonplace, was credited to God's sovereignty. Since my death as a man half a millennium ago, I have been divided from the Church and the Vatican. Free from their interference and the constraints of dogma, I have spent countless hours contemplating the divine and the nature of the world. Over time, certain truths have emerged as indisputable. One is that we have risen to the pinnacle of nature's hierarchy because we are her greatest killers. I have asked myself, *how can this be so, if it is not God's will?*"

I looked into Vlad's eyes to see if there was some sign that he was about to take a violent plunge off the deep end, but he was as calm and composed as I had ever seen him.

"Men in every age will speak about the will of God—that He wants you to believe this, or that, or worship this way or that way. Time has made liars of them all. God's will is made obvious only by what is irrefutable. The fittest survive. I am sure you have some knowledge of Wallace and Darwin's work on natural selection. I was not surprised when their theories came to prominence, though they shook the world to its very roots." He fixed me with an intense stare, his wide green eyes unblinking. "How could it be wrong to kill for survival, if it is so integral a part of God's plan for every creature, great and small?"

I'm not certain if he expected a reply. If God had any particular plans for me, He'd never mentioned them. And as for killing and the law of the jungle, my conscience told me we were supposed to rise above that. It had been a mistake for me to act otherwise. One I would not repeat.

"It is not my intention to start a debate on your right to self-preservation. Think on it. That is all. Now . . ." He paused to move Istvan's stool out of the way. "I have distracted you from your appointed task long enough. Forgive me. We will continue with your lesson." He gestured towards the coffin. "It will be easiest if you lie down."

I was only too happy to put an end to the conversation. I climbed in.

"How did Istvan begin?"

"He asked me to imagine myself as a shadow," I said. "Then I worked on trying to project myself outward."

"You have done remarkably well in a short time," Vlad observed. "But I would ask you—what is a shadow? It is a place sheltered from light. Without light, the shadow cannot exist. Begin with light. You have been to the tunnel. Close your eyes and visit it again."

I pressed my lids together and imagined the circle in the distance, faint at first, then, as I drew closer, the warmth of light all around me.

"Good . . . Now, with the light surrounding you, there is nothing to project your shadow upon, so you must become a living shadow. A thing of darkness that, like other black objects, does not reflect the light. You must absorb the light, draw it into yourself."

I pushed against the light and imagined myself appearing black, but it didn't work.

"Do not reject the light," he said. "Rather, draw it into your centre, all of it, so that what remains is just the black shape your inner, hidden light occupies."

I pulled the light inside and imagined myself as a shadow once more.

"Now rise," he said.

I stood. He was looking at me. I glanced back at the coffin. My body was lying there, eyes closed. It was like staring into a mirror.

"Your body is now a soulless vessel and will remain preserved until you return."

So I'd done it. I was a living shadow. A night stalker. An essence that was one with the night.

Vlad didn't give me time to celebrate. "We are not yet finished," he said. "You must learn to move as a shadow, a thing that exists where there is no light. To pass unnoticed is an invaluable skill. Quickly. We have little time."

And so, with his help, I practised moving. It was like nothing I'd ever experienced before. I could change my shape merely by willing it. In almost no time I could leak from shadow to shadow like a thing without form. I could twist and shrink and stretch. I was limited only by what shapes my mind could conceive. If only Charlie and Luna had been there to see me. It was thrilling, and it took me back to the first time I'd gone running with Mr. Entwistle. He'd helped me test my limits, and the strength I discovered in my body was empowering in exactly the same way as this. I felt as though I could stand alone against the whole world and come out without a scratch.

Vlad rested one hand on the pommel of his sword and the other on his hip, then announced that we were ready. He was looking at me intently again, and I saw something in his face that surprised me. It was pride. This from the man who had nearly ruined me.

I felt proud too. And excited. I probably should have been afraid. We were going to face the Changeling and his Horsemen. At the harbour they had been terrifying. But my fear was gone, and I owed this to him. Whoever said that truth was stranger than fiction must have lived through moments like this. Vlad and I, against the New Order. I would never have imagined it.

"I almost pity them," Vlad said, his fingers curling over the hilt of his sword. "Almost . . ."

CHAPTER 29

A JOURNEY IN THE DARK

I FOLLOWED VLAD through the secret door and into the room beyond. Stainless steel shelves and counters ran the length of the tile floor. A number of tall refrigerator units sat against the far wall. They were full of tiny vials I assumed were blood samples. There were computers, modern microscopes and centrifuges at several workstations, along with other pieces of equipment whose purposes I could only guess at. The entire room might have been lifted out of a medical research facility.

"I prefer the atmosphere in my old laboratory," Vlad said. "Istvan has been modernizing in my absence." He moved to the door, which had a sensor of some kind and opened by itself. "This way." He beckoned with a tip of his head.

I followed him to a set of stairs carved into the bedrock. They spiralled up a natural fissure in the stone. At regular intervals we passed doors of solid iron set into the rock.

Where do those go? I asked. Without lungs or vocal cords I had no means of speech, so I projected my thoughts, as I would with Luna.

"Those halls contain rows of prison cells," Vlad answered.

This must have been where Vlad stored the undead corpses Istvan had referred to—those who had broken Coven law and were sometimes raised up so Vlad could make use of their talents.

Where is Istvan? Isn't he coming with us?

"No. My good cousin has other tasks to perform. Ones that are essential if we are going to outmanoeuvre the New Order."

We continued upwards, level by level, past more rows of cells. I realized one of the prisoners in this vast collection must have supplied the blood that allowed me to move like this, as a living shadow. It made me a thief of sorts. I wondered if I should have felt ashamed of this. I didn't, perhaps because I'd been given no choice in the matter. Instead I felt alive with purpose. We were going to save Ophelia. Everything else was irrelevant.

Eventually we reached the end of the staircase. The last few steps were blocked by a pile of large stones. Vlad put his hand on the nearest one and paused, concentrating. Then he announced that the way ahead was clear. "To succeed tonight, you must be able to infiltrate the Council Chamber of the New Order. It will require that you sink beneath the earth, just as you must now rise through it to get outside. Think of this as a test. If you are patient, you will find spaces in the soil and gaps around the stones through which you can travel. See how you fare."

I touched the stone and felt myself slipping over its surface. Then I willed myself to shrink and searched out tiny pockets in the soil and seams between the rock and the ground. It wasn't difficult, just time-consuming, and it felt a bit uncomfortable because I couldn't see where I was going or where I had been.

When I emerged, Vlad was already outside. How he had managed it I couldn't guess. My surprise must have been obvious, because he put his hands on his hips and laughed quietly. "Istvan was right about you. You do our line proud."

My friends would have been stunned to see this. It was just as Istvan had said: I was one with the night, with the darkness.

Around me were the ruins of an old castle. The walls and towers had crumbled, but the stones and brick left little doubt that the battlements had once been very thick. It was set on the edge of a precipice. Far below, a river twisted like a black ribbon around the tall promontory on which the castle sat. It was a perfect landscape for what felt like my first real experience as an adult vampire. I had discovered my talent, and so had taken my first step into an exciting new world.

"You managed your first test admirably," Vlad said. "Here is the next. Pretend I am your enemy. See if you can slip away unnoticed."

I dropped so I was as slender as a thread, then travelled from blade to blade in the grasses at the base of the castle. Instead of moving away, I circled behind him, a more brazen move than my old self would have considered. When I rose again, he'd completely lost track of me.

"Not completely," he said. He turned and slashed his sword through the air. The stroke was so smooth that the blade barely made a sound as he drew it from the sheath. He stopped his swing at the edge of my neck. His control was phenomenal. "I could not see you, but I could sense your thoughts and so knew your intentions. You must keep your mind closed. Though you are a mere shadow, there are ways you can be hurt and imprisoned, perhaps even killed."

How? I asked, surprised.

"By a stronger night stalker, but as far as Istvan and I are aware, none save you exist." He sheathed his sword and turned his attention to the line of forested hills before us. "I have missed this place, Castle Dracula. It was shattered by a landslide over a hundred years ago but remains my favourite sanctuary." He took a deep breath. "I wish to walk the grounds as I did in older times. It will clear my head and help me focus on what must be done. It is far to Tirgoviste. I will not arrive in time to see the start of Ophelia's trial. You should go ahead so that one of us will see it in its entirety."

So I'm going alone?

"You are a shadow, little cub. A night stalker. As quick as thought. How could I keep up, even flying as a bat or raven?"

I hadn't considered his means of travel. I'd just assumed that I would scout ahead for him on a journey we would make together. The thought of having to go on my own took a healthy bite out of my confidence, especially since I wasn't as safe as I'd first believed.

What if you don't make it in time?

"Rest assured, it will not end until I am there."

How can you be sure?

"This trial is not about Ophelia. It is about the Changeling and his New Order, and me, and the old Coven of the Dragon. If they wanted to execute her, she would already be dead. No, it is me they want, and so I will give them what they desire, and we'll put an end to things."

But you're supposed to be dead.

"I would never let so small a thing as death stop me from saving Ophelia. The Changeling knows this, and so would expect me, even if I didn't tell him I was coming, which I did."

I was incredulous. *We'll be walking into a trap?*

"And walking out again. That part will be more difficult, but I have a loaded hand to play. And if I die, and Ophelia is freed, is that not a reasonable trade? What kind of husband would not exchange his life for that of his wife?"

I couldn't believe what I was hearing. He'd once been so crazy he'd threatened to feed my friends and me to the crows.

"A good leader knows when to take risks, and when to make sacrifices, even when he must sacrifice himself. But you know this already. To have confronted Death so your friends could escape the ship is proof enough. Now go, little cub, and see how they might remake the world, this New Order."

I don't know where I'm going.

He pointed to Polaris. "Keep the North Star on your left until you reach the Dimbovita River. Follow that south to Tirgoviste. On the north edge of the city you will see a small lake. The Prince's Church is there. You will recognize it by its three spires. Bordering this is the Prince's Court, my old seat of power, now in ruin. The southern tower is all that remains standing. There, deep beneath the earth, is a vault of stone and iron. It is the old headquarters of the Coven, and it is where Ophelia is being tried. Find out what you can. And shield your thoughts. Bury them deeply. You must not fail in this."

I did as he asked, then felt the tendrils of his mind digging beneath my own. He seemed satisfied. "I will see you at midnight."

He turned and walked down the hill. I watched him disappear, then realized what he'd asked me to do. Fly halfway across Romania and single-handedly invade the headquarters of the New Order, who'd been warned that trouble was coming, while he went for a stroll across the countryside. I would have laughed at the absurdity of it had it not been me heading into the lion's den. Then I realized that, contrary to what Vlad had said, this was not about him and the Changeling. It was about Ophelia. I would have sent my shadow dancing through the gates of hell if it would have brought her back.

With my eyes on the horizon, and Polaris on my left, I flew through the air at the speed of thought. The trees below passed like a scene from a movie run at fast-forward. Farms and villages shot past. Then I saw a dark, smooth streak in the landscape, the Dimbovita River, and turned to follow it south. It took only moments. Tirgoviste was spread below me, its streets and stores, sidewalks and houses. On the near edge of the city was the lake Vlad had mentioned. It was bordered by a park.

I had expected Tirgoviste to be a busy city, but it was small, quiet and sleeping. I shrank, then slipped to the edge of the Prince's Church. It was made of rose-coloured brick and looked more like a fortress than a place of worship. A tall, round tower with a square base sat about fifty yards away. Sandwiched in between were the ruins Vlad had mentioned. His former court was now just sections of wall made of the same pinkish brick. No trace of the roof remained. I hovered over the empty rooms for a moment, then sped to the base of the tower. There was no one around. Just me and the wind.

Once I'd taken a moment to collect myself, I drifted over the porous ground and let my essence sink in. I didn't go far before I hit stone. It wasn't natural bedrock. This stuff had been carved, like the vaulted ceiling of Vlad's lab. I inserted myself into a seam between two large, curving pieces of an arch, then emerged in an antechamber that was crowded, wall to wall, with vampires.

CHAPTER 30

THE TRIAL

I MADE MYSELF slender and passed from the shadow of one vampire to another, careful to keep my thoughts hidden. Beyond the crowded antechamber was a short hall, ending in an iron gate, like the portcullis in an ancient castle. Those outside jockeyed for the best position to see through the bars. Beyond were four guards. Each had a sword sheathed inside a dark overcoat, and I saw what might have been a shoulder harness for an automatic on the one nearest me.

The room beyond the portcullis was circular in shape, with a large set of double doors at the far end. Two sets of stairs, one on either side of me, rose up the walls and led to the back of an open balcony facing out over the next room. I could see the backs of the vampires who were seated up there, whispering and shifting like patrons at a movie theatre.

I moved into the room and up the stairs, then found myself overlooking the large oval Council Chamber. It had balconies on three sides. Beneath these were tiers of benches that made me think of a miniature coliseum. Every seat was filled.

Along the wall farthest from me was a raised dais. On it was a row of large chairs, sitting side by side behind a counter-like desk. Four figures, dressed in long, flowing crimson robes, sat in judgment there. War and Famine were recognizable by their faces and Death by his cowl. Pestilence was hidden behind a masquerade mask. His arms, neck and hands were covered in tight red cloth. The material was stained in places with tiny dark blotches, fluid from his leaking pustules. Despite this effort to make him presentable, the sight of him still filled me with revulsion.

Ophelia was slumped behind a table in the centre of the room. Her eyes were bloodshot and flitted nervously over those assembled, as though uncertain that any of it was real. Her body armour had been replaced with a simple cotton smock that I'm guessing had once been white. There were bloodstains on the sleeves.

Baoh was sitting beside her. Since our disastrous visit on the Dream Road, I had not heard from him and so had assumed that he was dead. The sight of him, poised and alert, was a tremendous relief. He straightened his orange habit, then leaned closer and whispered something in Ophelia's ear. She didn't respond but stared vacantly at the floor. When she pulled up a sleeve to scratch at her wrist, I saw that it had been slashed open. Her fingers found the edges of the scab and started to pick. Baoh reached over and gently pulled her hand away. She seemed oblivious. Her eyes never left the floor. I had never seen her brought so low, and it was heart-wrenching.

Without thinking, I started drifting towards her. Then, Famine, the Countess Bathory, turned her head in my direction. I quickly buried my alarm and darted out of sight. When I sensed her attention was elsewhere, I ventured closer to the edge of the balcony, hidden in the shadows of a man's boots.

". . . inappropriate to hold her responsible for the crimes of her husband." Baoh had left his seat and was addressing the Horsemen. He must have been acting as a lawyer of sorts.

"Ophelia kept the Impaler in check for centuries. Who knows the depths of depravity to which he might have sunk had she not been there to pacify him in his moments of irrationality?" Baoh looked around the courtroom. It seemed an odd gesture for a blind man. His skin-covered orbits seemed to sweep the entire assembly. "How many here might have fallen victim to his uncontrollable rages had she not mitigated his violent temper, time and again?"

"That only makes her complicit in his crimes," said the Countess. "There is no doubt that he was insane. The lawful course in such cases is to bring a formal charge before the officers of the court. Yet not once did she do this. Not once."

"Vlad *was* the court. How do you accuse a man of anything when the powers of prosecution and judgment lie with him alone?"

"That issue is not relevant to the original charge," said Tamerlane. "Only two generations in any one line can exist simultaneously. Ophelia spawned Vlad, who spawned this boy, Zachariah. A child! And in a single year, two more children in her line have been created. This Charles Rutherford and the girl, Luna Abbott. It is insupportable!"

"But hardly Ophelia's fault," Baoh replied.

"It is the eldest in the line who is responsible for maintaining the line's integrity," Tamerlane said. "That was a policy Vlad instituted himself."

Ophelia glanced over her shoulder in the direction of the doors, then looked down at the floor, indifferent.

"Does the accused have nothing to say in her defence?" Tamerlane asked.

Ophelia didn't respond.

"You must answer when addressed by this court!"

"There is no point in getting angry," Baoh said. "Had you wanted her to show more respect for these proceedings, you would have shown her more respect as your prisoner. No civilized nation on earth would deny someone the basic right to sustenance. She has been starved, and her wrists—"

"The court regrets that this extreme treatment was necessary," said the Countess. "The accused is possessed of psionic talents that make her dangerous. Bloodletting is not unprecedented. Vlad did this often to reduce the risk posed by those he detained. Ophelia would know this, of course.

"And she has flouted too many laws for us to assume she would submit willingly to any kind of cross-examination. Harbouring infected children. Facilitating the spread of the pathogen. Her line is three generations too long. If every family were so unscrupulous, the results would be catastrophic. Such wanton and unlawful behaviour is not to be tolerated!"

"Unlawful, yes," said Baoh, "but it does not warrant a death sentence. Not for Ophelia, who can hardly be made responsible for the behaviour of Vlad."

The Countess was unrelenting. "But these children were all wards of hers. She chose to shelter them. It is abominable!"

"And treasonous," added Tamerlane. "Have you no answer for this, Ophelia?"

She wasn't paying attention. Baoh placed a hand over hers and grew quiet. Her face calmed. She started to speak, then stopped herself right away. Famine was watching her closely. Her eyes were intense. Something sinister was happening.

"If the accused refuses to address the court, we will end this now," said Tamerlane. "No mercy can be shown to those who disregard the law. No mercy—"

"Mercy? Please!" said Baoh. "Frank and honest words should

be our currency. It was never the intention of this court to show mercy to the accused. This is a witch hunt. Nothing more."

"Enough," said the Countess. "None are above the law. You will mind your tongue, charlatan. This court has not forgotten the role that you played in helping the boy to escape us."

Baoh shrank. He had saved me from Pestilence on the Dream Road. Of course, they would know about that. The accusation was meant to muzzle him, and it did. But Famine's words had the opposite effect on Ophelia. Her eyes rose from the table.

"All of these accusations are true," she said. "It would be pointless to deny them."

A ripple of noise spread through those gathered. Their whispers rose in volume until the entire courtroom was alive with conversation. Even Pestilence sat up a bit straighter, a raspy gargle of surprise audible through his mask.

"Silence," someone whispered. It was Death, John Tiptoft. His voice was quiet, but there was no mistaking the centuries of force behind it. "You must have more than that to say in your defence, Ophelia. Do not be afraid to speak the truth here. Despite what Baoh insists, we have not passed judgment on you yet. Few are those whose sins are so grievous that they cannot make recompense. I would suggest you answer these charges with a more thorough explanation."

Ophelia glanced around the room once more. "I do not recognize the authority of this court."

"That will not save you, Ophelia," John Tiptoft said. "You will die with the sunrise, unless you can convince us you deserve leniency."

"For helping a child? He was Dr. Robert's son, and a better man . . ." She stopped speaking. Something was wrong. She was concentrating too hard. There was sweat on her forehead. Her jaw twitched. A moment later, she looked up at the Countess

Bathory and shook her head slowly back and forth. "You are not half as clever as you think, Elza. Your voice has no sway over me." Her eyes swept over the panel of judges. "I pity all of you. My ward, Zachariah, is not some child to be trifled with. Help him, nurture him, and your rewards will be great. Stand against him and you doom yourselves. He is the Messiah. The Child of Prophecy. He cannot be stopped."

"But he has already been stopped," said the Countess. Her lips curved into a wicked grin. "The boy is dead."

Murmurs rippled through the crowd when she spoke. I could hear Pestilence laughing quietly, blood bubbling in his mouth. All eyes in the courtroom passed to Ophelia, mine included. I thought these words would crush her, but she was made of sterner stuff than that.

"Zachary has died before—ending the reign of Vlad, and again when the Beast of the Apocalypse ran rampant in the New World. I have no doubt he will die again in the service of our kind. I have heard it whispered among the prophets that he will have nine lives. That his reign will last a thousand generations. Repent now, all of you, before it is too late."

"Your loyalty to the boy is misplaced," Timur said. "He cannot save your cause. The future belongs to us."

"Believe that, Timur, if it helps you. But the four of you were depraved in life, and you are depraved now. If the future were in your hands, I would weep for all assembled, but I have faith that it is not. Your nights are numbered."

Timur seemed unperturbed. "And yours have ended—"

"Unless you have something else to say in your defence?" interrupted John Tiptoft.

Ophelia paused for a moment, then raised her chin. "Only that I have no regrets. If guardianship of Zachariah passed to

182

me again, I would do as I have done. To have touched a life so pure is a reward beyond measure."

"He is the spawn of Vlad," said Famine. "The Dragon's Son. A parasite. There is a madness at work in him. I have seen it."

"Then you have gone where you have no business being," Ophelia snapped. "No doubt it was others who paid for your folly, and not you. But so it is with cowards."

Famine looked ready to respond, but she was cut short by John Tiptoft. "If you have nothing else to add in your defence, this court will adjourn." He stood. "We will announce our verdict at midnight."

There were murmurs in the crowd as the judges rose to their feet. Then a commotion in the hall started people chattering in the balconies. Tiptoft asked for silence. The gallery grew hushed. The doors at the back of the room slowly opened and Vlad walked in, his iron boots echoing loudly on the stone floor. Each left a bloody footprint on the ground. His Dragon armour was dotted with crimson spots. The four guards in the adjoining room obviously hadn't fared well keeping him out. I expected him to move as he usually did, in stops and starts that were dizzying to watch. Instead, he strode slowly to Ophelia's table and rapped an iron-clad knuckle against the edge of the wood a few times. His face was composed, but I could sense his fury boiling just beneath the surface.

"The court has already reached its verdict, Ophelia, and for your unwavering commitment to the preservation of order as a prefect within the Coven of the Dragon, you are acquitted on all charges and are free to go."

CHAPTER 31

SON OF THE DRAGON

V LAD LOOKED DOWN at Ophelia with a softness in his expression I never imagined he could possess. Her eyes were tearing up. A hint of a smile quivered on her lips, but I could tell she was still frightened. Thoughts passed between them, then his face hardened and he turned to face the spectators. When he unleashed his voice, the anger within it was colossal. It seemed to come from every point in the room.

"It seems the rumours of my destruction have been accepted as truth by too many, for here you sit idly by, allowing this offensive charade to take place. But I am not without mercy . . .

"For this act of disloyalty, you will all be forgiven. But understand, from this moment forward, you are either for me or against me. Once I have dealt with this usurper, this Changeling, I will find each and every one of you and ask a simple question: What have you done to help me and my Coven maintain order? I will not accept any pleas of neutrality."

The panic in the crowd rose to such a pitch, I was surprised I could hear anything over the sound of frantic hearts and shuffling feet. Although he had told me his presence was expected, those in the crowd were clearly shocked to see him. Many fled openly. Others made their way out more cautiously.

After a minute, only a handful were left watching from their seats. One I recognized. He was wearing a round-brimmed leather hat with red tassels and a tight-fitting black vest studded with rhinestones. His outfit had changed, but there was no mistaking the Arabian Elvis. He crossed his feet on the seat in front of him and lounged back with his hands crossed in his lap, the rings on each finger so thick that together they looked like a row of gem-studded brass knuckles. A muscular Asian woman was sitting beside him. Her thick dark hair was cut in a straight line above her eyebrows and at the back along her neck. Her green, almond-shaped eyes almost glowed in the dark. She whispered something to the King, who sat up a little straighter and looked in my direction. I wondered if she could see me.

Vlad ignored them. His attention was focused exclusively on the Horsemen, none of whom seemed surprised to see him.

Tamerlane was the first to respond. His skin blackened and he rose above the bench, his legs a serpentine coil of smoke. "Enough of your parlour tricks, Impaler. We can settle this ourselves, you and I."

Baoh started backing towards the large set of double doors at the back of the room.

Vlad smiled. "Timur the Lame, you claimed that if you rose from the dead the world would tremble. Well, men can tremble in laughter as well as fear. Do not flatter yourself. In this world of darkness, I have no equal."

Ophelia still hadn't moved. A tear spilled down one cheek and her hands shook. She looked as though she was about to have a nervous breakdown. I slid down the wall and moved towards the bench nearest her table.

Patience, little cub. Do not reveal yourself yet.

Tamerlane swooped forward. Vlad was enveloped in sulphurous smoke. For a second I lost sight of him, then his hazy silhouette came into view, arms spread wide, fists clenched. An explosion of light followed. Golden-yellow flame erupted from every square inch of him. He was on fire, just like the jet-black vampire Charlie and I had seen on the stairs of Iron Spike Enterprises. Vlad had self-immolated somehow. His fists shook, and the heat intensified. Smoke burned. Tamerlane cried out. Vapour and ash spun back to the dais. When Tamerlane took form beside the other Horsemen, his skin was charred and steaming.

The fire died. The darkness that fell was more complete than before. The candles in the chandelier above Ophelia's table had melted. Vlad's outer clothing had been incinerated and his armour was scorched black. The rest of him seemed unaffected. Not one hair on his head had been singed.

"You must do more than toss your cap if you wish to be lord here, Timur," Vlad said.

A wave of energy passed through me as Famine brought her voice to bear. I did my best to shield myself. Vlad seemed unconcerned.

"You wish to control my thoughts, Elizabeth. Tread carefully. Not all who die go to the light. We are the damned, you and I. Keep digging, and I'll give you a taste of the hell that awaits you in the next life."

The voice of the Countess faded and she drew back a step into the protective space behind John Tiptoft, who had risen from his seat.

"Fortune favours the bold, Bathory," Vlad said. "It will not favour you. You are a disgrace to your family."

Tiptoft reached inside his robe to where his sickle was belted and placed a hand over the grip. "You cannot stand against all of us, Vlad. Come to your senses. Your crimes are many, but not unforgivable. You and Ophelia must confess and atone."

"John Tiptoft!" Vlad exclaimed. "The Butcher . . . You have been irrelevant for so long, one easily forgets you are present. I will atone in my own way, by my own prescription. As for you, if you leave now and never interfere in my business again, I will not avenge myself for the dishonour you have done my wife, parading her about in this manner. That is my peace offering. Accept it or I will destroy you."

Tiptoft stepped off the dais and stopped several paces from where Vlad was standing. His confidence was unsettling. "You know that will not happen, Vlad. But it does not have to end badly for you. Agree to serve us, and your place in the New Order will be assured."

"Serve *us*?" said Vlad. "Who is this *us* you speak of?" His eyes passed over Pestilence, the Countess, Tamerlane and then Tiptoft. "I see only the depraved, the dispossessed, the delusional and a lapdog. Let your master show himself. I am beginning to wonder if he exists at all."

"He will reveal himself to you at a time of his own choosing, not yours. Stand down, Vlad. Your reign has ended. It is time for others to lead."

"Others?" said Vlad. "Perhaps you are right."

I heard his voice whisper in my head again. *Move behind me now. Let them see you. Remember, you are my progeny. A Dracula. Be bold. And terrible.*

I was already in position at the table. I rose up from the floor and stood behind Vlad. He was about half a foot shorter than me. I made myself even taller, and broader, so I'd stand out even more.

"I believe you are acquainted with my son. It seems his work is not yet finished. Like me, he has risen again. If my reign has ended, Tiptoft, it is only so that his can begin."

Tamerlane scowled, as though he could hardly believe his eyes. Pestilence backed away from his chair until his feet were rooted in the shadows along the wall. Tendrils of thought passed over me. Famine, the Countess Bathory, was searching the room. She might have been looking for my body—or perhaps she thought I wasn't real and was trying to find the source of my shadow. Tiptoft didn't move.

I drew my feelings inward, then I took Vlad's words to heart and changed my shape into something that suited one of the Draculista.

Vlad's father was named Dracul, which means "dragon" in old Romanian. Oddly enough, the word also means "devil." Dracula, the name Vlad made infamous, means "son of the dragon" or "son of the devil." Vlad must have liked the dragon handle better, because he made it his family symbol and, later, the symbol of his Coven. Since he was my vampire father, I was also the son of a dragon, and after years of indulging in comic books and fantasy games, my mind had no difficulty drawing from a catalogue of images one that was both awesome and startling. My arms became talons. Wings the length of the Council Chamber unfurled from my back. I dwarfed the company assembled as my torso stretched upwards past the top of the chandelier. This I crowned with a long head of teeth and horns and spikes that would have had *Tyrannosaurus rex* begging for a one-way ticket back to Jurassic Park.

Tiptoft seemed unimpressed. If I wasn't mistaken, he actually sighed as he drew his sickle.

"I am sorry it has come to this," he said. Then he stepped forward and attacked.

CHAPTER 32

TRIAL BY COMBAT

VLAD DID NOT have time to draw his sword before
Death was on him. He raised both arms and stopped a
stroke that was so fast and hard it made my shade ripple. Sparks
flew. Ophelia cried out. Vlad skipped back and pulled out the
Dragon Blade.

"Go, love," he said to Ophelia. "I will meet you in the tunnels."

She hadn't moved from behind the table. Baoh was gone. I
was angered that he would leave, but he was over twelve hundred years old and had probably survived to that age by avoid-
ing men like Vlad and Tiptoft.

They began to circle each other.

I spread my wings to block the view from the dais so Ophelia
could leave unseen, but she didn't budge. *You have to go*, I said.
We can't leave until you do.

Ophelia looked at me, confused. Until that moment, I don't
think she realized I was really there. Perhaps she thought I was
a trick of Vlad's. Some phantom conjured up to distract his
enemies.

You have to go, I said again.

Her eyes shifted from me to Vlad. A feeling of sick disappointment came over me. She wouldn't leave him. It didn't matter what I said.

Vlad was perspiring heavily. And he was losing. Tiptoft was faster. More precise. As their weapons sang through the air, punctuated by clangs and bangs and sparks, I realized that Vlad was the stronger of the two, but he was too exhausted for it to matter. The energy he had used to self-immolate had drained him. His chest heaved and his shoulders sagged. When Tiptoft took his next stroke, a clean overhead, Vlad brought his sword up too slowly to block it, and the edge nicked the bridge of his nose, opening a deep gash across it. Blood poured in thick ribbons down his cheeks.

I glanced back at Ophelia. Her eyes were locked on the Countess. The two were waging a silent battle. I moved between them, thinking it might release Ophelia from Famine's gaze, but it made no difference.

Pestilence took notice. He backed into the corner then dove into the shadow of the bench, emerging an instant later in the tiered seats behind Vlad. I shot across the room to attack him, but all I managed to do was cover him with my shadow. It was about as effective as smashing someone with a flashlight beam.

Pestilence leapt at Vlad's back, his hands stretched out for the Prince's neck. Vlad spun and grabbed him by the throat, then hurled him into Tiptoft. The taller man moved aside deftly. In one fluid motion, he switched his sickle to his other hand and caught Pestilence as he was tumbling to his knees.

"Stay out of this," Tiptoft snapped. "You insult me with your cowardly antics."

"If he shadow-jumps again, meet him in the darkness and kill him," Vlad said to me.

I wasn't certain what he meant, but it didn't matter. Pestilence wasn't the threat. Death was, and after a good half minute of fighting, he didn't have so much as a crease in his crimson cowl. Vlad was up to his usual trick of skipping through space without seeming to move, but Tiptoft wasn't fooled. Time and again he parried each stroke. It looked effortless.

I glanced at Tamerlane. He hadn't moved. I couldn't figure out why. Did he not think it necessary to help? Was he too hurt? Was there some kind of code—that you didn't interfere when two men were engaged in solo combat? Or was it something else? A deep malevolence was evident in his expression. It made me wonder if there was some animosity between the two Horsemen. I had assumed, since both served the Changeling, that they would work together, in the same way Charlie and I might, as friends, but things may not have been that simple.

As Vlad and John circled one another, I realized that the questions were irrelevant. Vlad was finished, whether Tamerlane helped or not. The Prince must have known it too, because he growled and let loose a flurry of clumsy strokes. One missed wide and carved a chunk out of the bench to his right. Tiptoft ducked the next, then met the last two cleanly with the flat of his blade. He flicked Vlad's sword aside and smashed a blow down on his arm. It bit into the armour and I heard the sound of bone cracking. Vlad fell to his knees.

"Will you yield, Vlad?" Tiptoft asked, wrenching his weapon free.

Vlad's eyes were glazing over.

"Kill him," said Tamerlane.

Pestilence started laughing. He took a step towards the shadows as if he might do the deed himself but saw me and stopped.

Zachary, Vlad whispered to me. *You must get Ophelia out.*

Tiptoft brought his sickle crashing down towards Vlad's neck.

The former Grand Master raised his arm to ward off the blow, but it got battered aside and the metal blade bit through the raised neck guard on the side of his breastplate. Blood splashed his cheek and ran down the inside of his armour. Tiptoft raised his weapon to the other side. In desperation, I hurled myself at him, but my shade just spread over his cloak. Vlad tried to lift his other arm, the broken one, but Tiptoft kicked it away. His sickle crashed down against the other side of Vlad's neck, opening a gash that mirrored the first.

Ophelia darted forward and reached for the fallen Dragon Blade.

Tiptoft raised his sickle. "Three strokes for the Trinity," he said.

Ophelia lunged forward as he swung. She braced the flat of the Dragon Blade across the back of Vlad's armour. When Tiptoft's weapon hit the black metal, his blade shattered.

Attack, someone whispered to me.

I quickly glanced around. The voice was familiar.

Strike now, he said. *Before it is too late.*

There were only a few vampires present. One was tucked into the shadows of the upper balcony. His long brown hair was pulled back in a ponytail, just as it had been on *L'Esprit Sauvage,* the ship in Montreal, when he saved me from Death. If Istvan was correct, it was the Baptist.

Shadows can go where light can go, he told me, tapping the side of his head near the temple.

He was right. Light could penetrate the eyes, and so could I.

Tiptoft's weapon was now short by a good foot of steel, but enough blade remained that when Ophelia attacked, he was able to deflect each stroke. Then he pushed her back so that she crashed into the table in the centre of the room. Before he could turn and take another swing at Vlad's unprotected neck, I shot myself at his eyes. I expected something supernatural to occur. If eyes were the windows to the soul, I thought I might come face to face with his inner self, but all that happened was I moved through his pupils and collided with the lens at the back of his eyeballs. It was about as spiritual as walking face first into a door.

Tiptoft slapped his hand over his face and stepped back. "Who are you, boy?" he said. There was no anger in his tone. He was genuinely curious, perhaps even amused. It upset me, because he sounded exactly like John Entwistle.

I was your friend once, I said. *When you were a better man.*

He didn't answer. But I heard Famine shout, "Stop them!"

I couldn't see what was happening, but there was a gap between the fingers of John's hand, so I slipped through. Vlad's Dragon Blade was lying on the ground. The large stone tiles around it were stained with blood. A long smear led to a bench, which was tilted upwards, like a trap door. Vlad and Ophelia were gone.

Tamerlane rose into the air, then settled beside the opening. "Meet me on the other side," he said to Pestilence. "Together we can finish this."

Pestilence hesitated, his eyes busily scanning the room. He seemed unwilling to shadow-jump with me present.

"Let them go," Tiptoft said. He was still holding his broken sickle. Half of the arc was in shards on the floor. He tossed the hilt aside, bent and raised the Dragon Blade.

"The Impaler is almost dead," Tamerlane said. "We may never have an opportunity like this again."

"It is not important that he die. Of what use is a dead enemy? It is more important that he was beaten, here, in his former court, with these few to bear witness." He waved to the upper balconies and to the benches where the handful of spectators remained, including the Arabian Elvis, the strong Asian woman who was huddled against him and the young vampire who was still watching me, intently.

I snuck into his shadow, then rose up his back. *You're the Baptist, aren't you?* I asked.

I am, he said. *To give light to those who sit in darkness and in the shadow of death to guide your feet into the way of peace.* He winked and looked behind me to where the Four Horsemen were standing. I glanced back and almost missed seeing him sink into a shadow on the wall. His sudden departure left me exposed.

Famine saw me first. "There," she said, pointing.

Tiptoft eyed me, unconcerned. "Tell your master that our offer stands. He would be wise to join his power to ours."

I am my own master, I told him, sliding to the floor. *And we both know Vlad isn't the type to take orders.*

"Then his fate is sealed, as is yours, Son of the Dragon. Unless you join us, I see pain and loss and death for you."

CHAPTER 33

CHANGE OF PLANS

I FOLLOWED VLAD'S blood trail through the trap door and emerged in a stone tunnel. It was only four feet in height, so when I found Vlad farther along, he was stooped at the waist, walking with Ophelia cradled in his arms. He appeared to be perfectly fine, although moments before his right forearm had been shattered and his neck nearly severed. There was only one explanation.

You drank from Ophelia!

He glanced backwards. "It was a sacrifice she made willingly. The path to safety is one that only I can navigate."

I wasn't sure how to respond. Or how I was supposed to feel, seeing Ophelia in a worse state now than in the courtroom. But a part of me must have realized that this was the only way forward. If Vlad had remained incapacitated, Ophelia and I might not have been able to get him out, and as willing as I might have been to leave him behind, she certainly wouldn't have. It would have left me in a dreadful bind.

"I will need you to keep an eye out behind us," Vlad said, moving forward at a crouch.

I don't think they plan to follow, I told him.

"And why not?"

Tiptoft told them not to. He said a dead enemy was of no use.

Vlad turned. He was suddenly standing at his full height. In the short tunnel, it should have been impossible.

"If rulership taught me one thing, pup, it is the power of deception. A dead enemy . . ." He laughed. "Tiptoft is posturing. A dead enemy is the best kind to have! No, he's too smart to be lured into this den of traps. These tunnels aren't safe for him, and he knows it. Tamerlane and Pestilence are another matter. Tiptoft just wants them tethered so they don't steal his prize. But they might not comply, so stay vigilant."

He stooped and continued down the tunnel. It was as if the ceiling dropped when he turned around. His pace remained slow. He was counting the stones on the floor as he walked over them. From time to time, he would take a long step to pass over a certain tile. The walls were lined with torch sconces. At odd intervals he'd pull one out, or rotate another. He never said why.

We passed several branches. Most he ignored. Only once, when we came to a dead end, did he appear lost, but instead of turning around he reached to his left and pushed in one of the stones in the wall so that it slid inward several inches. A loud clacking followed, like the unwinding of a chain, and the wall on the right swung open beside us. This led to more tunnels and branches.

Eventually we came to a fork. To the left were stairs going down, to the right, stairs going up.

"You must return to your body," Vlad said. "I will meet you back at Castle Dracula. My method of travel will be slower. The sun will rise before my return."

As soon as he mentioned travel, I thought of the speed of my journey here, flying as a shade over the Transylvanian Alps. He had arrived just minutes later.

How did you get here so quickly?

"Pestilence is not the only vampire who can move from one shadow to another. When there is time, I will show you how, but you must have the right blood in your system, and you do not."

He nodded for me to go up the stairs, opposite to the direction he was travelling, then readjusted Ophelia in his arms.

"Your journey back will be easy, but you will find your body exhausted, unaccustomed as it is to this form of separation. Go home now and sleep." He turned and began to walk down the steps. "Fly north towards Polaris. As you draw closer to your body, it will call you back."

I watched him descend out of sight. *Go home now and sleep.* He'd said it as though his ruined castle was a place I was safe and welcome. It seemed an odd remark coming from a man who was basically holding my friends hostage.

My instincts told me to follow him, at least until I knew that Ophelia would be all right. It seemed risky, leaving her in his hands. I stood unmoving for a time, thinking about this, and remembering something Mr. Entwistle had once told me about villainy: that whether we saw a person as good or bad usually depended on whether they served our interests or stood against them. Vlad seemed a much different person than the one who'd tried to kill me in my uncle's office. I wondered if he'd actually changed, or if I was just seeing him differently because circumstances had forced us to work together. I tried to be objective, to look at his behaviour as one of the spectators in the courtroom would have. In the end, it came down to one thing: he'd been willing to die for Ophelia. Villains didn't do that.

I slunk up the steps, hopeful that with Ophelia back we could regroup with my friends and start over. The stairs led to a dirt tunnel that connected to one of the city's underground sewers. I rose up through a manhole and found myself on a quiet city street. Polaris was clearly visible overhead. I rose towards it and felt something pull at me. It was subtle. I wondered if it was similar to the feeling that birds got when it was time to migrate. An instinct just said *this way*. I didn't have to think about it.

I followed the pull northwest towards my resting body, moving once again at the speed of thought. As I approached the castle ruins, I was aware that others were nearby. The lure of my body was strong, but a deeper instinct told me to stop. I took the shape of a small bat and flapped my way above a stand of trees. Shadows were visible through the canopy. Several people were running away from the castle. One of them was Charlie. Luna was with him. I moved closer, curious about what they were doing there and anxious to give them the news about Ophelia. As vain as this will sound, I also wanted to show off a bit. I dropped beside them, as silent as still air. They ran past without noticing.

Hey, you two, back here, I said.

Charlie stopped. Luna grabbed his arm and pulled him forward. "It's got to be a trick," she said. "Keep running."

He hesitated. "It sounds just like him."

Luna didn't break stride. "Don't you think Istvan would have said something if Zack were here?"

Annoyed, I shot ahead of them, then rose up from the ground, shaping my silhouette so that it would appear as my normal self, a young man in Kevlar armour. *Hold up. It's me.*

Luna froze.

"That can't be him," Charlie said. He drew a knife from his belt and assumed an offensive crouch.

Of course it's me, you knucklehead. Well, it's my shadow, actually. But close enough.

I felt Luna reach out with her mind. I welcomed it. Her face softened. "It's him, Charlie." She took a half-step forward, then stopped. "At least, I think so. You didn't die again, did you? Why do you look like this?"

Didn't Istvan explain?

"Are you kidding?" said Charlie. "That nincompoop is more tight-lipped than Ophelia." He scrutinized my shadow essence more closely, then he shot me a disapproving look. "You've got to be kidding."

About what?

"You've got your talent already, don't you?" He gestured to Luna, the knife hanging loosely in his hand. "I told you he'd get his talent first. This just takes the cake. The last thing we hear is that you're alive again—"

"Zack, what's happening to your legs?" Luna asked, interrupting.

I had no idea. The base of my shadow essence was starting to stretch back towards Castle Dracula, moving as if it had a will of its own. My surprise quickly turned to panic. I'm not sure how I knew, but my physical body was being moved. I reached out for Luna. *Help me!* The shadow of my hands ran the length of her arm and slipped off.

"Not that way," she shouted.

Charlie threw his hands up in the air. "Well, this sucks."

I flew backwards. As I did, a large, ominous shape rose up beside Charlie. It was Vincent. Before I could ask if he was okay, or what they were doing here, the ground blew through me like a cold wind.

I crashed into my body and stopped dead. The smell of decay was instantly nauseating. I took a breath and could taste the rot around me. It sounded as if someone was pounding the sides of my coffin with a mallet. It was my heartbeat. I raised my hands to cover my ears. As the coarse fabric of my robe rubbed against my skin, I gasped. It felt like a nail file. My senses had come alive, and every nerve was screaming. After a few seconds the sensations began to ebb. My pain subsided and the sound of my heartbeat dropped to its regular volume.

I pushed open the lid to my coffin and climbed out. After travelling unhindered, it felt odd to have to use my legs again. They were slow and unwieldy. A lone candle burned on the floor, casting huge shadows against the wall. I had been moved to a cell of some kind. A heavy wooden door bound with iron was slightly ajar in front of me.

Voices approached from down the hall. One of them belonged to Istvan. "This way," he said.

His footsteps drew nearer until he knocked at the door and pushed it open. The smell of death and corrupting bodies grew stronger, making my head shake. Instinctively, I closed my fingers over the handle of the Dragon Dagger still tucked inside my belt.

Istvan stepped inside. "I am relieved you are well. I'm told it can be a trial re-entering the body, especially for the first time. The senses awaken in ways that are unpleasant."

He moved out of the doorway to make room for the person behind him. It was Uncle Jake. He was wearing the same ripped T-shirt and leather coat he'd had on at Iron Spike Enterprises, but they were filthy now and reeked of sweat. The skin underneath his bloodshot eyes sagged as if he had not slept properly for days. Stubble covered his chin and scalp, and his skin, which was much paler than I remembered, was covered in patches of grime. His movements were stiff. It clearly pained him to walk.

A vampire with purple eyes had his hand around the back of his neck. It was the Arabian Elvis. He looked much the same as he had in the courtroom. Black tasselled hat with a matching leather outfit. Two modern automatics had replaced his old six-shooters. The barrel of one was pressed into the side of Uncle Jake's neck.

Istvan gestured for them to stop where they were, then turned to me. "I am sorry to do this, Zachariah, but there has been a slight change of plans. You won't be meeting Vlad here after all."

CHAPTER 34

TESTING THEORIES

I PULLED THE dragon-headed dagger from its sheath.

"Move and the Commander dies," Istvan said.

I looked at Uncle Jake and wilted. He looked positively wretched, and there was nothing I could do to help him. I suppose I should have felt some joy or relief that he was alive, but Istvan's betrayal obliterated everything but my sense of shock and outrage. My hackles rose and my stomach tightened. It wasn't supposed to be like this. Istvan was one of the good guys.

"What are you doing?"

"Only what is necessary. We are perched on the edge of an abyss, Zachary. The pathogen has spread out of control. There are too many vampires. If we fail to act decisively and the balance tips further, we will fall into a hell so deep not even God will be able to save us."

"This has nothing to do with Mr. Rutherford. You have no right to treat him this way."

"He will be allowed to go, *if* you co-operate."

It was just as Ophelia had said back in Montreal. If someone I cared about was taken, I could be leveraged.

"I'll do what you ask. Just let him go."

Istvan took the dagger from me and glanced at the shadow of my coffin on the wall. It shifted slightly with each flicker of the candle flame. Pestilence stepped out from that darkness. He was still clothed in red, although his mask had been removed. Another shadow-jumper followed him. It was the Asian woman with the shiny green eyes and thick black hair who had been sitting with the bounty hunter at Ophelia's trial. On her right hand I could see the Changeling's mark. In the other was a set of manacles. She stepped closer, secured them in place around my wrists and ankles, then tested them carefully, her movements quiet and efficient. When she was finished, I couldn't move.

"Now let him go," I said.

A shadow fell across Uncle Jake and I suddenly found myself staring at a completely different man. He was several inches shorter and his clothes had changed to a pair of black slacks and a matching T-shirt with a large, round, open neck embroidered with silver thread. His body was lean and well muscled, like that of a young man, but he must have been very old, because his irises were completely white. It would have taken centuries to bleach the colour from them. I couldn't guess his ethnicity. His face was perfectly proportioned, his skin tanned. He could have come from just about anywhere: the Far East, the Near East, the Middle East, South America or Europe. He definitely wasn't Inuit or African, but he might have been a mix of either.

I suppose I should have felt surprise. I was standing face to face with the Changeling. But mostly, I just felt stupid.

"Forgive us a small deception," the Changeling said. "The Baptist has been spreading a rumour that the true Messiah can see through my disguises. It comforts me to know that he is wrong . . . Unless you are not, in fact, the Child of Prophecy, and it is really the lycanthrope, Vincent, who escaped with your friends."

The Changeling's arm fell into shadow. When I could see it clearly again, the fingers had bonded together and were covered with something hard and chitinous, like the stinger of a scorpion's tail.

"The Baptist also claims that you are immune to my venom. I would like to test that theory as well."

He struck with alarming speed. A jolt of pain tore through my neck. It subsided slowly, leaving an itch behind. The itch became a burn. With each frantic beat of my heart, liquid fire spread through my body, first into my head and down into my chest, then into my shoulders and limbs. Every muscle grew taut. The edges of the manacles bit through the skin of my wrists. I fell sideways to the floor and watched as the veins in my forearms bulged and turned grey.

I had one chance. I closed my eyes and imagined the light of the tunnel. I drew it into my centre, so in my mind's eye I was nothing but a shadow. Then I willed myself to leave my body. It almost worked. My shadow essence started to rise, but the Changeling saw me right away.

"Where do you think you're going?" he asked.

An instant later, a shadow, identical in shape to him, emerged from his body, put its hands on my shoulders and shoved me back inside myself.

I stopped breathing. My diaphragm wouldn't relax. The pain grew unbearable. Then my heart spasmed, blackness took over and everything went quiet.

CHAPTER 35

UNDEATH

I DID NOT GO to the tunnel of light. There was no warmth, or sense of other. My senses had been stripped. I did not think or dream or feel. I had no self-awareness. No sense of time or place. There was only darkness and a silence so profound it was as if the entire world had vanished, and me along with it, so that nothing—not my body, my mind or my soul—existed at all.

This didn't last forever. In time, I became aware of myself again. The space I was in shifted. My mind felt as though it was full of water. I couldn't move, but my eyes were open a sliver. A blurry crack of light appeared beside me, then widened. I was in a coffin, and someone was opening the lid. Overhead was a huge bronze chandelier. It drifted in and out of focus as the muscles of my eyes began to work again. Orange-yellow candlelight cast dancing shadows on a circle of tall, thin, rectangular windows set inside a high dome. The areas between the window frames were covered with pictures of people with halos. This must have been a church.

A fuzzy shape appeared above me. A man in a cowl. There was an aura of power about him. When he bent closer to examine me, I noticed that he had a strange rune on his forehead. It was open, as if it had just been carved there with a knife. His hair and short beard were a mix of white and grey and black. I thought for a moment that it was an old friend, but something told me I was wrong.

"There is no cause for distress, John," said a voice from across the room.

The man, John, removed his cowl. Icy blue eyes swept over me. "I cannot endorse this," he said. "If this boy is who the prophets claim, he is a threat to us. He should be put to the torch, immediately."

Something in his voice jogged my memory—this had once been my friend, Mr. Entwistle. Now he was Death. They shared the same face, the same voice, the same confident, wolf-like mannerisms. It was just plain wrong. As unjust as the thought of being burned alive. Anger, helplessness, disappointment, frustration—I suppose I should have felt them all, but my body was still numb, and my mind groggy, and so I was spared everything but a sense that things were not as they should have been.

"The prophecy is a lie, John," the other man said. "A tool of the prophets, nothing more."

"Lie or no, the prophecy has a life of its own. The Baptist is still preaching it like gospel. He should be silenced."

"The Baptist is a paper tiger. Kill him and you make him a martyr. Let the man preach. He does us a service, for those who listen identify themselves with his cause and can be eliminated." The speaker moved to the edge of my coffin so I could see him clearly. It was the Changeling. He was dressed in a blue silk robe with long, flowing sleeves, all of it masterfully embroidered. The sight of him made my insides squirm. I tried to move. My right index finger rose a half inch, then fell.

"Did Istvan bring any news of Vlad?" the Changeling asked.

"Nothing encouraging."

"What have we to fear? His followers are dead, his store of bodies destroyed. It is his final, desperate hour."

Tiptoft clenched his teeth so that the muscles in his jaw twitched. "That only makes him more dangerous. I should have killed him at Ophelia's trial."

"That was not my wish, John. But things have changed. The war is all but over. Of our enemies, only Vlad and the Baptist remain."

So I still had allies. My left thumb quivered. Then the muscles of that shoulder flexed and relaxed.

Tiptoft looked skeptical. "There is that lycanthrope of Vlad's to deal with. The one who died and came back. The Impaler claims he is the true subject of the prophecy. That it isn't this boy at all. It is said that this shape-changer, Vincent, is Abaddon's son, that his father was the Beast of the Apocalypse, a creature no man could war against. Not even me."

My hand spasmed. Something pokey hit my little finger. It was the knife Vlad had given me—the Dragon Dagger. If Vincent was still alive, perhaps Charlie and Luna had escaped the castle and were alive too. I had to get out of there. I tried to sneak my hand closer to the handle, but it wouldn't move. I'd forgotten that my wrists and ankles had been manacled.

But there was another way. I imagined myself in the tunnel of light, then drew it into my centre. The next part, leaving my body, should have been easy, but when I tried to rise, nothing happened. I wondered if borrowed talents had an expiry date. Vampire blood broke down over time. It was why we had to feed so often. Could this have explained it?

The Changeling placed his hands on the side of my coffin. His eyes never left Tiptoft, but I could feel his presence pressing down on me. "You died, John, because you tried to reason with the Beast, to appeal to a rational side it did not possess."

"I have no memory of this."

"You have been many people, not all of them as useful as you are in this incarnation. The man who faced Hyde tried to walk the path of peace, and it proved his undoing. I have no need for such a man."

Tiptoft frowned. He looked suddenly uncomfortable. I felt an energy in the room that made my skin itch. I wasn't certain if it was my imagination or not, but the rune on Tiptoft's forehead seemed to stand out a little more.

"Do not be concerned about the werewolf. Vampires will not follow one of the unclean."

Tiptoft was rubbing the mark as if it pained him. A moment later, his eyes lost their focus, as though he was getting drowsy.

The Changeling watched him for a few moments. "What do you see, John?" he asked.

Tiptoft stared through the floor for a good half minute. Then his eyes widened and he took in the room as though surprised to find himself there. "This lycanthrope is formidable. We must separate him from Vlad. He will present a problem for us otherwise."

"Are you certain?"

"The future is never certain."

"You see a battle?"

"Yes."

"Where?"

Tiptoft paused. His eyebrows pinched together in an expression of uncertainty. "Underground. Paris maybe. Or Budapest. It is hard to tell."

"And the outcome?"

"I cannot see."

A long silence followed. I remembered that Mr. Entwistle had not been able to see the outcome of his fight with Hyde. He thought that it meant he was going to die, which was exactly what happened. I wondered briefly if that was the case now: if Tiptoft was going to die and couldn't see past his death.

My left leg twitched. Both men saw it. Neither seemed surprised.

"It is only one possible future you see, John. It is not what I have seen. Now, tell me why this boy's body has not been prepared. I asked you to revive him."

"I had some concerns. At Ophelia's trial, he claimed to be a friend of mine. He wasn't lying."

"He spoke truthfully. You were friends once."

Tiptoft looked down at me and began rubbing at his forehead again.

"That life is gone, John. I need you to remain as you are."

"There are other matters. It is well known that the boy was poisoned. If he is seen again, it will only fuel the rumours that he is immune, that he is the One."

"I employ many toxins, John. If I wanted him dead, he would be. Permanently. But I would rather that he join our cause. Like Vlad, he is a parasite. It would make him an invaluable asset."

"It is an unnecessary risk."

"He is little more than a child. What right do we have to lead if we fear him?"

Tiptoft glanced uneasily between us. "Very well. I will see it done."

There was a pause. "No, I will tend to him myself. It is time for you to gather our friends."

"Famine's legion? I thought they were to be disposed of."

"We will cull the herd after Vlad has been dealt with."

"As you wish."

After one uneasy glance in my direction, Tiptoft raised his cowl, then turned to leave the room. His slow, lupine gait reminded me again of Mr. Entwistle. The last time the two of us had spoken, he'd been sad. And terrified. He knew he had to face the Beast of the Apocalypse, alone, and he knew it would kill him. When I'd asked him if he was afraid of death, he'd seemed offended. "Heavens no," he said. "I've never been afraid of that." It was only later in our conversation that I realized the source of his fear. It was this other person he could become. Now those fears were realized. I had no idea how it had happened, but like Suki's death, and the death of Charlie's father, it was another wrong that needed righting.

Tiptoft's footsteps faded and I heard the sound of a heavy door banging shut in the wind. The Changeling looked down at me, his milky-white eyes impossible to read.

"I have followed your career with great interest, Zachariah. Since the death of your father, in fact. I am pleased you survived your foray into undeath with no ill effects." He reached in and began unchaining me. Once my hands and feet were free, he pulled my arm over his shoulder and hoisted me out. "Now come. A debt is owed, and it is you who must repay it."

CHAPTER 36

THE CHANGELING

MY TOES DRAGGED across the wooden floor as the Changeling carried me towards the altar. Hovering in front of us was a short, ornate cross of gold. It was sitting on a wall covered in tiny murals of Christian saints. The Changeling lifted me onto the altar. The stone was cold and hard beneath me. I wondered if I was going to be sacrificed in some kind of Black Mass.

"I would not have taken such pains to preserve you only to end your life now," the Changeling said. He shifted my head so that my chin was pointing upwards, then took a goblet from somewhere and tipped it over my mouth. Blood trickled down my throat. I waited for the rush, but instead of the usual euphoria, a steady warmth spread through my chest and limbs. My mind felt like jelly. Eventually I could sit up. The Changeling reached out a hand to steady me; without it, I would have toppled from the altar. Even breathing was difficult. My lungs felt stiff and would only let so much air in. I pressed a hand to my chest and rubbed the coarse fabric of my robe, hoping to enliven the skin underneath.

"You don't know Vlad as well as I do," the Changeling said. "Nothing he does is an accident. He chose those clothes for a reason."

I looked down at my habit. With my bare feet and belt of rope, I might have just stepped out of a medieval monastery.

"Have you read Vlad's biographies? There is a famous anecdote about him impaling a monk. In one version, the monk flatters him and is condemned for not telling the truth. In another version, the monk tells him the truth and is impaled for failing to flatter his patron appropriately." The Changeling looked at me closely. "Vlad wants me to think that, regardless of what you do, he is willing to sacrifice you."

He made it sound as though I were here by Vlad's design, and not his.

"The Prince is terribly crafty," the Changeling said. "He was fully aware that my servants and I would be ransacking his castle during the trial, and that we would find you. He chose Ophelia over his fortress, its store of undead bodies and *you*."

I remembered what Vlad had said to me about a leader having to take risks and make sacrifices. I should not have been surprised that he was willing to sacrifice me. Once he had Ophelia, what use would he have for me? In other circumstances, I'm sure this betrayal would have infuriated me. I should have been angry. But rage requires energy, and I was simply too tired to get worked up. All I could manage was a strange disappointment. Not in Vlad, but in myself. I should have predicted that he would turn on me. And I should have taken steps to protect myself.

Unless the Changeling was lying . . .

"So he knew I would be captured?" I asked. The words came out in a raspy whisper. My throat was raw from disuse.

"Captured, yes. And, no doubt, his hope was that I would perceive you as a threat and would want you eliminated.

But in that he is mistaken. I don't want to kill you. I want to redeem you."

He paused to give the words emphasis. *I want to redeem you.* I had no idea what he meant by that.

"It means I want to save you from your current state of sinfulness."

My current state was more tired confusion. I didn't like the Changeling plucking thoughts from my head, so I buried them as deeply as I could.

"Where are we?" I asked.

"The Prince's Church in Tirgoviste."

"How long have I been here?"

"Here? Less than a day. But you were in transit a bit longer."

He reached down to where my necklace was hanging and took the charm between his fingers. "Vlad is a brilliant deceiver. And daring. Such a shame about his mental instabilities. Ophelia thinks she can cure him of these defects, but in that she is mistaken."

He let the charm fall back against my chest. "Can you walk?" he asked.

I needed his help to reach the first row of pews. Lying on the floor in front of these was my coffin. Inside was the poisoned Dragon Dagger.

"You will need that in the nights ahead," the Changeling said. He removed it from the coffin, then pulled it from the sheath and placed the handle in my hand.

I couldn't believe he was arming me. The dried snake venom was still visible on the blade. One thrust and he would be finished. The thought had barely flitted across my consciousness when the Changeling shifted to the far side of the coffin, just as Vlad would have done. At the same time, my fingers spasmed involuntarily and the dagger clattered to the floor. I blinked and the Changeling was beside me again, handing me the knife.

"Who are you?" I asked.

He tapped the side of his head beside his eye. "A person who has been watching over you since your father passed away."

I didn't believe it. Then his face and body fell into shadow and I was suddenly staring at a dead ringer for one of the security guards at the Nicholls Ward. I didn't know his name, we'd never spoken, but I'd seen him there regularly. Darkness covered his face again and he turned into my psychiatrist, Dr. Shepherd.

"I have always been a friend to you, Zachariah."

I bristled at this. No one needs to be told who their friends are. "You took Ophelia," I said. "You cut her wrists—" My hands began to shake. I clenched them into fists. "You sent your Horsemen to kill my friends. They murdered Charlie's father. They killed Suki . . ." I had to stop speaking. I was too shaken to continue.

The Changeling glanced towards the doors. A strong wind was blowing outside. "Perhaps it is time for some honest discourse. But not too much. The truth is like a good meal, Zachary. It should be eaten in small bites and digested slowly. Take it all in one lump, and all you'll get is a bellyache."

I already had a bellyache. I wanted answers.

"You must first understand that much of what people do is for the sake of appearances. It was not my intention to harm Ophelia or you."

"Then why did you take her?" I asked.

"Ophelia had to be brought here to stand trial. She broke the law and had to suffer, if only mildly, to maintain the illusion of justice. Had I not acted, she would have kept you hidden in Montreal while the world burned. A bit of a paradox, really. She believes more ardently in the prophecy than anyone, and yet she refused to let you play your part. A mother's fear, I suppose." His gaze drifted to the church doors. Outside, I could sense tension and the presence of others, waiting.

"I needed you both here, and Vlad, too. He was of no use to me rotting on the shelf."

I thought of Vlad's remains, locked away in the photon torpedo, on the top shelf of the weapons depot at Iron Spike Enterprises. Those remains should have been left there.

"He was dead. Why would you want him back? He's your enemy."

"Allowing Istvan to resurrect him was the most efficient way to deal with his followers, the old Coven of the Dragon. Even after his death, many of them remained loyal. It would have taken years to smoke them out of their hiding places. But when news spread that Istvan had brought his casket to Romania, they popped up like mushrooms, and fell to my poison, one after the other."

I'd seen his handiwork: the grey-skinned corpses in Vlad's lab. But his explanation was faulty.

"I don't get it. You could have posed as Vlad any time you wanted and accomplished the same thing."

"True," he said. A shadow passed before his face. When it vanished I was staring at a perfect likeness of the Impaler. The wide face, the green eyes, the thick moustache. The sight of him made me dizzy. He looked at me and, for just an instant, his left eye looked larger than the right. I started to tip over. He reached out with his left arm to steady me. It looked longer than it should have. I pressed my eyes closed. When I opened them again, his proportions had returned to normal.

"I can appear as Vlad at will. But could I act as he does? Not without considerable risk. To plunge myself into that role is to plunge myself into madness. I would rather not. And even the Changeling has limits. He cannot be two places at once, leading Vlad's followers and leading mine at the same time. No, I prefer to work behind the scenes. It is safer, and the end result is a greater sense of detachment, which makes it easier to make decisions." Darkness passed over him again, and his face returned to normal. "It is easiest to remain as I am, and let Istvan work for me from the inside."

I thought of Vlad's cousin and his disappointing betrayal at Castle Dracula. But I also remembered him battling against War and Death on the ship in Montreal. The two didn't fit together—unless the fight was staged, and he had just been waiting to grab Vlad's coffin.

"Was Istvan with you from the start?"

The Changeling smiled. The question seemed to amuse him. "From the start? No. But he understands my motivations and supports them in his own way. You will come to understand in time that the real enemy is the pathogen. It spread quickly after Vlad's death. His followers should not have allowed this. By their own inaction, they have been condemned. Vlad's few remaining allies will be taken care of in the nights ahead. As the Messiah, you have an important role to play in this. It is the least you can do to make amends."

"Amends for what?"

"For ending Vlad's reign but not assuming any of his responsibilities. The Coven did nothing to control the spread of the pathogen, nor did you. Because you both failed in your duties, more people became infected than ever before. There is no cure for vampirism, Zachary. The only thing that stops it is death. So, who lives and who dies? Do you think these are easy choices to make?"

"You seem to have made them easily enough."

"Perhaps. But the real choice is made by others. I am not unlike your father in this regard. Just as he gave vampires the choice to stop killing, I let them decide to take my mark or not. Those who choose wisely live. It is a sign that they will respect my laws and my authority."

Was this what he wanted, for me to take his mark and serve his cause? If he knew me at all, he'd have understood that I would never do anything to hurt Ophelia. Nor would I ever bet against her.

"If you want me to take sides, forget it. I have no interest in your war with Vlad. I just want to get my friends and get out of here."

"That is not possible. You were not meant to be a spectator. Under my tutelage, you will become the perfect instrument for controlling the pathogen."

I didn't want to join his circus any more than I wanted to join forces with Vlad. "Do you know where Ophelia and my friends are?"

"Vlad has hidden them. You will find them when you find him. It is just one of the many tasks you will perform for me, once you take my mark."

I shook my head. It was as much an act of dismay as one of defiance. The thought that Vlad was still with my friends was unsettling. But taking the Changeling's mark was even more unthinkable.

"You will serve me, one way or the other." He glanced towards the entrance of the church. People were talking outside. It sounded as though a crowd was gathering. "I have business to attend to. You will remain here and think on what I have said. When I return, I will expect an answer. Will you take the mark and serve me, or join the rest of my enemies in oblivion?"

He walked towards the doors. They opened for him, and I caught a glimpse of a tall figure outside. It was Tiptoft. Tamerlane was beside him. There was an obvious tension between the two men. Beyond them was a crowd.

The Changeling turned before making his exit. "This vampire war is almost over. In a short time, the contagion will be under control. It is my gift to the world, and to you, since it was your mess I was cleaning. But a few loose threads remain that must be tied. Vlad is one of them. Help me find him and I will consider the bulk of your debt repaid."

I didn't consider myself indebted to him, and I had no interest in joining the likes of Famine and Pestilence, and having a mark carved into me.

"Are you familiar with Horace Walpole?" the Changeling asked. "'The world is a tragedy to those who feel, but a comedy to those who think.' The current of empathy runs deep in you. It is a blessing and a curse. You care for those you must destroy. It makes your task tragic, but it does not change what must be done." He fixed me with his white-eyed stare, his pupils wide and penetrating. "Are you ready to uphold the law and make the hard decisions? Who lives? Who dies? Who must be sacrificed? Think on it. Your fate is in your own hands. At sun-up . . ."

CHAPTER 37

REUNION

I SAT IN THE CHURCH PEW, my head in my hands, my brain on the verge of a meltdown. If the Changeling was being honest, Vlad had been brought back to life just so his followers could be killed, and he was now with my friends, who clearly didn't know that both he and Istvan had betrayed me. Istvan, who'd seemingly done his best to save us all on the ship in Montreal. Was it possible that he'd been in the enemy camp from the get-go?

And what did the Changeling mean about my sense of empathy, that it would make it hard to destroy those I cared about? Was he referring to my friends? If he thought I would ever hurt them, he was out of his mind. And yet, he seemed perfectly rational. Kind, even. And his interest in me felt genuine. Why else would he have posed as my old psychiatrist, and that security guard? It boggled my mind.

The faint creak of the door and the sound of the wind outside drew my attention to the entrance. The purple-eyed bounty hunter was approaching. He'd traded his round-brimmed, tasselled hat for a Stetson with an eagle feather, and his blue jumpsuit had more rhinestones than a cheap jewellery store. Beside him was the Asian shadow-jumper with the large muscles and straight-cut bangs. Her green eyes were luminescent in the candlelight. The two stopped on either side of the pew. I closed my fingers over the hilt of my dagger.

"*Don't*," the bounty hunter said, his hand on his pistol.

The woman pulled back the side of her coat. A sword was belted to her waist. "That would not end well for you."

I must have looked harmless, because she quickly turned her attention to the shadows along the walls. A few minutes passed, then a few more. I could practically hear my hair growing over the sound of us ignoring one another. Then a mechanical hum, faint and distant, rose quickly in volume until it became the familiar sound of a helicopter. The two vampires exchanged an uncertain look. Footsteps approached from outside. This was followed by the squeak of the door hinges.

In walked Ophelia.

Should I have expected this? Whenever I got into trouble, she was the first person who came kicking in the door. But the last time I'd seen her, she'd been unconscious from blood loss. Now she looked like the Angel of Death. A drawn rapier rested on the shoulder plate of her new Kevlar body armour, and her face had the no-nonsense expression she wore whenever someone was about to get it. I looked at my two guards, feeling an odd mixture of relief and pity.

The bounty hunter pulled out his automatics. Both had laser sightings. Two red beams passed over the tops of the pews, then rose to where Ophelia was standing. In the same instant, I heard a muffled sound like a person trying to quietly whistle.

Shrish.

The vampire flinched, dropped a gun, then reached up to the

side of his neck. When his hand fell away, there was a small, red hole in the skin beneath his ear. He raised his other gun, but before he could properly aim, he stumbled sideways and collapsed to the floor.

Another *shrish* followed. Something streaked through the air from behind the altar and sped like a bullet towards the woman with the black hair. She stepped sideways, drew her sword and slashed downward. I heard a metallic clink and the sound of something breaking as her blade sliced through the projectile, scattering broken pieces of it across the floor.

I pulled the Dragon Dagger from its sheath, stepped to my coffin and push-kicked it at her. She hurdled it without even looking.

Ophelia sprinted straight for us. "Zachary, get back!" she shouted.

I didn't move. My dagger was a bit short for a sword fight, and I was still woozy from my long rest, but I wasn't going to let anyone do my fighting for me.

The Asian woman clearly understood where the real threat lay. She moved for Ophelia and executed a perfect crosscut slash. Ophelia nimbly flicked her blade aside and shouldered her into the wall.

I heard another *shrish*. This shot was coming from the pews behind me. Something zipped past my hair and thumped into the woman's throat. She took an awkward step forward, then slumped to the ground. A small dart protruded from her skin.

Charlie rose from behind a row of seats at the back. "Did you see that shot? Right in the neck!"

I stared at my best friend, incredulous that he could be standing there. "How is this possible?"

Charlie held up a sleek firearm barely larger than a .22. "With the Sure-Shot Tranquilizer Rifle, anything's possible."

Ophelia laughed and moved closer. A familiar feeling of comfort washed over me. I was reminded of all the times in the Nicholls Ward when I'd become angry and frustrated, and she'd arrive to make everything okay.

"How did you know where to find me?"

"I'll explain later. It's complicated."

She reached up and cupped my cheek, then smiled and looked past me. Luna was standing quietly beside the altar, carrying a gun identical to the one Charlie had used. She was wrapped up in a new suit of Kevlar that was so tight I was amazed she could move. I stood gawking until my brain reminded me that it needed some oxygen, so I started breathing again, and it loosened up my tongue.

"How did you get in without me hearing you?"

She tipped the gun barrel backwards so that it rested on her shoulder, then walked over, her footfalls quiet on the wooden floor. "Zack, you're so out of it sometimes I could drive a tank past you and you wouldn't notice."

Charlie laughed. "It's funny because it's true. You're a total space cadet." He drew a knife from his belt and waved it at the two unconscious guards. "What do we do with them?" he asked Ophelia.

She didn't answer. Her eyes were on me.

"What do you mean *do with them*?" I asked, although it was clear enough what he meant. All the relief at seeing him and the others vanished with a chill.

"What do you think I mean, Friar Zack? If we let these two live, they'll—"

"They'll what!?"

"I don't know. What do I look like, a fortune teller? But it will be bad for us, whatever it is. This guy chucked a grenade in your face on Halloween night! Don't you remember?

Do you think he'd show us any mercy if our positions were reversed?"

"No," I said. "I'm sure he wouldn't. But it hardly justifies what you're considering. That man is harmless now. If you kill him, it will be murder. Is that really what you want—to be a murderer?"

He pointed his knife at me. "What I want is to stay alive for a few more days. The fewer of these idiots I have to worry about, the better my chances."

"Charlie, there has to be a difference between us and them."

"And if you have your way, there will be. They'll be alive and we'll be dead, instead of the other way around. You have no idea how bad things are. We can't let these people take over."

"What difference does it make who takes over if we act the same way they do?"

He ground his teeth together. His fingers were so tight on the handle of his knife it was a miracle it didn't snap. "I knew you'd be like this. I knew it! But you don't understand. These two have the Changeling's mark."

"Can it be removed?" I asked.

"I'm not certain," Ophelia said. She took my arm and turned me gently towards the door. "But we've got other concerns at the moment. And we can't get caught here when the Changeling comes back."

Charlie didn't move. "I'm telling you, we shouldn't leave these guys here like this. We'll pay for it."

Ophelia looked at me. "He's right. These two are lethal."

"Can we take them as hostages?"

"To what end?" Ophelia asked. "Their lives mean nothing to the Changeling."

"Why are we even debating this?" Charlie asked. "You were willing to kill on the ship to save our lives."

"Our lives were in danger," I said. "They certainly aren't now." I considered mentioning how badly that encounter had ended, but I didn't want to remind him of Suki's death. It might have pushed him over the edge.

"Can we fight about this later?" Luna asked.

"Now *is* later," Charlie said. "We need to make a decision."

"Is there room in the helicopter?" I asked.

Ophelia nodded. And that settled it. She walked back to the Asian woman, then drew her up over her back and started for the door. "Istvan said you would be poorly guarded, but this is ridiculous."

"Istvan's a traitor," I said.

Ophelia took the lead. "Yes, but to whom?"

"What does that mean?"

"It means things are seldom as they seem."

It wasn't much of an answer. Before I could say so, Luna slipped her arm through mine. She smiled. I stared. It was impossible not to.

"Where did you get the new suit?"

"You like?"

What could I say? It was round in all the right places.

"Hurry," Ophelia said. "The weather is changing. We don't want to get caught in a storm."

Luna helped me shuffle outside. Light flakes of snow were starting to fall. Down a set of stone steps was a jet-black military helicopter with retractable landing gear. Two rocket casings were mounted on each side. There was enough firepower in them to blow a hole in the fabric of space-time. The blades were kicking up such a wind I was amazed the church windows hadn't blown in.

"Where did this come from?" I asked. I had to shout so Luna could hear me.

"It was the one that was supposed to be waiting for us on top of Iron Spike Enterprises. Remember? Maximilian gave it to Vlad when they cut their deal. It's why it was gone."

I remembered Charlie's father flipping out when it wasn't on the landing pad. The thought of his death, and my part in it, put a nervous crimp in my stomach. I glanced at Charlie. He had the bounty hunter draped over one shoulder. I wondered if he'd forgiven me. I was going to ask Luna about it, but before I could, a shape moved on the edges of my peripheral vision. I stopped. There was something in the trees.

"Get ready for trouble," I said to Luna. Then I drew the Dragon Dagger and waited.

CHAPTER 38

FLY BY NIGHT

LUNA HELD THE tranquilizer rifle one-handed at her hip, the barrel pointing into the woods. Her other arm was fastened around my waist. Without it I might have toppled. I saw movement again, this time on our other side. Whatever was shifting through the trees was either shadow-jumping or faster than the Man of Steel.

"Over there," I said, squinting from the snow that was blowing around.

Charlie nudged me forward. "Keep the train rolling. If the horde comes back, we're going to be chop suey."

A human-shaped silhouette appeared in front of the helicopter. It was huge. Charlie seemed indifferent. He shifted the bounty hunter on his shoulder, then slipped past me and dropped down the steps three at a time.

"Hey, Vin," he said. "Anything suspicious?"

I stared at the figure as he moved closer. It was Vincent. I recognized him instantly, despite his impossible appearance. His size made it clear that he had turned, but somehow his human features had remained intact. His nose was a bit flat and his ears pointed back slightly, and he had the same wide, yellow pupils we'd come to expect at feeding time, but otherwise he looked exactly like the boy we'd adopted, albeit twice as large.

"Nothing around here but a bad smell, Charlie," he said, nostrils flaring. His voice was low but was lacking the raspy, animal quality of his father's. I'd never heard Vincent speak as a beast. He'd never done anything but flip out. "What's with that?" he asked, nodding to the bounty hunter.

"Hostage," Charlie answered.

Vincent's eyes returned to me. He smiled. His teeth would have put a mountain lion to flight. In one powerful leap, he jumped up beside Luna and me. At his full height, my forehead was level with his shoulder. He must have outweighed me by a hundred pounds.

"I knew we'd have you back in no time," he said. He reached out with one hand and took me around the waist, then ducked between Luna and me so his shoulder was under my arm. When he stood, it lifted me right off the ground. "You look terrible," he added.

He put his other arm around Luna. She let out a yelp of surprise, which made him laugh. Then he leapt down the stairs to the helicopter, carrying us both as if we weighed no more than a couple of feather pillows. Unencumbered, at a full clip, I couldn't have jumped half that distance.

"Hurry," Ophelia said. She was already inside the cockpit, closing the door.

Charlie dumped the body of the bounty hunter in the open cabin. His partner, the Asian woman, was already strapped, unconscious, into one of the seats. Charlie hoisted the man up beside her, then took up a position behind a Gatling gun I'm certain Arnold Schwarzenegger used in the second

Terminator movie. There was one pointing out each side of the helicopter.

Vincent stepped up behind the second Gatling gun. It looked small with him hunched over it. The entire chopper lurched under his weight. Luna climbed in next and offered me a hand. I collapsed into the middle seat in a row that was mounted on the wall separating us from the cockpit. Ophelia was on the other side, playing with the flight controls.

"You swallow some bad blood or something?" Charlie asked. "You look half-dead."

I wasn't sure how to answer. I was worried that he was still angry with me for having failed his father. "Are we okay?"

His answer was a confused look.

The hum of helicopter blades intensified. "Hang on," Luna said. She strapped a double harness over my shoulders, then did herself up beside me. The seat on my other side was empty. I was immediately mindful that Suki should have been sitting there. Istvan had said that there had been no time for my friends to mourn her death. I wondered how they'd been coping. When I reached out with my mind to find out from Luna, nothing happened. I couldn't hear what she was thinking, nor did she give any sign that she could hear me. The connection we had once shared was gone.

We rose unsteadily from the ground, swaying from side to side, as if Ophelia wasn't sure which way to go. Once we cleared the trees, she circled, then we whooshed off into the night.

"Where are we going?" I asked.

"We're meeting Vlad," Vincent said.

"Vlad?" I looked at Luna.

"Yeah. You know—thick moustache, husky build, long black hair, angry, brooding eyes. I'm sure you two have met."

It might have been the thought of seeing Vlad again, or the motion of the helicopter, but I started to feel queasy. "Very funny."

She seemed taken aback. "What's with you?"

I thought of what the Changeling had told me, that Vlad had knowingly given me up to be captured and killed. It might have been a lie, but my gut instinct said otherwise.

"Are you telling me you trust him after everything that's happened?"

"Hey, we already got the trust speech from Entwistle," Charlie said. "Don't you remember?"

"No."

"Last summer, when we were running around looking for Hyde. He told us not to get hung up on trust. Does that ring any bells?"

It did. Mr. Entwistle had told us to focus on what people wanted. If we understood their interests, we'd have a better idea of how they would behave.

"How is that relevant?" I asked.

Charlie nodded towards the cockpit, where Ophelia was sitting. "Vlad's main interest is right there. He risked his life to save her! You know that. You had a front row seat!"

This was true. His performance during Ophelia's trial had been both brave and selfless. But then he'd sent me back to Castle Dracula, where I'd been betrayed. I had no idea if that was just Istvan's doing, or if he had he been acting with Vlad's consent, but I had to get to the bottom of it.

"The Changeling said Vlad knew what was happening at his castle. That he wanted me out of the way."

"That's a lie," Vincent said. His tone was unusually sharp.

"Easy, Vin," Charlie said over his shoulder. "Zack's not up to speed yet."

"What does that mean?" I asked.

"It means Vlad's with us now. We thought you knew that."

"Are you forgetting that he tried to kill you?"

Charlie's eyes shifted upwards as he thought about it. "Yeah. You know, I sort of had forgotten."

"You've got to be kidding! He was holding you hostage!"

"Hey, keep your shirt on. Or that robe or whatever it is. You're supposed to be the forgiving one, remember? The Changeling kills anyone who doesn't take the mark. We'd be dead right now if it weren't for Vlad."

"And Ophelia," Luna added with a reproving look.

"Yeah, but Vlad gives the orders."

I couldn't imagine Ophelia being told what to do by anyone.

"If you thought Ophelia was controlling," Luna said, her lips nearly brushing my ear, "Vlad is in a league by himself. The two of them fight like cats and dogs."

"Someone's got to be the boss," Vincent said. "Vlad's amazing. He can do anything. Just look what he did for me."

"You got that right, Vin," Charlie said.

I looked Vincent over again. He might have passed for a vampire now, had his scent and yellow eyes not given him away. Was this Vlad's doing?

"He's still got some anger-management issues," said Charlie, "but you get past it. And Vinny's right. He's amazing. He's got a wonder potion for everything. Boils this. Distills that. A little eye of newt and tongue of frog, and presto, he's turned water into wine, or a pine cone into a hand grenade, or powdered blood into something edible. And the serum he makes for Vin. Well, you can see for yourself. All the power of the Beast, but no fleas, no fuss and no freaking out."

There was awe in Charlie's voice. It rattled me. When I'd last seen them together, Vlad had threatened to impale him.

"I don't get it. After the hell that guy put us through, how could you have anything to do with him?"

"How could *you*?"

"At the trial? What choice did I have?"

"What choice do *we* have?" Charlie leaned closer, his hands still locked firmly on the controls of the gun. "Vlad and Ophelia have been keeping us alive. You want a reason to trust him? Well, there it is. The Changeling and his Horsemen are killing everything in sight. It's always dark somewhere, and they're at it twenty-four seven. If they get their way, there won't be enough vampires left in the world to fill a school bus."

"Except the ones that take the mark," Luna said.

Charlie snorted in disgust. "That's no guarantee. According to Ophelia, half their army got buried at Iron Spike Enterprises, and they didn't care a whit. She said they arranged for it to happen that way, so it'd be easier to control infection rates. Who would do that, kill their own soldiers?"

"Well, they still have plenty to spare," Luna said. "They've had us on the run since the trial."

My head fell back against the top of the seat. The chopper jostled a bit, then tilted as we changed direction. For a moment, no one spoke. I was grateful for the quiet.

I'd been in tough spots before, but never had I felt so uncertain. Like a marionette with some unseen person pulling at my strings, I'd been hauled from one disaster to another. The rooftop of Iron Spike Enterprises. *L'Esprit Sauvage*. Ophelia's trial. Castle Dracula. The Prince's Church. It seemed I'd been powerless to exercise any control over what was happening around me. If that was going to change, I had to start doing things differently. The trouble was, I had no idea where to start. Allying myself with Vlad, a man I didn't trust, seemed a poor way to get the ball rolling.

While I sat brooding, trying to figure out how to manage my inevitable meeting with him, a dark ribbon of water appeared below, frozen along the banks but open through the middle, winding through the tree-covered mountains. The evergreens rising on either side had been dusted with a white layer of snow. In the still night air, it sparkled like tinsel on a forest of Christmas trees.

"You know," said Charlie, "this landscape has given me a brilliant idea." He looked at the two comatose hostages, then his eyes fell to the open river below us.

"You aren't thinking what I think you're thinking . . ." I said.

"I am."

"Charlie, you can't."

"Actually, it should be easy. Gravity will do most of the work." He started unstrapping the harness that was holding the Asian woman in her seat.

I looked at Luna.

"I agree with Charlie," she said. "It's brilliant."

Vincent laughed. I blanched.

"Think of it as a compromise," she said. "Drowning won't kill them permanently, but it keeps them off our backs for a while."

"Compromise," Charlie echoed, "the foundation of any healthy relationship." He pulled the woman from her seat. "If you have to, just think of it as a midnight swim for two people whose morals need a good cleansing."

I reached up and knocked on the glass separating us from Ophelia.

"What? You planning to tell on me?" Charlie asked, walking the body over to the edge of the cabin.

"Just getting a second opinion."

Ophelia's voice came over a speaker from the cockpit. "You going to lighten our load?" she asked.

Charlie gave her a thumbs-up.

"Brilliant!" she answered. "I'll take us down."

I felt the helicopter lurch and we dropped.

"Aren't we going to discuss this?" I asked.

"We just did," said Charlie.

The wind from our rotors caused the small section of open river to ripple along the surface. Two splashes later, we rose again and changed our bearings.

"See?" Charlie said. "I told you that would be easy."

Vincent laughed. "Moral cleansing. That was a good one, Charlie."

I looked from one to the other, then to Luna. "I can't believe you supported that!"

"It's better than the alternative. Vlad would just insist we cut their heads off."

"So we're really going to see Vlad." I felt my stomach twist as if I'd swallowed a knife.

Luna slipped her fingers through mine. "It'll be okay."

Vincent was watching us. His eyes strayed from me, to Luna, to our hands in a quiet, disapproving way. I remembered him stepping between us and casually putting his arm around her back at the church. I was guessing the two had become closer in my absence. I wondered if it was going to be a problem.

I closed my eyes and imagined the warm light of the tunnel all around me. It helped settle my stomach. "So, where is Vlad now?" I asked.

"Budapest," said Charlie. "He's taking us to meet the Baptist."

CHAPTER 39

BUDAPEST

LUNA'S FINGERS WERE still entwined with my own. I brought her hand to my lips. When I opened my eyes, I noticed that Vincent was watching us, furtively, from the corner of his eye. I tried to put it from my mind and squeezed what peace I could from Luna's calming presence. The moment didn't last.

"We've crossed the Carpathians," Ophelia said, her voice crackling over the cabin speaker. "We should reach the Hungarian border soon."

We were flying low to the ground. It was cold. Our breath froze in tiny white clouds that the wind quickly snatched away. Everyone was quiet. Vincent and Charlie were both hunched behind their guns, scanning the naked oak and beech trees of the foothills below. Luna let go of my hand and pulled out a pistol, then started loading bullets into the clip.

"What happens when we land?" I asked.

"Vlad will have a plan," Charlie said. "He always does."

Was I wrong about my vampire father? The Changeling

had suggested I hardly knew him, then went on to say that Vlad had betrayed me. If this were true, would Ophelia be supporting him? That might have been all of the answer that I needed.

I thought back to the first time I'd seen him, face to face, at Iron Spike Enterprises. Even when stark raving mad, there'd been limits to his violent behaviour. He'd refused to hurt Ophelia when she came to my defence. They'd been husband and wife for over five hundred years, and he thought my father had killed her. Should I have been surprised that he would take revenge? While I puzzled this out, mountains and forests, farms and villages passed unnoticed beneath me. I didn't snap out of it until Luna tapped my shoulder. We were flying over a wide river. The lights of a city were visible on either side.

"Budapest," she said.

I stared out of the cabin, thinking I might recognize some part of it. I'd been here with my father when I was seven. At the time, I thought he'd come to lecture at one of the universities, but he and my Uncle Maximilian had really been hunting Vlad. Nothing looked familiar. I knew enough to separate the two cities, Buda and Pest, on either side of the Danube, but couldn't remember which side was which. Both had a distinctive European feel. The streets were much narrower than the ones at home, and they wound like fishing line straight off the spool. The faces of the buildings were right up against the sidewalks, and they all touched side to side as if every inch of space was precious. The helicopter dipped closer to the river, sending tiny ripples across the surface. We followed it to a large castle-like building on the right that was straight out of a fairy tale. I counted nineteen spires, but it might have had more.

"Parliament," Ophelia said. "But we're heading there." She pointed across the river to a building that must have been at least two football fields long. There was a single dome in the centre. It looked like a fortified office building. "The Royal Palace."

We skimmed a short hill and rose over the palace, which was topped with small islands of copper roofing, all tarnished green. The city was quiet, but the lights of the building made it seem as though we were flying into a spotlight. Ophelia brought us down in an open courtyard near a statue of a horse.

The instant the wheels hit the ground, Luna jumped out, both pistols drawn. Vincent removed the Gatling gun from its housing, grabbed a long belt of bullets, slung it over his shoulder and followed. By this time, Ophelia and Charlie were already out.

"Man, you guys mean business," I said, jumping down.

Charlie laughed. Ophelia quieted us with a glance.

"Is this where we meet the Baptist?" I asked

"No," she answered. "We'll meet him in the labyrinth just before sunrise. This is where we meet Vlad."

Clustered around a fountain at the far side of the courtyard was a group of copper statues tarnished green like the roof. The highest, most prominent figure was a man holding a bow. He was standing over the body of a freshly killed stag. Vlad had his back to us and was admiring it from below.

"I don't understand," I said to Ophelia. "I'm not sure I ever have. What are you doing with that awful man?"

Ophelia paused. She'd been strapping her rapier to her hip. "I know this is difficult for you. And I don't expect you to understand. I owe him a debt that spans centuries . . . You can't imagine the weight of that." She adjusted her belt and gave everyone a quick inspection. "I left his side when your father caught up with me. He offered me redemption, and I accepted. Part of that arrangement involved cutting my ties with Vlad. I should not have been so selfish. Without me to keep him stable, he became something terrible."

"You've never been selfish," I said.

"You don't know what I've been. Your father was hunting me, Zachary. You've never asked me why he felt that was necessary, and I'm more grateful for that than you can ever know. I was not always as I am now."

I felt awkward in the silence that followed. I remembered that Mr. Entwistle had known her by a different name: Ilona. Although that was centuries ago, the thought that she had once been someone else was unsettling. I didn't want to think of her as anyone but Ophelia.

"I think that life is behind you," Luna said.

"It is. Or it was. Part of it has resurfaced." Her eyes drifted to Vlad, who was still facing the opposite direction.

"I don't want to have anything to do with him," I said. "I don't trust him. The Changeling said he gave me up. That he knew his castle was being ransacked and he let me get captured."

"The Changeling would want you to think as much. He would not want to see you and Vlad united."

She sighed.

I looked at her as you might look at a stranger, as if seeing her for the first time. I realized that, like me, she had no idea what was going to happen next, and she was flustered. She was used to being in control. This was unfamiliar territory.

"I am not asking you to trust him," she said, "or to like him or to forgive him. But realize that we have a fight to finish, and for that, we need his help. I know he's far from perfect, but there is a nobility in him. You need to recognize it, and help him to be his best person. Is this not what your father would have wanted?"

It was. I felt a sting of shame that she should have had to remind me.

Ophelia started walking away. I followed. Vlad turned when I took my first step, as if he'd been waiting for this one gesture, like the extending of an olive branch, before acknowledging me. His voice filled my head, drowning out the sound of our footfalls on the stone.

So, my progeny returns . . . Well, come forward, little cub, and we shall see if your abduction has proven fruitful.

CHAPTER 40

COUNTERMOVE

"**I** KNOW WHAT you're thinking," Charlie whispered. "This is gonna be fine. Trust me."

I reached under my robe and felt for my necklace. Luna took my hand. I searched her neckline. There was no trace of the golden-crescent charm.

"Welcome to the Royal Palace," Vlad said as we entered the nimbus of light around the fountain. "Beneath this building are the ruins of older castles. One of them belonged to Matthias Corvinus. That is him, above." He glanced at the statue of the hunter with the bow. "I think the likeness is quite good. Much preferable to the rotting corpse you saw in my lab. Matthias the Just, King of Hungary, Croatia, Bohemia, Duke of Austria, my ally and rival."

I remembered the name from Vlad's biography. Matthias Corvinus had betrayed him to his death. Vlad had been betrayed by Istvan, too, when they were young. As hard as it was for me to imagine, Vlad had forgiven them both.

His eyes drifted to the dragon-headed dagger still hanging at my waist. "The Changeling let you keep that? How interesting." It seemed that he was going to reach for the hilt, but he didn't. "Can you tell us what has happened since the night you were abducted? Do you know anything of the Changeling's plans?"

I eyed Vlad cautiously. He seemed more composed than I'd expected. More human. But there was no way for me to know if, underneath it all, he was trustworthy. Ophelia was right to say there was good in him. I'd seen it at her trial. And my father would have wanted me to recognize it. "The greatest measure of a man's soul is his capacity to forgive," he might have said. But he also said things like, "Someone needs to stand up to the bullies of the world."

I didn't even know who the bad guys were any more. Vlad. The Changeling. I didn't want to side with either of them.

The Dragon Prince was standing in front me, glaring at Ophelia. "What is wrong with this boy?"

"Give him time. He's thinking. Can't you tell?"

The two of them argued back and forth while I figured out what to say. It took a while.

"How is this supposed to work?" I asked eventually.

Vlad turned to face me. "Ah, so you've returned again, a second coming, this time in body *and* mind . . . How is this supposed to work? I'm not certain. I suppose we shall learn as we go."

"And what happens now?"

"You tell us what you know," he said. "You weren't gone long, but you must have learned something about the Changeling and his plans."

"Did he show you his face?" Charlie asked.

"He showed me several faces. But we spoke for only a few minutes. It was just before you guys showed up. I was dead the whole time. He poisoned me and . . . I don't know what happened. I woke up in a coffin. But it wasn't like the other times. I didn't go to the tunnel."

"You died but did not pass on to the next life," Vlad said. "Trapped in undeath, a state that would make it impossible for Ophelia to find you, since those who are undead don't dream and so have no voice on the Dream Road. Thankfully, we had a backup. Two, in fact. One was Istvan. The other was your necklace. My guess is, the coffin he used for you was lined with heavy metal. It would have blocked the signal."

"Signal? What are you talking about?"

Ophelia lifted the full-moon necklace from under my habit. There was a guilty look on her face.

"I had a duplicate made for you," Vlad said. "It contains a tiny transponder. I wanted you to wear it in case you got lost."

I looked for any signs that he was lying and found none. I was still skeptical. The idea that Vlad cared about whether I got lost, was poisoned by the Changeling or got fed to a pool of hungry piranha seemed about as thin to me as the fabric of my monk's habit, the same outfit that was meant to show the Changeling how little my fate mattered. Caring wasn't Vlad's style. Neither were transponders. I didn't know much about them, only that they sent out a signal that could be traced.

"How did you think we found you?" he asked.

I'd been very curious about that. Ophelia had brushed me off when I'd asked back at the Prince's Church. I'd assumed at the time it was because we were in such a hurry, but she probably wasn't keen to reveal that my necklace was a fake, transponder or no transponder.

"So, where's my real necklace?"

Vlad ignored the question. "Did he indicate why he didn't kill you?"

"He said he wanted to redeem me. That I owed him a debt, and finding you was how I was going to start repaying it, after I'd taken his mark."

Vlad's eyes jumped quickly from my right hand to my forehead. Both were unblemished. He nodded his approval. "And why were you so poorly guarded?"

"I got the sense he was using his soldiers for something else. Tiptoft and Tamerlane were there with the horde, but he flew them off someplace."

"Did he indicate where?"

"No. But he did talk about—how did he say it?—*culling the herd*. But not until he'd dealt with you."

"Culling the herd? Even though they have his mark? Interesting. What else did he say?"

I took a moment to run through things in my head. One statement in particular stood out: that, under the Changeling's tutelage, I could become the perfect instrument for controlling the pathogen. Mentioning it seemed risky. Vlad was composed at the moment, but his bouts of paranoia were a thing of legend, and I had no way to know how he might later twist this against me. Fortunately, there were other snippets of conversation worthy of attention.

"He said he likes to stay behind the scenes. That even though he can imitate you, he had Istvan resurrect you so he wouldn't have to. He says it's safer, and keeps him detached, so he can make decisions more objectively."

Vlad snickered. "What nonsense! He wasn't distant when he killed my friends. Did he speak to that?" Vlad must have read my expression, because he didn't wait long before continuing. "Did I not tell you in the tunnels how often men are served by saying one thing and doing another? He bloodies his hands often, and I doubt that will change any time soon." He looked away, his jaw twitching, as though wrestling with some inner demon. Ophelia put a hand on his arm. He seemed not to notice.

"How did he present himself to you?" she asked. "You mentioned several faces. Were any of them people you recognized?"

"Some," I said. Then I did my best to explain about the young man with the ancient eyes whose ethnicity I couldn't place. I also mentioned how he'd appeared as Uncle Jake and the security guard from the Nicholls Ward and, lastly, Dr. Shepherd, my old shrink. It took a while to cover everything. People kept interrupting.

"Hold on a minute," Charlie said. "You mean this freak's been spying on you since you were a kid?"

"So he says. Since my father died."

At the mention of my father, Vlad perked up. "Is this possible?" he asked Ophelia.

"I screened all of the people who had contact with Zachary at the Nicholls Ward," she answered. "I can assure you that none of them were vampires."

"Could you have made a mistake?" I asked.

"I doubt it. It is more likely that he plucked the images of those people from your memory."

Vlad's forehead knotted. His eyes strayed to the Dragon Dagger. He stared at it a moment, then held out his hand. "That's not the dagger I gave you."

He waved his fingers slightly as if to tell me to hurry up and hand it over.

I drew it from the sheath. The black metal blade was dulled along the edge where the snake venom had dried. I wondered if it would still be fatal if he crammed it in my belly. And I wondered if he'd knowingly given me up to be killed by his enemies.

"There was a bond growing between us the night of Ophelia's

trial," he said. "I know you felt it. Don't let the Changeling destroy it entirely. He would want you to mistrust me. How else can he ensure we don't unite to stand against him?"

Was that right? My memory was usually very dependable. But I'd been so focused on what happened after the trial, I hadn't thought much about what had happened before. I *had* felt a bond growing between us the night we rescued Ophelia. Vlad's pride in me had been empowering.

I placed the hilt of the dagger in his palm. He twisted it lengthwise in his fingers, then made a few phantom swipes through the air. "The weight isn't right." He raised his hand and swung it in a violent arc. For an instant, I thought he was going to stab me, but he spun the dagger instead and slammed the pommel against the metal armour of his thigh. The ruby in the dragon's mouth shattered with a dull pop, scattering shards of crystal across the courtyard. It was a fake. Vlad kicked through the pieces on the ground, then reached down and picked up a metal square about the size of a postage stamp. His eyes narrowed as he scrutinized it.

"Interesting countermove . . ."

"What it is?" Ophelia asked.

"Another transponder. It seems the Changeling is no stranger to technology."

He turned to the roof. A man stepped from the shadows above us. Vlad must have communicated something to him, because the man nodded, then secured a rope to the edge of the building and dropped over the side. He was surprisingly nimble for a human.

"Miklos is an old friend," Vlad said. "His family has served my house for generations. He will fly the helicopter to a safer location while we are underground. I will have him take both transponders with him."

Miklos's expression was hard to read. He had a full beard that climbed up his cheeks and hid most of his face. After a short introduction, Vlad handed him the transponders. A conversation followed between the two men in a language I didn't understand. When it was finished, Miklos scampered off towards the helicopter.

"I'm sending the transponders east," Vlad said. "It might fool the Changeling, though I doubt it. He seems to anticipate our every move. In the meantime, we have an appointment to keep. The dawn is nearing. It is time to meet the Baptist." He turned to Vincent. "You know what to do?"

Vinny smiled. "You betcha." He handed his Gatling gun to Charlie, slipped the ammunition belt from his shoulder and took off towards the wall on our right. It was at least twenty feet high and separated the courtyard from a parking lot beside the building. He hurdled it without breaking stride. I hadn't seen anything like it since Charlie and I went after his father, Hyde, in the Warsaw Caves.

"He shows exceptional promise," Vlad said, then he gestured towards the base of the fountain. "Now, you need to put your armour on. I had new suits made for everyone. After spending so much time in the same clothes, I'm sure you'll find the change agreeable."

A suit of Kevlar was lying on the paving stones. There was a *katana* beside it. Its sheath was crusted with gems. It would have cost a king's ransom. "You understand that in accepting these gifts you are pledging your support for our cause."

"And what cause is that?" I asked.

"Survival. At least for now. We are too few to consider any other course."

I understood. I also understood that I was stuck between the proverbial rock and hard place. The Changeling was on one side; Vlad, the other. A collision between the two was imminent, and if I wasn't careful, my friends and I were going to get ground up between them.

Vlad's few remaining allies will be taken care of in the nights ahead, the Changeling had said. It was clear now that he'd been referring to my friends. Although I didn't trust Vlad, Charlie had made a good point in the helicopter. I could trust Vlad's interests. To survive, he needed Ophelia, and the support of my friends and me. And we needed him.

When I was finished dressing, Vlad slipped his hand past Ophelia's elbow. Arm in arm, the two began walking from the courtyard. Without a word, Luna flanked them on the left. Charlie started backing his way out of the courtyard, the Gatling gun in one hand, the belt wrapped around the other. "Take the right flank," he said. "And keep your eyes peeled."

I glanced at Vlad and Ophelia. It was like watching the Royal Family with their body guards heading out for an evening stroll.

"You know how to use that thing?" I asked Charlie, nodding to the Gatling gun.

"Yeah," he said, raising the tip. "That's the dangerous end."

CHAPTER 41

THE LABYRINTH

WHILE WE CAUTIOUSLY exited the brightly lit court-yard, Charlie explained their system. He was rear-guard, Vincent scouted ahead, Ophelia watched one flank, Luna the other, and Vlad held the centre. I was supposed to take Ophelia's place so she could talk with Vlad, but I hung back to ask Charlie about Istvan. In Montreal, he'd taken a stand with us against the Horsemen, then retrieved my corpse and raised me from the dead. Why do that if he was working for the Changeling?

When I brought it up, Charlie shrugged. "Vlad says Istvan is a loyal friend. I like the guy and he hasn't taken the mark. But Luna thinks he might be trying to play both sides against the middle. You know, like in Halo? You let the Covenant and the Flood hash it out, then mop up the leftovers."

"I don't see the connection," I said.

"If Istvan helps us stay alive, both sides keep fighting and do more damage to one another. Then it's easier for him to swoop in and claim the throne."

I hadn't considered it, but the idea had merit.

"He hid us in his castle in Moldavia," Charlie continued, "then brought us to Castle Dracula just before you left with Vlad. We didn't know you were there, or that you were even alive. It was crazy weird when your shadow caught us in the woods."

Charlie then explained how Istvan had warned them that the Changeling was coming. "He told us to scram. He said he was going to get your body and meet us outside, but he never showed. I figure he got nabbed by the Changeling and had to cut a deal to save his hide, but Luna thinks the whole thing was a set-up, that he arranged to turn you over as soon as Vlad was gone."

"What does Ophelia think?"

"She won't say. You know how tight-lipped she can be." He paused to think. "But you know, Luna could be right. It's possible Istvan turned you over on purpose. He might have known about the transponder. Maybe he thought we could use you to find the Changeling." He shook his head as though disagreeing with himself. "Ahhh, who knows?"

Istvan knew. I wondered if I'd ever get to the bottom of it. "And what about Vlad?" I asked. "Do you think he had anything to do with it?"

"With you getting caught?" Charlie asked. "No, I don't think so. After you disappeared, he made finding you his top priority."

He looked straight at me as though challenging me to doubt him. I didn't. At least, I had no doubt that he was telling me the truth as he saw it. It didn't mean he wasn't wrong.

"So why didn't the Changeling kill you?" he asked.

I shrugged. If I was the Messiah, I was a threat. If I wasn't, I was still a young vampire in a family with too many generations. I should have been executed, or at least left in undeath.

"Do you think the prophecies are true?" Charlie asked.

"What, that I'm the Messiah? More like one of the Lost Boys.

And here I am following Vlad again . . . I don't know, Charlie. None of this makes sense to me."

"I hear ya."

"Are you doing all right?"

I meant to be more specific, to ask about Suki and his father and how he was coping, but he knew exactly what I was getting at. His eyes fell. "It's better when we're busy. But . . . I don't know. I don't want to talk about it."

I understood. I didn't want to talk about it either. "Are *we* okay?"

"Yeah. We're good. Hard to stay mad at a guy when he dies saving your life."

"What about Luna?"

"She's doing better. She was a mess when we got off the ship. Istvan dumped your body in the harbour, and we didn't know if he was going to be able to find it again, or if the New Order knew what he'd done and was looking for it. Then she had to tell her parents about Suki. That was a train wreck. But we've got you back now. If we can hook up with the Baptist, we might just make it out of this alive."

He was still facing the way we'd come, staring into the darkness with such intensity I don't think a dust mote could have slipped past him. He'd changed since Halloween. His restlessness was gone. In its place was a calm determination that chilled me, because I could sense the anger lurking just beneath. It reminded me of Vlad. I glanced to my left, where Luna was just as focused, her head on a swivel. In contrast, Vlad and Ophelia walked ahead arm in arm, their eyes on one another, arguing in hushed whispers.

Charlie nodded for me to take my place on the right. "Vlad wants eyes on all sides. He'll get . . . well, you know how he'll get. Better take your place."

I took up a position about a stone's throw from Vlad and Ophelia. They led us to a set of spiral steps that wound down to a street with beige and yellow buildings set tightly together. For just a second, it brought Charlie back into my orbit.

"Where's Vinny?" I asked.

"You won't see him unless he wants you to," Charlie answered. "He's more dangerous than the rest of us put together. If he ever goes nuts like his old man, we're going to have our hands full."

I understood. His father had been indomitable. It had taken a million pounds of falling rock to stop him.

We fanned out and continued along a winding street. Eventually, Vlad waved us into the backyard of a red-brick building. Protecting the back door was a locked iron gate. Vlad produced a set of keys, then led us down into a basement. "Budapest is famous for its hydrothermal caves," he said. "Hundreds run through these hills."

The place didn't look like a cave at all, more like a wine cellar. It was well lit, well travelled. The passages were wide enough for a tour bus, and the floor and walls were perfectly flat, finished in places with concrete or stone.

"It was a bomb shelter during World War II," Ophelia added. "Thousands of people could hide down here at a time."

"The Baptist is meeting us here?" I asked.

"Not here. Farther along—past this tourist area."

We kept walking through the dark, past walls that were painted with primitive pictures of Stone Age hunters and aurochs. At one place, there was a huge head carved from stone that looked as if it had sunk halfway into the floor. Past this was a chamber with a low ceiling. It was supported in the middle by a square stone column covered in ivy. A fountain had been set into each of the four sides. Instead of water, red wine flowed from each spigot, filling the damp, earthy air with a sour smell.

Vlad glanced at Charlie. My friend handed the Gatling gun back to Vincent. I hadn't even noticed that he'd rejoined us. Charlie drew an English longsword from his belt. He looked at the *katana* on my hip. I took it out.

"The Baptist is waiting just beyond this chamber," Vlad said. "Unless the Changeling follows the transponders to Snagov, we will likely be interrupted."

Snagov. It was another name from Vlad's biography, an island monastery where his body was thought to have been buried centuries ago.

Vlad reached under his cloak and produced a handful of pamphlets. He opened one and began to read. "The third great woe is upon us," it began. The rest read like a religious brochure straight out of Revelation. It talked about the Antichrist and the coming of the Messiah, how he would stare into the maw of evil and drive it from the face of the earth. He folded open another. This one was about a boy with nine lives who would walk through fire and drive the forces of darkness back into the abyss. In another, the orphaned son of the hunter, who had faced the Beast of the Apocalypse and ended the reign of the mad Impaler, offered up everything but a free trip to Disneyland.

Vlad showed me other pamphlets. One had a drawing in it that might have been me or Johnny Depp. The writing was Chinese, or maybe Japanese. "Romanian," he said, flashing another. There were more. "Swahili. Spanish. Dutch. Norwegian. Russian. This one is apparently a big hit in Argentina. Since the Changeling's rise, the Baptist has been distributing propaganda like this all around the globe. I have been trying to meet with him, but he has been unwilling to risk it. The Changeling has whittled away at both of us, and now, it seems, out of desperation, the Baptist is willing to join his strength to ours. It is you who will make this alliance possible. Are you ready?" He didn't wait for me to answer but walked to the wall and bent to the floor. "What direction am I facing, Luna?" he asked.

"North."

I had no idea how either of them knew, but obviously she had learned a thing or two since our lessons at Iron Spike Enterprises.

Vlad counted up six stones, then pushed one in. I heard a click, like a tumbler in a lock. A second stone, four over and one down, released some other mechanism behind the wall. I could hear a chain winding. A section of the cave wall swung inward. The opening was just high enough that we could duck in.

Vlad glanced back at all of us. "Be on your guard. We . . ."

He didn't finish. Instead, he turned towards Vincent, who was growling beside me. I felt a jab of pain in my gums as my teeth slid down. The odour of vampire blood came wafting out of the hole, masking the smells of dust and sour wine.

"There has been fighting here," said Vlad. Then he ducked into the cave and waved us forward.

CHAPTER 42

THE END OF WAR

"VINCENT, TAKE THE point," Ophelia said. "Luna and Charlie, guard the flanks. Zack, stay here and guard the exit with me."

Vlad shifted ahead, then nodded that it was safe to follow. This cave—irregular in shape—was more in line with what I'd expected when we entered the tourist area.

Luna didn't move.

"I'm with you," I said.

She ducked through the entrance. I bent to follow.

Ophelia took hold of my arm. "Zack . . ."

She was afraid for me, I could smell it. But what could I say? I was afraid too, for all of us. It was all the more reason to act.

Vlad was watching us closely. "He cannot lead from the rear, Ophelia."

She didn't let go. "If something were to happen to you again—"

"I'll be careful."

She didn't try to stop me when I darted after Luna.

Footfalls and the clash of metal weapons echoed from ahead, but the cave was honeycombed with side tunnels and the sounds reverberated up and down through the limestone, making it impossible to tell exactly where they were coming from. The smell of blood was strong, however, and that was what we followed. It wasn't long before Luna skidded to a halt. The yellowish-grey stone underfoot was stained crimson. I saw scuff marks. A vampire had been killed there, but the body had been dragged away.

Luna turned to speak, then her eyes widened and she pushed me sideways. A white, long-fingered hand covered with scars and pustules slashed through the air where my neck had been. She thrust forward with her sword. I heard a raspy cry of pain and turned to see Pestilence diving into the shadows. An instant later, he appeared ahead of us, then vanished again. I heard more clanging and followed the trail of blood. The smell of death grew stronger.

"Thanks," I said.

Luna ducked a low-hanging stalactite. "You're welcome."

"Where's Charlie?"

"That way." She pointed right.

I looked but didn't see him. The cave branched. The steel-and-oil smell of Vlad's armour led me onward. I could hear Vincent snarling. It seemed to come from everywhere. We found him around the next corner, thrashing madly within a cloud of sulphurous smoke. He looked more like a phantom than a being of flesh and bone. Vlad was farther up the cave. Sparks flew from his sword and armour as he traded blows with a taller opponent I couldn't see.

"Strange aeons have arrived, Tiptoft," Vlad said. "It is time for Death to die."

I slowed to avoid a collision with Charlie, who shot from a

tunnel beside me. There was blood on his sword blade. His sights were on Tamerlane. "He's mine, Vinny," he shouted.

War's curved scimitar was visible in the smoke ahead. Charlie closed in. Using his sword two-handed, he cut downward just behind the base of the scimitar's grip, right where Tamerlane's hand and wrist should have been. His sword whistled through empty smoke and the scimitar clattered to the ground. A second later it rose into the air again. Charlie parried it once, then thrust forward and missed. Vincent didn't. When the smoke cleared, I was reminded of his last drawing at Iron Spike Enterprises, the one of Doctor Doom with his arms missing, only this was a lot messier.

Tamerlane screamed and fell to a knee. Vincent was holding his arm and a good portion of his shoulder. He growled. The sound rippled through my chest like a jolt of electricity. Tamerlane turned to smoke and spun like a torrent down the cave. We followed at a sprint. Vincent passed us in two strides, Tamerlane's arm and shoulder still gripped in his clawed hand, spots of blood trailing along the floor and walls.

"He can't stay smoke forever, Vin," Charlie shouted. "Stay with him."

Tamerlane led us around the next corner to where Vlad was duelling with John Tiptoft. Both men were perspiring heavily. Vlad seemed to sense War's approach. Instead of turning to meet his charge, he stepped back against the cave wall. Tiptoft was fighting with Vlad's Dragon Blade. I expected him to press his attack, but his eyes locked on Tamerlane and he backed into the darkness, a mocking smile on his face. It seemed a strange decision until I realized what Vlad was doing. I dove forward and tackled Charlie to the ground before he got too close. Then Vlad self-immolated. In the darkness of the cave, the sudden explosion of fire and light from his body was dazzling. Through my closed eyelids, I could see his black silhouette encased in radiant energy.

Tamerlane screamed. He'd been caught in the halo of fire and the effect was devastating. Burning smoke condensed into something that resembled a writhing lump of human charcoal. He fell to the ground in a heap. Vapour rose from his skin, which was black and cracked and bleeding. His right shoulder and arm were still missing.

Vincent flew at him as if slung from a catapult, his mouth in an open roar, teeth bared, arms up and claws out. The Horseman rose and stumbled into the cave wall. The scimitar in his remaining hand glowed red from the heat of Vlad's fire. He took a clumsy swing. Vinny leaned back and the blade whistled past. Then his arm snaked out and, one rip later, he restored an aesthetic symmetry to Tamerlane's figure.

War gasped and fell to his knees. Vinny's jaws opened and snapped forward. I thought he was going to tear out Tamerlane's throat, but Vlad shifted forward, put a firm hand on Vincent's chest and held him back.

"This one is not for you, Vincent," he said. Then he locked eyes on Charlie, who was helping me to my feet.

Tamerlane's skin was changing colour as he healed. Black became red. Cracks became blisters. Blisters turned pink, then began to disappear. Charlie noticed too, but didn't rush. He picked up his sword, which he'd dropped in order to shield his face from the heat, and walked over to face the man who had killed both his father and his girlfriend.

"Make this quick, Charles," Vlad said.

My friend stopped in front of Tamerlane, then his face changed, twisting into something terrible. He started to shake.

I took a step closer. I knew what he was going to do and all the reasons for it, but that didn't lessen my sense of dread that he was taking a giant leap down a very dark path. Vlad shifted so that he stood between us. He nodded for Charlie to hurry. My friend was still shaking, grief and fury etched so keenly on his face it pained me to see it.

"You will be the author of your own calamity," Tamerlane whispered to him.

Charlie swung and Tamerlane's torso tipped sideways, headless, to the ground.

CHAPTER 43

BITTEN

CHARLIE LOOKED AS THOUGH he was about to have a nervous breakdown. Tears spilled from his eyes. His sword shook in his hands. He started to hack furiously at War's dead body. A guttural sound rumbled from his throat. It rose in volume until the whole labyrinth echoed with his rage and pain.

Vlad shifted beside Vincent. "Take him back to the fountain," he said.

Vincent slipped behind Charlie, took hold of him around the waist and picked him up. Charlie squirmed and tried to swing his sword at War again, but Vincent grabbed his arm and whisked him away. Luna fell in beside them. I couldn't hear her words over the sound of Charlie's shouting. He was incoherent.

"His anger and sadness . . ." Vlad said. "Time will dull their hold."

I hoped so.

"Did you see where Tiptoft went?" He was staring into the shadows.

"He slipped away when you self-immolated."

"I'll have my Dragon Blade yet." He tipped his head as if straining to hear something. "We need to get Ophelia."

"What do you hear?"

He didn't answer. A second later, a strange clattering sound, like a wave of stones falling on rock, began to build in intensity until it filled every cave and crevice. It was coming from the direction in which John Tiptoft had disappeared.

Vlad pushed me towards the cave entrance. "Fall back!"

In the next instant, a black, writhing mass of bodies exploded around the corner. At first it looked like a horde of giant insects scurrying across the walls, floor and ceiling of the tunnel, but they were vampires, dozens of them, howling to get at us. The shrieking and scuttling of nails on stone set my teeth on edge.

I let Vlad lead. He quickly shifted around the corner. Luna and the others were waiting there, debating which way to go. Vincent turned towards us. His nostrils flared and he roared. The sound was so loud I was amazed the cave didn't collapse. Then it did. The ground shook. Rock dust filled the air. Somewhere ahead of us the ceiling must have given way. Small rivulets of daylight shone pale in the swirling dust, bouncing off the tunnel walls.

"What was that?" Luna asked.

"A cave-in," Vlad answered. "They are trying to block our exit. If we can't get out, we'll be ripped to pieces."

I glanced back. The sudden tremors and shifting rock, or perhaps the unwelcome streams of sunlight ahead, caused the vampires at the front of the horde to stop their pursuit. They were only twenty or so feet away, a black, writhing wall of malice.

"Not this crowd again," Charlie said. His tears were still wet on his cheeks, and his breaths came in shudders.

"Do we run or make a stand?" Luna asked.

Before anyone could answer, Pestilence reappeared, springing from the shadows beside her. He grabbed a handful of her copper hair, yanked her head to the side and bit a chunk out of her neck. She screamed. I leapt at him, but he pushed her into me, then disappeared, smiling, into the darkness.

I took Luna by the shoulders to keep her from falling over. She pressed both hands over her neck. Blood gushed down her arms and torso. I lowered her to the ground, then put my hands over hers to try to stop the bleeding. It made no difference. Her eyes began to lose their focus.

"Hang on. Hang on!" I shouted.

She didn't respond. She was gasping for breath. I was losing her. There was nothing I could do.

Vlad leaned down to inspect her wound. She was barely conscious, and she moaned when he moved her hair out of the way. "This is bad. The wound will fester if left untreated. She'll need blood and time to heal. We must move quickly, back the way we came."

He flicked a hand at Vincent, who stepped over and scooped her up in his arms.

"No! Wait," I said.

Vincent took off. I couldn't keep up. He didn't get far before he ran into Ophelia.

"The way ahead is blocked," she said. "They have forced the ceiling down somehow." Then she saw Luna. "Oh, heavens. What happened?"

I tried to answer but started coughing. The air was full of dust. I waved a hand in front of my face and noticed it was covered with Luna's blood. So was my armour. I was shaking.

Vlad shifted beside us. Charlie was right on his heels.

"Is there another way out?" Ophelia asked.

"Not a short one," Vlad said. He followed with some words in Romanian, or Hungarian, or maybe Orcish, that sounded like sandpaper scraping over concrete.

"What about the Shadow Road?" she asked him.

"With so large a group, and her bleeding like a fount, it would be suicide."

I reached out so that I could take her back, but Vincent turned away protectively. "Where do I go?" he asked.

Several tunnels branched off to either side. Vlad pointed to his right. "That leads to the river. Follow it south. When you're clear, radio for Miklos. We'll hold them off and catch up later. On the Pest side. We can tend to her then."

Before I could voice any objection Vincent bolted. I started after him, but Vlad grabbed the back collar of my armour. "Vincent is faster. She has a better chance with him. You are needed here."

"For what?" I shouted.

"I'll go with them," Ophelia said.

"No," Vlad said. "Your place is at my side."

Ophelia glanced at me as if she might argue, but she said nothing. Vincent disappeared down the tunnel. The sight of him leaving twisted my stomach like a rusted coil. Vlad was still holding me back. I tried to pull free, but he wouldn't let go.

"We have to buy them time," he said. "Do as I say. They're coming."

The horde was on the move again. I could hear the clatter of many feet and an unholy shrieking that electrified my skin. Vlad pushed me to the side so we wouldn't get in each other's way.

Are you ready? he asked.

I wasn't. My place was with Luna.

The air began to swell with hate. I forced myself to breathe deeply despite the awful density of it. My body was still shaking, so I closed my eyes and imagined myself in the tunnel of light. A second later, the horde was upon us.

CHAPTER 44

THE HORDE

THERE WASN'T ENOUGH room for all of us to fight side by side, so Vlad and I stood in front. Behind us, Ophelia and Charlie spoke in hushed whispers. He rubbed his hand over his eyes and nodded. A moment later I heard her voice in my head.

Be like water. A thousand pounds crashing down the mountain. Fast. Fluid. And unstoppable.

After what had just happened to Luna, I felt more like Jell-O right out of the mould, quivering and useless.

The horde rolled forward like a wave. All of them were dressed in black, and the skin of their hands and faces had been darkened. It made it harder to see where one body ended and another began.

The first vampire in the group coiled and sprang. Clawed fingers stretched for my throat. I kicked him into the wall. I smashed my fist into the chin of another. It left my midriff exposed. The next vampire put a shoulder to my stomach and bowled me over. We hit the ground hard and a row of sharp nails raked my face. I pushed her off, but others arrived, kicking, tearing, screaming. Only my armour kept me from getting ripped to pieces. And Vlad.

A bright light flashed beside me. Vampires screamed. The pressure on my chest lifted. Vlad stood over me, his skin alight. He pulled one vampire from me and his clothes caught fire. Vlad hurled him into the others, then jumped forward. The horde melted away and I scrambled to my feet.

Charlie handed me my sword, then pointed to the tip. "That's the dangerous end. Use it." He pushed me into the tunnel on our left, opposite to the direction Vincent had gone with Luna.

"Famine has to be nearby," I said. "This is her work. It's her and Pestilence that we need to stop. We're just wasting our time with these others."

Vlad stepped towards the horde. For an instant, the flames emanating from his body flared yellow, then white. The heat was so intense, even from a dozen paces, that I had to turn away. The horde retreated to a chorus of agonizing screams.

"That won't keep them away for long," Ophelia said. "That way. Go."

She led us farther into the tunnel. The light behind me died as the flames from Vlad's body vanished. He shifted after us. His cloak and outer garments had burned away, leaving a dusting of ash on his dragon armour. The sound of the metal plates rubbing together was quickly drowned out by the screeching of the horde as they renewed their pursuit, clawing their way along the tunnel.

I came to a fork and stopped. "Which way?" I asked.

One tunnel burrowed deeper into the earth, the other rose upwards. Fresh air was streaming from it.

Vlad glanced up. He climbed slowly, his breath ragged. Ophelia followed. Before Charlie and I could fall in behind her, the mob arrived. The vampire in front was faster than the others and came scuttling across the ceiling. He saw me and dropped. I threw an uppercut. Bones crunched and he collapsed on the floor.

Charlie dispatched a tall vampire with teeth like a piranha, then grabbed my shoulder, pulled me back and tossed something in the air. "Flash-bang!"

I closed my eyes, ducked my head and covered my ears. The boom that followed deafened me anyway. Smoke was suddenly everywhere. My sense of direction was off and I started stumbling the wrong way.

Charlie grabbed me and pulled me back. "Haven't we been over this before?" he shouted. "When a guy shouts *flash-bang*, you cover your ears!"

"That's exactly what I did!"

He started pulling me up the tunnel. A few dizzy steps later, I collided with Ophelia, who took my arm and led me in the direction Vlad had disappeared. He'd been moving so slowly I assumed we'd catch him right away, but after travelling down a good length of tunnel he was still out of sight. The smell of his charred armour was gone. I wondered if we'd missed a turn, then a cluster of small stones rained down from above. I looked up. Where the tunnel widened there was a seam in the rock. Vlad's shoulders were braced under the cave roof and his feet were on the bottom of the fissure. Veins bulged on his neck as he strained to collapse the tunnel.

Charlie bounded past. "They're right behind me."

I moved to follow, but someone took hold of my legs and I was tackled to the ground. The face of the vampire overtop of me had been blackened like the others, but there was no mistaking the shiny green eyes and perfectly cut hair of the vampire Charlie had tossed from the helicopter. She had a sharp stone in her hands and started smashing it into my ribs. I grabbed her arms, then heard a snarl and a crack, and the roof started coming down.

CHAPTER 45

BETWEEN A ROCK AND
A HARD PLACE

I'D BEEN IN a cave-in before, the night Charlie and I went after Hyde. If experience had taught me anything, it was that experience was useless. There is no defence against a million pounds of falling rock.

Bits of grit and dust fell into my face and eyes as I tried to kick the vampire off my stomach. I didn't have time for a wrestling match; the rest of the ceiling was going to follow in an instant. I spun my *katana* and jammed it into her throat, then twisted the blade to wrench her off. Once freed, I rolled to my knees, ripped the blade clear and jumped as far as I could. A boom followed, then a blast of dust shot past. A painful ringing filled my ears and I started coughing uncontrollably.

The woman was squirming behind me on the ground. Her mouth contorted in a scream, but instead of sound, blood bubbled forth and gushed from the hole I'd punched in her voice box. Her legs were buried under a large pile of rock that sealed the tunnel, floor to ceiling. Another vampire had been trapped as well. A hand was sticking out beside her, unmoving, the Changeling's mark clearly visible on the darkened skin. Some attempt had been made to blacken the thick rings that decorated each finger, but there was no mistaking the owner. The rest of the bounty hunter's body would have been crushed to ruin.

The woman's pain must have been extraordinary. The sight of her frantic thrashing had my stomach doing somersaults. Charlie was calling from down the tunnel, but I couldn't leave her like that. She would have killed me given the chance, but had my fate been different, it might have been me down there, writhing in pain with a mark on my hand and a mind that was not my own.

I put my sword down and grabbed one of the larger stones pinning her legs to the floor. She tried to push me away. The effort knocked her out. I caught her shoulders before her head hit the ground, then put a hand over her throat to stop the bleeding. Pulling her clear was going to involve moving a few thousand pounds of stone. She'd bleed to death before I was finished, so I tore off one of her sleeves and used it to bind her neck. Then I started hauling the larger rocks out of the way.

I heard footsteps behind me. Vlad was there. He shifted forward, raised his sword and swung for her neck. I quickly grabbed his shoulder and pulled him off balance so his blade arced wide. He turned and pushed me up against the wall. He was shouting, but I could barely hear him.

"Whose side are you on?" he said.

I'm not sure how I would have answered if Charlie and Ophelia hadn't appeared at that moment. Vlad must have sensed their arrival, because he let go of me an instant before they would have seen.

"What's the holdup?" Charlie asked. He bent, picked up my *katana* and handed it to me.

"That woman bears the Changeling's mark," Vlad said. "In moments she could awaken. Her screams will bring others. We cannot allow that."

"Wait a minute," Charlie said, inspecting her more closely. "She's the one from the church. Her friend is the bounty hunter. How did she even get here? She should be sleeping with the fishes."

"She's a shadow-jumper," I said.

"Wonderful. Those freaks are like portable telepods." He put two hands on the grip of his sword and lined her up for a clean overhead.

I stepped in the way. "That's not going to happen."

"It is not for you to decide," Vlad said.

"What if we can remove the mark? She might throw her lot in with us. Wouldn't that be better?"

Vlad didn't answer. He and Ophelia were talking silently with one another. Her face was grave.

"Let me try something," I said.

Charlie grudgingly stepped back as I crouched beside her. I put my palm over the mark on her hand, then closed my eyes and imagined the woman's skin as it should have appeared, smooth and unblemished. Nothing happened. I concentrated harder, willing the mark to disappear. Nothing. Next, I used the edge of my sword to cut a shallow groove across the top of my palm, then I pressed my hand against her mark again, wincing with discomfort. I figured that if I was the real Messiah, maybe something in my blood would make this work. But it seemed that every time life presented me with a valid test—like seeing through the Changeling's disguises, or resisting his venom—something that would prove that I was the one the prophecies were really about, I came up short.

"There has to be a way to do this."

"We won't discover it here," Vlad said.

Something in his tone unnerved me. Our eyes met. An understanding passed between us. He wasn't going to leave her alive.

I stood. Killing Tamerlane was one thing. He'd known exactly what he was doing when he murdered Suki and Uncle Jake, and he had shown no remorse. Killing this woman was different— like executing an insane person, someone who had no grasp of what they were doing. I'd spent enough time around the mentally ill to know how wrong this was.

I held Vlad's gaze, set my feet at shoulder width, put two hands on my *katana*, raised the tip and pointed it at his chest. And another understanding passed between us.

CHAPTER 46

SIGNS AND SIGNALS

VLAD'S MOUTH SPLIT into a wide grin. "So, it seems you *are* capable of killing on principle. All I need to do is threaten to take the lives of your enemies."

I didn't let my guard down. There was no way to know if his levity might suddenly vanish beneath a torrent of rage.

"Perhaps there is some way to restore her mind, but we are out of time. There is a parking lot above us. If we are lucky, the way will be clear and we can join Vincent in Pest. We must leave, immediately."

Vlad didn't strike me as the kind of man who deferred to others. I waited for him to make his exit first. He seemed to be waiting for me to do the same.

At Ophelia's prompting, Charlie turned to leave. Then footsteps echoed down from the tunnel ahead. A man emerged. He was tall and handsome, with a moustache like two half moons and a streak of white in his tawny hair. If he was surprised to see us, he gave no sign.

Vlad rubbed his chin. "Istvan, this is unexpected."

"Truly? You know I never stray far from where the action is." He stroked his moustache. "It is hard to maintain my status as a triple agent, playing you and the Changeling off against one another, if I remain too far behind the scenes."

Vlad chuckled at this. "Well met, cousin," he said.

"And you. You seem remarkably well intact, despite the Changeling's attempts to kill you."

"The Horseman's attempts. The Changeling remains aloof, regrettably."

Istvan waved a hand in front of his face to move the dust away, then made a fist, pressed it against his lips and coughed gently. "The puppet master is always closer than you think. This was an important meeting, you and the Baptist."

"You knew of it?" Vlad asked, scratching at his throat.

"Not until now, or I would have been here to witness it. Tell me, are the rumours true? Is Tamerlane dead?"

"Quite," said Vlad. "But I cannot take credit. Most of the work was Vincent's. Charlie dealt the final blow, as was his right."

"So now there are but three. The balance of power is shifting."

"Not far enough."

Istvan turned to Charlie. "Did you know, it was rumoured that inside Timur's casket it was written, 'Whoever opens my tomb shall release an invader more terrible than I'? His body was exhumed by the Russians for examination in 1941. Two days later, Hitler launched Operation Barbarossa. An interesting bit of history."

"There is more to that story, is there not, cousin?" Vlad said, adjusting his belt.

"There is," Istvan said. He pushed a long lock of hair away from his eyes and tucked it behind his ear. "Before the assault on Iron Spike Enterprises, the Changeling opened Tamerlane's tomb yet again so that, as War, he could lead the horde. And not a week later, I resurrected Vladislav so we could secure Ophelia's release. And so a more terrible invader was released. Fascinating how history repeats itself, don't you think, Charles?"

Charlie did not have time to respond before Vlad attacked. He shifted forward and rammed his sword through Istvan's chest. He aimed for the heart, but Istvan twisted so that it pierced his other side. I took a step back in surprise.

A raspy moan escaped Istvan's lips. "Were my gestures not faithful?"

"They were, all of them," Vlad said, twisting the sword. Judging by the look on Istvan's face, it was excruciating. "My chin, your moustache, your mouth, my throat, my stomach, your ear," Vlad said. "A pointless exercise, it would seem. Thankfully, Istvan only calls me Vladislav when he is upset with me. A small mistake, but a revealing one." Vlad pushed the sword deeper. "Where is my good cousin? Did you kill him?"

Istvan's face went flat and his pupils turned a chalky white. I'd seen those eyes before. It was the Changeling.

"Why would I kill such a useful man?" he said. "Did you not think he could be valuable to me, despite his loyalties to you?" All evidence of the Changeling's pain vanished. He put a foot on Vlad's thigh and jumped back. Vlad's blade slid from his torso. The wound it left behind sealed instantly.

Before he could say more, Ophelia closed in and struck. The Changeling brushed her sword aside with his open palm, then pushed her into the tunnel wall. Charlie and I moved in and swung at the same time but from different sides—me high, Charlie low. The Changeling's body turned to mist. Our swords passed right through him and he flowed back against the cave wall, then reassumed the form of Istvan.

"The signalling was a clever idea, Vladislav, but I was able to pluck the details from Istvan's mind. Your cousin foolishly believes that he can shield his thoughts from me, but there is no defence that I cannot penetrate with time and patience."

Ophelia nudged me sideways. The four of us fanned out, blades up.

"Have you learned nothing? Put your weapons away and accept the hand that fate has dealt you. Take the mark or be destroyed."

Vlad hesitated as if in doubt, then shifted so that he was right in the Changeling's face, his sword thrust forward. It would have taken the Changeling through the heart, but that part of him had turned to mist again. His arms remained solid, however. One hand closed around Vlad's throat. The other pushed his sword to the side. Once the blade was no longer sticking through his misty torso, he solidified, and that same hand passed into shadow. It reappeared an instant later with the fingers fused together. They were encased in a scorpion's shell, the end tipped with an envenomed stinger.

Vlad dropped his sword and grabbed the Changeling's forearm in his hands. At the same time, Ophelia lunged forward and swung. Her timing seemed perfect, but the Changeling's stinger turned to mist just as she would have severed it. Then he pushed Vlad at her. She managed to step out of the way, but Vlad wasn't so lucky. His heel hit a stone and he stumbled backwards. The Changeling shifted so he was right beside him as he fell. He swung with his stinger. I was close enough to parry. My blade bit into the surrounding shell. He grimaced, tore it loose and swung for Vlad again. This time, Ophelia stepped in the way. She swung her rapier at his neck with one hand and pulled Vlad sideways with the other.

I missed what happened next. Charlie had taken hold of my collar and pulled me back. I heard him shout, "Fire in the hole!"

The air around me detonated. Red, orange and yellow sparks

lit up the cave, peppering every bit of my exposed skin with burning metal. The effect was identical to the canister shot his father had used against Tamerlane. I raised an arm to shield my eyes, but the damage was done. A thousand sparks had burned golden trails across my field of view, so when I opened them the cave looked like a glowing electric spiderweb. I couldn't see a thing.

"After him!" Charlie shouted. I heard footsteps disappear down the tunnel.

Vlad's voice exploded in my head. "WAIT!"

My eyes began to clear and I could see from his expression that something was terribly wrong. Ophelia was lying on the ground at his feet. She was clutching her neck. Her face was contorted with pain and the skin under her chin was turning grey.

CHAPTER 47

ULTIMATUM

VLAD KNELT ON the ground beside Ophelia. "Oh no . . . Oh no . . . This cannot be." He put a hand under her head, cradling it from the rock as he spoke to her. "Why would you do such a thing? That stroke was intended for me . . ."

Grey death washed over Ophelia's face. Her breathing grew shallow. Then it stopped.

Vlad scooped her up in his arms. "Go after Charlie," he said to me.

I stared at Ophelia's face, too stunned to move. Her skin had turned the colour of ash. Her eyes were vacant and lifeless.

"We cannot lose them both," Vlad shouted. "Go . . . Go, or your friend will suffer the same fate as this! GO!"

I stumbled down the tunnel. My vision collapsed into something so narrow I barely saw the walls around me. A surreal feeling followed, as though my senses were muted and what I smelled and heard and saw was filtered through air too thick to breathe. Ophelia was dead. She wasn't coming back. And there was nothing I could do about it. Nothing but run. It was just like that day in Libya when my father died. I could barely see. Tears poured from my eyes. I sped blindly down the tunnel, but I was really back in Libya, in that ancient city, my feet tirelessly pounding down streets of sand. The rock walls were ruins. My body was hollow, my mind numb.

I ran in circles. Tunnels looped and doubled back. I had no sense of where I was. I didn't care. All I remember thinking was that if I ran far enough I would come to a place where things were right. My father would be there. And Ophelia. I would be a kid again and everything would be as it was supposed to be.

But that place did not exist. And nothing I did could change it.

Eventually the tunnel grew so steep I had to climb to continue. Ahead was a faint light. The sun was up outside. I could smell the open air. Then the ground flattened out. I heard voices and stopped.

"... dead?" said a woman. It was Famine. She was just around the corner.

John Tiptoft spoke next. "And you are certain that the boy is alone?"

There was no answer.

"Can you find out where he is?"

A few seconds later, Pestilence stepped out of the shadows below me. The steep part of the tunnel was at his back, so I was out of sight. He slunk away from me, bent over like a thief in the night.

I heard a noise behind me. Before I could turn, the keen edge of a longsword was pulled up against my throat.

"What was the first thing you ever killed?" Charlie asked me. "Whisper. And if I feel you digging in my head for the answer, it will be the last thing you ever do."

Charlie's other arm was wrapped around my chest. In that hand was an incendiary grenade. He had taken the pin out and was holding the lever closed with his fingers.

"It was a red squirrel," I answered quietly, mouthing the words more than saying them. Then I pushed his blade away, turned and swung. The edge of my *katana* stopped against the side of his neck. "Where did it happen?"

"My cottage on Stoney Lake," he answered, a bit too loudly. There was a look of shock on his face.

I put my finger over my mouth as a warning to be quiet. "It's me," I whispered.

"Yeah, I hope so."

I lowered my sword.

"I forgot you could move so quickly," he said.

I smiled.

"Yeah, it's you. Who else would blush from a compliment?" He glanced down the tunnel. "Bathory and Tiptoft are up there."

"I heard them."

"Where're Vlad and Ophelia?"

I looked at him. Words failed me. My eyes began to water and I felt the muscles in my neck tighten. He glanced down, then handed me his sword. I took it and watched, bleary-eyed, while he put the pin back in his grenade. He slipped it into his belt beside a gas canister, then took his sword back. "The Changeling . . . He got her, didn't he, with his stinger?"

"Yeah."

"They were both moving so quickly. I hoped . . ."

He didn't finish.

"Vlad's very close to an antidote, you know. Very close. He'll get her back. He will. I know it."

I was having trouble seeing and had to look away. I had no idea what to do. Pestilence was behind us. It wouldn't take him long to reach the cave-in. He'd probably double back and would find us unless we got out, but Tiptoft and Famine were ahead, blocking the only obvious exit. Without Vlad and

Ophelia, we had no chance of escaping. Even if Vlad had an antidote, it wouldn't do us any good. Dead or alive, I'd probably never see Ophelia again. Or Luna. I didn't even know where she was. I should never have let Vincent take off with her. All that blood . . . I started pulling at my collar. It was getting hard to breathe.

Charlie grabbed me roughly by the shoulders. "Keep it together. If you fall apart now we're both dead."

He was right, and I had no right to lash out at him, but I did just the same. It seemed getting angry was the only thing that would keep my sadness from taking over. That would have shut me down completely.

"If you don't get out of my face, Charlie, I'm going to kill you myself."

He took a step back and smiled. "That's more like it!"

I stared at him for a few seconds, then wiped my eyes clear and shook my head. He was still grinning. I couldn't help myself. Despite all that we'd suffered, I had to smile back.

"How do we get into these messes?"

"I've been asking myself that since preschool," he said. "I guess it's a talent."

"Yeah," I said, and wiped my eyes clear. A small measure of calm was returning. "I wish I had some good news. Pestilence is looking for us. We've got to get out of here."

Charlie nervously picked at the grip of his longsword. "If we go ahead, we face Tiptoft. Do you think we can take him?"

"Didn't you just chase after the Changeling all by yourself?"

"My grenade did a number on him. He was hurt, and I wasn't thinking. Tiptoft is fresh. And he's lethal."

"If you can deal with Bathory," I said, "I can deal with John."

"You sure?"

"No. But what choice do we have?"

We started forward at a crouch. The cave continued to grow brighter as we rose closer to the surface, forcing us to squint. We came to a dead end. Above us was a concrete ceiling about three feet thick with a car-sized hole in it. Fingers of rusted rebar stuck out along the inside of the opening so that it looked like the gaping mouth of a grey-skinned monster.

"Hold this," Charlie said, handing me his sword again. He jumped to the lip of the hole and pulled himself up. Once he was clear, I leapt straight through.

"Show-off," he whispered.

We were in an underground parking lot. A cement mixer sat against one wall, along with an assortment of equipment: hoses, shovels, picks, orange pylons and a pile of large I-beams. Otherwise, the place was deserted.

Charlie reached for his sword. I kept it. "I have an idea," I said.

"So far I don't like it."

"Trust me. Just keep going."

We didn't get far. John Tiptoft stepped from behind a concrete column. Vlad's Dragon Blade was in his hands. His cowl was pulled back so we could see his weathered face and salt-and-pepper whiskers. Famine was behind him. Beyond that, a ramp spiralled up to the level outside. The light filtering down was strong. The sun must have been well above the horizon.

"That's far enough," Tiptoft said. "Drop the swords."

I shook my head. "That's not going to happen. But if you put down the Dragon Blade and kick it over to me, you might just leave with your head attached."

CHAPTER 48

DUELLING WITH DEATH

FAMINE TOOK A step back.

"What do you think is going to happen, youngblood?" Tiptoft asked. "Do you think Vlad is going to save you? His safe houses have been torched. The last of his tombs has been razed. And now Ophelia is dead. He and all who align themselves with him are finished."

"So is Tamerlane," Charlie said. "He's a good head shorter now." He reached out to take his sword back.

I held it away. "You'd better get going," I said to him. "Make sure the others are okay. I'll deal with these two." I handed him my sword. I mean no offence to Japanese swordsmiths, but a *katana* is basically just a long razor blade. When a man is in armour, you might just as well be whacking him with a willow wand. Tiptoft wore platinum and Kevlar, just as we did. I needed Charlie's sword to beat him down. It was heavier.

Charlie accepted the *katana*. "I'm not leaving."

"He's trying to save your life, boy," Tiptoft said.

"No, actually," I said, "I was trying to save yours."

He laughed.

"You forget how well I know you," I said. "In your last life, you were killed by a werewolf. You knew you had to face him, and you knew you were going to die because you couldn't see anything beyond that moment. Just the cold dark of the grave. You told the Changeling that you couldn't see the end of this battle. We both know why, don't we? It's because you're going to die down here."

Bathory took another step back.

"I don't believe in killing," I said, "Charlie has a different opinion. And after what you've put us through, if he stays, I have no doubt that after we beat you down he'll lop your head off."

Tiptoft didn't hesitate. His first blow fell so hard against my sword it nearly shattered my arms. I jumped back and circled towards the entrance of the garage. Charlie flanked him on the other side. Against two of us, Tiptoft had to be careful.

Famine slipped behind a pier. *You will fail*, she said. *Then you and your friend will die.*

I forced my voice into her mind. She winced as though I'd slapped her. *I have already succeeded. Vlad has escaped with Ophelia.*

He has escaped with a corpse.

He's going to bring her back. What do you think they're going to do to you when that happens? Run while you can, Bathory. Your voice has no power over me.

Her eyes flitted nervously from me to Charlie. *Perhaps not over you . . .*

Charlie's face contorted in pain and he fell to his knees. The *katana* slipped from his fingers.

Tiptoft rushed him. I leaped between them and blocked an overhand stroke, then took the next one in the ribs. Even though I was wearing the best armour this side of an Abrams tank, the air shot from my lungs. I couldn't let him know I was weak, so I went on the offensive. He deflected my blade away, then circled again, waiting.

Charlie pushed himself to one knee. Sweat dripped from his forehead. Another jolt of pain arched his back. I saw the fingers of the hand nearest me spread wide from the shock of it. The other hand was at his belt.

"What is the matter, child?" Famine mocked. "Have you no witty words for me now?"

He answered by swinging his hand forward. He was trying to throw something at her. Famine sent another blast of pain through his body. The shock of it arrested his arm in mid-swing. Instead of flying through the air, the object dropped at his feet.

"Oh no!" He looked at me. "Gas bomb!"

There was no bang, just the sound of a can bouncing on concrete. It spun in tight circles, filling the air with a yellow, chalky gas. Bathory coughed and disappeared behind the growing haze. Tiptoft ignored it and attacked me. His blows were so powerful, and the Dragon Blade so heavy, it was impossible to hold my ground. I got pushed back towards the exit ramp. The yellow cloud continued to thicken until my friend was completely obscured. I had to hope there was a gas mask on his utility belt, because with Tiptoft between us, there was no quick way to fish him out.

I faked an overhead and tried to circle around him, but Tiptoft sidestepped me easily, then started a barrage that backed me up even farther. I tried to get past his guard, but he parried all my attacks with a precision and fluidity that seemed supernatural. On technique alone, I realized I'd never beat him. It didn't matter how empty my mind was, or how in sync I felt with the light of the tunnel entrenched in my mind's eye, he was simply better. So instead of trying to hit him, I made the Dragon Blade my target and hammered at it again and again. Fast, hard strokes.

The kind that sent shivers through your arms. His weapon was heavier. Slower. It was more difficult for him to keep it in place. He had to back up to buy himself time.

I didn't let up. His breathing deepened, his chest heaved. He was surprised. So was Famine. She had crept up after us and was watching from behind the nearest pillar. The yellow cloud behind her was beginning to drift away. The canister had emptied. Charlie was going to be exposed in a matter of moments. I needed to draw them away, or he was going to be easy pickings.

I retreated several steps towards the exit. It was painfully bright. The light wasn't direct, but the skin on the back of my neck began to tingle, then burn. Any closer and I risked a fatal suntan. It was there that I had to make my stand.

When we re-engaged, I faked a low crosscut. Tiptoft dropped his blade to parry and I swung for his hilt. Every ounce of my strength was behind it. I thought if I knocked the Dragon Blade aside, maybe I could land a decisive blow to his person, but it didn't play out that way. My sword shattered.

Tiptoft slammed the Dragon Blade across the side of my leg. When I dropped to a knee he bowled me over. I hit the concrete and rolled for the cool shadows beside the ramp. Tiptoft was right on me. He dropped his foot on my chest and stopped me dead. A heartbeat later, I felt the tip of his sword against my throat.

"I wasn't lying, boy, when I said that I saw pain and loss and death for you. You should have taken the mark."

CHAPTER 49

AN UNEXPECTED TURN OF EVENTS

JOHN'S WEIGHT SHIFTED and his arm rose slightly. Before he rammed the sword down, something stretched from the shadows and pulled the tip of the blade aside so it sparked against the asphalt. I was staring at a metal gauntlet. Ash coated its surface. A second gauntlet closed over the blade closer to the hilt. Vlad pulled himself from the darkness and wrenched the weapon from Tiptoft's hand.

"And I wasn't lying when I told you to accept my peace offering or be destroyed. I remain a man of my word."

John took a step back. He was so focused on Vlad that he didn't see me hook my foot around his ankle. He tripped backwards and sunlight hit him flush on the face. He screamed.

Vlad raised the Dragon Blade for the killing blow, but a pale, thin arm reached out of the shadows from exactly the same place he had appeared. Thin white fingers took hold of his breastplate and pulled him off balance. I turned and saw a toothy smile fade into the darkness. Vlad spun and thrust his sword into the shadows, but Pestilence was already gone. His gargling laughter echoed down the lot.

Meanwhile, Tiptoft had risen to his feet and was running up into the light, his cowl pulled over his face. That way was certain death, but it was the only path he could take that we wouldn't follow.

I pointed to the thinning yellow cloud of gas ahead of us. "Charlie's in there," I said.

Vlad straightened up. His movements were slow. After self-immolating several times during our last battle, he must have been exhausted.

"I'm not as tired as you think," he said. He held the Dragon Blade up in one hand and examined the perfect symmetry of it. "Its return is an omen." He reached down and helped me to my feet. "You did much better than I expected."

"You were watching?"

"From the shadows, yes. Just waiting for the right moment." He shifted closer to Charlie, appearing first in one area of darkness, then another, until he was clear of the sunlight. I had to run through it. The back of my neck was blistering when I caught up to him.

"Is Luna safe?" I asked.

"Time will tell."

"What about Ophelia?"

"I . . . I should have sent her back with Vincent and Luna before the Changeling appeared. I thought she would be safer with me. If I cannot bring her back . . ."

He waved his hand in front of his face. Charlie was a lump on the ground. I started coughing, my eyes watering from the tear gas. I had to close them and nearly missed Vlad's transformation. His body turned to fog and his armour fell empty to the pavement. He began to swirl in a cyclone, pushing the yellow gas away. Once it was dispersed, the fog spun back inside his armour. The metal plates rose into the air and assumed their proper arrangement. Inside, Vlad became a man of vapour and shadow, then a solid being of blood and bone. He bent and picked up Charlie.

"The crystals in the gas will have damaged his lungs. He will need rest and blood before he fights again."

I looked around for my *katana*. It was on the ground where Charlie had dropped it. A thin film of yellow dust had settled on it. I tossed the broken grip of Charlie's longsword away, then picked up the *katana* and wiped it clean.

Vlad's eyes were red-rimmed and bloodshot. "I will take him to the others. You cannot follow me on the Shadow Road, so I will send Vincent to keep you safe. Not even a being as powerful as the Changeling would try to tackle a lycanthrope so close to the surface while the sun is up."

He stepped into a shadow and disappeared. I stared at the cinder blocks for a few seconds, then put my hand against them, marvelling that something so solid could be used as a doorway.

The light was growing in intensity, enlivening the pain in my neck and hands. I sprinted back to the hole that led to the caves. The shadows within beckoned like a cool bath. When I stepped to the edge, something smashed against the back of my head. My knees buckled and I crumpled to the asphalt.

The Countess stood over me, a wedge of concrete in her hands. I'd forgotten about her. A wicked smile spread up her cheeks. She reached down and pried the sword from my deadened fingers. *I told you that you would fail. That you would die.*

She had. And I had laughed her off.

Not this time, she said.

CHAPTER 50

OUTLAWS

MY HEAD WAS REELING. I tried to lift my arms to protect myself but they weren't responding.

Famine raised the *katana*, a smug look of triumph on her face. It quickly turned to alarm when a dark shape rose up behind her. She glanced back to see the dark-haired vampire with the luminescent green eyes standing in her shadow. The woman's arms were bare. The black sleeve I'd used to bind her neck was tied around her forehead, the bloodstain dead centre, like a crimson star in a night sky. The other sleeve had been torn off and was wrapped around her knuckles so that it hid the Changeling's mark. When Famine saw this, surprise, then panic danced across her gaunt features.

The woman hammered Famine in the stomach. She crumpled. As she fell, the woman twisted the *katana* from her hands.

I tried to stand but I was too dizzy. A goose egg throbbed on the back of my head. I touched it gingerly, and my fingertips came away bloody. Then someone took hold of me under the shoulders. I looked up into a pair of purple eyes. The bounty hunter had climbed from the hole and was pulling me to my feet. His hat was gone, and he was covered, head to toe, in rock dust. One of the lapels of his jumpsuit had been torn off and was wrapped around his hand so that the Changeling's mark was covered, just like the woman's.

"Can you stand?" he asked, guiding me carefully from the edge of the hole. His eyes fell to Famine, who was curled up on the asphalt, her thin arms crossed in front of her face. "Kill her, Min," he said to the green-eyed woman.

She pointed the *katana* up the ramp. Dust swirled in a column of sunlight shining down from the level above. "We have killed enough on her account. Let the sun have her."

"You wouldn't dare!" Famine said. "I am the voice of the New Order. You must obey."

"Must I?" Min said. She took the Countess by the arm and yanked her to her feet. "You are gravely mistaken."

"Both of you swore loyalty to the Changeling. To betray him is death."

"Better to die free than live enslaved."

"Please," Famine said. Her eyes closed and her voice echoed deeply through the recesses of my mind. *Have mercy.*

"You shall have mercy," Min said, "in the same measure you would give us."

"This is a mistake," I said.

Min wasn't budging. "We have been badly used. Justice must be served."

The bounty hunter grabbed Famine's other arm and the two dragged her towards the light. Her pleas became threats. Threats became offers. Offers became one long, depressing wail. Then they cast her into the sunlight. I was stunned by how suddenly it happened. There was no trial, no verdict or last words of appeal. Just a piercing scream. Famine's hair caught fire. She scuttled back towards the darkness, but Min was there waiting and kicked her back. Soon her skin was burned black and riddled with blood-red cracks. Flames spurted from her clothes.

"Enough," I said, stumbling past the edge of the darkness. I couldn't watch a person die that way, regardless of what they'd done.

The back of my neck was already burnt. In the strong sunlight, it felt as though someone was pouring boiling water on it. I snarled as it smoked and cracked. Famine had stopped screaming. Most of her skin had crumbled away. When I picked her up, my fingertips hissed. She weighed nothing. I quickly scrambled back to the shadows.

Min raised the *katana*. "She must be destroyed."

The bounty hunter drew a pistol. "Min is right. If she's raised up . . . well, I can't have anyone messin' with my mind like that again."

"You broke her hold once," I said. "After that, she can't make you do anything."

"It was you who broke her hold," Min said. The way her eyes held mine, I wasn't certain if this was a question.

"I tried to remove your mark," I said, "but it wouldn't come off."

"The mark is the Changeling's," she said. "Famine's voice is a separate matter. She speaks for him when he wills it, but the power to compel is hers alone. You broke that power in the caves."

"I couldn't have," I said. "I did nothing . . . I just held your hand. Maybe something happened when you went unconscious, or maybe it was the pain. But it wasn't me."

Min and the bounty hunter looked at each other for a few seconds, then she handed me the *katana*. "That's not how we see it."

The bounty hunter holstered his pistol. His eyes fell to Famine's corpse. "What will you do with her?"

"I don't know," I said. "She might have information we can use against the Changeling."

"Please use it quickly," Min said. "We still bear his mark." She held up her hand. The rune was covered, but it bled through the cloth so that the strange symbol was visible once more. "When he finds us, he will kill us."

"Then we'd better make sure he doesn't find you."

Min smiled, then stepped back and hissed. The bounty hunter drew both guns and pointed them past my shoulder. I turned. Vincent was standing behind me. He looked ferocious. There was still blood on his pants and under his nails from his fight with Tamerlane.

"It's all right," I said. "He won't harm you."

The vampires retreated to the edge of the hole. I understood. Fear of the werewolf was in our blood.

Min took a step back and dropped out of sight.

The bounty hunter hesitated. "We'll be fugitives now. Outlaws with no rights."

"Not for long," I promised.

He flashed me a quick military salute, then stepped back into the darkness.

Vincent growled. "Why did you let them go? We've got to kill those freaks."

"Not those two."

"What's so special about them?"

"They just saved my life," I said.

His eyes fell to the corpse in my arms. "Who's that?"

"Elizabeth Bathory."

His upper lip quivered, exposing a long canine. "She's the worst of them. We should toss her in the sunlight."

"We can't. She has information we're going to need."

I shifted Famine in my arms. My fingers were burnt and

blistered. I was all but useless. When I tried to move, a wave of nausea nearly floored me.

"You okay?"

I wasn't, but I had other things to worry about. "What about Luna? Is she all right?"

"Vlad says she'll be fine once we get more blood."

"Where is she?"

"With the others. They're on the Pest side under a pub. It smells bad there. The others don't mind, but I don't like it."

"Is Charlie there?"

"Yeah. Vlad brought him through the shadows. His lungs and throat are a mess, but he'll be okay."

"And the Baptist?"

Vinny shrugged. "Nobody saw him. Hopefully, he's not dead." He stood on the lip of the hole and looked in. "We should go. Someone might come down here to park."

"Which way?"

"Not down there." He walked over to a pile of I-beams and tore the tarpaulin off them. "We've got to go up into the sun."

CHAPTER 51

A VALUABLE DISCOVERY

VINCENT SPREAD THE tarp over me, then slipped under the front edge so he could hold it in place. "There's a hole outside that leads to another bunch of tunnels. They're safer. It's not too far."

I felt a moment's apprehension. Perhaps Vlad's paranoia was rubbing off on me, but the fear that Vincent might tear the tarp away once we were in the sun was suddenly very real. He was very close to Vlad, who wasn't exactly the president of my fan club, and his feelings for Luna were obvious.

"You sure you want to take her?" His eyes fell to Famine's scorched body. "If you get sun-shock and drop her, I'm not pickin' her up."

I'd never heard the term sun-shock, but it was easy to guess the meaning. "I'll manage," I said. "Lead away."

He took off at an easy run. I did fine until we got outside in the full light. It was like having my skin scrubbed with sandpaper. I thought I was going to combust. At the edge of the lot was a short concrete wall we had to jump. The tarp rose

291

like a parachute and my hair caught fire. I landed on a well-groomed lawn. One of the Countess's hands snapped off and vanished in a flash of flame. Just ahead, a section of earth had collapsed into one of the caves. The shade was like a magnet. I jumped down and bolted from the light. My hands were black, cracked and bleeding.

I laid Famine down against the cold stone. Her skin and outer tissue had all burned away. A trickle of water dribbled down one of the jagged walls. My skin hissed when I filled my hands and doused my face. The same thing happened when I splashed it over her. Moaning, I collapsed against the wall.

"We can't stop here. Those freaks haven't reached this section, but if one does and starts screaming . . ."

"I'm not worried about the horde," I said. "With Famine dead, they won't be the same crew of mindless personality disorders we saw earlier."

"Maybe not. But it doesn't mean they're on our side."

He had a good point.

Standing was difficult, but I made my way along, wincing, with Famine's corpse cradled delicately in my arms. My burns started to heal, but not as quickly as they should have. I needed blood and a long rest. My skin soon grew itchy. I wanted to scratch myself raw. It slowed me to a snail's pace, which agitated Vincent. He kept running ahead and then doubling back, as if it might hurry me along.

"I'm going to go ahead," he said finally. "It's not good to keep Vlad waiting."

He took off.

A few minutes later, I heard the grating sound of Vlad's dragon armour. It was still coated with ash and dust. "We need to keep moving," he said. "Pestilence is still looking for us." The Dragon Blade was resting on his shoulder. There was energy in his expression and movements that had been missing earlier, and his skin colour had returned.

"You've fed," I said.

"Yes. Miklos brought several of his kin so that you can feed as well. Once you are restored, we will rejoin the others and plan our next move." His eyes passed from me to the Countess. "Bathory was depraved in life. She has never been anything but a deranged narcissist. You should have let her burn."

I was tired and forgot to shield my thoughts: namely, that men would have said he was just as depraved, but when I'd had the chance to destroy him, I hadn't.

He shifted so he was right in front of me, the tip of his sword at my throat. I had to back up to the cave wall to keep from being cut open. The Changeling's *truth-in-small-bites* comment came to mind. Even tiny morsels could be bitter to swallow, I supposed. The only sound in the cave was the rasp of his breath as he considered what to do.

"You would not have survived in my time," he said. "Your enemies would have buried you alive."

What could I say to that? It was probably true. But at least I would have died with a clear conscience.

Vlad snorted, then lowered his blade and shifted away. I followed, carrying the Countess, until we reached the area where Miklos was waiting. He was wearing night-vision goggles. Two young girls were huddled nearby. Identical twins. Their hair had been braided down the sides and they were wearing dresses with puffy sleeves that reminded me of two old-fashioned dolls. Both were pale. In the darkness, neither of them could see. Their expressions were blank, as though they were sleepwalking. The smell of blood was in the air.

Hunger knotted my stomach. I shifted Famine's body so I could scratch at my neck. Vlad said something and Miklos walked over. He was holding a chalice. When he spoke, his accent was thick, and his words unusually formal, so it took me a moment to figure out what he'd said.

"From Draculista to Draculista. Please accept the blood of my kin. May it preserve you through the ages."

I thanked him and raised the cup. The smell was intoxicating. It took every ounce of my willpower not to drink. Instead, I held the chalice over Famine's mouth and let the blood dribble in. Miklos's solemn expression turned to astonishment, then anger. He shouted something to Vlad, then tried to take the cup away. I pushed him back gently, but the cave floor was damp and slick, and he lost his footing.

"Have you lost your wits?" Vlad snapped. "This man is a direct descendant of my house!" He grabbed hold of my arm, but I planted my foot in his midsection and pushed him back. He drew the Dragon Blade and closed in.

"Wait!" I shouted. "Look."

He planted the tip of his sword against my chest but kept his eyes on Famine. Where the blood touched her, she was regenerating. It was a fascinating sight, and Vlad, despite his anger, was captivated.

"We need to question her," I said. "She'll have information about the Changeling, and she might know what has happened to the Baptist."

Famine's skin had burned away, so we saw her muscles first. They turned pink, and then red. Skin formed. It was seethrough at first, like cellophane, but it quickly turned to alabaster. But that wasn't what caught my eye. I saw what wasn't there. Then she coughed. The sound woke both girls, who started shrieking. Miklos scampered back to offer them what comfort he could. The Countess started to thrash as though she were on fire again. Most of her skin was still missing. She screamed. The power within her voice was phenomenal. I would have blacked out, but Vlad stepped in and drove the Dragon Blade through her heart. Her scream faded to a whisper and her limbs stopped moving. He drew the blade out and poised it as if to cleave her head off. I stepped in the way.

"Not everyone is worth saving," he said.

It hardly mattered. He'd put an end to things, at least for now. But we had learned something of immeasurable value. "There's not a mark on her," I said.

Vlad quietly examined her corpse. Her body was still charred in the areas untouched by blood, but around her neck, the burns were gone and the skin was white and free of blemishes. There wasn't a trace of the Changeling's runes anywhere.

CHAPTER 52

THE GRAVE

"DO YOU KNOW what this means?" I asked.

Vlad didn't answer me. Miklos was trying to comfort his children. The two men spoke for a moment in what I guessed was Romanian. Then Vlad shifted closer, the Dragon Blade hanging loosely in one hand.

"Miklos is more than just my servant. He is our host. To spurn the gift of his daughters' blood is a grave insult. Laying hands on him in anger is many times worse. The pub where your friends are resting is his establishment. He has forbidden you to enter. I will try to change his mind and repair some of the damage you have done. Until that happens, you must wait here. I will return at sunset. You should be safe, so long as you don't stray." He shifted beside Miklos and whispered something, then sent him and his daughters on ahead. "Sunset," he added. Then he was gone.

I found the driest bit of floor and lay down. Despite the tension surrounding Vlad's departure, my thoughts were hopeful. If the sun had removed Famine's mark, the same might have happened for Tiptoft. I wondered if that might help him remember who he was, or rather, who I wanted him to be.

Sleep came quickly. I didn't stir until Vlad nudged me with his boot. I stretched and yawned, then sat up. He was holding a spade in each hand.

"Night has fallen," he said. "We must go."

I inspected my hands. The skin was still pink and scarred. I needed blood. "Are we meeting the others?"

"Not yet. There is a person we have to find." He put a hand under my arm to help me up, then handed me a spade. "Come. We have some digging to do."

We left Famine's body under a pile of stones. Once the cairn was finished, he led me deeper into the caves until we were well outside the city. He seemed remarkably calm. I searched for signs of yesterday's anger, but none were evident.

Eventually, the cave we followed opened on a steep bank at a bend in the river. I could still see the distant lights of Buda and Pest rippling on the water.

"Where are the others?" I asked.

"Back in the city," he said. "They have placed their faith in us. We must not fail them."

"What about the Changeling?" I asked. "And the Horsemen?"

"Gone to lick their wounds, I would imagine."

"And the Baptist?"

"Probably dead."

He led me to a dirt road set within a forest of very young trees. They looked cold and naked in the winter air. Vlad had oiled his armour. He wasn't shifting; he walked with quiet, carefully measured steps. He pulled up suddenly and turned to his left, then started counting paces. His eyes scanned the dead leaves littering the ground.

"There," he said, pointing to a large rock that rose several feet from the earth.

We walked over to it, then he stood on top and faced south. Ten paces later, in an open area between two oaks, he rammed his shovel into the ground. I went to work beside him. The top layer of earth was frozen, so our progress was slow. For a time neither of us spoke, then my curiosity got the better of me.

"Who are we looking for?" I asked.

Vlad didn't answer. His spade hit a rock and sparked. He jumped down into the shallow, man-sized hole we'd dug and pried the large stone loose with his thick fingers. It must have weighed several hundred pounds, but he hefted it with ease.

"The Changeling has destroyed the undead vampires I had resting in Curtea de Arges, Castle Dracula, Fagaras, Giurgiu, St. George's in Tirgoviste and Suceava. They are gone, and with them the talents I might have possessed. Of my sanctuaries, none remain that are safe. All of my former allies are either dead or have changed sides, with the exception of your friends, who in our world are little more than children. All I really have left is Ophelia. When I complete the antidote, she will take her rightful place with me. It will be as it once was, before you and your wretched father ruined everything."

The hackles on my neck rose. Vlad reached behind his back and removed a tranquilizer rifle from under his cloak.

"It was clear to me as we entered the cave to meet the Baptist that she cared more for your safety than for mine. I cannot risk that she might turn from me to you at some time when my life is in the balance. I cannot have her loyalty divided."

He pointed the gun at me and pulled the trigger.

Shrish.

I tried to jump out of the way, but I was so surprised I forgot to shield my thoughts. One of my legs spasmed. This was Vlad's doing. The dart hit the fleshy part of my throat. I grew dizzy, then collapsed face down into the hole we'd dug. I couldn't move.

"I replaced the tranquilizer with a paralytic agent," Vlad said. "I didn't want you to sleep through this." He flipped me over and started shovelling dirt onto me.

"I hope you can forgive me for allowing the Changeling to abduct you. Istvan was already working with him closely, and I thought the offer of you and Castle Dracula might further their relationship, but the Changeling is too cautious. He kept Istvan at arm's length and, to my chagrin, neither killed you nor forced you to take his mark. It is obvious that he sent you back only to get to Ophelia and me."

The moon was rising. Vlad was pensive, and for a time I heard nothing but the scrape of his shovel as he piled more dirt on me. With each passing moment, my distress grew until it seemed it would crush me. I couldn't move. I was completely helpless. And I was going to die. This alone wouldn't have scared me, as I'd been to the tunnel of light and knew it for what it was, a place of healing. But there is an instinct to survive in all living things, and coupled with this was a bitter sense of failure, and of being used and deceived and betrayed. My spirit railed against the injustice of it, and against my powerlessness. And against the awful truth that I'd never see my friends again. That neither Luna nor Charlie would ever know that I was stuck in a hole, or that Vlad had put me there. It seemed that once I was buried, the truth would be buried with me. If I'd been able, I would have screamed murder until the sky cracked open.

"I never believed in the prophecy," Vlad said at last. "Not even when it was applied to me centuries ago. The son of a great hunter. An orphan who would be born again. Nonsense. Or so I thought. But Vincent has made a believer of me. I told you that you would regret keeping him alive."

I regretted a lot of things, but raising Vincent after his father's death wasn't one of them. I only wished he could have been there so he could see Vlad for the monster he was.

"I think he has taken quite a liking to Luna. I must confess, I have encouraged this attachment where I could. It will help her deal with the pain of your death. And once they are closer, it will give me another tool with which to leverage him. You must admit, he is certainly better at taking care of her. You seem to have developed the nasty habit of dying just when you're needed most."

He stopped shovelling. One side of his mouth rose in a smile. "You have only yourself to blame. Of what use are you to me if you would rather save my enemies than kill them?"

If I could have spoken I would have quoted Abraham Lincoln: "Do I not destroy my enemies when I make them my friends?" Mr. Entwistle had taught me that. No sooner did I think the words than I realized how badly I'd taken this advice to heart. I'd never made any sincere effort to befriend Vlad. I hadn't forgiven him, nor had I expressed any gratitude for his keeping my friends and me alive. Had I acted differently, I might not have been in this mess.

"You fool yourself," Vlad said. "Friendship for men like me is impossible. The entire relationship is based on equality, and none are my equal."

He threw a shovelful of dirt on my face. I tried to close my eyes, but my lids were paralyzed, like the rest of me. More dirt fell. The night sky disappeared. The sound of the shovel was muted as soil filled my ears. My next breath was nothing but dirt. Some air snuck in, but not enough. What little oxygen I had trapped in my lungs soon disappeared. Then the pressure in my chest and head was too much and I passed out to the muffled sound of Vlad patting down the soil of my grave.

CHAPTER 53

LÚ-YÍNG, THE
SHADOW ROAD

I'M SURE DYING can be terrifying for those who've never tried it, but the act itself is surprisingly simple. Your heart stops and you go to the light. I expected the warmth of it to surround me, but it didn't. I wondered if this meant I was undead again. Stuck once more between life and death.

I felt an odd pressure against my chest and I began to sink. I thought of something Vlad had said, that not all who died went to the light. It occurred to me as I sank into the dark earth that I didn't deserve to go to the tunnel. On the ship, *L'Esprit Sauvage*, I'd broken a promise to myself. I had killed. And I'd done nothing to atone for it.

As I sank, my image stretched behind me. It was similar to the streak you see in a photograph if a person moves while it's being taken, only the trail I left was like a black flame. Two hands were clasped around my torso. Like my body, they seemed to blaze with a dark energy.

Don't panic, youngblood, a man said. *You're in good hands.* I recognized the dry crackle of his voice but couldn't remember his name. A moment later, my feet touched down on solid rock. Everything around me was shades of black. Fissures, spires, tunnels and jagged edges. If you took the earth, stripped it of soil, water and life, then blasted it half to smithereens and sucked out all the colour, it would have looked just like this. Something like ash floated in the air. It was so thick, I couldn't see more than a dozen feet in any direction.

A bald figure took shape beside me. He stood no higher than my shoulder. Long eyebrows floated over his eyeless orbits. Like me, he glowed black, though his clothes were etched with lines of silver, like a photo negative.

"Is this hell?" I asked him.

"Not unless we took a wrong turn somewhere."

"So I'm still alive?"

"I hope so. Because if you're dead then so am I, and I've missed my last chance to visit Walt Disney World."

I squinted to see better through the ash, but it was no use. "What is this place?"

"It is a plane of existence that intersects with our own. A realm of negative energy."

"What does that mean?"

"You don't need to know, youngblood. You just need to listen." He took me by the arm. "But first things first. Do you know who I am?"

I shook my head.

"Do you know who *you* are?"

I thought for a moment. Nothing came to mind.

"Well then, son of the hunter, remember . . ."

Darkness stretched from his mind and enveloped me. Images swam before my mind's eye. I saw a city of stone through the eyes of a child. I reached a fallen temple. My father was there, buried under pieces of the roof. Devastated and confused, I ran until I saw two red eyes staring at me from the darkness. A creature darted out and bit me. Pain and death followed. Later I was in a mental ward, my arms strapped behind my back. I was ravenous and tried to bite a nurse. Then Ophelia arrived and made everything all right. When I was older, she trusted me to leave the ward. So I did. And I ran, and ran, and ran. My feet were a blur. Other images swam through my head. Dreams of my father. My first visit from Maximilian. Charlie's cottage. Meeting Luna. How could I have forgotten someone so beautiful? Vrolok, who was really Vlad. Mr. Entwistle. Meeting Baoh on the Dream Road. Facing Hyde in the Warsaw Caves. Iron Spike Enterprises collapsing. Suki dying. My whole life played out for me in seconds.

"Do you remember now?" Baoh asked.

"Yeah, I do."

"Well then, Zachariah, it is time for you to fulfill your destiny."

He made it sound so easy. "Isn't my body buried in a hole?"

"You *were* buried," Baoh answered. "But I have moved you. Does the ground not feel solid under your feet?"

I shifted my weight and felt the same pressure I would have anywhere else.

"You are here in body and spirit. We just need to find the right doorway and send you back."

"What do you mean, doorway? What's going on here? Why did you bring me here if we're just going to leave?"

"Think of this as a shortcut." He pointed to a textured wall of rock beside us. A section of it looked smoother than it should have, as if someone had sanded it flat. "Can you see through that? You are not a shadow-jumper, so your vision may be impaired here."

When I moved closer to the wall, I could see that the smooth patch was really an opening. It led to another cave, one that looked strangely distant, as if the threshold between where I was and where I was looking contained an invisible lens that pushed the image farther away.

"Yes, I can see another cave. Why does it look like that?"

"The cave appears distant because it is not actually here."

"Then where is it?"

"It is back in the real world, the world of matter and light."

"How do I get back?"

"You shadow-jump. You have seen Pestilence do this, eh? Jump from shadow to shadow."

I had seen him do it. Vlad, too. I'd never understood how.

Baoh snickered, then stepped forward. As he passed through the opening, he stretched and shrank so that by the time he had taken one step and turned around it was as though he had been transported to a place that was a good hundred feet away. He waved. I raised my hand. A second later he returned. First his foot, then the rest of him grew large as he stretched back through the portal. He did it in one step. It was the most bizarre thing I'd ever seen.

"How do you do that?"

"I have the right blood," he answered. "Were you so blessed, you would see shadows for what they truly are: not just areas sheltered from light, but doorways that lead from our physical plane of existence to where you stand now."

"And where is that, exactly?"

"This place has many names. Most would mean nothing to you. I call it Lú-Yíng, the Shadow Road, although it is really a whole world unto itself. A place of perpetual darkness. The perfect refuge for creatures of the night."

He reached his hand through the shadow-portal. I saw it emerge in the distant cave, a hundred feet away again, connected to an arm stretched so far it would have made Plastic Man jealous.

"So now you know the secret of shadow-jumping. One does not move from shadow to shadow. One moves from one world to another, using shadows as the door."

"Can you teach me how?"

"There isn't time. The Changeling's servants have overrun all of Vlad's strongholds. The Impaler is desperate. Without Ophelia, he will become his worst self. This has happened before. You know the consequences well enough."

I did.

"The Changeling—you must face him, too."

I couldn't confront either of them on my own. "Are you coming with me?"

"I cannot. One does not survive as long as I have by taking sides."

"But you're taking sides now!"

He placed a finger over his mouth and glanced over his shoulder. "What happens in the world of shadows stays in the world of shadows, eh?"

"What about the Baptist? Could he help me?"

Baoh jumped as if I'd kicked him in the pants. "The Baptist? Don't be crazy. The Changeling *is* the Baptist. Didn't you know?"

I stood in silence for a moment, scanning his face for signs of uncertainty. "You must be mistaken. The Baptist has been preaching about the Messiah."

"Yes," Baoh agreed. "It is how he roots out those vampires who are in hiding. Especially the young. They know they aren't safe from Vlad or the Changeling, so they stay underground. Disguised as the Baptist, he wins their confidence. Once they are comfortable enough to arrange a meeting, he sends the Horsemen to kill them."

This must have been wrong. The Baptist was one of the good guys. He'd saved me from the Horsemen on the ship in

Montreal, and he had helped me at Ophelia's trial. "That can't be right."

"We cannot linger for a debate, Zachariah. We aren't the only ones who travel through this world. And there's nothing to drink here. You look like you could use a stiff one. I know I could. Come." His dark body began to shift at the edges.

"Where are we going?"

"We need to find the right door," he said. "I need to get you some help."

His dark essence flared, then began to shimmer. Pale silver lines rippled through the fabric of his clothing. A second later, he rose off the ground and stretched out like a man taking flight.

"You have travelled as a night stalker, eh? Travelling the Shadow Road is not much different. The body will act as the mind wills. Hurry. Time is precious."

I wasn't certain what to do. I felt just as solid and heavy as I did in the real world. Only my appearance had changed.

"Imagine that you are weightless. A being of light and darkness floating in a world without gravity."

He reached down. I took his hand. He pulled gently and I rose into the air.

"This way." He nodded ahead, then started to drift, his body undulating as though caught in some kind of ethereal current.

I willed my body to follow, and it did, just as he'd said it would. A thrill rippled through me. I was flying again, just as I had the night of Ophelia's trial.

Baoh led me past spires of rock into a tunnel so choked with ash my sight was limited to a few paces. He moved without hesitation, slowing only once to let a group of shadows flit past. They were small, globular shapes that stretched and flattened, then curled up slowly, flattening again at regular intervals to propel themselves through the ether.

"Denizens of the shadow world," Baoh said. "These ones are harmless, but that is not always the case."

Once they were past, he led me down another tunnel, then slowed and dropped to his feet. We had reached another opening, an irregularly shaped window through which I could see back into the normal world.

"So that's a shadow?" I said, pointing to the opening.

"On the other side, yes. But to those who shadow-jump, it is a portal that leads to and from the Shadow Road."

I moved closer and peered through the shadow-portal. On the other side was a cave. Lying on the rocks was a corpse.

"Is that a vampire?" I asked.

"Yes."

"What am I supposed to do?"

"Do what is right."

"Could you be more specific?"

"That cave is near the Royal Palace. It will lead you to your friends. Go now and find them."

"And what about that dead vampire?"

"You will need to find blood."

I didn't have any leads, and I'm not certain I would have used any to revive a stranger. "Who is it?"

Baoh didn't answer. He was looking over his shoulder. "Pestilence is coming," he whispered.

I glanced over my shoulder. A dark cloud was approaching.

"It is his essence you see—his evil."

I have no idea how Baoh recognized him. There was nothing human about the thing that slithered closer. It looked more like a billowing eel than a person. I heard a gargling hiss as it wormed its way towards us. When it touched down on the ground, it assumed the familiar shape of Pestilence, although he retained a loose, ethereal quality that made me think of a

307

ghost that was somehow both shadow and vapour. His face was large in proportion to his body and undulated at the edges as he eyed us both.

Baoh took a step back. Like Pestilence, the edges of him were shifting.

Pestilence laughed. Blood gargled in his mouth. It didn't take long for me to figure out the source of his amusement. Baoh was planning to run.

CHAPTER 54

DUELLING SHADOWS

BAOH'S BODY FADED until he was nothing more than a thin wisp of shadow outlined in silver. Then, like a cold breath on a winter day, he disappeared completely, leaving me alone with Pestilence.

You are not alone, Baoh said. *Go through the portal. I will lure him from here. Do not linger. There are many creatures in the world of shadows more dangerous than vampires.*

What about you? I asked.

Baoh floats like a butterfly but stings like a bee. He is not easily caught. We will meet again. Go.

Although I could no longer see him, I felt a gentle pressure push me through the opening. A weird stretching sensation followed, similar to what I'd experienced when he'd dragged me from the grave, only this was much faster. My feet were suddenly slipping on hard stone. Colour and light returned. I had to jump sideways to avoid a torch that was stuck in the floor. Curling tendrils of smoke gathered in a sooty cloud just under the ceiling, drifting slowly in a draft from farther down the tunnel.

I turned back to the portal. It was like looking the wrong way through a peephole. The images beyond were so small I could scarcely resolve them. Two shadows—one black, one streaked with silver—coiled around one another like smoke, morphing through a dizzying array of shapes. The melee was unlike anything I'd ever seen. Snake versus crane. Crocodile versus shark. Urchin and octopus. Spear and rope. Spider and hydra. Mantis and fish. Wasp and lion. Fist and shield. Bear and dragon. Eagle and tiger. Each permutation lasted only an instant and left me with no real sense of who had the upper hand. For a full minute, I stared. Then the shadow etched in silver exploded into a train of butterflies that scattered in all directions so that only the black cloud remained.

Pestilence waited a moment, then his thin-fingered hands reached out of the shadows. I took a step back and gasped as the torch in the floor scorched my hand. I'd forgotten about it. As he pulled himself into the room, I grabbed it and shoved it at him. Light spread over the rock, closing the portal and trapping his legs on the Shadow Road. He hissed in anger and started squirming. The torch flickered in my hand. In his shifting shadow I caught a glimpse of something moving towards him. It was a butterfly. Following right behind, like a fish chasing a lure, was something that looked like a giant eel. It was larger than a whale, but moving twice as quickly; the squeamish, sinuous rhythm of its body was weird and otherworldly. Then I caught a glimpse of its head—a thick, tube-like opening, ringed with hooks and spines and rows of pointed teeth—and my whole body flared with a kind of terror I didn't think was possible.

Pestilence's shadow continued to shift as my torch flared in the drafty cave. It left enough of a door to the Shadow Road that he was able to wiggle forward, but not quickly enough.

The worm-like creature lunged for the butterfly. Baoh swerved deftly aside so the mouth struck Pestilence instead. It caught one leg just as he was about to pull himself clear. The Horseman screamed and flailed. Bones cracked. Flesh ripped. His finger-nails gouged tracks in the rock as he was pulled out of sight, leaving a profound silence behind.

It was a few seconds before I could move. My hands were trembling and my heart beat so fiercely it shook my armour. I held the torch in front of me like a sword, then gave every shadow in sight a light bath. After a moment, I realized how silly this was. If anything like that giant worm were capable of crossing into this world, human history would have been painfully short.

I waited, hoping Baoh would appear. After a few moments it was clear that, true to his word, he wasn't taking sides. Twelve hundred years of habit was obviously hard to break. I took a deep breath, pushed that disappointment from my mind and turned my attention to the dead vampire on the floor. The corpse was tall and wrapped in a funeral shroud. I folded the top back to see the face, which I recognized despite his burns. Weathered features. Icy blue eyes. Long black hair streaked with white and grey, just like his whiskers. And without a trace of the Changeling's mark on his forehead.

CHAPTER 55

THE RETURN OF JOHN ENTWISTLE

JOHN WAS LIGHTER than he should have been, a sure sign that it was going to take a lot of blood to bring him back. I picked him up and started following the draft, knowing it would lead to fresh air. The cave wound past other tunnels, then came to a dead end. I turned, thinking I'd try another branch, then saw several shapes moving towards me. They were vampires.

I set John's body down and stepped in front of it, my hand on my sword. Three vampires became four, then five. The closest to me was Min. The bounty hunter was behind her. He turned back to the others, then spoke in a language I didn't understand.

"You have returned," Min said.

"I have."

Her luminescent green eyes wandered over me.

"Are you sure it's him?" the bounty hunter asked her.

She reached out to shake my hand. When I took it, she pulled me sideways and used her other hand to draw out my *katana*.

"Same sword," she said. "If he's the Changeling, our hopes are already dashed."

He looked satisfied.

"The Changeling hasn't come for you?" I asked.

"No," Min said. "But many others have gone missing. Our hope is they have fled, but we suspect he has killed them. Rumour has it he now searches for his Horsemen, but they are gone."

"They're more than gone. They're dead. All of them."

She pushed my sword back into the sheath and flashed a dangerous smile. "So you *are* the Messiah?"

I felt my face redden. "I'm just trying to stay alive."

"We can help." She glanced at the bounty hunter. "Others are waiting ahead. Hassan can lead you to them. I will keep watch." She moved towards the shadows. I felt a newfound respect for her, knowing what might be waiting on the other side.

"Be careful."

I picked up John's body and fell in step behind the Arabian Elvis, Hassan. Although he was still dressed in black like the others, he'd smoothed his hair back in a coif that made him look more like his former self. He led me down a low-ceilinged tunnel to a wider space where a larger group was waiting. All of them had bound cloth around their foreheads or hands to cover their marks.

"Is it him?" one asked.

"He has the boy's trappings," Hassan answered. He reached to his belt and pulled out a curved dagger. "Hold still." He raised the tip to my cheek, made a small scratch and sniffed the blade. "*Happy ending.* He's a youngblood." He winked at me. "Sorry . . . tough crowd."

I understood.

"Who's that?" One pointed to the corpse in my arms.

"Death," said another.

Several vampires hissed.

Hassan backed up a step and drew his automatics. Two red dots from his laser sightings fixed themselves on John's head. "Is that the Changeling's first in command?"

"He was," I said.

Other vampires rose from where they were resting and moved closer. I heard snatches of conversation. None of them were in English, but the gist of them was clear. They wanted his head on a platter.

"*Fool, Fool, Fool.*" Hassan's purple eyes were intense.

I drew my *katana* and cut a small gully across Mr. Entwistle's wrist. As I feared, the tissue was completely dry. "I'm going to need as much blood as you have."

"To bring him back?" Hassan said. "That's madness. He'll kill us all. He bears the mark. We all do."

"His mark is gone," I said. "It burned off in the sun."

He inspected John's forehead carefully. "So it can be done!"

"It can."

"And when he comes back, he will help us?"

"I hope so."

"And if not?"

I considered my options. "If he's still Death when he wakes up, then I'll have to kill him."

HASSAN DIDN'T TELL me where the blood came from, and I didn't ask. We doused John with it, then poured it down his throat until two crimson ribbons spilled down the sides of his cheeks. The burns on his skin disappeared, then we hit that magical threshold and, presto, his eyelids fluttered, his chest heaved and his heart started up. A second later he coughed up a mouthful of blood. His fingers closed over a rock and he broke it in his hand. A low moan followed and he opened his milky-blue eyes. For a few moments he stared at the ceiling, then he raised his head just long enough to size us up.

"I take it I'm not in Kansas any more."

The air was tense. Most present were nervous. Some were angry. I was guessing Tiptoft hadn't been a gentle master.

"Do you have any of the good stuff, boy?"

"No," I said. "We've given you all the blood we have."

He closed his eyes and let his head fall back. "I don't mean blood, damn it. I need a shot of whisky."

CHAPTER 56

CATCHING UP

THE SUNLIGHT HAD burned the rune from John's forehead, but when he looked at me, it was clear he had no idea who I was. Everything else was as it should have been. His voice, his mannerisms, his quiet confidence. He was surrounded by strangers, some of whom looked as though they'd just crawled out of the abyss, but he was as relaxed as a tourist in a spa.

"Do you know who you are?" I asked.

His eyes passed over us. "King of the Under-dwellers?" He thought about it for a few more seconds. "Well, I'm sure if it's important, it will come back to me." He reached up and grabbed my arm, then pulled himself to his feet. It took him a moment to adjust to his new elevation, then he patted the top of his head. "Where's my lucky hat?" He reached for his silver flask—one he kept in the pocket of a coat he was no longer wearing. He looked at me and his eyes narrowed. "Who are you? And what have you done to me?"

No one moved. Hassan and the others were watching us closely.

"You died in the sun," I said. "It removed the Changeling's

mark. We gave you blood and it brought you back. And here we are."

He seemed to digest this slowly. His face was flat and his eyes were distant.

"We need your help," I said.

He reached for his missing hat again, then looked down to where his coat pocket and liquor should have been. "Trouble with the coal miners' union?"

"Not exactly."

"Where are we?"

"Budapest. In the caves near the Royal Palace."

"What is it with vampires and caves?"

I had no idea. At least it was dark.

"How long have I been asleep?" he asked.

"Less than a day. And you weren't asleep. You were dead." I turned to Hassan. "Last I heard, my friends were in Pest hiding under a pub. Can you find out where?"

He nodded curtly. "Consider it done." He peered into the shadows and signalled with a flick of his finger. Min stepped into the light.

"Vlad is with them," I added, "so be careful."

He grunted an affirmative, then he and Min started barking orders in about twenty different languages. The horde dispersed in an instant. A few stayed back, including Hassan, who directed them to fan out in a protective pocket around John and me.

"Will you help us?" I asked him again. "I need to find my friends and get them out of harm's way. They're with Vlad Dracula."

"So the Impaler is alive again?"

"He is."

"And he has your friends?"

"He does."

"And they're under a pub?"

"Yeah."

He clapped me on the back. "Well, let's hope they're still serving."

THERE WAS MUCH to explain and little time. Mr. Entwistle listened intently as we moved through the matrix of caves. Each time we came to a new branch or tunnel, someone would be waiting to point us in the right direction. I started by telling him how we'd met—that he'd crashed a stolen police motorcycle through the front doors of the Nicholls Ward when I'd been a patient there.

"I have no memory of this, boy," he said. "But I have a good nose for people. I trust what you're saying is true. What name did I go by then?"

"Mr. Entwistle."

His forehead knotted. "Mr. Entwistle? I never go by *mister*. Too impersonal. It's always John." Then his face lit up. "Yeah, John Entwistle, the bass player from The Who. Always liked their music." He sidestepped a cluster of stalagmites. "Go on."

"You died fighting a werewolf." I went on to explain how he'd been buried in a cave-in and had then been dug up and resurrected by the Changeling. Somehow, he'd reverted back to an earlier persona, John Tiptoft, the Butcher of England.

"That sounds impossible," he said. "I put that man behind me centuries ago."

"The Changeling is powerful. The vampires you saw when you woke up were followers of his until last night."

I told him about the Countess Bathory. How she had enslaved them, before Min and Hassan cast her into the light. "Her death

318

freed the others. Most have run away or been killed. There don't seem to be many left."

"And Elza Bathory was behind it . . ." He frowned. "She's been nothing but dust and bones for centuries, boy, and should have been left that way."

That's basically what she was, dust and bones, with a lot of char on top.

"Why don't I remember any of this?" he said. "I used to have a brain like a sponge."

"Maybe death wrung it clean."

"Maybe," he said. "Names would help. You mentioned Vlad. Who else is with him?"

When I mentioned my friends, I got nothing but a vacant stare. It was different when I told him about the Changeling and his Horsemen. His forehead became a mess of wrinkles.

"Elza's bad enough, but a vampire would have to be nine-tenths crazy and one-tenth mental to bring back vampires like Timur and de Sade."

"The Changeling's not crazy," I said. "Cold-blooded maybe, but not insane. Your transformation into Tiptoft would have been his work." I then explained how the Changeling read minds and used the information to imitate people. Lastly, I mentioned his venom. "If he kills you, your death is permanent."

"Boy, a vampire would have to be older than Rome to do half of what you're saying. How much of this are you certain of?"

"All of it."

John stood thinking, his eyes roaming over the cave floor. We were getting closer to the surface. The air wasn't as heavy, and the mouldy smell of the earth was mixing with the odour of cold, wet concrete.

"I sense you aren't lying, but perhaps you were deceived. A

319

vampire with that kind of power and influence could have top-pled Vlad and his Coven centuries ago."

"So why didn't he?"

"There's only one reason I can think of. He didn't want to." He grumbled something under his breath. "What does it all mean, boy?"

I had no answer for him. It seemed our conversation was over anyway. Min appeared and waved us ahead. "Your friends have left the pub. We believe they are coming here."

John let out a disappointed grumble. "Left the pub? Ahhh! Well, there's no helping it, I suppose." His eyes wandered up the tunnel. "Can we get out of here? I'm starting to feel like a corpse in a coffin."

We travelled farther along until we reached the hole Vincent and I had used to get underground. A patch of sky was visible above, overcast and backlit by a hazy half moon. John bent his legs and jumped through the opening. I'd forgotten what an amazing leaper he was. I followed and was surprised to discover myself in the ruins of an old building. There was no roof, just the footprints of the old rooms. Around these were the stunted remains of ancient brick and stone walls, two or three feet in height. A light dusting of snow covered everything. I spied a few vampires keeping watch at either end of the lot. Several more were on the rooftop of the neighbouring Royal Palace. Otherwise, the place was like a ghost town.

The sounds of traffic drifted over from the far side of the building. I tested the air, but all I could smell was snow and wet brick. Then my ears caught the whir of helicopter blades. One of the vampires on the palace roof was pointing towards the river. I drew my *katana*.

John dropped to the ground in the shadow of a ruined wall, then pulled me down beside him. "Put that away. The metal shines like a beacon."

I slid the blade back in the sheath, then raised my head above the wall.

"That's a US Battlehawk!" he said, surprised. "Looks like it's had some custom work done."

I didn't know anything about that, but there was no mistaking the helicopter my uncle had given Vlad. The landing gear was out. It settled on the grass between several sets of paved walkways in the courtyard of the Royal Palace.

Vlad stepped from the cabin. He was carrying the Dragon Blade. Luna followed. My stomach tightened. She turned towards us and for a moment I had a window to catch her attention, then Vlad waved her towards the statue of Matthias Corvinus, still standing vigil in his hunting garb. Vlad stood out in the open and stared up at the roof. Hopefully, the vampires who had been keeping watch earlier had the sense to get out of harm's way.

Charlie and Vincent were still aboard the helicopter. Each was perched behind a Gatling gun.

"Better sit tight," John said. "Those are Dillon M134s, the fastest-firing guns in the world. If they get trigger-happy, anything out here larger than a moth is going to wind up with more holes than a screen door."

The helicopter started to rise. Charlie and Vincent stayed in the cabin, searching the grounds for something. I could see Miklos in the cockpit, speaking into a headset. He turned the copter and hovered over the building.

"What do you make of that?" John asked.

I shrugged as Charlie and Vincent leapt down onto the roof and took up separate positions. Their eyes remained fixed on the courtyard as Miklos pulled away.

"Those are your friends?" John asked.

"Yeah."

"I recognize them. Well, those two, anyway." He flicked a finger at Luna, then Charlie. "They seem all right. You made it sound as though they were hostages."

"They were. Now they're recruits. But they don't realize how dangerous Vlad is, and what he's done."

John hummed in quiet understanding. We watched without speaking for a few minutes.

"Funny," he said at last. "They aren't going inside the palace. And they've made no effort to hide. They must be meeting someone here."

I glanced around but saw no sign of anyone. "What should we do?"

"Why are you asking me? Isn't this *your* party?"

"I don't remember getting an invitation."

Snowflakes began to fall. Vlad and the others still hadn't moved. No one was speaking to anyone else. The mood was very sombre.

"Maybe it got lost in the mail," John said.

"I doubt it. I'm the last person Vlad wants to see." I then explained how he'd lured me out into the woods and duped me into digging my own grave.

"What do you think he told your friends?" he asked.

I had no idea. Certainly not the truth.

John smiled. "Any reason we shouldn't stroll over and ask him?" He stood and offered me his hand.

"I'll introduce you to him," I said, rising.

"No need. I knew him even before he became a vampire. He was just as unpredictable back then." He winked and brushed a few flakes of snow from his shoulders. Then we jumped the wall and walked across the courtyard.

CHAPTER 57

REVELATION

VINCENT WAS THE first to see us. He tapped Charlie's shoulder. I raised my hand. Charlie waved back.

Luna left the fountain and walked towards me. A walk became a jog. A jog became a run. She whispered my name. If the two of us had been alone, this would have been a perfect happy ending. But Vlad said something and she stopped. He shifted forward so that he stood between us, then glanced back over his shoulder.

"Vincent?"

Vincent was already on the ground, Charlie in tow. They padded over. "It's him," Vincent said.

"Are you certain?"

"Yup."

"What about this one?" Vlad pointed his sword at John.

Vincent's nostrils widened slightly. "Might be the Changeling. Might not be. But he was in the caves."

"Are you certain?"

"Hundred per cent."

"Step away from Zack," Charlie said.

John raised his hands and backed away. "We've very exposed out here. Do you have any idea what you're doing?"

"Improvising," Vlad said. "We certainly weren't expecting you. But since you are here, perhaps you could shed some light on where the Changeling is, and what he's up to."

John shook his head. "I can't help you there."

"What about his identity?"

"If I ever knew who he was, the memory is gone now. But some old ones seem to be making a comeback. Hi, Charlie. Hi, Luna."

Luna smiled. Charlie nodded, a bit more seriously than I would have expected.

Vlad turned his eyes on me. "Well, you must know something, little cub. Speak up."

I hadn't anticipated any of this. I'd thought Vlad would be shocked to see me, but he was just his brooding, determined self. Luna looked at me expectantly. Charlie was staring too, an "out with it" expression on his face. Even Vincent was waiting for some kind of answer.

"Who is the Changeling?" Vlad asked. "Our little stunt in the woods should have flushed him out."

His wide eyes wandered impatiently over my face. I stared back, unspeaking. He'd just buried me alive, and now he was acting as though it had never happened. Any anger I might have felt was dwarfed by my incredulity. Ophelia insisted there was nobility in him. I couldn't see it. I wondered if my father had, and how he would have dealt with this. I could imagine him standing there in his fedora and khakis, sketch pad or brush in hand, examining some trinket he'd unearthed. "Every person should be the hero of their own life story, Zack," he would have said. "So how should a hero behave?"

The answer was painfully simple. A hero does what's right, and always stands up to the bad guys.

I felt the tip of Vlad's sword against my chest. He was looking at Luna. "Can you bring him out of this?"

"I can try," she said. Then she noticed I was back in the real world and nodded for me to say something. I glanced down at the Dragon Blade. Vlad lowered the tip.

"I have nothing to say to you except . . . *Leave.* Stay out of our lives. If I see you again, you'll regret it."

"*I'll regret it? I'LL REGRET IT?*" Vlad puffed up so I thought his armour might pop. "Pup, you have answers, and now is the time to share them. I have done what I can for your friends, but I'm at the end of my rope." He was practically frothing. "I told you when I saw you last that we had someone to find. That someone is the Changeling. I am certain he was watching us from the shadows. Why else would I have acted like that, and said those things? You must have learned something. Your presence here is all the proof I need. Speak up!"

His moss-coloured eyes passed frantically over my face, then remained fixed on the top of my head. He shifted closer. "Why isn't there any dirt in your hair? How did you escape? Who saved you?"

The questions seemed to surprise everyone. He obviously hadn't told them I'd been buried alive. I reached up and pulled my fingers along my scalp. There wasn't so much as a grain of sand up there. It must have had something to do with travelling into the shadow world. The dirt must have stayed behind.

"The Changeling wants you alive. He must, or he would have killed you before. So who saved you?" Vlad pointed a finger at John. "It wasn't him. He was dead. So are the other Horsemen. The horde has dispersed. The Changeling has no allies left.

Don't you see? There are no other players in the game. *Whoever saved you was the Changeling! Who was it?*"

Baoh had saved me, but I wasn't going to drag him into this, not with Vlad ranting like a madman. He was out of his tree. I hadn't seen him so incensed since the night he tried to kill my friends and me at Iron Spike Enterprises.

Luna stepped between us. The moment her hands touched me I felt my insides melt. "Zack, please. We need an answer."

There was such hopefulness in her eyes that, in the end, I couldn't keep it from her. "It was Baoh," I said. "Baoh saved me."

"Say that again," Vlad said, his face twisted in confusion. I might just as well have told him it was the Pillsbury Doughboy.

"Baoh."

Vlad's breath hissed out in icy disgust. He dropped his Dragon Blade, tip first, into the snow so it stood up like a cross. John, meanwhile, was staring at my face as though I must have made a mistake.

Luna put her arms around me. "We knew you could do it. Vlad said you put yourself in incredible danger, but that you'd come through for us."

By the sound of things, he'd omitted a few details.

"Baoh . . . ?" Vlad muttered to himself. "That sideshow phony! He's as harmless as a housefly. Damn it, pup, you can curse me for a fool. I'm sorry. I truly am. I thought our little gambit would reveal the last piece of the puzzle, but it was all for nothing. For nothing. We're finished . . ."

CHAPTER 58

MISPRONUNCIATION

I DON'T KNOW if it was the presence of Charlie, and the familiar way he'd waved to me when I'd first arrived, or the feel of Luna's arm around my waist, and the thought of her running to meet me, but I was suddenly homesick. I longed for a night run through the streets of Peterborough and some time alone with the people I loved most. Something told me that if I didn't sever the ties between my friends and Vlad soon, I would continue to lose them, one after the other, until my whole world was just an empty shell.

"Sorry to disappoint you," I said to Vlad, "but I don't care if the Changeling is really Peter Parker, the Spectacular Spider-Man. I'm leaving." I pulled back from Luna so I could look at her more closely. "I have no idea what Vlad told you, but it was a lie. I didn't put myself in danger. I wasn't on any secret mission. He drugged me, buried me alive in the woods and left me to suffocate. That's where I've been. In a hole."

The courtyard was suddenly very quiet.

"Now that's the Vlad we know and love," Mr. Entwistle said. He had his arms crossed over his chest and he was staring at the Prince with eyes that were smouldering.

"This doesn't concern you, Tiptoft."

"I no longer answer to that name, Impaler."

Vlad shifted so he was directly in my line of sight. "If you think I don't care about your well-being, you are mistaken. I do." He glanced at Mr. Entwistle. "Is that a lie, Butcher? I'm told you can detect any falsehood in a man's words."

John stepped up beside me. "Whether you care about him for his sake or your own I wouldn't venture to say. Regardless, burying him alive isn't the best way to show it."

"A calculated risk. I knew the Changeling wouldn't let him die, not after sparing him that first time. I have no doubt Baoh was sent to save him."

Luna stared at him. The colour had drained from her face. "Did you arrange for Istvan to give him away that first time?" Her voice was a hoarse whisper. "Did you? Was that all part of your plan?"

"No," Vlad answered.

"You're lying," I said.

He glared at me. "And how do you know? Because the Changeling told you? The same person who killed Ophelia? You would take his word over mine?"

"You're both liars," I said. "And I don't trust either of you."

"What else have you lied about?" Luna asked.

Vlad scooped the Dragon Blade from where it was sticking from the ground. "You should never accuse a man without proof."

"You said you sent Zack on a mission."

"I did. And it is true. He simply didn't know it."

John snorted.

"I played the cards I was dealt," Vlad said. "The only connection we have to the Changeling is that boy."

Luna took hold of my hand. "I think we're finished here."

"Why did you lie?" Charlie said, his eyes fixed on the ground.

Vlad snorted angrily. "Not a lie. An omission. Would you have agreed to stand by me if you had known?"

"You had no right to put him at risk," Luna said.

Vlad made no apologies. "I knew if he were in danger the Changeling would save him. And if not, we could go back to the woods and bring him back ourselves."

"Unless our enemies dug him up first and torched his corpse," Charlie said.

"If they wanted him dead, they would have killed him when he was their prisoner."

"That's nonsense," Luna said.

"No, it isn't," said Mr. Entwistle. "I may not approve of Vlad's methods, but he's right about this. The Changeling has more than just a passing interest in the boy."

"His name is Zachary."

"Remembered by God. A fitting name for a messiah."

"The Changeling doesn't believe in the prophecy," I said.

Mr. Entwistle scratched at the whiskers on his chin. "Does anyone know what the Changeling believes?"

"He told you the prophecy was just a tool of the prophets. A lie. You believed him."

"That means nothing," he said.

"I thought you could tell when a man was telling the truth."

"The Changeling is no ordinary man."

Vlad eyed us both. "Perhaps we should talk to Baoh."

"I'm not going anywhere with you," I said. "And I have no wish to endanger Baoh by drawing attention to him."

"Endanger Baoh," Mr. Entwistle said, snickering. "Not likely.

I remember that old crackpot. He's as tough as a Grape-Nut."

"Are we talking about the same guy who visits you on the Dream Road?" Charlie asked. "The prophet?"

"That quack is no prophet," Vlad scoffed. "He can't tell you any more about the future than your average horoscope."

"What about the Baptist?" Charlie asked.

"The Changeling and the Baptist are the same person," I said.

Vlad's expression flared. "Who told you that?"

"Baoh told me. He said the Baptist was just a disguise the Changeling used to find vampires who were in hiding. Once he knew where they were, he'd send in the Horsemen."

"How would Baoh know that?" Luna asked.

"Good question."

"Who is Baoh, anyway?" Vincent asked. "You know you all say his name a bit differently?"

"Mandarin words are confusing," Mr. Entwistle said. "They mean something a bit different if you change your inflection. The proper pronunciation is *Baoh*. It means precious, like a jewel. Something like that. But you can also pronounce it *Baoh*." He paused, so we could appreciate the difference. I didn't catch one. "In that case, it means nurse or governess, someone who protects others."

"Wrong on both counts," Vlad said. "It's pronounced *Baoh*. It means violent and cruel."

Everyone looked at him.

"It's true," he insisted. "It can also mean to suddenly injure someone."

"I can't really hear a difference," I said.

Vlad smiled. "How good is your Mandarin?"

I think he knew the answer.

"I still have trouble picking up the subtle nuances in people's inflections," he said. "Context is critical."

"So the meaning of his name changes. You don't find that suggestive?" Luna asked.

"No," Vlad said. "Mandarin words are like that." He paused, thinking. "But if we consider those different meanings together: precious, someone who looks after others, but who can be violent and suddenly injure. Those all describe the Changeling. Perfectly, in fact."

"So you're saying it's Baoh?" Charlie asked him.

"No, it cannot be. He was a friend to Ophelia for five centuries."

"Didn't he also help Ophelia at her trial?" Charlie said.

Vlad's eyes narrowed. "Yes. Strange that the New Order would allow it. And let him escape the courtroom."

"After helping me on the Dream Road," I added.

Vlad's voice came alive. "Could it really be him? He has convinced the world that he's little more than a harmless coot. In five centuries he hasn't shown any obvious interest in the politics of our kind. A perfect front. The last vampire on earth I would have suspected. Baoh . . .

"We must get to the bottom of this. I am going to visit the good prophet. If he really is the Changeling, it is time to put an end to things."

CHAPTER 59

SUMMONS

MR. ENTWISTLE LOOKED at Vlad with an expression of doubt on his face, one eyebrow much higher than its neighbour. "Sorry for tempering your enthusiasm with a dose of reality, but if Baoh is the Changeling, then he's way out of our league. You might just as well try to paint the sun black."

"I want answers," Vlad said. "I'm not going to spend the rest of my life wandering about with one eye over my shoulder waiting for him to strike. It is time to end this."

"How will you even find him?" John asked. "He disappears for years at a time."

"Aren't you his second in command?" Charlie said to Mr. Entwistle. "Put that cowl back on. We could set a trap—"

"That won't work," I said. "Baoh brought me to Mr. Entwistle's corpse after it had burned in the sun. He'll know we're on the same side now."

"This is foolishness," John said to Vlad. "If Baoh is the Changeling, and you press him, how will you protect yourself from his poison? It is fatal, instantly. There is no antidote."

Vlad reached into a pocket on his belt and pulled out a stainless steel vial. "In that you are mistaken, John. I have created one. Our only dose is in this tube."

He held it up for us to see. A silent war between hope and doubt started inside me. I wanted his words to be true, but I felt I couldn't trust anything he said. None of my friends seemed surprised by his revelation. I guess they must have known.

"Why haven't you used it on Ophelia?" I asked.

"It is too risky," Vlad said. "I might raise her up only to see her killed again. And if both of us died, who could make more? No, I am keeping this as insurance against the Changeling. I'll make more once he has been dealt with."

"You could bring Ophelia back and then make more."

"Where?" he asked. "And with what? I am out of materials and have no place to work."

Should I have been surprised? He knew that if we believed he could make more, we'd protect him until the sky fell in hopes that he might eventually restore Ophelia. But before I could voice any further objections, Vincent started to growl. Min was approaching.

"It's okay," I said. "She's cool."

I felt Luna grow rigid beside me. I should have picked a better adjective.

Min stopped a good ten paces away. More vampires appeared from the shadows. Several jumped down from the roof. The air was very tense, punctuated by the guttural rumble still emanating from Vincent's throat.

"It's fine," I said. "They're here to help."

I poked Charlie gently on the chest. "Recognize anyone?"

Judging from the colour of his cheeks, he did.

"She saved me from Famine after Vlad carted you away. Would have been hard to do if you'd taken her head off."

"Point taken," he said.

Min stepped to one side and waved for someone to come forward. Hassan, the bounty hunter, was escorting a figure towards us, the barrel of an automatic pressed tight to the man's neck. He had a moustache shaped like two crescent moons, the same colour as his tawny hair, which was streaked with white over the left side.

"We found him in the woods beside an empty grave," Min said. "He asked to speak to you."

"Is it my cousin?" Vlad asked Vincent.

Vincent's nostrils flared. "Yup. It's Istvan."

I nodded to Min. She, Hassan and the others moved back so that Istvan stood alone.

"I am glad you are all well," he said. A smile crept up his cheeks when he saw John. "It is good to see you are your old self again. Or rather, your new self again." Then he looked at Vlad and me. "The Changeling would like to see you both. Come. Miklos is waiting in the helicopter."

He turned, expecting us to follow. Vlad shifted beside him. There was no hostility or surprise in his face, no evidence of mistrust or anger.

"You might have saved me a lot of bother if you'd just set this meeting up at the beginning."

Istvan laughed. "You are mistaken, cousin, if you think I have that kind of influence."

Both men turned back when it was obvious I wasn't following. I was still holding Luna's hand. We'd been separated too many times already.

"You cannot safely refuse this request, Zachariah," Istvan said. "I am sorry. You must obey."

I looked at Luna. She looked at Charlie. He looked at Mr. Entwistle.

"We will all go," John said. "I have questions of my own that need answering."

Istvan frowned. "The Changeling is a follower of the old ways, John. He does not approve of child vampires or those he deems unclean. If you bring the shape-changer and these young ones to his temple, they will not come out alive."

"It is a parley, Istvan," John said. "The rules are ancient and inviolable. It is forbidden for him to harm us."

"These vampires are too young to be protected by any law, old or new. And Vincent is a lycanthrope. Our laws do not pertain to him."

"Perhaps it is time to re-examine those laws," John said.

"Perhaps . . . but the Changeling might be more set in his ways than you would wish him to be."

Mr. Entwistle looked at Istvan with an expression that surprised me. Had I not known him, I would have thought he was afraid. "I will not take his mark again."

"And I have no wish to take it even once," Istvan replied.

"You never took his mark?"

Istvan pulled back his hair. He always wore it loose, so I'd never seen his forehead clearly. It was pristine. So was his right hand. "The Changeling never asked me. It was what allowed me to play the role I needed to play."

Vlad smiled at that.

"You're worse than Benedict Arnold," Luna said. "You have no loyalty to anyone."

"I am loyal to a cause," Istvan said. "And I love Vlad and Ophelia both. Never doubt that. Her loss touches us all. If you feel betrayed, trust that time will exonerate me. But . . ." He gestured for us to get moving. "The war is now over. It is time to negotiate the peace."

CHAPTER 60

TERMS

I'D BEEN TO the temple before—with Ophelia, the night she introduced me to Baoh on the Dream Road. The sun had been shining. The light and warmth of it had created a surreal quality that was now missing in the cold dark of the mountaintop.

Tibet. The Roof of the World.

Our breath froze and disappeared in the night air. Istvan led us to the temple doors and rang a small gong that was sitting on the stone floor. One door swung inward with a creak.

"This is a holy place," Istvan said. "Your weapons must be left outside."

Vlad set the Dragon Blade beside the door.

"Are you for real?" Charlie asked.

"Yup," John answered. "It is forbidden to bring weapons to a parley."

Charlie dropped his utility belt, then started shedding knives, guns and explosives. So did Luna. By the time they were finished, there was a small arsenal sitting on the paving stones.

Luna tapped the handle of my *katana*. "Oh, right," I said, unbelting it quickly.

She glanced at John. "What about you?"

He reached into his overcoat and pulled out a flask. "This isn't a weapon," he said, unscrewing the cap. "It's a crutch."

He took a haul of whisky, then readjusted the top hat on his head. It and his other belongings had been in the Changeling's safekeeping, unearthed in the Warsaw Caves when his body was exhumed and delivered by Istvan. John now looked exactly as I remembered him.

Istvan led us through the temple doors. Inside, rows of fluttering candles sent shadows dancing along the timbers of the ceiling. Waxy smoke mixed with the pleasant aroma of incense. A small fire was burning in a square hole set in the floor. It was mostly coals now. Just beyond, near a small shrine to the Buddha, stood Baoh. He had his arms folded across his waist, his hands hidden by the long, flowing sleeves of his orange habit. He nodded to Istvan. There was no stiffness in his movements now. I guess the time for acting was over.

"Had I known I'd be talking to an apparition, I would have stayed home," Vlad said.

"You have no home to go to, Vladislav. And a man does not reach my age by placing himself in danger unnecessarily, particularly when he invites three vampires to parley, and six show up."

Vlad chuckled quietly, but I sensed his unease. I looked at Baoh more closely. His body seemed real until I noticed the floor beneath him. Wood deforms when you stand on it. The difference is slight, but anyone with vampire eyes could see the boards under his feet carried no weight. We were talking to a ghost image.

Baoh's eyeless orbits changed. They were shrouded in darkness, then his eyelids snapped opened, revealing the milky irises of the Changeling. "Time is precious," he said, "so I will not waste yours with pleasantries. These are my terms. Vlad, you will be induced into a state of undeath. All of your properties, monetary assets and titles will be transferred to me. Your body will be taken to Snagov, which will remain in the possession of Miklos and his family. A reward for his loyalty, however misplaced."

Vlad's face began to redden. His jaw clenched while the Changeling continued.

"Istvan, you will join Vlad in undeath. I will also take possession of your assets, deeds and titles. I understand this was less than you were promised, but, given where your true allegiance resides, I am disinclined to trust you. And I am not pleased to find my home putrefied by the presence of one who is unclean." Baoh's eyes shifted to Vincent. "You should not have brought this animal here. It is as thoughtless as it is insulting."

Istvan started to speak, but Baoh cut him off.

"Zachariah, you have never posed a threat to me, and although you are young by any standard, no sane person would accuse you of mental instability, the only justification we have for terminating the young. You will be allowed to leave, but only after we deal with your friends."

I stared into the murky depths of his eyes to see if they offered some clue as to what he intended, but they were like lenses too thick to see through.

"It is convention in the vampire world that one does not pass the pathogen to another person until one's progenitor is dead. Vlad broke this tradition when he made you. Ophelia was still alive. I overlooked this because of how much I admired your father and because of a long-dead prophecy that made me curious about the outcome of your infection. However, I am now staring at a family of four vampires, two of whom spring directly from you. Certainly the Chosen One must set a better example. As Luna was the last in your line to be infected, she must join Vlad in undeath."

Luna was beside me. I could smell her fear.

"What about Vincent?" I asked.

"He is unclean. He is to be terminated, immediately."

"Baoh," Vlad whispered, his teeth clamped firmly together. "You are a fool if you think we will agree to these terms. This meeting is over." He turned to go.

"I think not," Baoh said.

"It is forbidden to harm guests at a parley," Mr. Entwistle said.

"You are correct, John. But you violated my terms when you entered this temple, as only Istvan, Vlad and Zachary were invited. And weapons were forbidden." He looked at Charlie. A *who, me?* look came over my friend's face. "In your left boot, Charlie, there is a knife."

Charlie looked down. His face turned red. "That was an accident!"

"Arguably, your entire life has been an accident! It changes nothing. Luna, you must prepare yourself for undeath. I will give you a moment to say goodbye. Do not be dismayed. Vlad and Istvan will confirm this—in a state of undeath you will not suffer or age. Your body will not corrupt. In time, you can be raised up again."

As he finished speaking, his image began to fade. Smoke from the incense burner swirled through him, then he disappeared completely.

"Watch the shadows," Mr. Entwistle said. He moved towards the centre of the room. We all formed a circle, staring outwards.

"What did he mean, unclean?" Vincent asked.

"He means you forgot your deodorant, Vin," Charlie said. He pulled out the incriminating boot knife. "Should I get our weapons? They're right outside the door."

"No," Vlad said. "Baoh will have moved them." He glanced at John. "What chance do we have?"

Mr. Entwistle's face was grim. "I fear this won't end well for you."

"No. I knew that already. But a leader must be willing to make sacrifices."

I didn't doubt he'd sacrifice all of us to save his skin. But this didn't have to end badly for everyone.

"This is crazy," I said. "Vlad and I can stay here with Istvan and figure this out. The rest of you should head for the hills."

"It is too late for that, Zachariah," Istvan said. "The Changeling has offered us his terms and we have rejected them. He won't let us go."

"Even the Changeling can't be in two places at once. If he's here dealing with us, he can't be chasing the others."

"Forget that," Charlie said. "We're staying. End of story."

"You would never leave us behind," Luna said. "Don't expect us to do that to you."

"He's coming," said John.

Vlad seemed to sense this as well. His eyes were fixed on the temple doors. He spoke to Vincent without turning. "You know what to do?"

"Yeah," Vinny answered. One side of his upper lip rose, exposing a long canine. He was coiled up like an adder, his fingers loose, claws bared.

The double doors opened. A young-looking vampire was standing just outside the threshold, dressed as a Shaolin monk. His head was shaved and his eyebrows were dark and manicured.

"It is time," he said. Then he stepped into the room.

CHAPTER 61

APPARITIONS

A YOUNG VERSION of the prophet stood before us, looking as he had when he walked the earth over twelve hundred years ago, seven hundred years before Columbus set sail, five hundred years before Genghis Khan sat a horse, three hundred years before the first Christian Crusade, when Charlemagne ruled in France and Vikings first set their sights on the churches and monasteries of Britain.

"Will you agree to my terms?" Baoh asked. "Or will we do this the hard way?"

"The hard way it is," Vlad said.

Charlie laughed. He was picking his teeth with the end of his knife. He nearly dropped it when Baoh stepped out of himself, moving sideways and standing still at the same time. One person became two. Two became four. Four became six. Then the last in the row stepped sideways, leaving a seventh duplicate behind, one Baoh for each of us in the room.

"I thought you said he could be in only one place at a time?" Charlie said.

"His words, not mine."

"How do we deal with this?"

I shrugged. The only story I knew about vampires that came close to this was a Russian folk tale my father had read to me as a child. A group of villagers, having been tormented by a local vampire, formed a mob, captured the vampire and set about trying to burn it. When they threw it on a pyre, it exploded into a host of snakes and toads. The villagers had to kill them all, knowing that if even one survived, the spirit of the vampire would live on. We were standing face to face with seven Baohs. Did we have to kill them all? Were they real people or just ghost images, like the apparition we'd been talking to earlier? I had no idea. Fortunately, there was someone in the room with *true sight*.

"Charlie, that one!" Mr. Entwistle said, pointing to the figure on the far left. He started running towards it. Vlad shifted across the room. Meanwhile, all of the other Baohs scattered. One leapt onto a shelf covered in ornamental jars. One slid under a table. Others disappeared into shadows and emerged on the far side of the room. They didn't stop moving.

Charlie threw his knife at the figure Mr. Entwistle was attacking. I don't know how they kept their eyes on the real target—it was a live shell game. As the knife somersaulted through the air, one of the Baohs grabbed Luna and pulled her in front of the spinning blade. It hit her throat just below her chin and she crumpled to one knee. It happened so quickly, there was nothing I could do. As I started towards her, eyes wide and heart pounding, Vincent leapt forward and slashed at Baoh. He wasn't quite fast enough. The prophet became a puff of vapour and slipped through a crack in the floor. I blinked and all the Baohs were gone. I blinked again, and they were back in the room, having risen from shadows along the walls, behind the table, under benches or chairs and in the beams of the ceiling.

One stepped out of the fireplace. I could see from the floor that he had more weight than the others. Charlie noticed too. He push-kicked the table across the floor, but we were both fooled. The table went right through and crashed into the wall.

Mr. Entwistle swung at one and missed. "He's moving from apparition to apparition," he said.

Luna pulled the knife from her throat and pressed a hand over her voice box. Blood ran through her fingers. I wasn't sure how to help her. She waved me off just as one of the Baohs emerged from the shadows beside her. I threw myself at him in a flying tackle, but it wasn't really him and I landed face first on the floor. At the same time, another grabbed Istvan from behind and pulled him into the shadows beside a column. The apparitions all vanished, then reappeared in different locations. Istvan was gone. My guess was he'd been trapped on the Shadow Road.

"Can you breathe?" I asked Luna.

"I'll be fine." She pulled her hand away from her neck. The opening had sealed and was turning from pink to alabaster. She grabbed my belt and hauled herself to her feet.

The real Baoh slammed into Charlie. The two disappeared behind a bench. I heard a crunch, like bones breaking, then Charlie went flying through the air and collapsed into a heap near the fireplace, knocking a row of idols off the mantel. Vlad shifted behind the bench where the Changeling was waiting. I jumped over, too, Luna at my side, but instead of the prophet, we saw Charlie lying on the ground, his neck twisted at an impossible angle. I spun to the fireplace, realizing that Baoh had jumped free in the guise of my friend. Four Baohs rose up from the shadows to surround me. Any one of them could have been real.

"There," Mr. Entwistle said, pointing to Vincent. The apparition behind him had a stinger in place of a hand. The barb glistened with poison. Instantly, the hands of the other apparitions changed. They converged on Vincent. He slashed at two and bit a third, but they were ghosts. Then he roared as the real Baoh slammed a poisoned barb into the back of his leg.

Vincent spun. He caught the Changeling on the chin with a backhanded uppercut. It would have sent anyone else through the roof, but Baoh turned to mist and disappeared into a shadow behind a ceiling joist.

All of the apparitions disappeared again, then emerged around Vlad. One put an arm around his neck and pulled him backwards. "Do you really have an antidote, Vlad?" he asked.

"One dose," the Prince answered.

"We shall see how effective it is."

The Changeling jabbed Vlad's neck with his stinger. The Prince stiffened, then growled. It quickly became a cry of pain. Luna and I raced towards him, but Mr. Entwistle stepped in the way and held us back. At the same time, Vincent collapsed to the floor.

The skin of Vlad's neck started turning grey. Seven Baohs circled him. Vlad started to smoke, then he self-immolated. None of the apparitions around him were affected by the heat—save one. Vlad shifted so the two were face to face, then took hold of Baoh in a bear hug and turned up the heat. The rest of us had to back away, but Baoh's skin didn't so much as blister. The prophet was centuries older, and in the world of vampires, seniority was everything. He put a hand on Vlad's throat and raised him off the ground. One by one, the apparitions merged with the original until only one remained. He forced Vlad to his knees.

"There is no antidote for the Changeling," he said.

Vlad's eyes were pinched shut. Grey spread over his face. The flames sputtered and died. Somehow, he managed to force his eyelids open just a sliver. There was a wicked grin on his face, all teeth and anger.

"The antidote is working just fine."

He took hold of Baoh's wrists and hung on. It was the last thing he did before he died. Then Vincent attacked. I'd been so focused on Baoh, I'd neither seen nor heard him. No one had. Nor had anyone suspected that Vlad had given the antidote to him. But there was no mistaking the tiny vial that dropped from Vincent's hand as he sprang across the room. It shattered when it hit the floor. Empty.

Baoh shifted to his left, but Vincent followed him like a bloodhound, his claws whistling through the air in a blur. He caught Baoh in the face and the prophet's skin tore open. Before his next blow landed, Baoh turned to mist. Vincent jumped right in the middle of it, just as he had with Tamerlane, his claws swinging wildly.

"Here," Mr. Entwistle shouted. He handed me two lighted candles from a shrine to the Buddha. Luna already had a pair and was thrusting them into the shadows. It took me a moment to figure out what she was doing, then I followed suit. So did Mr. Entwistle. We surrounded the cloud of mist, causing all of the shadows around it to jump. Each was a portal to the Shadow Road, but none stayed in place long enough for Baoh to leave. Sooner or later he'd have to solidify. Then Vincent would rip him apart.

But Baoh had other plans. He solidified behind Luna, his arm around her waist, her body like a shield between him and Vincent. "Stop or she dies," he said. Then he raised his poisoned barb to her throat.

CHAPTER 62

STALEMATE

INSIDE A HEARTBEAT, Vincent was rock still. Nobody moved.

"That's better," Baoh said. "This would have been much easier if you'd simply agreed to my terms."

Mr. Entwistle turned his back and walked to where Charlie's body was lying in the centre of the floor. He carefully set my friend's neck. "Your terms were unacceptable. You knew we'd never agree. So, what will it really take to end things?"

"I will settle for nothing less than what I ask. There are still too many vampires in Ophelia's line. And this one," he glared at Vincent, "is a lycanthrope. It isn't to be tolerated."

"I swore an oath to his father," I said.

"Yes, the Beast of the Apocalypse. If the prophecy is correct, then this *thing* might be the Messiah. Where do you think he will lead our kind? To death and damnation. I will not allow it."

Mr. Entwistle's hat had come off in all the action. On the way over to me, he scooped it up, then set the candles down so he could take a sip of his whisky. "You don't have to kill this boy."

"He is unclean."

"That wasn't his choice."

"It matters not. His kind are a threat."

"But *he* isn't," I said.

"That is not for you to judge. His bite is lethal. What if he makes others like him? Our people will not be long for this world."

Baoh took hold of Luna's hair and pulled her head back. The poisoned barb glistened in the candlelight.

"You two should take Charlie and go," Vincent said. His yellow eyes bounced from John to me, then back to Baoh. "My life for Luna's. Seems like a bargain to me."

Baoh looked skeptical. *Does he mean that?* he asked me.

His question told me something important: he couldn't read Vincent's thoughts, or he'd have known.

It doesn't matter, I answered. *I promised his father I'd look after him. I'm not going back on my word.*

Even if it kills you?

I was glad that Luna couldn't sense my thought—that I didn't expect anyone to get out of the room alive. Then I saw what Vincent saw. The knife that Charlie had thrown, the one that had struck Luna's throat, was tucked up against her forearm. Her eyes were furious.

"Zachary," she said. "If Vlad made an antidote, then so can we. Stop dithering and do what you have to do."

Mr. Entwistle took another pull of whisky and picked up a candle. The bouncing flame bathed his face with a sinister light. He might have been John Entwistle now, but I could see in his eyes that a part of the Butcher remained. "Luna has a point. And there are three of us."

"Four of us," she said.

He smiled, but not with humour. It gave me chills.

And that settled it. I rubbed my tongue over the bottom of my teeth. "I love you," I said to her.

She answered by jamming the knife into Baoh's thigh. That was when we moved.

CHAPTER 63

THERE IS NO ANTIDOTE . . .

O F ALL THE things I've ever had to do, watching Luna die was the hardest. To this day, I'm still not sure if the Changeling meant to do it or if his hand moved involuntarily when she buried the knife in him. He gasped in surprise and the barb grazed her neck. She didn't stiffen the way Vlad had, so I didn't notice at first. I was too focused on Baoh.

Vincent reached him first. Baoh swung with his poisoned stinger but missed badly. Then he turned to mist and rose out of striking range. As the knife in his leg clattered to the floor, John took a swig of whisky, then held up the candle in his other hand and spat the booze out in a fine mist. When the alcohol made contact with the flame, it combusted in a bright orange and blue cloud. The fire burned through the fog. It also caused the shadows to shift, so Baoh wasn't able to escape to the Shadow Road.

Baoh solidified, smouldering, near the ground in front of Vincent, who grabbed his arms, hauled him off his feet and snapped his jaw forward in a vicious bite. It would have ended things right there had the Changeling not been a Shaolin monk. His whole body was a weapon. He kicked a foot into Vincent's chin, pulled his arms free, stepped off Vinny's chest with his other foot and did a perfect backflip. Vinny's teeth broke. His eyes were suddenly wide. In all the time I'd known him, I don't think he'd ever been hurt.

Fortunately, Mr. Entwistle was on his wing, and when he started swinging, Vincent moved forward to re-engage. I would have followed their lead, but I stalled when I saw Luna. Her skin was turning grey. She fell to her knees.

I was at her side in an instant. I took her in my arms, but there was little comfort I could offer. Her death was coming and she was scared. She tried to speak and couldn't. Grey crept up her neck, spread over her cheeks and surrounded her pale green eyes. I stared, helpless, as the light within them faded, then vanished.

An intense heat blasted my face and hands. Vincent howled in pain. Baoh was a dark shadow in a column of flame. He had self-immolated, just as Vlad had done earlier. Vincent must have been holding him when it happened. Mr. Entwistle hauled him backwards, but the damage was done. There was little he could do but try to smother the flames with his coat.

I set Luna gently on the floor and rubbed a hand through her hair. Then I closed her eyes. My skin began to burn. I stood and walked towards Baoh. He saw me approaching and the heat intensified. I'm not sure what he was expecting—that I was going to back away because he was on fire? No amount of pain was going to stop me. He'd just killed Luna. There was only one answer for that.

He tried to hit me. Had he not been self-immolating, it would have been the beginning of the end, but I knew from observing Vlad that it took great reserves of energy to keep those fires burning. Baoh couldn't do it and mount an effective attack at the same time.

I slipped under his punch, pushed his stinger away, grabbed his arms and pulled him close. Surprise lit up his face. He hadn't anticipated that. Were my thoughts buried? Had I emptied my mind? No. It was just luck. My flesh was melting. I was screaming. There was nothing inside my head but pain. And instinct.

I sank my teeth into his neck.

His energy began to wane instantly, then his blood went to work on my system, healing burns and firing my muscles to Herculean levels. He was an elder. His power was phenomenal. And then it was mine. I squeezed. His ribs cracked. He was caught like a mouse in the coils of a constrictor. He couldn't breathe. As I stole more of his blood, he began to age, slowly at first, then rapidly so that he soon took on the familiar appearance of an elderly man, though his eyes remained intact. His strength began to fail. It forced him to decide: try to escape or keep himself alight. He couldn't do both.

He chose escape. I knew it before he moved. I could read his thoughts as easily as I could with Luna after we shared blood. He thrashed his arms and tried to kick free, but I wasn't budging. My arms were hardened steel.

He started turning into mist. I couldn't stop him. He drifted through a crack in the floor. I heard John shouting, "No! *Noooo!*" first in alarm, then in frustration.

"He's not getting away," I said.

As Baoh sublimated, the entire process was laid out for me, step by step, his thoughts as clear to me as my own. I let myself drift apart until I was nothing more than a cloud of disconnected molecules, all held together by my consciousness. Moving was tougher. Each particle, once freed from its neighbours, wanted to separate completely and drift away. I had to pull at the edges of myself so that I wouldn't expand and disappear. It took a moment to get the hang of it, but eventually I managed to herd myself through the same crack and into the darkness under the temple.

Baoh was hiding. When I appeared, his fear rose so that it seemed to fill the whole space we were sharing. Some light filtered down through the cracks above, enough to form shadows. He used one as a portal and slipped through. I peered into the realm of Lú-Yíng, saw my reflection in the darkness beyond and moved towards it. With his mind open like an instruction booklet, I might just as well have been following tracks he left behind in the sand.

Baoh was a thin black cloud in a colourless world. There was barely enough energy in his essence for him to move. I enclosed him in a sphere as dense as lead. He spun and rolled and twisted, searching for a chink in my armour, but there was none. I pulled him back into the world of light and matter and literally squeezed him back into his body. As he solidified, so did I. He would have fallen over had I not reached out and taken hold of him by the scruff of his neck.

"There is no antidote for justice," I said. Then I held him off the ground and started to throttle him.

CHAPTER 64

THE PUPPET MASTER

I SQUEEZED UNTIL I felt Baoh's windpipe begin to collapse, then I forced him to his knees and let go.

"You have some explaining to do."

He tipped back against the temple wall, gasping. His hands rose to his neck and he touched it gingerly, the indentation of my fingers still clearly visible in his skin.

"Are you calm enough to listen?" he asked, his voice old and crackling once more.

I folded my arms over my chest.

"And is this truly necessary? You should have enough pieces of the puzzle by now to discern my grand design."

"I don't want puzzles. I want answers."

"Apparently." He hacked several times, cleared his throat, then stood unsteadily, his hand against the wall. "Did I not preach about your rise to power as the Baptist? Have I not, directly or indirectly, guided you through every phase of your journey here? When we were in the Prince's Church, I told you that, with my help, you could become the perfect instrument."

"What are you talking about?"

"I'm talking about you, and the various personae I assumed to help you on your path to this eventuality."

I started at him, stupefied. He was making it sound as though I was his pet project. Then I considered his words more carefully. As the prophet, he had warned me on the Dream Road about the New Order, and later, outside of Budapest, removed me from the grave Vlad and I had dug. In the guise of the Baptist, he'd tried to save me from Death on *L'Esprit Sauvage*. Had I taken his leap of faith, I would have made it to safety. Later, in the courtroom, he'd helped tip the scales just far enough that Vlad, Ophelia and I could escape. Was it possible that he'd orchestrated events so that, at the end, we'd be standing here like this, face to face?

I couldn't believe it. "You put a bounty on my head!"

"And yet you survived, with my help. That bounty and your numerous escapes were essential in establishing your credibility as the Messiah. The danger had to be real, your accomplishments fantastic, for you to earn the reverence of those who have survived."

"I don't want to be revered. I want my friends back."

I glanced around the room. Vincent lay near the far wall. He was a boy again. His torso and inner arms were charred black. So was the skin on half of his face. Charlie's body was twitching on the ground, healing. Beyond it was Luna, her face grey, her features rigid with pain.

He'd killed Luna . . . My hands shook. A tremendous power was at work in my body, and it raged. Steam rose from my skin. I understood at that moment what people meant when they said their blood was boiling. Mine was threatening to ignite. Waves of heat rose from my arms. I grabbed Baoh by the throat again and forced him back to his knees.

"I should kill you for what you've done."

He put his hands on my wrist. My grip must have been too tight because he couldn't speak. I loosened it but did not let go. He started wheezing. After a few difficult breaths, he spoke.

"So we are finally at the last stage of your development. Are you prepared to make the hard decisions? Who lives? Who dies?"

"Who lives? Who dies? No person should get to decide that. Not you. Not me. Not Vlad. Not anyone."

Charlie sat up. Mr. Entwistle's eyes bounced from my face to my fists, then to the tiny flames that had appeared on my wrists and hands. Others flared and disappeared along my arms and shoulders. Baoh turned his face to avoid being burned.

"If I killed you right now," I said, "how many vampires would line up to dance on your grave?"

"I would," Charlie whispered hoarsely. "Do it!"

"Not yet," I said, pointing towards Luna's corpse. "Not until you bring her back."

Baoh's hands were still on my wrist, trying to relieve the pressure of my hand on his throat. I gave him just enough room to breathe. "Do you think my venom can be neutralized by some potion you synthesize in a lab?" he asked. "It cannot be done. I was not lying when I told Vlad that there was no antidote for the Changeling."

"What about Vincent?" John asked. "Vlad's antidote worked for him."

"No," Baoh said. "That abomination is a lycanthrope. His blood is not the same as ours. His immunity is his own."

His words confirmed my worst fears—that Luna was gone forever. My arms caught fire, then my chest and shoulders. For a fleeting moment, a glimmer of hope appeared deep within Baoh's milky eyes. Was this what he wanted, for me to lose control and self-immolate? It was a terrible energy drain. If I burned all the fuel in my tank and he survived, would it put us back on an equal footing? I took a deep breath, then another, the tunnel of light firmly entrenched in my mind's eye. Slowly, the flames turned from orange to red to deep blue, then faded completely.

"There is a way," I said. "There is *always* a way. You're going to find it, and you're going to bring her back for me. Then you're going to find each and every survivor of this war, every man, woman and child you wronged, and you're going to earn their forgiveness."

I pushed him towards Luna's body. He stumbled to a knee, then rose awkwardly and rubbed at his throat.

"Noble words," he said. "But I am afraid you are mistaken. I do not seek forgiveness, yours or anyone's, and I have done enough for you already."

"He's stalling," Charlie said. "You need to finish this."

Baoh cringed. "I have controlled this outbreak," he said hastily. "And I have destroyed those who would be your enemies, including Vlad and all his generals. Feats accomplished while you trained, or slept in death, or in undeath. Is there any blood on your hands? Little. It is mine that are stained. Genius, is it not, to become the villain whose defeat legitimizes your rule? And all the while, preaching your virtues as the Baptist. Do you think others, like Min and Hassan, would have accepted you without it?"

I wasn't buying it. "There were other reasons the Baptist did his preaching. You told me so yourself. To lure people out of hiding."

"True. But in time, you will come to understand how necessary that was. Too many were infected. Too many."

He sensed my anger rising again, and his hands rose, as if imploring me to listen. "When we first met on the Dream

Road, did I not tell you that I was a media man? That I give the people what they want? They want heroes. People larger than life. So I have given them you. Child of prophecy. Messiah. The orphan who bested the Changeling and will remake the world. You will bring hope to the survivors, those who would dance on my grave, as you so kindly put it. Let them dance. I care not. What matters is that the vampire population is stable once again, and all the power-mongering vampires who would turn the world upside down to gain your throne have been destroyed. You should be thanking me. History will credit *you* for this accomplishment."

"*Thank you?* For killing Luna? For killing Ophelia? For all the innocent lives you've ruined?"

"The blow that killed Ophelia was intended for Vlad. But it is done, and perhaps it is for the best. Did you not just say yourself that there is no antidote for justice? Ophelia broke the law. Or should I say, she broke herself against it. The punishment for her crimes is death. It is unfortunate, but I did my best to make amends. Did I not reunite you with John, so that, in her place, you would have someone of experience to guide you?

"And Luna was an accident. But if you had listened to me in Montreal, and put Charlie and her into a state of undeath, none of this would have happened! You made the decision to keep them alive—"

"So you're saying this is my fault?"

Baoh rolled his shoulders back and stood a bit straighter. A measure of confidence was returning to his tone and the cadence of his words. "Luna should never have been infected in the first place. You know this. Charlie and you are now all that remain of your line. Two generations. Lawful by the ancient canons. This is important. You cannot enforce laws as the next Grand Master if you don't obey them yourself."

"There isn't going to be another Grand Master."

"So you say. But if you look at any organization, you will always find one person at the top. Just one. The emperor, the king, the czar, the president, the chairman, the prime minister, the pope. Whether you choose to call yourself the Grand Master or something else, people will look to you for leadership. This is my doing."

"You really expect me to believe that you arranged this from the start?"

"Your belief or disbelief does not concern me. And if you must know, the person I wanted in charge was your father. But Vlad killed him, and so I tried my best to help you become the man you are. And you are as perfect for this role as I could make you. That is why you are going to take charge and form a new government, and it is why you're going to let me live."

"Because I owe you?"

"In part, but also because a time will come when you will lose your mind, as all vampires do. Power corrupts. Absolute power corrupts absolutely. I have seen it time and again. It is why Baoh does not choose to be at the helm. Rather, he seeks the best helmsman. You are my choice. But even you will fall from grace, Zachary. Who will step in to provide a remedy when that happens? It will fall to me, as it always has. A person outside the system. One who cannot be the Grand Master himself, not permanently, because he must sleep for years at a time, and so can't oversee the night-to-night management of our species."

Charlie bent and picked up his knife, which was lying on the floor near Luna's corpse. "Zack, you can't let him walk out of here."

John moved closer. His eyes fell in shadow. For just an instant, he looked like Death again. "No one's going anywhere."

Baoh shrank from him. "Endpoint Psychosis awaits us all. When Zachariah begins to go mad, will you kill him, Charles? Will you, John? Even if you saw the need and had the resolve, would you be powerful enough to do it? I think not. Zachary has the blood of an ancient in his system and is more than a match for anyone alive in the world. He must pass only this final test. Can he place reason and logic above personal revenge? Will he let me go, or begin a descent into self-serving depravity?"

"So this is what you do?" I asked. "You play God, like a demented puppet master pulling our strings."

"It is what needs to be done. And yes, it is I who do it. Centuries ago I managed to get Ophelia and Vlad in power without my interference being discovered. I was behind your father's rise to fame. None were aware of it. This time, I was not so lucky. My role is now revealed. It does not make it any less important. And I cannot fulfill it if I am dead."

Charlie looked at me, then at Baoh. "You slimy weasel," he muttered. "I ought to fill you full of holes."

"Easy, Charlie," I said.

He scowled, then pointed his knife at me. "You're dithering again."

"Not at all," I said, snatching the blade away from him. "I just don't think one person should get to decide who lives and who dies."

Baoh's face took on a smug expression. Then he gasped when I rammed the knife into his chest. The tip of the blade sliced straight through his heart. His eyes opened wide and blood pooled in his mouth. He gargled something incoherent and tried to free the blade from between his ribs, but I kept my hands firmly on the grip.

"Questions of life and death should be decided by juries," I said. "I will make certain that no one person ever has that authority again. But the question of who gets to be *undead* is one I'm very comfortable answering at the moment, and since you won't repent, Baoh, you're going to be sleeping in undeath for a very, very long time."

CHAPTER 65

TWO WEEKS LATER

I EMERGED FROM the Shadow Road in the old lab of Castle Dracula. The mood was sombre. The New Order had disposed of the corpses Vlad had been trying to save, but they'd been replaced by others. Istvan was one of them. I'd found him grey and lifeless on the Shadow Road. It surprised me how disappointed I was about this, not only because of the questions I would have asked about his role in this story, questions that now could never be answered, but because, deep down, I believed he had a kind soul and that I would have benefited from his friendship. His betrayal at Castle Dracula, which had me both incensed and confused weeks ago, now seemed hardly a betrayal at all, given what I knew about the Changeling and his goals. Istvan had said back in Montreal that we were often treated better by our enemies than by our friends. Had he lived, we would have had much to discuss about this, and many other things besides.

The photon torpedo rested beside him. Baoh's body was locked inside, sleeping indefinitely in undeath. Vlad was there, too. The Prince. My progenitor. I stood in front of his coffin, wondering.

"Still trying to figure him out?" Mr. Entwistle asked. He was hovering over a rack of test tubes behind me.

"I guess so. I just . . . I still have no idea what to make of him."

"What do you mean?"

"All that stuff about burying me alive so he could find out who the Changeling was. And before that, claiming he had no part in giving me up after Ophelia's trial. And saying he cared about me. Was any of it true?"

John chuckled. "Does it matter?"

I turned away from Vlad's corpse. "Doesn't the truth always matter?"

John looked pensive for a moment. "That's not what I was getting at. You need to make sense of this. I understand. But there are certain things you can never be sure about. You need to come to terms with that, because in the end, knowing or not knowing, it changes nothing. Your situation and responsibilities remain what they are. Did Vlad abandon you to the Changeling? So what if he did? He also orchestrated your rescue. Did he lie about his reasons for sticking you in that hole? Again, so what? He kept your friends alive. Isn't that adequate compensation?"

It was. But I still wanted clarity.

"You want to know if you were right not to trust him?"

I hummed a yes.

"You know how I feel about trust. We talked about it last summer."

I did. He'd told Charlie and me we'd be better off focusing on what a person wanted and how they planned to get it. Then we could decide whether to help them or stop them, according to our conscience.

"Do you know what Vlad wanted?" he asked.

"Power," I said.

John didn't look convinced. "What man ever wants just one thing? We all want control over our lives. But what about love? Comradeship? Respect? Forgiveness? Understanding? A family? Perhaps a son? Someone to shape in his own image." He paused, watching me closely. "In what measure did he want these things, too? Do you have any idea?"

"No." I looked down at the floor. "I never bothered to find out."

"And that was a mistake. Learn from it. And don't be too hard on yourself. Vlad wasn't exactly the sharing type, and you had a lot on your plate. You still do."

I turned back to the corpses. Beside Vlad was Luna. I didn't have the strength to look at her face. My eyes fell instead to the half-moon necklace hanging from her neck. Vlad had taken it from her, but it was where it belonged now. I took the gold charm in my fingers. It was cold. I let it drop and turned away.

"Any luck?" Mr. Entwistle asked me.

"No."

I plopped myself onto a stool. I had been searching all of Vlad's old haunts for Ophelia's body. He had hidden it, and no one knew where. If I didn't find it soon, it would be too corrupted to save, even if we found an antidote.

"What about you?" I asked. "Any closer?"

"No. It seems Baoh was honest about one thing, at least—Vincent's immunity was his own. His blood is different, and it's a toxic stew. The parts that are most useful for combatting the venom are fatal to us."

Vlad's corpse stared at me from across the room. I heard his voice in my mind. *There is always a way . . .* I was beginning to doubt that.

"How are you holding up?" he asked.

I shrugged. I didn't want to talk about it. And I didn't want people telling me everything would be fine. Or that Luna and Ophelia had gone to a better place. What I wanted was to stay busy. There was no other way to avoid falling apart.

I heard footfalls in the room outside the lab. The secret door opened and Charlie stepped in. He had his cellphone open and was furiously tapping buttons with his thumbs. "You find her?"

"No."

His tired eyes wandered over all of the chemistry equipment, then settled on Mr. Entwistle. "Tell me you've got some good news, at least."

The old vampire shook his head. "Not on the antidote front. But we mustn't surrender to despair. We're privileged. It would serve us well to be mindful of that." He started clearing dead rats from the counter. None had survived the experiments. "We get to remake the world. Think on that. No more Coven. No New Order. No entrenched institutions to try to change. We get to build a society from the ground up. From scratch."

Charlie pulled out a stool and sat down. "Yeah . . . Well, privileged we may be. But world building is going to have to wait." He started reading from his cell. "Min checked in earlier. There's trouble in Paris. A vampire has been killed in the crypts below the city. Territorial feud most likely. We're needed there right away. A blood shipment to Amsterdam has disappeared and a few women have gone missing. They've gotta be connected. A kid got spotted in Shanghai. Nine or ten years old. Could be a vampire, could be a lycanthrope. We'll need to find him and figure something out. He's the first infected child we've had to deal with, so we've got to watch our step. Whatever we decide, there's bound to be some grumbling."

"We'll bring him back here," I said. "Anything else?"

"Yeah. Somebody who calls himself the Pastor is demanding your execution. He says you're an abomination and a heretic. The bounty is a billion US dollars."

"Is that all I'm worth? It used to be ten billion."

Charlie slipped his phone into the utility belt circling his armour. "It's enough to get people's attention. We were going to draw straws to see who gets to collect."

"Very funny," I said. "But I guess you'd better call a meeting. Can you send word to Hassan that he's needed here?"

Charlie threw up his hands. It lacked the energy of a typical outburst. "It's almost sunrise!"

"We're two hundred feet underground, Charlie. I'm sure we'll be safe."

"I need my beauty rest."

"No one's arguing with that," Mr. Entwistle said. "I feel tired just looking at you boys."

"We'll live," Charlie and I said together.

Mr. Entwistle reached for his top hat and slapped it on his head. "I think a meeting can wait until tomorrow night."

"Exactly," said Charlie. "We can tackle this later."

"Aren't you the guy who wanted me to be more assertive?" I asked. "Now *is* later. You know the rules. Good news we get to sleep on, bad news we have to act on."

Charlie's eyes were at half-mast. "You ought to respect your elders more. You're becoming a tyrant."

"Take it up with the vampire union. We have work to do."

He rose from his seat. "No rest for the weary."

"It's no rest for the wicked," Mr. Entwistle said.

Charlie sighed. "Not with Zack in charge."

CHAPTER 66

IMMUNITY

M R. ENTWISTLE GRABBED his overcoat and headed for the modern lab next door. "You two get some rest. I'll consult the others. We can see what they recommend, then decide on the best course of action."

Charlie listened until his footsteps faded through the next room. He yawned and sat back down. "You okay?"

"I hate that question."

"Yeah. So do I. Not sure why I asked it." He glanced at the corpses. For a spell neither of us spoke. In the silence, a deep fatigue took hold.

"Can you believe it?" he asked. "All that stuff the Changeling said about wanting you in charge?"

I didn't know what to make of it. Just like Vlad's explanations, it seemed there were reasons to believe and disbelieve all of it. "I wonder if he would have said something similar to Vlad or Istvan, if they'd been the last ones standing."

"I've wondered that too. But they weren't. It was you. Ophelia was right. So was Luna."

I took a tired breath and let it out slowly. Their faith hadn't been rewarded. My eyes started watering. "I sometimes wonder if everything that happened, all the fights and escapes and disasters, if it was all just a juggling act. If Baoh didn't really care about me or anyone else, just the results."

"What do you mean?"

I had to take a minute to think my way through it. "I mean that he helped me, and resurrected Vlad, and used Istvan, and did all that other stuff just to keep both sides in fighting shape. That way, enough people would be killed to get the pathogen under control. He might have been content to leave anyone in charge."

"What does Entwistle say about it?"

"I didn't mention that last bit to him, but I think I know what he'd say. That we should get comfortable with the fact that we'll never know. And that it doesn't matter anyway, because we've got work to do."

"Yeah. We do." His shoulders slumped. He looked ready to pass out. "Was it worth it?" he asked. "All of this. Being *the Messiah*. Beating the Changeling. Getting to run the show."

"I don't know if we had a choice about most of this, Charlie."

"No. We didn't. But if you did have a choice, would—?"

"No. I would trade all of this for five minutes . . ." *at Stoney Lake with the girls*. The words got stuck in my throat.

"I hear ya," he said, staring at the wall. "I never imagined it would be like this. I thought, if we lived, that it would be a triumph. Or at least . . . I don't know, a relief maybe. But this . . . I think this must be how Endpoint Psychosis starts. The minute I slow down, I get angry. Or sad. I just think, what the hell was the point?"

I shifted beside him. He started. "I hate it when you do that."

"Sorry. It seems to happen when I want to move quickly,

367

when I don't think about it." I reached out and helped him off his stool. "The secret is to stay busy, because there *is* a point to all of this. There's a boy in Shanghai who needs looking after. He'll be hungry and confused. And there are vampires in Amsterdam and Paris who need us too. So you've got to hold it together, because I can't do this without you."

He didn't smile. Neither did I. But he understood. "Let's get out of here."

"Yeah."

We exited the old lab and entered the modern one. The New Order had destroyed all of the equipment that was there. We were waiting for new stuff—microscopes, centrifuges, refrigerator units. That kind of thing. I would stock blood from Min and Hassan and the other vampires who would help us form the next government. The League of Vampires. Different from Vlad's Coven or the New Order. Less a hierarchical secret police and more an open, democratic body. John was working on the details. With his help, we'd also study the pathogen, with the added bonus that any blood stored here would be at my disposal, should our work require me to make use of other talents—although, with the Changeling's blood in my system, it wasn't necessary at the moment. Perhaps it never would be, if I discovered a way to parasitize Baoh without bringing him out of undeath. It was an idea I would explore later.

I walked over to our only refrigerator and took a small stoppered test tube out of a rack. "I need to run this up to Vincent."

"I can do that," Charlie offered.

"We'll both go. I want to see how he's doing. Do you know where he is?"

"Top side, with the twins."

I held the liquid up to the light. It was an extract from wolfsbane. It would keep him from turning into the beast. Without

Vlad's secret serum, Vincent was either a young man or a health hazard. He spent most of his time playing with Miklos's twin daughters. It helped him fill the void, with Suki, Luna and Ophelia gone.

We climbed until we reached the top of the stairs. The large stones Vlad had used to block the entrance had been moved. Castle Dracula was being rebuilt. It would be a fortress again. We were also constructing a war memorial. A wall of names and a simple pair of statues. And so Suki Abbott and Commander James Rutherford would soon be standing vigil over a list of the innocent dead, a monument to Charlie's love and despair.

Vincent and the girls were on the scaffolding. One of them was perched on his shoulders, swinging a stick in the air. Charlie and I stood, transfixed, as they laughed and played amongst the ruins.

"Life goes on, doesn't it," he said.

"Yeah. Ready or not."

One of the girls spotted us. "Will you play?" she asked. "We're killing dragons."

"Maybe tomorrow night," I answered.

She frowned. "You always say that."

I always hoped it would be true. "Ask me again tomorrow. The sun will be up soon. I need to get underground."

Vincent set her down and walked over, a boy trapped in an adult body. I handed him the extract. He forced a smile. Things were still a bit strained with us. Luna was at the centre of it. Maybe the prophecy was, too. I had no idea what Vlad had told him while I was a hostage of the Changeling's. That seemed to have been the time when Vincent came into his own. It was certainly when he fell for Luna. I'm not sure if he blamed me for her death, or himself, but he missed her terribly. I felt sick about it, in part because it made us rivals of a sort, but also because he now thought of himself as ugly and useless. I would have to change that.

"We're going to have a meeting now. Would you join us?"

"I don't know," he said. His head was turned so the worst of his burns would be hidden. He looked much better than he had two weeks ago, but he didn't regenerate as quickly as we did. It would take another few months for the scar tissue to disappear. At the rate he aged, he'd look like a man in his thirties by then.

"May I?" Charlie asked.

Vincent nodded. Charlie reached up and turned his head so we could inspect the burns.

"They're getting better."

"Yeah, slowly."

"How are your lessons with Hassan going?"

"Good," he said. "But I'm slow now. And weak. I couldn't beat a mosquito."

"We have to work on an antidote for Luna," I said. "But once we have it, we'll get busy duplicating the formula Vlad made for you. Be patient. It will happen in good time." I rapped his chest with my knuckle, right over his heart. "You've got it where it counts, Vin. That was very brave, back in the temple, going after the Changeling the way you did."

We'd talked about this before. I knew what he would say even before he spoke.

"I let him go . . . he caught fire and I let go."

"No, Vincent. You held him just long enough. And you were willing to die for your friends. For Luna. Your parents would have been proud."

Charlie put a hand on his head and playfully pushed him back towards the girls. "You'll be the top of the food chain in no time. We'll buzz you when the meeting's ready to start."

"Okay," Vincent said, then looked away, smiling.

AFTER THE MEETING, Charlie and I headed down to the room we shared one level above the lab.

"Did Vinny seem okay to you?" he asked.

"I guess."

"You still think the prophecy is about him?"

I opened the short, iron-bound door and stepped to the side so Charlie could go through. "Vlad must have thought so. He's a good match. Orphan. Blood drinker. Died and came back. Son of a vampire hunter."

"*The* vampire hunter," Charlie said, ducking under the lintel. "Hyde was in a league all his own."

"Exactly. And Vinny could see through the Changeling's disguises."

"Smell through them."

"Same difference." I closed and latched the door, then opened the lid to my coffin. The beds we'd ordered hadn't arrived yet. "Baoh couldn't read his mind, either."

Charlie sat on a stool and started shedding armour. "I didn't know that."

"Yeah, and he was the only one immune to the Changeling's venom."

I was too tired to get undressed. My eyes were closed before my head hit the satin liner.

"He wasn't the only one," Charlie said.

"Only one what?"

"The only one immune to the Changeling's venom."

My mind was already half asleep. I couldn't remember ever feeling so exhausted. I opened my eyes, but I'd lost the thread of our conversation. "What were we talking about?"

Charlie yawned and lay down. "Vincent," he said. "He wasn't the only one immune to the Changeling's venom." His breathing slowed.

"Was someone else immune?"

"Hmmm?"

"Was someone else immune?"

"Yeah . . . of course."

I waited for him to finish, but he'd fallen asleep. I looked for something to throw at the side of his coffin. Nothing was in arm's reach so I pulled off a boot and chucked it at the lid. The first one missed. The second one sounded like a canister shot.

Charlie sat up in alarm. "What was that? Was that a bomb?"

"No, it was my boot," I said. "Who else was immune?"

He lay back down. "You woke me for that? Man, for a genius, you're a real dim-wit." His voice slowed. "The Changeling . . . he must have been immune. You think he'd run around with his stinger dripping like that if it could kill him?"

I hadn't thought about it, but of course Baoh was immune. Why hadn't it occurred to me? "Do you know what this means?" I asked. I had the Changeling's blood in me. If he was immune, then I was, too. And blood could be shared . . .

Charlie answered with a gentle snore.

I put my hands on the sides of the coffin, or I meant to, but I was too tired. Sleep claimed me before I could rise.

In the next moment I was falling over the edge of a ship. Charlie was watching from the deck. John was beside him, dressed in Death's cowl, the hood pulled down. A top hat was in one hand, a sickle in the other. I landed in a river and got swept away. I fought to stay above the plumes of white water and got washed, breathless, onto a small beach not unlike the one at Luna's cottage, where she'd taught me to swim. My armour and weapons were gone. I was wearing running shoes and hospital scrubs—the same ones I'd had back at the Nicholls Ward. I stood. There was no one around. Just the bats and chirping insects. The night was clear and fresh. I started running.

The beach turned into a pine forest. It grew so thick with undergrowth that after a time I couldn't see where I was going. Branches and leaves slapped at my face as I called out Luna's name over and over again. My foot got caught in something. I pitched forward and crash-landed in a clearing of granite, moss and juniper. I looked up to see Ophelia standing there. She was smiling, eyes soft, her hand outstretched to help me to my feet. I stood and smiled. The warm, comfortable light of the tunnel surrounded her with its familiar glow.

She put a finger over her mouth, then pointed towards the shore. I turned to look, saw the pines along the beach. A half moon rising over the water. Ripples of light glimmering on the granite rock. And a flash of copper-coloured hair.

ACKNOWLEDGEMENTS

I imposed on many friends in getting this project off the ground. My thanks go out to Charles Marriott, Mark Swailes, Shawn Mowry, Chris Spicer, Erin Brady and Gail Ladouceur; my brothers, Jake and Charlie; my daughter Bea; and my mother, Julia Bell, for reading early drafts and providing invaluable feedback. *New Order* passed through many iterations before taking on its present shape. For the staff at HarperCollins, and to those they commandeered to help get this book ready, your effort and patience is much appreciated. Thanks to reader Colin Thomas and proofer Natalie Meditsky. Greg Tabor and Alan Jones did a great job on the cover. Thanks also to Melissa Zilberberg for her advice and support through all three novels. Although my original editor, Lynne Missen, left while this project was still in its infancy, she helped nudge it gently in the right direction. Catherine Marjoribanks, whose keen eyes helped steer me from disaster in my first two novels, came through again with another fantastic copy edit. Thanks also to Maria Golikova for her assistance down the stretch, to Catharine Chen for her insight through the final drafts and to Hadley Dyer, who came on board midstream and had to make sense of the nonsensical—this would not have happened without you.